Pra

"This book is a remarkable literary expedition that keeps you breathless up until the very last page … a must read—with a glass in hand."

— Yves Dubuc, CBON FM Radio-Canada website:
"100 must read Canadian novels"

"Quite a fictional story built on the real history of single malt. Surprising, entertaining, and well researched."

— Martine Nouet, *Whisky Magazine* (French edition)

"Daniel Marchildon knows how to distill life … His new book fabulously combines his two passions … He meshes a good story with a good History while recounting a turbulent family saga stretching across two continents …"

— Paul-François Sylvestre, *L'express de Toronto*

"… a whisky story accessible to all … to be savoured very quickly! There's no risk, as far as I can see, of being disappointed by the author's knowledge of Scotch: he knows his stuff!"

— The UP Berry whisky club blog

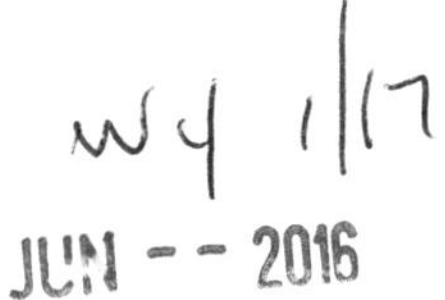

the WATER *of* LIFE

Uisge beatha

DANIEL MARCHILDON

Published by Odyssey Books in 2015
ISBN 978-1-922200-26-6

www.odysseybooks.com.au

A Cataloguing-in-Publication entry is available from the National Library of Australia

ISBN: 978-1-922200-26-6 (pbk)
ISBN: 978-1-922200-27-3 (ebook)

The Water of Life (Uisge beatha) as translated by Mārta Ziemelis, originally published in French as *L'eau de vie (Uisge beatha)* in 2008 by les Éditions David, Ottawa, Canada.

https://thewateroflifebydanielmarchildon.wordpress.com

* *A lexicon of all Scottish Gaelic words and expressions is included on page 311.*

DANIEL MARCHILDON

as translated by Mārta Ziemelis

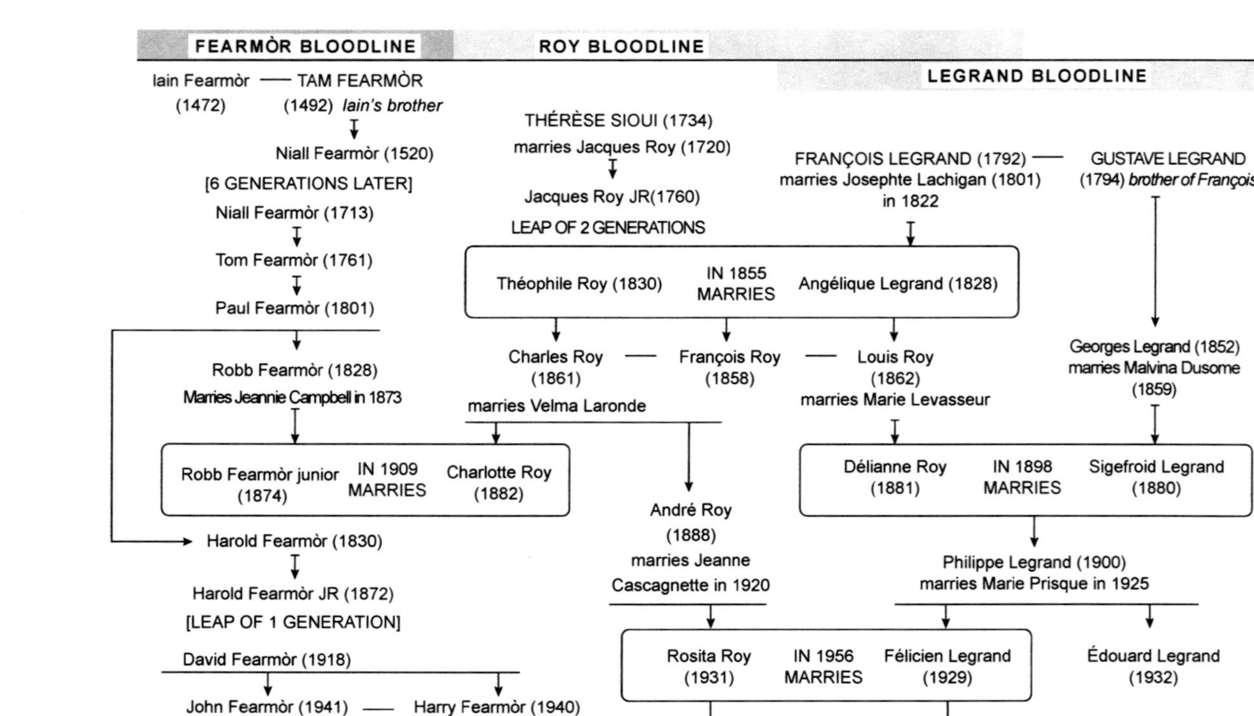

FEARMÒR BLOODLINE
ROY BLOODLINE
LEGRAND BLOODLINE
Iain Fearmòr (1472)
TAM FEARMÒR (1492) *Iain's brother*
Niall Fearmòr (1520)
[6 GENERATIONS LATER]
Niall Fearmòr (1713)
Tom Fearmòr (1761)
Paul Fearmòr (1801)
Robb Fearmòr (1828)
Marries Jeannie Campbell in 1873
Robb Fearmòr junior (1874)
IN 1909 MARRIES
Charlotte Roy (1882)
Harold Fearmòr (1830)
Harold Fearmòr JR (1872)
[LEAP OF 1 GENERATION]
David Fearmòr (1918)
John Fearmòr (1941)
Harry Fearmòr (1940)
Robert Fearmòr (1960)
THÉRÈSE SIOUI (1734)
marries Jacques Roy (1720)
Jacques Roy JR(1760)
LEAP OF 2 GENERATIONS
Théophile Roy (1830)
IN 1855 MARRIES
Angélique Legrand (1828)
Charles Roy (1861)
marries Velma Laronde
François Roy (1858)
Louis Roy (1862)
marries Marie Levasseur
André Roy (1888)
marries Jeanne Cascagnette in 1920
FRANÇOIS LEGRAND (1792)
marries Josephte Lachigan (1801)
in 1822
GUSTAVE LEGRAND (1794) *brother of François*
Georges Legrand (1852)
marries Malvina Dusome (1859)
Délianne Roy (1881)
IN 1898 MARRIES
Sigefroid Legrand (1880)
Philippe Legrand (1900)
marries Marie Prisque in 1925
Rosita Roy (1931)
IN 1956 MARRIES
Félicien Legrand (1929)
Édouard Legrand (1932)
Élisabeth Legrand (1957)
Louise Legrand (1960)

Part I

I. Elizabeth, Lighthouse Point

Better to die before Lighthouse Point does. This thought, making its way through her anguished mind, surprises her.

The sky is already darkening, even though it's only early afternoon on this November day. Elizabeth Legrand, steering her pleasure boat under the influence of a rough hangover, must choose between two paths. Open water, or a channel leading to Lighthouse Point and running behind the large rock dominated by a whitewashed lighthouse. No longer hesitating, she points the bow towards the open water and pushes the throttle to the limit. Her vessel begins to leap about on the waves, its course set for a destination unknown to Elizabeth. She's heading into emptiness—into the heart of Georgian Bay and its latent, deceptively calm yet omnipresent strength. At any moment and without warning, this vast, rock-walled pot of water can start to foam like a saucepan of milk left on the stove for too long. Elizabeth means to go on until …

When she nears the Tortoise Islands, she abruptly cuts the engine, abandoning her boat to the movement of the waves. The drifting craft approaches these islands, strung out across the mouth of the very channel where Elizabeth's parents died one winter. She turns her back on the islands, gazing at the bay instead. Today's overcast weather clouds the view, and so she can only imagine the distant Bruce Peninsula, normally visible from Lighthouse Point. At the peninsula's tip lies Tobermory, a town that borrowed its name from a small, Scotch-producing fishing port on the Isle of Mull off Scotland's west coast. She contemplates the bay before her: 1,350 square kilometres dotted by 30,000 islands and islets, and swept by waves that have swallowed two hundred ships—and twenty inhabitants of Lighthouse Point.

Beneath the water's surface, flotsam and jetsam, shipwreck debris and even fully intact bodies lie on the bottom of the bay, where the lack of oxygen slows their decomposition.

"I'll rejoin my mother, return to the waters that witnessed my birth." This idea comforts Elizabeth.

With a gesture of resignation, Elizabeth tosses the anchor overboard and watches the rope uncoil. Everyone will believe her motor broke down. Its carburettor has always been a capricious beast; her friend Ghisèle and the others have seen her battling the damn thing hundreds of times.

Her resolve strengthening, Elizabeth is determined that the gloomy evening she just lived through will be her last.

Still, it had got off to a good start. The entire population of Lighthouse Point village—thirty people—had gathered in the Bar au Baril to toast the departure of Sylvain, the last local single man aged under fifty. Following in the footsteps of the rest of the village's youth, Sylvain is moving away to look for work—more specifically, to Toronto. As of this departure Elizabeth and Ghisèle, both a year shy of forty, now hold the title of youngest people in Lighthouse Point. This community, just like all the rest along the northeast coast of Georgian Bay, is slowly emptying because it can't hold on to its sons and daughters—they abandon coastal life for the city, often against their own deepest wishes.

For Elizabeth, last night's party turned into a wake that pushed her to drink more than her fill. Mostly beer, since the small amount of Scotch on offer disappeared quickly. Ghisèle even had to drag her home and plop her down on the sofa. Whisky would never have floored her so badly.

Lighthouse Point is slowly dying, and hopes for nothing more than a peaceful death. With little money to rely on, Elizabeth can't afford to wait for this death any more than Sylvain and the others before him could. Nevertheless, she no longer has the strength to leave, at least not like that. Oh, she tried fifteen years ago. Living off next to nothing, she wandered across Canada, then through Europe. One day she found herself in Scotland, face to face with a truth she could no longer deny: for her, it was impossible to live anywhere else than at Lighthouse Point.

And yet, though she's happy enough to live alone in her parents' house, today Elizabeth must confront another truth: she no longer has the means to go on living like this. In a month's time the ice will freeze up all along the coast and …

The motorboat is dragging its anchor along, and Elizabeth hears it scrape the bottom of the bay without catching. Listening to this sound, she thinks, *Well, Louise will certainly be happy.* The reefs are approaching rapidly now. She need only wait; this won't take very long. Louise, her younger sister, will at last have the house all to herself, and …

No! Not in this water. In the water of life instead.

Elizabeth perks up her ears. Her whole body shudders with horror. She really heard that voice, a woman's voice. But around her there's nothing but grey water, waves battering the hull, and the wind mussing her long brown hair.

In the water of life.

"What water of life?" cries Elizabeth, feeling lost.

Then, suddenly, she understands. *How can this stranger possibly know what no one else does?*

She turns the key, and the motor responds with a growl that is immediately choked off. Elizabeth spits out a curse: the faked breakdown is now all too real. Panicking, she rushes towards the motor. Barely fifty metres separate her from the chain of islets where the waves are determined to take her. She fiddles with the anchor rope, desperately hoping to stop this fatal trajectory long enough to restart the motor. No rocks or crevices come to her aid, and so she turns to the motor, her last hope. Fighting to maintain her balance, Elizabeth pops off the motor's cap, pulls a screwdriver from the toolbox, and tries to jam it into the throttle valve. But the tool falls and starts rolling around on the bottom of the boat. On all fours, Elizabeth grabs it and, distraught, tries to insert it once again. This time it stays in place, and she returns to the helm.

"Come on, for Chrissake!" she mutters, turning the key. There's a mechanical cough, then silence. Elizabeth looks grimly at the rocks about to crush her boat any minute now. Once she's in the glacially cold water, her chances of surviving more than fifteen minutes will be zero. She tries the key again.

The motor spits out steam then starts, at long last. Elizabeth pushes the throttle to carry her craft away from the reefs. Once out of danger, she hauls up the anchor. Hands still trembling, she heads for shore and the lighthouse. Elizabeth is now thoroughly determined to drink from the cup she's never dared to bring to her lips. But she remains fearful that the water of life may let her down—yet again.

2. Scotland, 1494

Friar Iain Fearmòr crossed himself and knelt on the stone-tiled chapel floor. The poor Benedictine monk's body was frozen by the salty air of the Firth of Tay, a narrow bay on the North Sea that licked the north-east coast of Scotland. Despite the cold, he focused on his prayers. Ten other friars were doing the same in the uncertain dawn, trying to break over the Chapel of St Dionysus, one of three belonging to Lindores Abbey.

A few candles faintly lit this sacred place—a stone building established at the beginning of the 13th century, which made it almost as old as the abbey itself.

"Grant that I should be successful, because the salvation of so many souls depends on it." The monk sought to invoke divine help in carrying out his mission, which could prove fatal. He had, for that reason, hesitated very much before accepting it. Was he even really sure the mission was worth the risk?

After an hour, the numbness in all his limbs told him that he had prayed enough, at least for now. He got up and, moving very slowly so as to allow the circulation in his legs to start flowing again, left the chapel. Outside, the October wind whipped the sea, pushing it to crash against the rocky coast with all its strength.

South of the abbey, the village of Newburgh seemed to be holding its breath while calmly waiting for sunrise. Hurrying, Friar Fearmòr entered the monastery stable, found a donkey already harnessed to a cart, and set out.

Twenty minutes later, he arrived at Robert Bruce's house, where he greeted the farmer and handed him a paper covered with fine handwriting in Latin. The peasant, who couldn't read, questioned the friar with his eyes.

"It's an order placed by the Exchequer," Iain explained. "I'll read it to you: 'To be handed over to Friar John Cor by order of the King, for the purpose of producing *aqua vitae:* eight bolls of malted barley …' Present this paper to the King's officers and you will be reimbursed."

The commoner could only agree with a nod. Despite his frustration at losing a considerable portion of his barley harvest, the peasant hardly wanted to risk opposing the king's bidding.

Friar Fearmòr followed the farmer to his barn. While he helped load the cart with barley, he reflected that taking what belonged to the king was a serious crime, and that in order to risk a venture like this, he must be mad.

* * *

Ten days later, Iain found himself, along with other monks, feeding the fires burning beneath three stills with dried peat—under the watchful eye of Friar John Cor, a man nearing fifty years of age. The men observed the vapour as it started to form inside the coils attached to the head of each still.

"This art fascinates me," Iain exclaimed. "From where did we acquire it?"

The monk's curiosity intrigued Friar Cor. "To tell the truth, no one knows. From Ireland, maybe. Apparently this art has existed for a long time, perhaps for even as much as seven centuries. Why are you so interested, brother Fearmòr?"

The monk, hiding his nervousness with difficulty, hesitated a little before replying: "Making *aqua vitae* fulfils a personal need, the need to … to create."

The friar, the monastery steward, accepted this explanation, cleared his throat and continued his lecture: "The fundamental principle to keep in mind is that the boiling point of spirits is lower than that of water. For this reason, once heated, they separate from the water in the wort. When it comes in contact with the cold air in the coil, it turns liquid again."

The monks had set up the stills outdoors, near a burn, one of the countless small streams that flowed in the Scottish countryside. But even in the open air, they were bothered by the foul smell produced by the stills and peaty fires. Nonetheless, Iain felt a certain kind of exaltation, like a believer communicating with God in a sacred place, enveloped in a cloud of incense.

Shortly afterwards, the process described by Friar Cor took place. As the precious clear liquid dripped from the coils, the monks carefully gathered it in stoneware jars. When Friar Cor judged that the stills had given up all their alcohol, he declared that they were done for the day.

While Iain and the others applied themselves to sealing the jars, Friar Cor expressed his satisfaction. "King James IV will be pleased with our plentiful output this year."

"So how our *aqua vitae* is used must remain the king's prerogative?"

This question unsettled Friar Cor. "It also serves to heal the sick at the monastery."

Realising that he had sparked Friar Cor's disapproval, Iain tried to hide his blunder with a second question. "Is the king really investigating the properties of our *aqua vitae*?"

"It seems so."

Faced with Friar Cor's curt reply, Iain decided to stop talking and apply himself conscientiously to his distilling work.

A few days later, in the evening, Friar Fearmòr made his way to the monastery storehouse. Among the numerous jars Iain found the object of his search: the perfectissima. The monks actually produced three types of spirits, known by Latin and Scottish Gaelic names: simplex or *usquebaugh*, distilled twice; composita or *testerig*, distilled three times; and *usquebaugh-baul* or perfectissima, the product of four distillations—and so strong that it was said drinking two consecutive spoonfuls of it could be fatal.

Iain chose five jars and decanted a little *aqua vitae* from each into a small flask, taking care to replace the stealthily removed liquid with water. By doing so, he could hope that no one would ever notice the disappearance of the stolen spirits, which represented only a tiny fraction of the three hundred and forty litres distilled by the brothers. Besides, because of their high alcohol concentration, all types of *aqua vitae* were drunk only in small spoonfuls, or greatly diluted in water. There was, however, always a risk. And if his crime were ever discovered, Iain didn't dare even to imagine the punishment he would receive.

Shortly afterwards, in the solitude of his cell, the monk contemplated the flask. After three weeks of taxing work, he had yet to taste the fruits of his labour; in fact, he would never be allowed to taste them. Even though he would soon have to part with these spirits, he began to think that, all the same, he had the right to a small reward—namely, the chance to satisfy his curiosity.

He lifted the jar's lid. A strong smell invaded his nostrils. He dipped his index finger in the liquid and, after a few seconds of hesitation, put it in his mouth.

An intense fire overran his taste buds. Once the shock of this first contact had passed, he felt both dazed and strangely lucid. He decided to take a swallow of perfectissima—just one.

This time his entire body ignited, for ten whole minutes. The monk felt a divine euphoria and clarity of mind. He understood that the scope of his mission went beyond simply delivering the flask. No, he had to add an element to the elixir's contents that would ensure its success.

In the reassuring silence of this tranquil spot, he rubbed his hands together and hiked up the lower part of his habit. Under normal circumstances, the act he was about to commit was a sin; tonight, however, through the intercession of His *aqua vitae*, God had just granted Iain permission to do it. And thus he did.

The friar had to wait a few weeks before he could venture to Newburgh without attracting suspicion. In the village, he found the house where he had been instructed to go. There, he handed the flask of *aqua vitae* over to a young man who left immediately for Dunfermline, the seat of the Scottish court, to deliver the precious elixir to the daughter of the chieftain of clan Fearmòr.

This young woman, Màiri Fearmòr, had been offered in marriage to Andra Haig, the son of clan Haig's most influential patriarch. This union was meant to forge an alliance between the two rival families and bring peace to a large part of the country, torn between its various warring factions.

And yet, before agreeing to hold the wedding, the Haig family had invoked the right to resort to handfasting. According to this old custom, the husband had the right to take his future wife as a concubine for a year and thus ascertain her fertility. At the end of these twelve months, if the woman still wasn't pregnant, the man could return her to her family and refuse the marriage.

Though loathe to do so, the Fearmòrs had no other option but to agree to this request. And so Màiri Fearmòr had lived among clan Haig for six months now, with no results. The Fearmòrs had therefore called upon one of their own, a monk of the abbey of Lindores, to obtain some *aqua vitae*. The *uisge beatha,* as the Scots called it in their language, was known for being able to heal a great many illnesses and, since its name literally meant "water of life", everyone believed it capable of creating fertility.

If the *aqua vitae* successfully brought about the birth of a child and sealed the hoped-for union between the clans, the Fearmòrs agreed, in exchange, to assure the propagation and strictest possible observation of the Christian faith among their own.

Neither Iain Fearmòr nor anyone else ever found out how Màiri Fearmòr had used the *uisge beatha*. Had she drunk it herself? Had she administered it to Andra Haig without his knowledge? Had she perhaps done both?

Nevertheless, when Andra Haig took a three-months-pregnant Màiri Fearmòr as his lawful wife in May of 1495, Iain Fearmòr knew that his *uisge beatha*, and the few drops he had added to it, had brought about the unification of the clans of Scotland. More importantly still, they had assured the eternal salvation of his family. The monk felt an entirely paternal pride in these results.

Yet he hardly suspected that in the coming century, this beautiful unification of Scotland, land of the holy water of life, would collapse in the face of English invaders—and that the monks would lose their hold both on Lindores Abbey and on the science of distillation.

3. Elizabeth, Lighthouse Point

When she passes in front of the lighthouse again, Elizabeth waves her hand; this gesture is an automatic reflex instilled in the days when her uncle, the former lighthouse keeper, lived there with his family. Even though the lighthouse has been automated and its residence empty for twenty-five years, Elizabeth can't stop her hand and its useless wave. Maybe her uncle or her paternal grandfather replies, in their own invisible way.

As she enters the channel behind the point on which the lighthouse stands, Elizabeth guides the boat without having to think, narrowly avoiding the many reefs hidden underwater. Fifteen minutes later, she cuts the motor and lets the boat drift into its slip next to the dock, like a horse returning to the stable.

She fastens the mooring lines and climbs the ten steps that lead to the house, a rustic building perched atop a rock, with a view over a large bay leading to the open water. Going inside, she puts on a CD of Cuban jazz, drops into a rocking chair and lets her eyes wander around the room. This house, the first building erected on Massassauga Bay, was built by her great-grandfather in the 1890s. Successive generations have grafted new rooms onto this very rudimentary, functional structure, without the slightest consideration for aesthetics. "And what am I going to add to it?" Elizabeth asks herself.

Rocking to the frantic rhythm of the music, Elizabeth remembers the last time she danced, the last time she felt a warm body against her own. Thirty-nine years is too young to have memories that already seem so distant. And yet …

She hesitates again. What if the mysterious voice was wrong? She climbs down the steps to the cellar cut from the rock. Digging into the granite of the Canadian Shield is difficult, and to make a hole in the rock, her grandfather had learned to use dynamite by trial and error, one explosive blast at a time. This room, built to store perishable foods, hides something else.

Elizabeth pulls a key from her pocket and sticks it into the padlock. This is only the second time she's been down here. The first, ten years ago, was just for a cursory inspection. With the padlock undone, she still hesitates to open the door. What exactly is she afraid of now, finding a skeleton?

Suddenly, the phone rings. She turns around, but stops herself. "I can't turn back, not now." After five rings, the answering machine kicks in, and she regains her calm. She pulls the door open and stretches out her trembling hand towards the interior wall. A rush of apprehension chills her, as though she were about to steal something. And yet what she's come here to take is rightfully hers.

The naked light bulb hanging from the ceiling gives off a gloomy light that silhouettes several wooden barrels and cases of bottles. Inside one of the cases, her fingers brush against smooth, curved glass. Pulling out the bottle, she studies her loot in the dim light.

Her Uncle Edward's voice echoes in her head: "Along with the house, your parents left this to both of you. It might be worthless, but keep it safe, and above all, don't mention it to anyone ..."

Did her uncle really say this to her? She's starting to doubt it, even though the memory seems so real.

Like a tomb robber, Elizabeth abruptly shuts the door, closes the padlock and quickly climbs back up to the kitchen. She puts the bottle down on the table and pours herself a large glass of water. At this moment Elizabeth is absolutely certain that her parents drank this whisky and, what's more, that if they had lived longer they would be with her tonight, offering her this dram. She calmly uncorks the bottle.

Strong fragrances flood the room. Elizabeth's nostrils react—out of joy or horror, she can't say which. The scents of the sea, of the north wind and of Georgian Bay swim in the air dominated by this powerful smell of water transformed through its contact with rock, peat and heather.

Five minutes go by. Elizabeth pours a long draught of the liquid into a triangle-shaped glass, a promotional item from the Glenfiddich distillery, and then begins to agitate it. On the side of the glass, the decal face of William Grant, the founder of Glenfiddich, sporting his Glengarry army cap, smiles at her.

Around her, the room pitches like the deck of a sailboat running from a storm in the open sea. This smell of water, so familiar and so alien at the same time, won't stop bombarding her. The glass brushes her lips when, suddenly, she remembers an essential element is missing: fresh water. A few drops of Georgian Bay water will draw out the natural oils of this whisky, aged like no other on Earth. She runs a drop from the tap and catches it in her glass. The reaction is immediate.

A sparkling patch, like an oil stain, shines for a brief moment and disappears. Elizabeth recoils in horror. She has the clear impression that she saw a woman's face in that stain, a stranger's face, but nonetheless familiar.

She grips the glass tightly in her hands; all she sees now is the very dark, straw-coloured liquid. After a long moment, she succeeds in controlling the shiver running up and down her body. Could she be reliving Doctor Jekyll's experience, venturing into a forbidden realm? Does this whisky have the power to transform her? And if so, will it be for better or worse?

A deep doubt gnaws at her. The solitude and the isolation are taking their toll on her; she can no longer deny it.

She doesn't have a choice anymore; she has to see this through to the end. The soul of the released spirit is commanding her to drink it.

The whisky enters her mouth. She suppresses an instinct to spit; she's never tasted liquor this strong. This whisky comes to her from another century, from a marriage, from a legendary crossbreeding, in fact. The fireworks exploding in her mouth spread through all her limbs, reaching her heart and her brain at the same time. This euphoria, both so sensual and so cerebral, makes her moan. Her heart pounds wildly. Flashes of enlightenment fill her head, one after the other. Oh, yes! The whole world will know this ecstasy, this sweet bliss, thanks to her—or rather, thanks to her, and to the three generations of Legrands who came before her, and to ... Her thoughts stop short.

She takes another swallow. This time she feels only gentleness and comfort.

"And thanks to the mystical powers of Georgian Bay," she says to herself. "Yes, in order for this whisky to be reborn, I'll have to tell the story of how it came to be." Elizabeth is the only one capable of doing it. "And what's more, its saga will continue through me."

She notices, with surprise, that her glass is already empty.

"One is enough, two are too many, and three are not enough," she recites aloud, remembering the Scottish proverb.

Without hesitating, she pours herself a second glass. The whisky has waited more than a century for its odyssey to add a new chapter to the annals of Lighthouse Point. And this chapter won't be the last. The secret of the past will be sacrificed in order to ensure a future.

"*Slàinte* to you, Glen Dubh!" Elizabeth cries, clinking her glass against the bottle.

4. Scotland, 1534

After thirty years of contemplative life, facing the confusion of the dirty, busy streets of Edinburgh was a shock for Ewen Ban. A year ago, the Statutes of the Realm decreed by King Henry VIII had forced him to leave monastic life. This decree had disfranchised the monasteries, allowing the English sovereign to distribute their lands to his followers. Now in his early fifties, Ewen had lost his purpose in life. With the closure of Lindores Abbey, he had been thrown out onto the street, and it was for this reason that he found himself in the Scottish capital, searching for his salvation, or at least for a way to live out, with a clear conscience, the few years left to him in this world before moving on to his eternal life in the next.

"St Giles' Cathedral?"

The passerby Ewen had just stopped looked him up and down with a scornful glance before pointing the way with a finger. "You're already practically there."

Ewen had barely understood what the gentleman had muttered to him before disappearing. He continued on his way, reassured that he had achieved his goal, at least his first one. To start with, he must pray. After that, he would seek out Iain Fearmòr's blood brother. He had to at least try to keep the solemn oath made to his old teacher. Only then could he go back, with complete peace of mind, to the land of his childhood, to where he had lived before the monastery.

In front of St Giles' Cathedral, a colourful mob of merchants boisterously hawked their wares.

"Drink *aqua vitae*."

This exhortation from one of the vendors attracted the ex-monk's attention. The merchant, who was in fact a barber-surgeon, was catching fire about his goods.

"Moderately taken, *aqua vitae* slows ageing, fortifies youth, helps with digestion, lightens the mind, cheers the heart, heals strangulation; it keeps and preserves the head from whirling, the tongue from lisping, the guts from rumbling, and the bones from aching."

Despite himself, Ewen stopped for a minute at the barber-surgeon's stall as he continued proclaiming the virtues of his product.

"It can even perk up an old man like you."

For a long moment, Ewen eyed the flasks of *aqua vitae* under the vendor's suspicious gaze. "May I have a sniff?" he asked.

The barber-surgeon uncorked a small flask and held it out to the former monk clad in simple peasants' clothes. "All right. But it's a penny for a taste."

Ewen moved closer to the open flask. His nostrils covered the neck and breathed in noisily. This deep breath and the smell that came with it made his head spin, transported him to a world possessing its own distinctive flavours, aromas and murmurs that made it both spiritual and very carnal.

"So, old man, do you want a taste?"

The seller's question pulled Ewen out of his pleasant daydream. Dumbfounded, he could only shake his head and dash briskly for the door of the cathedral. "Prayer, yes, prayer." He absolutely had to ask for divine counsel.

Inside the stone building, his eyes adjusted to the gloomy candlelight. This heavy atmosphere, designed to crush the average believer before the greatness of his God, had the opposite effect on the aged monk, accustomed to decades of daily prayer. The cold and hardness of the stone floor against his knees gave him a feeling of wellbeing. Comforted, he threw himself enthusiastically into prayer and meditation.

The smell of the *aqua vitae* still lingering in his nostrils, he watched the thread of his memories unroll before him. Ewen was twenty years old again. He was keeping a close eye on the fire under a still as the monastery steward, friar Iain Fearmòr, explained his wishes.

"I will share all my knowledge with you, but on one condition. If I am unable to pass it on to clan Fearmòr before my death, you, brother Ban, will have to do so in my place. Swear before me and before God ..."

That had been in 1504. Ewen had been living at the monastery for a year, and friar Fearmòr had been initiating him into the art of distilling *aqua vitae*. With the years, his mentor had succeeded in refining the techniques of distillation, thus increasing production and ensuring a greater share of *aqua vitae* for the monks of the abbey, who used it to successfully to treat a number of illnesses. The friars charged with milking the cows even coated their udders with it, claiming that it improved the yield and quality of the milk. Like a good student, Ewen had himself soon become an expert in distillation and, when friar Fearmòr died five years later, the monastery had entrusted him with the responsibility of producing their *aqua vitae*.

But now the abbey no longer existed, and Ewen still had to fulfil his promise.

In front of a statue of Saint Columba, the first to spread Christianity in Scotland, he prayed. Had this missionary also brought the science of distillation from Ireland? No one could prove it, but Ewen believed that he had.

Revitalised, he left the cathedral, determined to seek out Tam Fearmòr, but afraid that the man would refuse Ewen his help in fulfilling his dead brother's vow.

* * *

Ewen recited the Lord's Prayer as he watched white smoke rise over the fire. Although the sky was starry on this November night, he saw nothing but the darkness filling the space under South Bridge, the most discreet spot he had been able to find. The heat of the fire he shared with the still, a damaged vessel it had taken him a long search to acquire, was starting to permeate his numb limbs.

He would never have imagined himself one day simultaneously invoking the Divine Spirit through prayer, and alcoholic spirits through distillation, in a place like this. Since Tam had unequivocally refused to entrust his fourteen-year-old son, Niall, to the ex-monk so he could become his apprentice, Ewen saw only one way to convince the recalcitrant father: let the *uisge beatha* plead in his favour.

He had successfully traded his services as a scribe against a few bushels of good-quality barley. After malting it for two weeks, he was now finally able to move on to distilling the wort. However, he remained unsure of what the results would be. The water he had drawn from the Water of Leith, the little river that snaked across Edinburgh, was of mediocre quality, just like the few pieces of dried peat that he'd been able to scrounge for fuel. At least all the essential elements were gathered and, with the Lord's help, he would succeed in drawing true *aqua vitae* from them.

Approaching the fire and its acrid smoke, he examined the vapour finally starting to form inside the coil. He wouldn't have to wait much longer. For a moment he thought of Niall Fearmòr—a sturdy young lad, at least by the look of him, and quick-witted too. The memory of Tam's voice cast a shadow over this thought.

"It's illegal! The barber-surgeons are the only ones in Edinburgh allowed to make *uisge beatha*."

Exactly, Ewen had argued back. That's why he proposed to take Niall far away from Edinburgh, to the Highlands, to a valley that ran along the river Spey. In his native region, all the ingredients necessary for *aqua vitae* were of high quality and easy to procure. There, Ewen could initiate Niall into the art of distillation in complete peace and quiet, with no risk of imprisonment.

Since this argument hadn't been enough to persuade Tam, a desperate Ewen had evoked the gloomy prospects awaiting Niall in Edinburgh. In this city one had to fight for jobs, each as mediocre as the next, against tens of unemployed people. What kind of future could a young man like Niall hope for in this city overpopulated with shabby, miserable wretches?

Despite being unable to answer the question, Tam hadn't given in.

Drops were starting to form in the coil, and Ewen busied himself gathering them. The *aqua vitae* would have to succeed where Ewen had failed. Once the still had given up its spirits, Ewen let the fire die down. The night had been long, and dawn was already coming. That evening, the fate of *uisge beatha*, or at least of its passage into the Fearmòr lineage, would be decided.

* * *

Tam Fearmòr stared suspiciously at the glass in front of him: was this damnable man of God willing to go so far as to poison him in order to get his son? Ewen tried to reassure him by telling him that if he tasted the *aqua vitae*, he would understand why Niall had to learn how to make it.

"So why don't you drink some first?"

The question surprised Ewen who, despite hesitating for a moment, reached out to pour himself a glass.

"No, take mine," said Tam, pushing the vessel in front of his visitor.

It finally dawned on Ewen why Tam was ordering him to drink first. Rather than taking offence, he decided to laugh about it, bringing the glass to his lips to take a long gulp, exaggerating the gesture so far as to let a trickle of the liquid flow into his white beard. He finished off the scene with a sigh of satisfaction and an air of such total rapture that Tam was impatient to have his drink.

A few seconds later, all the troubles of the day vanished as the *aqua vitae* set the walls of his throat ablaze and re-energised all his limbs.

Glasses of whisky, along with stories, followed one after the other. Tam told Ewen about his misfortunes, and about his grief at living in destitution. At last, he agreed that Ewen should take Niall far away from the infectious poverty here. In this valley where Ewen was proposing to bring him, this Gleann Dubh, Niall couldn't do worse than in Edinburgh.

"I'll entrust him to you, but on one condition."

Ewen's eyebrows gathered in a question—a simple movement which, at this moment, required an enormous effort of concentration.

"Before leaving, you'll fill ten small casks with this *uisge beatha* for me."

Ewen raised his glass in agreement, emptied it in one go and then let himself fall to the ground, giving in to a deep sleep. He could sleep in peace. His promise would be kept, and the science of distillation of the monks of Lindores wouldn't be lost. The weight that had just been taken off his shoulders would be carried by others: the Fearmòrs. However, for this, he should have called upon a race of giants—for the task would prove to be not only great, but completely superhuman.

5. The New World, 1611

The winter had been long and hard, but neither as long nor as hard as his first in this country, two years ago—and much less gruesome as well.

Estienne Buslé gazed at the last blocks of ice of the season, tossed about by the wind on the vast inland sea which, six months earlier, he had crossed to end up in the Wendat village of Toanché. Samuel de Champlain had entrusted him to the Algonquians in exchange for Savignon, the son of a leader of the Wendat nation, at the beginning of the previous summer. When, in early October, the Algonquians had broken camp to undertake what had to be a journey of a considerable distance, he had participated in the preparations without saying a word. Buslé had watched the tree leaves transform the landscape into a forest of fire. Aware of being the first man of his race to gaze upon this country and its dazzling beauty, this peasant's son had felt like a lord.

At one point, the expedition had crossed a completely open lake, exposed to the whims of nature. Following this, when the canoes had been portaged around rapids emptying into a much narrower river, enclosed between steep rocky walls, Buslé had felt very relieved. He had noticed a change in the look of the rock, now much smoother and more rounded, almost soft.

After passing a number of waterfalls, the travellers had portaged around one last series of rapids. This time, Buslé's breath had been taken away. On the horizon, the colours of the sun melted into the sea. Before him, there was nothing but open water; however, both to the north and south, Buslé saw islands, rocks.

The next day, he had been surprised to see his Native companions effortlessly orient themselves in the maze of islands and narrow channels so harmoniously blended with this immense body of freshwater, as large as a sea. From the rock, which had gentle maternal curves, grew dense forests. The young Frenchman believed he was entering a natural realm, a true new world.

Euphoric,Ouslé had landed in the territory of the Wendats*, with whom he had then spent the winter. Today he remembered another, very different spring, namely the spring of 1609. Standing in front of the Habitation de Québec, both a fort and a settlement, he had, for the first time, watched a parade of ice sheets on the St Lawrence River—all the while counting himself lucky, after grim months of suffering and deaths, to be among the eight survivors of the group of twenty-eight from the previous autumn.

Wintering among the Wendats hadn't been easy either. He hadn't enjoyed the intense cold any more than the Natives. Bruslé had discovered that these people, hardened to the harshness of the season, were similar to the Algonquians and at the same time very different. They were settled and lived in fortified villages, in large wooden huts covered with bark. Agriculture, practiced exclusively by the women, ensured food was available most of the time—particularly ground, boiled corn. Unlike his first hosts, nomads dependent on the vagaries of hunting and fishing, the Wendats lived a stable existence. With the melting of the ice, the Algonquians had once again set off for their hunting grounds. Before, Bruslé had asked Iroquet's permission to stay in Wendake.

Iroquet, leader of the Algonquians, had found the idea excellent. The presence of this *Agnoha*, or man of iron, was turning out to be inconvenient. By entrusting him to the Wendats, the chances that he would survive and could one day be returned to Champlain would improve.

Bruslé got up and headed back to the village. In the Wendat huts, the close proximity caused by winter had allowed him to further his learning of his hosts' language. The arrival of spring and milder weather encouraged the Wendats to spend most of the day outdoors. Totiri, a child of ten with whom Bruslé had developed a friendly relationship, assured him that once the fine weather arrived, the Wendats hardly slept in their longhouses at all.

Back in the village, Touché was surprised to discover a large number of men and women gathered in a longhouse. Grouped around a sick elder, they were heatedly discussing something. Placing himself discreetly near one of the two entrances located at either end of the building, Brulé listened attentively.

"A feast?" cried a young voice that Brulé recognised.

"No, Totiri," replied the afflicted old woman.

One after the other, others in the group suggested objects or food dishes, to which the elder always replied with a no. Estienne Brulé realised that this had to be one of the Wendats' collective healing rituals. Several times over the past months, he had seen them partake in this type of activity. The dream of a man or woman suffering from an illness was supposed to contain the remedy they needed. So, when the sick person announced to the others that they had dreamed of their cure, the whole village tried very hard to guess what the remedy was. Whether it involved an object or an action, all the Wendats, accompanied by the chanting of their priests or shamans, cooperated wholeheartedly to ensure at least the symbolic fulfilment of this dream.

This time, the participants in the collective ritual seemed, at least to Brulé, particularly enthusiastic. Was this due to the popularity of the sick woman, Andiora, or simply to spring fever?

"*Andacwandet*?"

The word had come from the mouth of Tiena, a girl who was about sixteen years old and whose name meant "blue jay". There was a pronounced silence when old Andiora nodded affirmatively. Then shouts filled the air and people scattered in all directions. Brulé had never seen the Wendats so excited.

He grabbed Totiri in passing and demanded an explanation from him.

"*Andacwandet,*" the young boy replied simply. "You'll see."

Totiri stretched out his hand towards Brulé's beard and patted it for a minute before adding, in a teasing tone, "Or maybe not."

With that, the boy snuck away before the Frenchman could find out any more. Thus, Brulé remained the only person in the village with hair growing on his face and his curiosity unsatisfied.

* * *

Even after his question had been answered, Bruslé remained curious. In fact, even more than before, to the point where he wished he could participate in the ritual.

Throughout the whole day, the village had busied itself preparing the *andacwandet* ceremony. The two shamans overseeing the ritual had asked all the single girls to choose among the village's bachelors a partner for the night. At dusk, the young people had been brought to Andiora's longhouse and invited to indulge in sexual pleasures in her presence, just as she had dreamt it, in order to drive away her illness.

Bruslé had taken up a place near a fire outdoors, close by Andiora's longhouse. He regretted that he hadn't gone elsewhere, farther away. The thought of all these young people giving themselves over to erotic rapture, with the blessing of their priests, made him shiver. His eyes didn't really see the flames dancing in front of him. Despite his scruples, he devoted all his attention to his hearing. The chanting of one of the shamans, a succession of syllables punctuated by the regular, monotone beat of a tortoiseshell rattle, floated in the air of the full-moon night.

Bruslé jumped when he felt a warm hand touch his face.

"Come, I've chosen you."

By the glow of the fire, Bruslé recognised Tiena. He hadn't been surprised when none of the young girls had approached him for the ritual. They had no reason to consider him one of their own. His complexion, his beard, his clothes and his still shaky knowledge of their language were constant reminders that he was a foreigner. So this unexpected invitation astonished him. In matters of physical love his knowledge remained limited to feeling unfulfilled desire.

Sensing his hesitation, Tiena drew Bruslé's hand to her chest. The Frenchman let her lead him to the longhouse. As he passed from the bright moonlight to the dim glow of the fire indoors, Bruslé's heart started racing. The atmosphere was surreal: smoke, bodies lying here and there on the ground, the shamans' repetitive chants. Andiora, perched on a platform, watched everything, her toothless mouth smiling. Tiena guided Buslé to a space on the ground, on a fur, quite close to the others. Too close. His eyes, now adjusted to the soft glow, glanced at parts of bodies, thighs, hips, breasts, moving to the rhythm of lascivious moans, mostly uttered by male voices.

Wasn't this how the priests of his country described Hell? All that was missing was the Devil's pitchforks. Since leaving France, Buslé had distanced himself from the hollow doctrine of the priests and their oppressive religion. Even so, at this moment he realised just how much he was still, despite everything, influenced by his religious upbringing.

Denying his wild lust for this girl would have been impossible. Tiena's hand slid under his shirt and aroused his senses. He nibbled her neck. An exuberant energy rose in him. But suddenly the stifling atmosphere got the better of his desire; this being his first time, he didn't want to experience the momentous rite of passage like this.

He abruptly tore himself from Tiena's arms, his eyes full of regret. Stumbling, he found himself outside, ashamed and bitterly disappointed at the same time, filling his lungs quickly with cold air. What would Tiena and the Wendats think of his behaviour? In their language, which didn't seem to have words capable of expressing complex emotions, he knew he wouldn't succeed in making them understand.

At the entrance to the longhouse, he discerned a silhouette. Buslé's reluctance fell away. He embraced Tiena passionately and felt the warmth of her body, her cheek against his beard. At the time he had entrusted him to the Algonquians, Samuel de Champlain had ordered Buslé to apply himself studiously to learning the native languages, so that he could become a skilled interpreter. The young Frenchman had just learned a lesson that would serve him well throughout his entire interpreter's career: genuine emotions don't need to be translated into any language.

He led Tiena away to the outskirts of the village. Shortly afterwards, under the full moon and in the cold air, guided by this blue jay with skin like satin, Buslé discovered ecstasy.

The next day at dawn, the shamans declared the *andacwandet* over. Proud and happy, Buslé returned to the village with Tiena. From this day on, the stream of life that flowed within him would now be joined to that of the Wendats, uniting him with their land and their blood.

Two days later, Andiora announced her complete recovery.

6. Scotland, April 19th, 1746

"Gleann Dubh!"

The two words had crossed his lips without his having to form them. His eyes had contemplated the rolling hillsides, coloured by vibrant purple heather. Did his expression resemble his ancestor's, which had gazed upon these hills for the first time almost two hundred years ago? A flood of emotions, more restless than the rush of the river Spey visible in the distance, stirred his senses and made him want to run. He wasn't sure in which direction. Should he plunge into the valley or leave it for good?

Niall Fearmòr felt a great sense of pride to be returning home to the land that had reared and nourished him with its water and its barley. Three days ago, on the battlefield of Culloden, he had heard the pastor John Maitland consecrate crumbs of oatcake for Communion with *uisge beatha*, for lack of wine. And then, Niall had been thrown into the battle that had destroyed everything, especially hope.

The weight of such a great shame, the shame of the defeat that the clans had just suffered at Culloden, lay heavily on Niall's shoulders, weighing down his steps. He had fought for Scotland, had rallied to the young prince Charles Edward Stuart, whom he had followed into exile in France. Disembarking beside the Pretender in 1745, he had believed that Scotland would finally be freed from the English yoke. Despite the first victories and the taking of Edinburgh, Prince Charles had unfortunately decided to meet the English army, commanded by the ruthless Duke of Cumberland, on the field of Culloden. To make things worse, not all of the country had rallied behind its prince. The English troops had included just as many Scottish soldiers as the Pretender's army—which, badly routed, had left behind one thousand dead. Charles Edward Stuart had fled Scotland, as Niall Fearmòr should have done.

And yet the pull of the Gleann Dubh, of the Dark Valley of his birth, prevented Niall from walking away.

He had taken three days to cross a distance normally covered in one. He had lost blood from a shoulder injury, and he had been forced to travel carefully in order to evade the English patrols still searching for all those who had escaped their bullets and bayonets. Cumberland's army, driven by a singular brutality, had massacred just as many fugitives as fighters.

His stomach empty, a weakened Niall entered the valley, his senses taking in each bit of birdsong, each breeze and each smell like the words of a familiar, welcoming hymn. At the edge of the *Sruth fuar,* one of the three streams that meandered down the slopes of the Gleann Dubh, he found the path that would take him back home.

Since his departure for France, he had had no news of his family. During his walk, he climbed up the opposite side of the valley he had just crossed, fearing that the news he was about to receive would be even sadder than the news he was bringing.

When he reached the place to cross the *Sruth fuar*, he hesitated for a long time. He could continue straight to his parents' house, or go slightly back upstream to see whether, by any chance … He knelt, like a believer at a religious service. His fingers broke through the water's surface and formed a container of flesh, like a *quaich,* the type of small chalice the locals used here for drinking whisky. The icy cold pierced his battered body. He sprinkled the wound in his right shoulder with water and slowly leaned, prostrated himself, over the stream. His lips touched the surface of the water like a lover kissing his beloved upon returning from a long separation.

Niall got up in one quick movement. His head was spinning. The midges, those tiny, barely visible little black flies, formed a thick, constantly moving cloud. But Niall ignored them. Water trickled from his thick beard. He headed upstream; he'd go to the house afterwards. He hurried, suddenly feeling a sense of urgency, a fear that he had returned too late. Maybe his father was no longer around to make the whisky.

He finally arrived, crossing the edge of a forest that only a Fearmòr, or a close friend of the clan, could navigate.

Even before the hut clinging to the bank of the stream came into view, he was reassured by the smell. Thick smoke reeking of peat floated away through a hole in the roof. He moved forward and opened the hut door.

He saw before him the image engraved in his memory: a man standing next to a peat fire beside his still. If the man hadn't been more bent, whiter-haired and more wrinkled than his memories, he could have believed that ten years had not passed, that he had never left the Gleann Dubh.

Niall hugged his father. This reunion left them both equally amazed. Though they had barely exchanged a few words, the father was already handing a small jug to his son.

"Let's drink to your return."

"*Slàinte*!" toasted Niall, bringing the jug to his lips.

He let the whisky rest in his mouth for a moment. Niall smiled and held out the jug to his father. Now he was truly back in his own land, for it was not only all around him, but inside him as well.

"Och! There'll never be another whisky like my father's."

His father agreed. Niall asked for news of the family: of his mother, of his sisters Isobel and Maggie, of his brother Seamus.

"Your mother's well, she'll be happy to see you. But the others …"

Niall's fears were confirmed.

"They've gone away," his father said simply. "There's no way to live off the land here anymore."

So his brother and his sisters had all left the Highlands for the south, driven away by the unaffordable rents demanded by the landowners more and more resigned to the English occupation.

"If your mother and I are still clinging to our little plot, it's only because our lands are too craggy to serve as pasture, and because I still manage to sell my peat-reek. Damn the English!"

Niall drank some more whisky. The warmth comforted him like a balm on his wounded heart.

"You've come from Culloden?" his father asked, pointing to Niall's shoulder.

At least he had been spared the pain of announcing their defeat.

"We heard of it yesterday," his father continued. "I was sure you'd be there. But I thank God that you didn't fall to their bullets."

Niall drank again. He heard the wort boiling in the still, the sign that alcohol was about to separate from water.

"It's almost time," he said.

His father, attaching the coil to the still, nodded.

"You'll hide here, Niall. However hard they look for you, they won't find you."

The first drop condensed in the coil. Niall felt his blood boil as he watched life leave the water, to be reincarnated as *uisge beatha*. In the warmth of the bothy, he was rediscovering his taste for life. His father handed him an oatcake and a bit of cheese.

No, the English won't find me, thought Niall. *In any case, I'll never be the same again.* He took a bite of the oatcake. *Now it's me that has to find myself.*

7. MacPhearson, Toronto

"If you can authenticate it, do you realise the impact your discovery will have?"

"I do. And sure I can authenticate it. In any case, the whisky speaks for itself."

We'll see about that, John MacPhearson, proprietor of the Dearg Room, Toronto's most posh Scotch bar, says to himself. His eyes turn from his glass to Elizabeth Legrand.

"*Slàinte*!"

Despite his painstaking efforts, MacPhearson is unable to hide the pleasure that is giving his hard-edged face a look of warm cordiality. He senses many aromas: mellow, woody, peaty, joyful. A sublime tickle creeps up and down his whole body, as though he was twenty years old again and running naked through grassy fields. Fiery tongues lick the inside of his mouth, kiss him, and make him tremble.

She's right, thinks the man of fifty. *This miraculous find will create a great stir and I've got to exploit it with all my skill.* He reflects a moment more, before saying, "If you have the merchandise delivered to me along with all the necessary proofs of origin, I could sell it for you on consignment. I'll gladly make this whisky known to connoisseurs the world over, and put it up for sale—while retaining a modest percentage of the profits as my commission, of course."

He waits for a reaction. Meanwhile, Elizabeth studies the large bar behind MacPhearson, an impressive showcase of bottles of every stripe, including a few very rare ones. The Dearg Room even offers cask strength whiskies for a select group of Scotch connoisseurs. She takes a mouthful of the excellent 38-year-old Bunnahabhain that MacPhearson offered her in exchange for a glassful from the bottle she brought along. The comforting liquid on her tongue whispers the words she seeks.

"I don't just intend to simply offer the world the oldest single malt whisky on Earth. I want to give the Glen Dubh a new lease on life."

MacPhearson doesn't hide his growing annoyance. This mysterious-looking woman intrigues him, but frightens him as well. Frustrated by her wall of secrecy, he boils with irritation.

"The oldest known bottle of whisky to date is a Tobermory from 1869, which sold for $15,000. More recently a bottle of Macallan 1926 went for $85,000. If, as you claim, your Glen Dubh dates from 1856, it would be worth still more. How many bottles of it do you have?"

"Let's say ten, for now."

MacPhearson makes some swift mental calculations. "Why aren't you being open with me?"

Elizabeth stares at the man. "Okay. I want to use this Glen Dubh to create a new whisky."

MacPhearson swallows a gulp of spirits and looks at Elizabeth as though he were hallucinating. *This extraordinary whisky can't possibly be real—and the insane woman who brought it to me even less so.* And yet she is speaking to him with the greatest possible seriousness.

"In the short term, I'll re-invest the profits of the sale, to combine part of the Glen Dubh with other whiskies and create three new blends—which I intend to put on the market two years from now."

"And in the long term?" MacPhearson poses the question without any hope of getting a coherent answer, as that seems beyond Elizabeth Legrand. He absolutely mustn't miss out on his chance to get his hands on the entire cache of this whisky.

"I mean to create a new single malt which will be the equal of this Glen Dubh, or even better."

"And where do you hope to achieve this?"

"At Lighthouse Point, where I live."

Flummoxed, MacPhearson drains his glass and prepares to ask for another. However, he thinks better of it. *Another dram of this incomparable Scotch and I'll start believing in her crazy plans.*

"Well?" asks Elizabeth.

MacPhearson takes a firmer tone. "Why would I trust you? What do you really know about Scotch?"

"Mr MacPhearson, like many Scots, you doubtless enjoy the occasional wager?" Elizabeth doesn't wait for a reply before continuing. "I propose a bet that you're sure to win. I'll select five whiskies from your menu. Behind my back, you'll pour me a dram from each bottle. If I can't correctly identify the five, either by aroma or by taste, I'll let you keep my bottle of Glen Dubh."

The proprietor of the Dearg Room gazes at her for a long moment.

"And if you succeed?"

Elizabeth smiles. "You simply accept my offer, and we fix your commission at five percent."

The utter self-confidence of this woman baffles him. She surely isn't capable of doing what she suggests.

"First make your selection, and then I'll tell you if I'll play."

Elizabeth takes the whisky menu, two pages long, and scans it rapidly. She writes the names of five whiskies down on a piece of paper, assigning each a number, and passes the list to MacPhearson.

"Very good," he says, noting that Elizabeth hasn't chosen the easiest whiskies to identify. He gets up and walks towards the bar.

"Number the glasses, make a second list with the numbers and their corresponding whiskies and bring it to the table."

Taken aback by Elizabeth's request, MacPhearson controls himself. *It's true that, if I was in her shoes, I'd ask as much.*

Shortly after, he returns with a tray containing the five numbered glasses, a large glass of water, and the list, which he places face down on the table. Elizabeth begins immediately, dissecting the contents of each glass with an intense gaze.

"This is a twelve-year-old Talisker." She moves the glass of amber-coloured liquid away from the four others."As for the rest, I'll have to at least nose them."

MacPhearson is hypnotised by this woman's little game. She bends over each glass to inhale its aroma. Her fingers move again.

"Glenfiddich, eight years old, and Bowmore, twelve years old." While speaking, Elizabeth has shifted the glasses. "The last two I'll need to taste, just to be sure."

Completely astounded, MacPhearson watches her carefully pick up the two remaining glasses, one after the other, and lift them to her lips. Each time, she allows the spirits to flood her mouth like a rising tide, which she savours for a long moment. Her whole body, her entire being, is suddenly illuminated by the warmth radiating from her face.

"This one is the ten-year-old Tomintoul," she announces, touching one of the two glasses. "An extraordinary dram. And the other is the twenty-four-year-old Macallan."

Like an actress who has just spoken the last line of a play, Elizabeth waits for her audience's verdict. MacPhearson turns over the sheet of paper.

"Five out of five!" he exclaims, incredulous. "Where in the world did you acquire such a talent for whisky?"

Elizabeth shrugs her shoulders and, satisfied, savours once again the Tomintoul—a whisky produced by the distillery located at the second highest altitude in Scotland. She doesn't know where her gift comes from. She has been told that her parents were connoisseurs of Scotch, but they barely sampled more than four or five varieties, and not the costliest ones at that. From the moment she became of age, Elizabeth has been able to "memorise" the appearance, the nose and the palate of whiskies after only a single tasting. At Lighthouse Point, her surprising ability has never been of much use. Today, a certain intuitive feeling pushed her to take a risk.

"You win. Tomorrow I'll get in touch with the Scotch Malt Whisky Society and get the ball rolling."

Smiling, Elizabeth raises her glass. "We've both won," she points out. "To the new Glen Dubh."

MacPhearson takes the glass of Bowmore and clinks glasses with his new associate. Then, taking the bottle of Glen Dubh in his hand, he runs a finger across its age-yellowed label.

"Do you know what 'Glen Dubh' means in Scottish Gaelic?"

"Naturally," replies Elizabeth. "'The dark valley'."

MacPhearson sets the bottle down. *And I'm venturing straight into it with my eyes closed.*

8. Scotland, 1757

Gazing out the window at the gloomy day, Lord Charles Sutherland turned toward his guest, Duke Reginald Redgrave, and cursed.

"This country of rain and fog will be the death of me!"

Drawing away from the window with a disappointed air, he dropped into the armchair facing Redgrave's.

"I fully empathise, dear friend. Since my arrival here, I've observed how the weather is more often than not abominably dreary."

"I miss being out in polite society and enjoying the company of the people of Edinburgh terribly," Sutherland complained. "If I hadn't inherited my uncle's damned estate, I'd still be in the city."

Redgrave, a Scottish Lowland noble of small means, did not share his host's disparaging view of the Highlands. He would have been grateful to own this estate. For him, this country held out great possibilities. He had been here for less than six months and, by mixing in the best society, was searching desperately for a possible business partnership, or for a marriage with a generous dowry. Redgrave had taken to visiting Sutherland, an idle young bachelor constantly seeking amusement. The duke tried to cheer up his friend.

"But you must admit, my dear Sutherland, that your situation is highly enviable. Your clan's farmers and this vast estate provide you the means to live quite comfortably with almost no effort on your part."

Sutherland rose and paced agitatedly, like a caged lion. Finding himself in front of the fireplace, he began to poke the fire with jerky movements.

"Yes, of course, but ..."

Since the defeat of the Jacobites at the Battle of Culloden in 1746, Charles Sutherland and the other clan chieftains of Scotland had drawn growing profits from the land. Though he was of the same blood as his farmers, Sutherland felt no compassion for them. He continually raised their rent to the very limits of what they could bear. The landowners, with the support of the British government and its powerful army, shamelessly exploited the people.

"The only possible distraction for a gentleman in this place is hunting—which I admit is good here. And yet, most days, this horrid climate renders such entertainment impossible."

"Luckily, there's the whisky!"

Redgrave's comment made Sutherland smile. Indeed, this dreadful country's whisky could release a man from boredom, at least a little. For some weeks now, Sutherland had found in Reginald Redgrave a most agreeable tasting companion.

"Aye, at least there's the whisky," repeated Sutherland, heading for a small table upon which stood a carafe of spirits.

The young man generously filled two glasses, handed one to his guest, and raised the other to his lips. Redgrave took the offered glass, sniffed its contents and asked what he was drinking.

"Taste it, my dear friend, and you'll tell me yourself."

Over the course of his visits to the local upper-class homes of the area, Redgrave had discovered the native drink of the Highlands and developed a taste for it. These spirits were of a far superior quality to those distilled in the Lowlands. He took a mouthful.

"Ferintosh?" he guessed.

"Well done, Redgrave. Your sophistication does you honour."

The two men drank. Redgrave was glad to see his host relax. Refilling their glasses, Sutherland emptied the carafe and rang the bell to summon his valet.

"Do you have other whiskies besides this very agreeable Ferintosh?" inquired Redgrave, in whom the Scotch had just planted the seeds of an idea.

This question pricked Sutherland's pride. "I assure you that my cellar contains the finest selection of whiskies legally—and even clandestinely—available in the area."

"Excellent!" Redgrave said quickly. "A few days ago, I was a guest at a party hosted by the Earl of Winchester. We played a most amusing game."

Sutherland's unbridled passion for all sorts of games was well known. The lord's eyes betrayed how impatient he was to hear the rest of the story.

"The Earl held a tasting. Upon my word, there were five different whiskies, and each guest had to identify them by flavour alone."

"And you fared well at this game?"

Seeing the lord's suddenly wide eyes, Redgrave knew that he had hit his mark.

"Aye, very well indeed; I correctly identified four out of the five."

Sutherland's valet, Niall Fearmòr, a tall, rangy man, entered the room.

"Well! This game intrigues me, Redgrave."

So the lord ordered his butler to seek out six different whiskies from the cellar, and to pour one glass of each whisky for himself and for his guest. He also instructed Niall to take careful note of each glass and its contents, for it would be up to him to judge the tasting.

"Very good, milord." Niall, face impassive, left to carry out his orders.

Excited, Sutherland rubbed his hands together and emptied his glass in one long draught. "Oh, we're going to have a marvellous time, my dear Redgrave."

The duke, whose finances were nearly totally depleted, hoped so as well. His winnings from the Earl's party would barely suffice to pay for his return to Edinburgh. So now he had but two options: play for high stakes or leave empty-handed.

Niall returned with two trays, each loaded with six glasses full of whisky—some very light in colour, others much darker.

"Have you noted the contents of each glass, Niall?" inquired the lord.

"Yes, milord," replied the valet, pulling a sheet of paper from his vest. "Every glass is marked with a different number which, in turn, corresponds to the name of a whisky I have written down."

Sutherland seated himself in the armchair facing the duke. Niall had placed both trays on a table between the two gentlemen.

"Here's how we proceeded at the Earl's," Redgrave explained. "First we did a general tasting, then we named each whisky."

Thus, the two contestants would state their guesses by turns, and Niall would then confirm if they were right or wrong.

The two drinkers applied themselves to the task. Redgrave was happy to encounter some familiar flavours, thus allowing him to immediately identify a Glen Turret, the very same Ferintosh drunk a few minutes ago, and a Talisker, recognisable through its particularly peaty accents.

"Tell me, Redgrave, during your tasting at Winchester's was there no betting on the results?"

Sutherland's increasingly glassy eyes fixed themselves on Reginald, who was relieved to hear this question, for it spared him from having to bring up the subject himself.

"Aye, there was, and it did add to the pleasure of the game. If you're keen, why not wager a hundred pounds on each guess."

Such an idea pleased the lord enormously, and he happily turned to his six glasses for a second round. Redgrave did so as well, now confident that he had the correct answers. Even if one of the whiskies proved problematic, with a score of at least five out of six he would win.

"You know, my dear Redgrave, to a man of my position, money doesn't mean very much. Our little game would interest me more if we added an element of chance, and far higher stakes as well."

"What did you have in mind?" Redgrave concealed his unease with difficulty.

"Niall," commanded the lord, "go and fetch two pistols. Load just one."

Asking no questions, Niall left the room. Redgrave felt a drop of sweat beading on his forehead.

"Every time one of us gives a correct answer, he'll select a pistol and give it to the other."

"And in the case of an incorrect answer?"

The lord's mouth shaped itself into a deceitful grin. "Well then! The man who has made a mistake will point the pistol selected by his rival at his head and pull the trigger."

Niall, who had just returned with the pistols, placed them on the table between the two men. The lord illustrated what he meant by pressing one of the weapons against his ear.

"And if I win I'll live, but if we both succeed, the contest will have served no purpose."

As he spoke, Redgrave felt sure he had hit upon the argument that would convince the lord to give up this mad scheme.

"Agreed. In the case of a draw, I'll give you half of my estates. If I lose, you'll have them all. I'll write out and sign a testamentary note."

Without waiting for a reply, Sutherland rose and made his way to a desk, where he began to write swiftly. Returning to Redgrave, the lord handed him a paper on which he had, in effect, jotted down his promise.

"But … I … have nothing of comparable value to offer in exchange," Redgrave stammered.

"Your honour and your life will suffice."

This unexpected response seemingly decided the question. Redgrave felt his thoughts grow muddled. He could no longer return penniless to Edinburgh, where his numerous creditors were impatiently waiting for him. And if he came out the winner of this horrible bet, he'd finally have the means to make his plan a reality. Namely, he wished to apply a new economic model to the Highlands—the same model that was making the landowners in the Scottish Lowlands wealthy. Over the last few years, clan chieftains had populated their holdings with sheep and raised them quite profitably. However, this had required that they evict those farmers too poor to pay their constantly rising rents. The sheep population had multiplied tenfold, while the numbers of "human livestock" had fallen dramatically. Newly destitute families were pushed out to the coast, where they barely survived by fishing and gathering kelp. The Clearances, as the Scots called them, were emptying the Lowlands of their inhabitants.

He glanced at Niall, who was maintaining his impassive demeanour. Was this a game orchestrated by master and servant simply to humiliate him?

"I'll even let you go first and, if you make a mistake on your first attempt, you won't have to pull the trigger."

Not thinking, Redgrave took a draught of whisky. In order for the lord to expose himself to such a risk, he had to be very sure of himself—just as sure as Redgrave was about five of the six glasses before him. And, thanks to the favour Sutherland had just granted him, if he began with the glass he was unsure of, he would run no risk. Why should he have qualms about stripping Sutherland—a man who did not appreciate his own wealth—of half his fortune?

"I accept," said Redgrave at last, after a long silence.

"Then let's drink one last time and move on to the moment of truth."

Both bettors left no more than a few drops in their glasses. The duke picked up the last glass in the row on his tray.

"I'll start with number six," he said gravely. "There is no doubt that this is a Kilbagie from the Lowlands."

The two men turned to Niall, who consulted his sheet of paper.

"His lordship the duke is correct."

"My turn, then," cried Sutherland, pointing at the third glass to his right. "My number three is a Gilcomston, recognisable by its heathery, smoky notes."

The valet confirmed that he was right. Redgrave continued with his own number two, a Ferintosh, and Sutherland with his number five, which was the same whisky. The duke correctly identified his number one as a Balblair, and the lord went on to name his number four, a Glen Turret. The Talisker, in its turn, was correctly identified by both men. Redgrave felt jubilant when he successfully named his Glen Turret, thinking, *Now, all I have to do is name the …*

"Gleann Dubh," announced Sutherland, holding his sixth tasting glass in his hand.

"No, milord is incorrect."

Amazement distorted the master's face.

"What?"

"Milord's number six is not Gleann Dubh."

Without a word, an offended Lord Sutherland gestured to Redgrave to choose a pistol. Frightened by his host's gaze, the duke selected one of the weapons, which the lord precipitously pressed against his ear.

"Don't do this, Sutherland," Redgrave pleaded. "Grant me half your estate and we'll say the game is over."

Lord Sutherland's face took on a strange expression, for his eyes seemed to say "Yes" even as his mouth hardened.

In the next instant, the terrible echo of a pistol shot filled the room, followed by the acrid smell of gunpowder. Lord Sutherland's body slumped down on the ground right next to the pistol. Horrified, Redgrave bent over his inert companion. He turned to Niall, who was looking steadily at him, as though awaiting orders from the estate's new proprietor.

"This is ghastly, Niall. How could we have committed such an irreparable act?" As he spoke, Redgrave had approached the table and picked up the second weapon.

"If I had chosen this pistol instead, we wouldn't have come to such a terrible end. If I'd been obliged to shoot, would I have done it?"

Redgrave was still looking at the gun in his hand, and as though to answer the question, he pointed its barrel at his chest, miming the deed he had described. He squeezed the trigger.

A gunshot sounded, and the duke, grimacing with incomprehension, fell dead in his turn. Very calmly, Niall walked up to the little table and picked up his late master's sixth glass. A finger of liquor remained, and Niall swallowed it, toasting the corpses with "*Slàinte*."

"Ah! What a marvellous whisky, this Gleann Dubh of my father's", thought the valet.

No one would ever know that in telling his master that his number six was not a Gleann Dubh, Niall had lied. In order to remain in the Highlands, he had been forced to enter into the service of this despicable clan chieftain, who played the Englishmen's game. While loading both guns, Niall had resolved to leave Scotland once again. The horror stories of the Lowland Clearances were beginning to spread. Sooner or later, the clan chieftains of the Highlands would follow in the footsteps of their southern counterparts.

Niall would enlist in the British army, and even if he never saw his country again, at least he would be leaving with a slightly lighter heart.

9. Elizabeth, Lighthouse Point

"What do you think?"

Ghisèle has been walking around the old depot site with Elizabeth for an hour. As they toured the scrap heaps, the abandoned railroad track, the dilapidated stone-and-wood hangars, she'd listened to her childhood friend outline her plan.

The time she spent abroad, and now the solitude, have changed her. Ghisèle is no longer sure she recognises this person who, in all seriousness, is entertaining crazy ambitions. She feels her body shudder—with cold, because of the north wind sure to bring snow, or with fear?

"It doesn't seem like a very practical plan."

Converting this abandoned depot, accessible only by boat, into a distillery is sheer insanity.

"The location is ideal!" Elizabeth retorts. "The distillery can take its water from the river and the bay. With one or two boats, it'll be easy to import the ingredients we need and export the finished product."

Elizabeth gathers up a stone and throws it into the water as hard as she can. It breaks the water's surface with a crash. Watching the concentric waves calms her down for a minute.

"You've never been to the Isle of Skye in Scotland. Believe me, what we have here is naturally just as good as what they have over there."

Ghisèle isn't convinced. "Maybe, but here we don't have peat or salty air."

Elizabeth's eyes scan the horizon, gazing at something dancing on the whitecaps.

"But we have the water," she says slowly. "Not sea water, not the stream water of the burns of Scotland, but the water of our freshwater sea."

Despite Ghisèle's incomprehension, Elizabeth, riding a wave of emotion, continues.

"Our water is magical; it's transformed the Glen Dubh that my family kept all these years. What we're going to make here isn't whisky, Ghisèle, but magic. We're going to create something more than just spirits. We're going to distil life itself, the very essence of the mythology of whisky."

Ghisèle studies her friend's features, then the wind-whipped waves. She takes a great gulp of air charged with particles of fresh water from this inland sea. Though she knows better, the need to believe in this magic, her ticket and everybody else's to surviving at Lighthouse Point, trumps her scepticism for a moment. But her pragmatism—inherited from her ancestors who had to cling to the edge of this granite coast by relying solely on themselves for more than a hundred years—catches up before the dream takes hold of her.

"Even if the distillery could succeed, the municipal council is bound to judge Desroches' real estate project to be a safer bet."

Elizabeth smiles enigmatically. "Desroches only has money on his side, while I ..." The wind ruffles Elizabeth's long hair, suddenly giving her a wild and witch-like air. "I have magic and the Glen Dubh on my side. My distillery, the New Glen Dubh, will restore Lighthouse Point's legendary power without compromising its natural environment."

With long steps, Elizabeth moves towards the boat moored near shore. Ghisèle has the impression she's just heard an oracle. But what exactly did it predict?

10. Québec, September 13th, 1759

"*Where are they?*"

"Shut up. If you have to talk, do it in French, you idiot."

In the half-light of fresh dawn, Niall couldn't judge the effect of his words on the young soldier, who, like him, was scrutinising the shore, searching for the enemy.

The officer who had entrusted them with this mission the day before hadn't seemed at all convinced it would succeed. But such were their orders. If the invaders wanted to leave this cursed country before the onset of winter, they had to please General Wolfe and attempt one last assault on the fortress that British artillery—positioned on the other side of the river at Pointe-Lévis—had reduced to a pile of rubble. And if army command was calling on this squadron drawn from the 78th Highlanders Regiment to carry out this almost suicidal undertaking, it was not only because of their legendary ferocity, but because these veterans—formerly allies of the French against England—spoke French. At least, enough of it to fool any enemy sentinels they might encounter while disembarking and scaling the cliffs of L'Anse au Foulon Cove. During the night, the squadron had climbed into boats that had then been allowed to drift. And this morning, despite being exhausted, all of Niall Fearmòr's senses were strained in anticipation of the battle.

All of a sudden, a young man's tense voice reached them from the darkness.

"*Qui vive? Qui vive?*" *(Who goes there?)*

A few feet away from their boat, on shore no doubt, they heard the rattle of firearms.

"*La France et vive le roi.*" *(Frenchmen, and long live the king.)*

The voice of Captain Fraser, commander of the squadron, sounded confident and firm. Nonetheless, Niall wondered whether the French would be deceived.

"They're our troops with the supplies. Let them pass."

Niall had to hold back a long sigh. The ruse had worked, and the boat went on sliding silently along the water for another twenty minutes. At five o'clock in the morning, when Captain Fraser and his troop set foot on the bank, they could clearly see the almost sixty-metre-high slope, which they soon set about climbing, pressing themselves flat against the hard and soaking wet rock wall.

Niall had taken the lead of the squadron, and the ten soldiers following him had to be just as miserable as he was. This difficult ascent continued for almost two hours; the men groping, a few centimetres at a time, rifles slung over their shoulders catching the branches of the shrubs bravely clinging to the inhospitable rock.

More than once Fearmòr had narrowly avoided a fatal fall into the river at their feet, saved by a quick reaction or a superhuman effort. He almost regretted it. Niall sensed that the summit was quite near. Once in place, the squadron had to hold this position so other troops could follow and launch the assault. Another, smaller group of soldiers was disembarking farther upstream from Québec—a deceptive ploy to distract the defenders' attention towards the opposite side of the city.

Finally Niall reached a flat surface where, cautiously, he crawled a bit further before rising to his feet. He heard the rustling of the men creeping along behind him and, relieved, whispered to them in French: "One last effort lads! We're at the top."

"Who goes there?"

Niall turned abruptly towards the silhouette that had just hailed him. He pictured the man two metres in front of him, clad in the grey uniform of the *Compagnie de la Marine Franche* soldiers. For three months now, British bullets had pierced this uniform all too often. In the faint light, he made out the barrel of a rifle pointed at him.

"The king's troops. We're the reinforcements."

Niall was surprised by the calm in his own voice. He listened carefully for any noises coming from behind him. If any one his men attacked the sentinel, who was certainly not alone, their operation would be compromised.

"Very well, hurry up then."

Youth, the finest thing in the French army, the finest thing in the world—Niall had detected it in this voice trying hard to sound in control, and in the abrupt gestures of the lad as he rapidly moved away. The squadron waited for two more minutes before resuming its advance. The creeping dawn was beginning to reveal the vast field in front of them. They spread out and, without encountering any opposition, took control of the position manned by the French soldiers. Now, all they had to do was hold it as the invaders gathered in the hopes of drawing the French army outside the city walls.

Executing the next step of the plan, a Highlander positioned himself in a visible spot at the top of the cliff and, using a lighted lantern, signalled to the attackers to begin the offensive.

Thanks to the Scottish Highlanders, the Battle of the Plains of Abraham could begin. The 35th Regiment would follow in their tracks—a regiment made up of Irishmen just as miserable as the Scots. These men, like them, were fighting for the empire of the country that had ruined theirs. The future of a continent lay in their hands. And yet, even if they proved victorious, those hands would remain empty.

11. MacPhearson, Toronto

GLEN DUBH: AGELESS

This new product, resulting from the recent discovery of a very old whisky, ironically comes to us from the New World. The Dearg Room, the very respectable Scotch bar in Toronto, Canada, just recently announced the notice of sale of ten bottles of Glen Dubh, a single malt whisky from a Scottish Speyside distillery that ceased production in 1919.

It was believed that the last drop of this whisky, much prized in those days, had been consumed in 1918. John MacPhearson, proprietor of the Dearg Room, can confirm that this authentic Glen Dubh dates to at least 1913 and, quite probably, to forty years earlier.

The ten bottles of this Glen Dubh will be offered on the world market with a huge price tag. To dispel any scepticism about this claim, Mr MacPhearson invited several of the greatest Scotch experts to a tasting in his Toronto bar. We participated in this session two weeks ago and, in the opinion of all those present, the results are conclusive: this is a single malt of extraordinary quality, superior to everything currently available the world over. There is clear evidence that this whisky has benefited from an ageing process of an unprecedented duration in the history of Scotch, and that it has taken place in a climate and location with very distinctive characteristics. All the great clubs of Scotch connoisseurs will wish to obtain it for their members to savour it, even if only once.

At the auction sale, which will take place next January 12th, we can expect fierce competition and breathtakingly steep prices.

OUR TASTING NOTES

A subtle nose, which lightly tickles the nostrils, evoking a cool breeze and fragrances of trees and wildflowers.

A dark amber colour, but with a barely discernible green sparkle.

A marvellously complex mouthfeel, in which contrasting flavours collide and then blend harmoniously. Essences of coffee and chocolate mingle with hints of wood and seafood. The primary taste is very bold, almost brutal but, after a few seconds, yields to a sublimely smooth, even ethereal finish. The flavour lingers in the mouth for a very long time.

What's more, this whisky goes straight to the heart, a unique phenomenon.

John MacPhearson finishes reading the article in *Whisky Magazine* with satisfaction. He then tapes it to the wall, just to the left of the bar. Next, he steps back to admire from a distance the photo accompanying the text, a picture of the Dearg Room's proprietor, smiling, a bottle of Glen Dubh in his hand. The caption underscores the bottle's probable value.

MacPhearson sips a Bowmore as he relives the magnificent tasting event in his mind. Now his bar has become world-famous. Even before the articles appeared, several whisky clubs had tried to circumvent the auction sale by making more than just enticing offers for the Glen Dubh. MacPhearson is now certain that he can double the starting auction price. *Elizabeth Legrand is going to earn herself a nice wad of cash.*

He reaches the bottom of his glass and sighs. The damned Glen Dubh has already changed his life. Since tasting it, other whiskies have lost their shine. To resist the temptation of uncorking another of these bottles, which have been waiting so long, he must constantly remind himself of the hefty commission he'll collect. He would very much like to rediscover the euphoric feeling kindled by the Glen Dubh. He must, however, leave this pleasure to the rich—at least for the time being.

And if Elizabeth really does have more bottles of this whisky? The possibility both comforts and troubles him. *I can't let the little scatterbrain waste it.* In spite of Elizabeth's confident air, MacPhearson knows she can't possibly create a good Glen Dubh-based blended whisky. And he's made enquiries about Lighthouse Point. This picturesque, quietly disappearing coastal community is an impossible location for a distillery. Turning it into a hot vacation spot or a luxurious summer cottage development, as suggested by the local promoter with whom he talked, would suit it infinitely better.

Anyway, he doesn't see how Elizabeth will rally the locals around such a crazy idea. *Yes, after the auction sale I'll have a serious talk with her*, MacPhearson tells himself. *Once she gets her hands on the money, if she really has more whisky, I'll have no trouble persuading her to put it in my care.*

12. Québec, 1759

For several hours, Niall Fearmòr had been walking through the edge of a dense forest clinging to the mountainside. This walk, strangely enough, reminded him of the one that had taken him from Culloden to Gleann Dubh thirteen years ago, with the exception that the hills and valleys he was roaming today were covered in strapping trees. No bushes, no heather. And this time he was crossing the countryside as a victor; it was he who was chasing the last resistance fighters, rather than fleeing at their side.

And yet, in his heart, the capture of Québec inspired in him an even greater sadness than he had felt after the defeat at Culloden.

He laid his rifle on the ground and sat leaning against a tree. All these battles, all this spilled blood, for nothing. Faced with the impossibility of ever beating the English, Niall had joined them in the hope of quenching his thirst for violence at the expense of others. From Kamouraska to Pointe-Lévis, for about forty leagues along the St Lawrence River, he had seen the English troops burn villages and parishes whole.

All he had sought was to drain away the belligerent rage consuming him, and to carve out a place of his own in this British Empire—which, with his help, had just seized yet another immense territory.

Nonetheless, the day Niall had seen Captain Montgomery, a barbaric officer, massacre two French prisoners in the cruellest and most inhuman way possible—prisoners whom Captain Fraser, with Niall's help, had just handed over to him—he had understood that there was no place for him in this new empire, no matter how immense it proved.

Niall looked off into the distance. In the fading light, he could just make out what had to be a farmhouse, built in the particular style of this country subjected to a frightfully harsh climate. He had left his troop of Highlanders a few hours ago. None of them had wanted to continue their hunt for enemy fighters so far away from the conquered city, since they dreaded the possibility of being forced to spend the night at the edge of this inhospitable forest.

But Niall had decided to continue on his own. He'd rejoin the troop the next day if he didn't manage to finish the search and return to camp before dark. Captain Fraser, commander of the Highlanders, to whom this dangerous, thankless task had been entrusted, had let Niall do as he pleased. In the regiment it was well known that getting in Fearmòr's way when he was hell-bent on doing something meant arousing his fury—possibly leading to serious, even fatal, consequences.

So Niall had ventured out on his own, visiting the rare farms down the length of this concession road without finding the slightest trace of armed men, or even of human beings. Both civilians and soldiers had probably fled while awaiting the battle's last gasps, and its definitive end.

An easy target for marksmen hidden behind barns or thickets, the soldier nonetheless wasn't afraid to walk about alone, in broad daylight, in his red uniform. Taking a bullet to the heart would have freed him from this abyss, in which he could no longer move forward or backward.

So it was stepping firmly that he went up the pathway leading to the stone house.

* * *

Inside, Thérèse Roy watched the approaching man with apprehension, since he was visibly armed. Her first instinct was to flee, but she ruled out this option, knowing that it was impossible. She would need to face this ordeal calmly.

She cast a glance at the large knife used for slaughtering pigs. If it proved to be necessary, she wouldn't hesitate. She resolved to take the initiative; that would put her in a position of strength. She abruptly opened the door and, once outside, planted herself solidly on both feet, giving herself an air conveying both firmness and pride.

* * *

Hearing the door open, Niall, whose battle instincts took the upper hand, had frozen right away, crouching slightly in readiness to shoot. The glint of the setting sun fell upon the silhouette with long black hair. Lowering his weapon, Niall went forward, trying to look reassuring.

"I come in the name of His Majesty the King of England. We mean you no harm. Québec has fallen."

He was close enough to the woman to see her face clearly. He saw her surprise upon hearing him speak French. He was also surprised to discover the nature of the person before him.

"So what do you want?"

The voice of this pregnant woman with native features didn't match her blue dress any more than Niall's voice matched his uniform.

"I need to make sure that you're not hiding any soldiers here and …" Niall hesitated, unsettled by the woman's beauty. "I'd like a little water if you have any."

Since his arrival on the continent, Niall had seen some of the indigenous women of New France, but none were dressed like Frenchwomen or spoke their language.

"Come," she said dryly.

Niall followed her into the house. The woman, who couldn't be older than twenty-five, plunged a ladle into a bucket, filled it and held it out to the soldier. Niall drank greedily.

"Are you alone here?"

Before she could reply, Niall's stomach let out a series of rumbles that made her smile.

"I barely have anything to eat. There's some salt pork and bread left, if you'd like some." Without waiting for the answer, the woman went to a pantry and took out a jar and some bread, which she put on the table. "I don't have any utensils. They were all melted down to make bullets."

Niall wondered whether this last comment was meant as a jibe, or simply a genuine excuse. He approached the table and went to prop his weapon up against the wall. He quickly scanned the room, pausing briefly on the knife near the window.

"Are you alone?" he asked again.

She nodded, but laid her hands on her stomach, as if to say that, very soon, she wouldn't be.

"Eat. You can search afterwards."

Throwing caution to the wind, Niall laid down his weapon and took a seat. At least he wouldn't die with an empty stomach.

"What about your husband?"

"He's at war like all the others."

The meat certainly tasted better than army rations. Niall almost said, "If he wasn't killed, he'll come back soon." But he thought better of it.

"And children?"

"Only the one I'm expecting."

Niall swallowed a few more mouthfuls. "You …" He didn't exactly know how to ask, neither in French nor in English, and in Scottish Gaelic still less. The woman, however, had sensed his curiosity.

"I'm Huron. My husband is French. My people live in a village near here."

Niall would have liked to ask why she had married a white man, but he asked her name instead.

"Thérèse Roy."

"Sergeant Niall Fearmòr."

Despite the hunger still tormenting him, Niall stopped. He didn't want to take too much from his hostess's provisions. He could at least return to his rations, while the inhabitants of this poor country, following a summer of scorched-earth policy that the British invaders had applied to the letter, now faced a winter of scarcity.

"You speak French well."

Niall explained to her that he was Scottish, but had spent time in France. In spite of Thérèse's curious look, he cut his explanations short.

"I'll conduct my search before it gets dark."

He got to his feet and picked up his weapon again. Thérèse showed him that the only rooms were the one they were in and two small bedrooms upstairs. The farm, of modest size, was comprised of a barn and a stable for the horses.

Niall first made a brief inspection of the bedrooms. There was little furniture, and even fewer places to hide. He cast a glance under the bed all the same, for form's sake, but also in order to lightly touch the quilt and inhale its smell of domesticity, of woman. The last night he'd spent in a bed had been a very long time ago.

Thérèse took him to the barn, where he found two pigs and a cow. The smell of straw and manure briefly took him back to his father's farm in Gleann Dubh. His inspection finished, he saw the young woman back to the house. Darkness was now total.

"I'll spend the night in the stable," announced the soldier, without preamble. As though excusing himself, he added, "It's too late to return to my camp. I'll leave early tomorrow morning." He turned on his heels, as if executing a military manoeuvre.

"I'll give you a blanket. The nights get chilly."

Niall followed Thérèse to the house, where she set water boiling on the fire in the fireplace.

"Surely you'll have some herb tea?"

She lit a lantern. This brightness gave a different radiance to her dark skin and to her features, made them even more unfathomable for Niall. Were her eyes those of a charlatan or a sorceress?

"Tell me about your country." At this moment, Thérèse's yearning for distant lands had to be as great as his.

Niall began describing Scotland, its valleys, its rivers, its burns. He even spoke to her of his father's whisky, of its magical properties. Words often failed him.

"But why did you come here?" Thérèse served the herb tea, a mix of various mints, with a soothing aroma.

Niall didn't know the answer. He could no longer tell the truth any more than he could lie. "The English defeated us ..." He explained the Clearances to her, painting a stark picture of the misery filling the industrial cities like Glasgow and Edinburgh.

"The French did more or less the same thing to us." Thérèse had spoken without bitterness. There was even a note of compassion in her voice, as if she was trying to console the Scot by pointing out that, although from two different continents, they were both the victims of the same colonial ambitions. "I even have some of their blood in my veins."

Surprised, Niall questioned her with his eyes.

"My great-grandmother's mother, who was called Tiena like her mother, had a French father, named Hoatatexa, or 'the burned man', in our language." Thérèse grew quiet and drank for a long time in silence.

"Life will be better under English rule." Niall sensed that she didn't believe it any more than he did but, doubtless out of pity, she said nothing. And yet he was on the winning side.

"If I had been lucky enough to be born in my ancestors' land of water, I'm sure I'd return there."

Niall didn't hide his surprise. "Where is your land of water?"

"The place is called Wendake. It's many leagues to the west."

"And you've never been there?"

"The elders of my village talk about it. When the French came to live among us at the beginning of the 1600s, that's where my people, my ancestor Tiena, lived ..."

After the fall of their nation, brought about by European illnesses and war against the Iroquois, some of the surviving Hurons had followed the French to Québec.

"There's no longer anyone among us who has seen the territory of our great-grandmothers."

Thérèse went upstairs and returned with a blanket. Niall got up in turn, accepted the blanket and went to the door. Thérèse lit a second lantern, which she gave him.

"I'll leave at dawn and I probably won't see you again. I thank you very much."

Thérèse smiled. Her hair, black as the night and encircled with a halo by the glow of the lantern, gave her an air of solemnity. "I sense that you won't stay here much longer, sergeant. Good night and a safe journey."

The air outside had gotten much colder. Niall was happy to have the blanket, and felt a peaceful weariness. He went to the barn and, guided by the light of the lantern, found himself a pile of comfortable looking hay. He expected to sleep like a log and, as soon as he'd settled in, his exhausted body drifted off completely.

A few hours later, Niall was half-woken by the torment of having to urinate, which prevented him from staying in this wonderfully restful state. He vaguely sensed the movement of the barn door opening. However, it was only when a body threw itself against him that Niall fully awoke to see the glint of metal driving towards his chest. His left hand managed to seize the wrist clutching the weapon, but his right found itself immobilised by a solid grip. His movement had checked the knife's momentum, but the blade was still advancing, gaining ground little by little.

The point of the blade hovered just above the left side of his chest, and he felt himself weakening. Strangely, he was comforted, because soon everything would be over.

The wheeze of a dying man echoed in the night. The blade that had just cut into the soldier's flesh had suddenly stopped. The force opposing Niall's was no longer resisting. He pushed off the body stretched out on top of him.

His eyes, now accustomed to darkness, picked out Thérèse's round silhouette at the door. She let out a cry and ran out of the barn.

The body next to Niall was completely immobile, the knife—the one the soldier had decided not to confiscate—still clutched in its stiffened hand. Niall leaped to his feet and ran to catch Thérèse. He took her by the arm and stopped her flight. Still panting, he couldn't speak.

"Did you kill him?"

It took Niall a few seconds to recover and understand the question. "No. But he's dead."

Thérèse shook her head. "If only he'd let you leave."

"Your husband?"

A long silence followed, until Thérèse finally broke it. "He came back from the battle injured. When the news of your patrols reached us, he hid in the woods."

Niall, who had been holding Thérèse firmly, dropped her wrists.

"I didn't want him to kill you. I knew it was useless. He didn't have enough strength left."

He'd almost had enough strength, thought Niall. Unable to support such a strain, the wounded man's heart had probably given in.

"What are you going to do with me?"

Niall let himself drop onto a log. A thread had just broken inside him as well. He would never again be able to kill. "We'll bury him come morning."

He wasn't destined to die here. So he had to set off again, and find a way to survive. After leaving this farm, he'd find a way to return to Scotland as soon as possible.

"I didn't really love him. I was forced to accept this marriage. But my life without him won't be any easier."

The Scot looked hard at her. Who would end up having the more difficult life: he or she? His hostess's herb tea had, perhaps, altered their destinies. But he asked himself whether that would be for the best or for the worst.

Part II

13. Elizabeth, Lighthouse Point

The tension is nearly palpable among the thirty Lighthouse Point residents—the whole community—gathered in the Bar au Baril. Meetings used to be held in the Saint Venerius chapel of Lighthouse Point. But owing to the poor state of the old place of worship, which is virtually never used anymore, the bar has supplanted it as the town hall.

"I thank you all for coming," begins Alvin Desroches, a stocky man of fifty, the one who called the meeting.

"It's not as if we had a million other things to do."

Angéline Bresette's caustic tone reassures Elizabeth, who puts her feet up on the case in front of her. Desroches ignores the comment.

"As you know, I've submitted a proposal to the municipal council. It's a golden opportunity to save the village. But I need your support."

Standing in front of the bar, Desroches extols the benefits of his real estate project. The construction of thirty luxury residences will make the old carcass of the railway depot disappear, create jobs and bring in property tax revenues.

"Without this development, Lighthouse Point is finished," he concludes.

A church-like silence fills the bar. Desroches grins with satisfaction. Elizabeth decides it's time to go on the offensive.

"That's not what we need."

There's a new silence, but one of amazement this time.

"Get real! Beggars can't be choosers," points out André Grisé, a man in his sixties, nicknamed Captain André because he practically lives in his boat.

"I've got another idea." She only has one weapon to persuade them—a sizeable weapon, it's true. However, if it proves ineffective, she'll be lost. Elizabeth calmly puts her case on the bar next to Alvin Desroches.

"I've just put ten bottles of Glen Dubh up for sale."

The room explodes into a noisy shambles.

"Where did you find them?" Angéline Bresette's question manages to silence the group.

Elizabeth hesitates before putting all her cards on the table. "They've been in my family since my great-grandparents' time."

The cacophony resumes with even greater intensity.

"I want to use the money from this sale to bring Lighthouse Point back to life."

Stunned, the audience listens to Elizabeth fervently unveil her distillery project. Unlike Alvin Desroches, she has no business plan, no numbers—just her passion, her unwavering conviction. Lighthouse Point possesses all the necessary elements for this venture to succeed: first the water, then the base material—the old Glen Dubh—and, finally, the abandoned depot that can be converted.

"You say we'll have to wait two years before even being able to sell the first bottle of your famous blend. We'd be nuts to board your ship of fools!" The objection comes from Catherine Roy, a descendant of Théophile Roy, one of the first inhabitants of Lighthouse Point.

"Not my ship, but yours. You'll be its shareholders."

Even Ghisèle can't believe her ears, since Elizabeth hadn't breathed a word of this idea to her.

"I'll issue vouchers for the new whisky. You'll be able to buy the number of cases you want, and the money will be invested in the distillery."

"Why do you want to revive such a sad memory?" asks Catherine forcefully. "The Glen Dubh has already done enough to Lighthouse Point."

"But it's not the same Glen Dubh anymore!" retorts Elizabeth. She pulls a bottle from the case and brandishes it in front of the crowd. "Time, air and the water of the bay have changed it. It's become good and gentle." In spite of the sceptical looks, Elizabeth continues: "I swear to you that this new Glen Dubh doesn't have the same character as the old one. It deserves the chance to right the wrong it did to Lighthouse Point." Elizabeth uncorks the bottle and goes behind the bar, where she starts to pour the dark liquid into glasses. "Drink some and you'll see for yourselves."

Elizabeth has already filled five glasses, and keeps on pouring as she tells her audience the probable value of the bottles of Glen Dubh appraised by John MacPhearson. Some in the crowd calculate the price of each of the glasses on the bar. None among them has ever tasted a glass or a bottle or even a meal so pricey. Torn between fear and temptation, the Lighthouse Point inhabitants don't dare move.

When Alvin Desroches slides over to the bar, the others rush to follow. There's no way that he'll be the only one to profit from this manna from Heaven. Eight decades have passed since the Glen Dubh left its indelible mark on Lighthouse Point. Today, the people who still carry the scars of that event will decide the whisky's fate.

14. Scotland, 1780

His weariness had lasted for months. And yet it wasn't physical, not the kind felt after a hard day of work. No, even at sixty-seven years old, Niall Fearmòr's body still had the vigour needed to perform the labour of farming and distilling.

What was really wearing him down was fighting a war of attrition. For twenty years, he had been relentlessly opposing an unjust regime and system, by wielding the only weapon he and his family had against an all-powerful government: whisky. And even if he could pride himself on having won more often than not, Niall suffered from the feeling of bequeathing an unfinished struggle to his son, a hopeless war for his people's independence.

"Even a stupid exciseman should be able to find it."

The comment from Tom, his eldest son, aged nineteen, pulled Niall out of his thoughts. Yes, the spot where they had put their old still was nicely situated. This little nook on the bank of the *Sruth fuar* had even, several years ago, once been used for distilling.

The two men lit a fire, shifted a few rocks and trampled down the grass all around, to create the impression that the place had been used for some time. Their task done, father and son sat down on a rock and contemplated the flames.

"I'll tell Donald to send the exciseman to this spot tomorrow."

Niall nodded his approval. His son devoted himself to the clandestine distilling of whisky with the same ardour that had inspired Niall after his discharge from the army and return from Canada.

Fearmòr senior pulled a flask from his vest, uncorked it and took a long swallow. The weather was particularly wet, and the whisky had the effect of a ray of sunshine. Niall smiled and held out the flask to his son, who downed a good gulp. Fine drops started to fall from the sky, but the men continued drinking and watching the dancing flames defying the rain.

Niall's white hair shed a drop of water, which ran down his face. He loved this land of water, his land of water, with all his heart—this land a young aboriginal woman from the other side of the world had told him to return to. Some days, Niall surprised himself by wondering about the fate of the woman who had changed the course of his life. Without knowing it, she had been right: transforming water, breathing the life of whisky into it, had given meaning to his own existence, given him a way to fight by creating rather than destroying.

"We should go home, Father."

Niall got up. The intensifying rain had put out the fire. Going down the *Sruth fuar*, they passed two other old bothies. One always had to stay a step ahead of the exciseman. This civil servant, responsible for collecting taxes from distillers on each litre of spirits produced legally, also had to stop those who distilled in secret without paying His Majesty his due—and the latter were much more numerous than the former.

Every increase in the tax on whisky—and they had been frequent—had had the effect of pushing more Highlanders to go underground to make their whisky. The rises in taxes on bushels of barley had even set off riots, like the Shawfield Riot in Glasgow in June 1725, or the Porteous Riots in Edinburgh in 1736. In 1774, a law had been passed to forbid the possession of stills of less than a hundred gallons. Five years later, the authorised size of stills for personal use had been reduced from ten to two gallons. In the Highlands, people expected from one day to the next that private distilling would be declared illegal outright. Even so, the Scots considered whisky a natural resource that didn't belong to anyone, no more than the water of the burns or the salmon they fished in the rivers crossing the estates of rich landowners.

Shortly after his return to the country, Niall had buried his parents and then taken the family farm in hand. Agriculture on this steep, rocky terrain barely produced enough to live on, but he had carried on the distillation tradition with great care, devoting himself to it body and soul, experimenting with different types of barley. With time, the "Fearmòr Gleann Dubh", as it was called in the area, had carved out an enviable reputation in a good part of the Highlands, and even beyond.

Niall had married a local girl, twenty years younger than himself. With the secondary income from the whisky, the couple had raised a family of three boys and two girls. Over the years, the whole clan had been called upon to aid in both making and distributing the whisky.

The excisemen succeeded each other, and even though their task stayed the same, they applied themselves to it with a degree of zeal that varied from one man to the next. Niall himself had been caught in the act twice. Both times, the confiscated whisky and still had constituted a much more costly loss than the fine imposed by the magistrates. As a rule, these judges sympathised with the distillers, since they often consumed the fruits of the accused's labour. Nonetheless, the presence of excisemen hindered whisky distilling and sales. And for two years now Alistair Geddes, a gauger from the southern Lowlands—and, what's more, a Scot—had constantly been increasing the number of arrests of distillers, bringing their trade to a standstill.

Furthermore, the scourge Niall had been expecting for years was beginning to descend on the poor tenant farmers of the Highlands, evicted to make way for sheep pastures. In spite of this, Niall believed that one day his daughters would make good matches, and that he'd have the means to establish his sons on their own plots of land. However, he asked himself what would be his legacy to Tom, the son who was the most interested in whisky?

Once at home, the two men dried themselves off. Shortly afterwards, Tom set out for Donald's place to let him know that he could tip off the gauger about the location of a clandestine still and collect the five-pound informant's reward. The exciseman would come to confiscate the old, unusable equipment that Tom and his father had just set up near the burn. Donald would then give them two thirds of the reward, which would cover part of the costs of buying replacement equipment. One day, the excisemen would surely catch on to the ploy. In the meantime, the distillers would keep using it to recoup a little of the money paid to the Crown.

"I'm tired." Morag, Niall's wife, came to sit beside him. This admission said a lot.

"Tom is ready to take things in hand." Niall asked for nothing better, but he was afraid for the future.

Tom came back an hour later and announced that Donald was off to make his false denunciation.

"That's good, son," Niall remarked. "Next week we'll start distilling again. There's a caravan being organised to send barrels south in a month's time."

Shortly after, Niall went to bed. Nonetheless, he couldn't sleep; he had to find a way to get the exciseman Geddes to leave, whatever the cost. The means to this end were doubtless extreme, but necessary. The future of his whisky—and of his son as well—depended on it.

15. MacPhearson, Lighthouse Point

For ten minutes now, MacPhearson's unease has been growing at a frightening pace. The boat, besieged by the waves, is moving forward with difficulty in the swell. He didn't think it was possible to get seasick on Georgian Bay.

He's already missing the comfort of his Audi, which he had to leave in Parry Sound, a small port town two hundred and fifty kilometres north of Toronto. The water taxi had picked him up half an hour late—because of the heavy waves, claimed the captain, a stocky old sea dog frank enough to admit laughingly that he doesn't know how to swim.

MacPhearson watches the rocky coast, unable to drive away his grim thoughts. *It would be difficult for anyone to keep his head above such choppy waters.* He begins to resent Elizabeth for forcing him to take this trip. She had insisted: if he wanted to meet her, he'd have to come to Lighthouse Point where, what's more, he'd be able to see the distillery.

He had grudgingly given in. He's determined to keep her from committing the irreparable at all costs—namely blending the pure Glen Dubh with other whiskies.

MacPhearson goes to throw his cigarette butt overboard when a gesture from the captain stops him. He resigns himself to burying it in his pocket.

She really doesn't realise what she's doing, thinks MacPhearson, once again considering the object of this journey, which is beginning to look like an odyssey. In fact, the success of the sale of the Glen Dubh had surpassed his wildest dreams. Encouraged by the articles written by Scotch specialists, the most prestigious whisky clubs in the world and a select group of billionaire Scotch connoisseurs had fought a ferocious bidding war during the auction sale. MacPhearson had been ecstatic, as had Elizabeth. Nevertheless, even this success had not pushed Elizabeth to sell the rest of her reserves at a sky high price. Quite the opposite—she had spent her money to set up the New Glen Dubh distillery. *I can't let her do this*, MacPhearson repeats to himself, calculating the potential value of Elizabeth's other bottles one more time.

His gaze falls to the port side of the vessel. In spite of the hot, brilliant late May sun, the waves of the open water, even bigger and whiter than those tossing the boat in the channel, are hardly reassuring. What's more, on the starboard side, the little boat is being assailed by the backwash of the breakers after they crash against the smooth rock walls with a roar.

"Will we be there soon?"

The captain gestures vaguely and replies in his French-accented English:"In ten minutes, if we manage to pass the point with the lighthouse."

The boat leaves the relative security of the channel and enters an opening at least a kilometre wide, where the water is boiling like overheated soup. MacPhearson holds tight to his seat and the captain clings to the wheel. The boat climbs and crashes heavily onto the next wave, shaking the hull and all its contents.

The vessel progresses, pitching against the waves and, ten minutes later, it arrives opposite a rocky cliff dominated by a nervously blinking lighthouse. MacPhearson is still recovering from his anxiety when a quay and a few houses appear.

Shortly afterwards, the craft, still subjected to the agitation of the waves, hugs the shoreline where abandoned, ghostlike structures stand. It finally draws up behind another vessel moored to a long, recently built dock. Twenty metres from the dock stands a fully restored building.

MacPhearson climbs onto the quay, where Elizabeth is arriving to welcome him.

"You're lucky; only Captain André would risk going out on a sea like this."

The taxi leaves, and Elizabeth announces, "Welcome to the New Glen Dubh distillery. You're our first visitor."

A strange shock surprises MacPhearson. He's amazed to feel honoured. He, who has visited Scotland's most prestigious distilleries, has never felt so moved. And yet there's nothing very impressive about the building, although MacPhearson has to admit the location is enchanting. He puts up a front, using his most sceptical tone.

"You call this a distillery?"

Elizabeth's enthusiasm seems rock solid and, worse still, potentially contagious.

"Don't put too much stock in appearances. No doubt the clandestine bothies of the Highlands didn't foreshadow the elaborate distilleries of today either. We're just waiting for the arrival of a few barrels to start creating our first blends."

The reminder of the future that Elizabeth Legrand is reserving for the most valuable bottles of Scotch in the world makes MacPhearson shudder all over again. Following his hostess, he enters the premises of the New Glen Dubh, listening patiently to her explanations.

"... our storehouse will be in the building over there. We've already designed a system for rolling the barrels between the dock and the distillery."

The vast structure, where a series of skylights lets in daylight, makes a strong impression on MacPhearson.

"Up until the 1960s, this was the lumber yard. The wood arrived by water as logs, and left again by train as planks."

Everywhere there are signs of ongoing restoration work—tools and bits of wood.

"Our offices will be here, and, on the other side, the malting room."

MacPhearson feels increasingly like he's being plunged into a dream world. This project seems even more insane to him, now that he's on site. A cell phone rings. Instinctively MacPhearson pulls his from his jacket pocket. Elizabeth is already waving hers.

"It's mine," she says, bringing the phone to her ear. As she talks, Elizabeth struts over to a desk covered in papers. "Perfect. I'll be waiting for them, then." She jots something down and hangs up. "The barrels of Glenfiddich have arrived in Toronto."

Elizabeth takes MacPhearson by the arm and they go into another large room. "In two years, I'll have the stills installed here."

A few steps take them to the next room. *A primitive church from another era …* thinks MacPhearson as he enters the stone-walled room, the future storehouse for ageing the barrels. Elizabeth points out the barrels, lying empty for the moment.

"You know a lot about the industry," MacPhearson concedes. "Have you studied Scotch?"

"I spent some time in Scotland," Elizabeth replies. "I even worked as a tour guide at the Glenfiddich distillery for a summer."

The reply doesn't satisfy MacPhearson. "But that doesn't give you the knowledge necessary to open a distillery, and especially not the craft you need to create blends."

Elizabeth slides her hand down the length of a barrel. "No, you're right. In fact I have something else, I …" But Elizabeth doesn't finish her sentence, and simply adds: "Come, let's share a dram."

Disappointed that he can't pierce the mystery of this enigmatic woman, MacPhearson has no choice but to follow her. As they pass her desk, Elizabeth opens a drawer and pulls out a bottle and two glasses. Outside, they sit on patio chairs at a table in the sun. Seeing her fill the two glasses, MacPhearson is barely able to contain his elation.

"Enjoy, Mr MacPhearson," says Elizabeth, raising her glass, "because this is probably the last time you'll taste Glen Dubh in this form. *Slàinte*!"

MacPhearson's glass stops a few centimetres from his lips. "Since you've brought it up, I want to talk to you about that. You're going to …"

But the ringing of a cell phone cuts him off. Elizabeth points at MacPhearson's jacket pocket. "Yours this time."

MacPhearson puts down his glass and answers. Turning to Elizabeth, he asks: "My wife wants to know when I'm going to be home. If I call the captain in an hour, how long will it take me to get back to Parry Sound?"

Elizabeth considers the water offshore. "The wind's blowing strong from the east. Here we call that 'a three-day blow'. No one, not even Captain André, will venture out into that. You'll just have to grin and bear it."

MacPhearson, stunned, mumbles "I'll call you back" and hangs up. He drinks a long draught of whisky. Its warmth gives him a reason to smile. "At least now I'll have plenty of time to convince her."

16. Scotland, 1780

Niall's hesitation had lasted for months. During this time, he had been irascible, and he took it out on his loved ones. In the end, he'd resigned himself to the fact that it was time to act.

Towards seven in the evening, after telling Morag that he was going to the village to have a drink and get caught up on the latest news at the Cratur House pub, he left home on horseback. The night was dark, which was perfect for his plan. Leaving the main path leading to the village, he took a less-travelled road instead, where two men from the Lowlands, hired for the occasion, were waiting for him.

Niall hated resorting to these untrustworthy-looking strangers, but caution had pushed him to choose men from well outside the area. He went over the plan again with the two henchmen, who were on horses as well, and barely visible in the darkness. He gave them half of their fee and promised them the rest once the deed was done. With Niall leading, they went silently on their way. He prayed within himself that nothing would force him to postpone this dirty business, because he doubted he'd be able to summon up the resolve to stage the caper a second time.

Fifteen minutes later, Niall motioned to the other two that they were at the chosen spot, a bend in the road. He moved aside and watched the two men get down from their mounts and position themselves for the ambush. Geddes wouldn't be much longer. Every Tuesday evening, the exciseman was in the habit of going to the Johnstones' to play cards with distinguished locals. This evening, he wouldn't get there.

A few minutes passed. Despite the mild late August weather, Niall had goose bumps. Suddenly, he heard the trotting of a horse. His two thugs, positioned on either side of the road, raised their heads. Niall's heart started beating furiously when he picked out the long shape of a rider. He gripped the cudgel attached to his saddle.

The horse was moving forward at a slow trot. Geddes had nothing to fear, since this rarely used road was of no interest to brigands. When the two men leapt towards their victim even Niall, who had been anticipating this action, jumped. Geddes' horse reared up, and for a few seconds that seemed an eternity to Niall, the rider fought off his assailants with his riding crop and remained mounted. Finally, lashed by the fear of seeing his scheme fail, Niall spurred his horse and, attacking Geddes from behind, hit him with his cudgel, causing him to fall. The two other aggressors pummelled the exciseman, cursing loudly.

"This is a warning. Leave the area, or you'll get much worse than this."

Niall had retreated to his vantage point further away. Had Geddes recognised him during the attack? If that was the case, it was too late now. He just hoped the exciseman would accept his defeat and leave.

The two henchmen went on beating their victim, who no longer offered the slightest resistance.

"Enough!" shouted Niall, beside himself.

He had instructed the thugs to beat up the exciseman, not kill him. A supreme disgust filled him, and a thread broke in his heart of hearts. *I'll never distil another drop of whisky again*, he swore to himself. *I don't have the strength anymore.* Searching in the folds of his coat for the money, his fingers brushed the loaded firearm he'd brought in case Geddes shot at them. He thought again: *If Geddes recognised me, he'll have me arrested.* Could he run that risk?

Before letting their prey go, the two henchmen made sure that it wasn't moving anymore. Satisfied, they pulled away, and Niall contemptuously threw them a bag with their due.

"Now get lost."

The two men didn't make him repeat himself; they remounted their horses. However, they had barely set off when they heard a gunshot. They looked at each other questioningly and, by mutual agreement, fled at full gallop. The rest of this story was none of their business.

The small pistol he held in his hand fell to the ground, and Geddes lost consciousness. A few metres away, Niall, who had taken the bullet right in the chest, staggered before falling.

The next day, when the two bodies would be found on this obscure stretch of road, no one would ask too many questions. The bloodstain on Niall's cudgel and the firearm found on the ground next to Geddes would suffice to establish the version of the facts that everyone would choose to believe. The exciseman and the distiller had insisted on engaging in a deadly duel that neither of the two adversaries could hope to win, even at the cost of his life.

A more attentive examination of the surroundings and of the corpse of the man beaten to death would doubtless have revealed the true nature of the attack and the lethal retaliation. But everybody would be satisfied with making each of the two victims into a hero in his own way—each one becoming another legendary figure among the many others in the land of whisky.

17. Elizabeth, Lighthouse Point

"… So you see, I've been entrusted with a kind of mission."

They're still sitting on the patio chairs in front of the future distillery. Two days have passed since the beginning of this conversation. Two days during which John MacPhearson, rather than convincing, has let himself be convinced—but to do what? To believe in this faith Elizabeth has just explained to him, to understand it—as though understanding a faith was possible? Or to believe in playing the game because, even though it can't take him to Heaven, following this path will at least lead him out of Hell?

MacPhearson studies the features of the woman savouring the Tomintoul for which he had to pay an outrageous price at the Bar au Baril in order to leave with the whole bottle. Her face resembles this landscape, which he's beginning to find increasingly appealing—possessing an undeniable beauty, albeit rugged, carved out by the water that has curved and softened the rock. Cheeks made for letting tears flow, not for holding them back. Clear blue eyes and long brown hair undulating in the wind, like pine needles.

What if there is even a grain of truth in what she believes? MacPhearson starts to fear that the whisky, today's Tomintoul just as much as the first day's Glen Dubh, is beginning to cloud his judgement. The "three-day blow" is nearing its end; the waves are getting calmer and Elizabeth has offered to take him back to Parry Sound by boat. MacPhearson is almost sorry to leave.

"Let's suppose your distillery were to succeed—and you'll notice I'm speaking hypothetically. Your vision is still too narrow."

The change in Elizabeth's expression reveals that MacPhearson has chosen the right angle and hit the mark.

"If your blends turn out to be drinkable and sell well, you'll have the capital you need to set up the distillery. But the economic benefits for Lighthouse Point will be limited. If you really want to create jobs and attract money, you need more than just whisky. And you've got the resources you need, provided you make the effort to use them properly."

Although intrigued, Elizabeth remains wary. She has noticed a shift in her guest's attitude—he's fallen under the spell of the waves and the wind.

MacPhearson has had a comfortable stay with her in the apartment she's had fitted out at the distillery. Once there is actually whisky on site, Elizabeth will have to live there in order to keep a permanent watch over it. Yesterday, the wind had calmed enough to let them go to Lighthouse Point. In the Bar au Baril, her visitor had met a few of the locals. Accustomed to hearing MacPhearson talk up a storm, Elizabeth had found him strangely dreamy and attentive.

"Lighthouse Point could become a destination, a fountain where people would come to soak up its whisky, its water, and its history."

Elizabeth hesitates. This scheme goes far beyond hers. "You mean like organising tours of the distillery ..."

"Yes, and much more," enthuses MacPhearson. "Can't you see the millionaires' sailboats pulling up alongside your dock? Then, once they're here, you let them visit and drink, of course, but also eat and putter around in the area. There could be a hotel, or at least a bed and breakfast. The Bar au Baril has enormous potential ..."

"There was once a hotel here," says Elizabeth. "My great-great-aunt worked there."

MacPhearson detects a disapproving tone in her voice. He tries to recover. "That's all long term. We'll see. First of all, there's your whisky. If it turns out to be good, you'll have to work hard at spreading the news throughout the wonderful whisky world."

"And you're up to that challenge," finishes Elizabeth teasingly.

MacPhearson feels relieved to be on more solid ground. "You bet I am. What I did with your Glen Dubh was a masterstroke."

Elizabeth knows it. Over the next hour, MacPhearson expounds his marketing plan for her whisky, that is if he becomes its exclusive distributor. Elizabeth is won over by the idea. Later, when she drops MacPhearson off at the Parry Sound town dock, the deal is done.

"... provided that your blends are marketable," MacPhearson declares, as if he were reading out an article from a contract.

"Come back to confirm it in eighteen months," says Elizabeth, to seal the agreement.

Playing the game is the best option, MacPhearson concludes. But the game looks like it could be long, and he has to resign himself to playing it to the end. *If she's willing to believe in me, I'll try to believe in her a little, and we can both come out winners.*

18. Scotland, 1820

Geordie Proudfoot waited for the verdict with just as much fear and anticipation as the accused, Tom Fearmòr. The trial before a judge had gone expeditiously and without a hitch—not surprisingly, since it was an open and shut case. The accused had been arrested on the road to Dufftown. He and his son, Paul, had been driving a cart with ten barrels of whisky destined for smuggling. If, at the time of the arrest, the exciseman Proudfoot hadn't been accompanied by two sturdy fellows he'd recruited for the operation, there was no doubt that Tom and his son would have put up a fight. The Fearmòrs, inveterate distillers, didn't give in easily.

What's more, this was the third time that Tom Fearmòr had been brought to court for the same offence. It seemed like nothing could dissuade him from continuing to make his whisky—which Proudfoot, like countless others, could affirm was excellent, because he had tasted it.

The judge, a new magistrate in this district, had not yet picked up the bad habit shared by most of his predecessors—namely that of consuming the merchandise of the offenders he was called upon to judge. Proudfoot could therefore hope that, for once, the judge would apply the law to the letter. However, the magistrate had retired before announcing his verdict, which was a bad sign.

An hour later, the judge had returned, and his serious voice rang out. "This court finds the accused, Tom Fearmòr, guilty and imposes on him a fine …" The judge paused, and his eyes went from Proudfoot to the face of the accused. "… of one hundred and fifty pounds."

The room filled with protests. This was a considerable sum. From now on the tone was set: the judge and the exciseman would work hand in hand to wipe out the plague of clandestine distilling in this mutinous district, the Highlands. Proudfoot gloated.

"Failing that, the accused will serve a year's jail time."

The judge's gavel punctuated the sentence and he left the room, leaving those attending the trial in shock. Everyone knew that Tom Fearmòr didn't have that kind of money. If he went to jail, his family would be deprived of its main provider. A wave of indignation shook the crowd, and Geordie Proudfoot slipped away discreetly, before this anger, for lack of a better target, could fall on him.

Outside, the two men Proudfoot had hired the day before were waiting impatiently. The gauger had promised to pay them their due after the trial. He tried to placate them.

"My friends, now that the court has come to a decision, I can collect the money for the confiscated whisky and then pay you."

Reassured, the two others fell into step behind Proudfoot. Encouraged by the shining sun, Proudfoot felt happy—a rare occurrence, especially on trial days. Did he love his job? Proudfoot couldn't really say. With Fearmòr's arrest, he had confiscated one hundred gallons of whisky, which brought the total number of gallons he'd taken from clandestine distillers during nineteen years of service up to twenty thousand. The exciseman meticulously recorded all the details of his confiscations in a notebook. Certainly, he took great pride and satisfaction in a job well done; no other gauger since the creation of the position could brag about having confiscated that much whisky. But did he love this work? If faithfully doing his duties had earned him a decent salary and the respect of those around him, maybe he would have felt the same passion for his work as the clandestine distillers did for theirs. Meanwhile, contrary to the enormous contempt Proudfoot endured, his salary remained tiny.

The trio finally arrived at the station where the confiscated goods were kept under lock and key. On the way there, Proudfoot had rented a cart to transport his loot. Once the accused was found guilty, half the money from the sale of the confiscated whisky went, by all rights, to the exciseman who had made the arrest. In fact, he drew the greater part of his salary from the sale of this whisky, which became legal after the payment of customs duties.

Proudfoot signed a paper promising that he would pay the government what it was owed on the goods. Next, with help from his associates, he loaded the whisky onto the cart. Armed with the certificate attesting to the legality of the whisky, he then went to an inn, still followed closely by his two lapdogs still waiting for their pay.

The innkeepers, required to sell spirits for which customs duties had been paid, always bought the exciseman's whisky. In almost all cases, the bootleggers' peat-reek proved to be of eminently superior quality to the rotgut distilled legally. In fact, the distillers of legal whisky rushed their work to make their production profitable, as it was subjected to taxes on barley malt and spirits. Today, Proudfoot had Gleann Dubh to offer, so he expected to pocket a pretty sum.

Confident, he entered the inn and called out to the proprietor. Luck was smiling on him, he announced. For an exceptional price, he could become the proud owner of ten barrels of premium whisky. Proudfoot was surprised by the innkeeper's reaction, or rather by his lack of one. Looking impassive and sounding bored, the publican offered him a quarter of the asking price.

Offended, Proudfoot repeated that this was Gleann Dubh, a fine whisky offered at a very good price.

"There's nothing forcing me to buy this whisky."

This rebuff made Proudfoot turn on his heels. Outside, he took his cart to a second inn. His offer was met with the same coldness, and an equally outrageous counter-offer. It then dawned on Proudfoot what was going on. The news of the exceptionally high fine imposed on Tom Fearmòr had preceded him. The publicans, sensing that their clientele wouldn't drink this whisky if it benefited the exciseman, had taken the position of offering a ridiculous price for the Gleann Dubh, even if it meant losing the chance of acquiring it. It would doubtless be necessary for Geordie Proudfoot to go all the way to Glasgow to find an innkeeper who wouldn't be on Tom Fearmòr's side. And he didn't have the means to take that kind of trip, especially since he still had to settle the customs duties on the whisky and pay his two accomplices. Resigned, he demanded a few more pounds from the innkeeper, who finally gave in. When the clientele found out that they were enjoying this excellent whisky at the exciseman's expense, they would drink both to the health of the establishment's proprietor and to the Fearmòrs.

Proudfoot pocketed the money and paid his helpers. The two men went into the inn to order a dram of Gleann Dubh, which they felt they had earned. Alone and depressed, Proudfoot started on his way home. Once the customs duties and the rental fees for the cart were paid, he would only have two pounds left—even less than the pay given to his assistants. His wife would complain yet again that his service to His Majesty didn't even bring in enough to feed his five children.

He drew some small consolation from the fact that he had, at least, dealt a hard blow to all the bootleggers, and especially to Tom Fearmòr. Passing in front of the inn where he'd made his first stop, he noticed a much bigger crowd than was normal for this time of day. He questioned a fellow who was coming out of the establishment. The man, who didn't know Proudfoot, at least not personally, smiled while telling him that, inside, people were drinking in honour of Tom Fearmòr.

"After his trial, a collection started right away. It took two hours and a lot of persuasion, but we gathered enough money for Tom to avoid going to prison."

Proudfoot cursed through his teeth. Grumbling to himself about injustice, he swore that, whatever the cost, he would defeat the bootleggers and Tom Fearmòr.

19. Scotland, 1821

Tom watched his son turn over the barley spread out on the barn floor. The malting had just begun. Over the next two weeks the two men would take turns repeating this task, so that the sprouts could grow and produce their maltose. Paul handled the *shiel,* a wide square shovel designed especially for this task, with dexterity, applying supple, graceful movements. Tom started to think that, when he was Paul's age, his father had probably sometimes watched him in the same way.

"We'll be able to distil in a fortnight," Paul declared, without lifting his head from his work.

Tom confirmed his son's prediction. There was nothing left for him to teach Paul about distilling. At the age of twenty, the young man had acquired all the necessary knowledge; now, only years of experience could perfect his art. Tom felt certain that once the Gleann Dubh was in Paul's hands, it would remain unchanged. With time, he might even find a way of perfecting their whisky even more, if that was possible. However, Tom hadn't been able to pass on to Paul a nonetheless vital skill: the cunning to escape the increased vigilance of the gauger Proudfoot and his henchmen. And the reason for that was very simple: he didn't know how to evade this surveillance.

"I can finish on my own, Dad. Go and rest a little."

Paul's voice reminded Tom of his own tone, which had been gentle and confident at that age. He had probably said something similar to his father the day before his death. During the last months of his life, Niall Fearmòr had seemed to carry a heavy burden, his features appearing drawn and his eyes lacking their usual fire.

Tom went back to the house, where his wife, Megan, served him a glass of whisky. It was late, and he was sleepy. Nevertheless, his fatigue didn't come from work or from old age. Since his most recent conviction, he was plagued by worry and weariness, no doubt the same afflictions that had weighed down his father. Today, having reached the age at which his father had passed the *uisge beatha* torch to him, he better understood this man who had remained a mystery to him for a long time.

But the torch Tom was preparing to pass on to his son burned more faintly than the one inherited from his father. After Niall Fearmòr's death, the excisemen in the district had, for several years, slackened their efforts. Still badly paid, and fearing the same fate as Geddes, they saw no reason to risk their lives to enforce a law that the Highlanders bragged about flouting.

The arrival of Geordie Proudfoot had disturbed this fragile peace.

Tom took a long, soothing swallow of his whisky. Its warmth comforted him on this chilly October night. A year had passed since the men of the area had pooled their money to save him from going to prison. Today, like all the other clandestine distillers, he found himself unable to export his whisky. Proudfoot had increased his efforts with renewed zeal, to the point of successfully deploying a surveillance network impossible to evade. To add to the distillers' frustration, this year's barley harvest had been especially good, and this promised an abundant production of *poteen* or clandestine whisky—a product they'd unfortunately be unable to get to their thirsty clients.

"Water," Tom murmured to himself. This thought jerked him out of the light sleep he'd fallen into. He emptied his glass right to the last drop. The solution was there, in the water of the sea. Starting tomorrow, he'd go to Lossiemouth to take the necessary steps. Clandestine whisky would flow once again, but in a different direction.

* * *

As on each of their return trips from Lossiemouth, father and son felt invigorated—spurred by successfully concluded business for one and by love for the other. The Fearmòrs benefited from these excursions which, for a year now, had given Tom new hope and Paul a more promising future.

"You're expecting to marry your lass Shona?"

The point-blank question embarrassed Paul. He held the horse's reins firmly in his hands. His meetings with Shona MacGregor took place when he accompanied his father to the port of Lossiemouth, thirty kilometres north of Dufftown. Since the exciseman and his henchmen had succeeded in cutting off the land routes going south, Tom had turned to the north and the sea. He and Paul would leave during the night, their cart loaded with whisky, and arrive at Lossiemouth at dawn. They would then transfer their cargo into a boat and row it to meet a ship anchored offshore. The schooner transported their merchandise first by sea, then up the river Clyde all the way to Glasgow.

Shona's father provided them with the rowboat and this had allowed Paul the opportunity to meet and court the young woman. The people of Lossiemouth, who took advantage of the Fearmòrs' trips to stock up on Gleann Dubh, liked the two distillers. Their mission accomplished, father and son usually rested in the village before returning home at nightfall.

Paul's life now practically revolved around seeing Shona. And yet, he still hadn't thought seriously about the step he needed to take if he wanted to be able to see her every day.

"I'm considering it, Dad, but I don't want to move too fast."

Tom patted his son on the back. "You'd do better not to move too slowly."

Paul was still staring at the road. Tom felt confident that his words had had the desired effect. The time was ripe. Since recent whisky sales had replenished the family coffers, Tom was in a position to help Paul get settled.

Of course, exporting whisky along this diverted route meant a longer distance to travel, higher transport costs and a decreased profit margin. But, for these very reasons, Proudfoot hardly suspected them of using it.

Tom, who had created his own good luck, was extremely careful not to reveal the key to his success to anyone. He was nonetheless aware of the great debt he owed to his colleagues and friends in the Dufftown area. Very discreetly, he had approached a few other distillers and offered to sell one or two barrels of their whisky, without taking a commission. This generosity had a secondary purpose: preventing his peers from becoming envious.

* * *

Geordie Proudfoot rubbed the scar on his right wrist. This injury, one of the forty permanent marks left by blows suffered during twenty years of fighting the distillers, was particularly sensitive to salty air. In fact, Proudfoot hated the seaside. He felt lost there. The sea's immensity gave him a feeling of powerlessness. This emptiness beyond his control stretched as far as the eye could see; it was an expanse that even the powerful British navy couldn't completely dominate, and it scared him stiff. He preferred the hills and valleys of the interior of the Highlands, where the eye could spot every traveller on the open heath for leagues around.

Here on the north coast of Scotland, even armed with a spyglass, his attentive eye could only watch the coast and the horizon. Having arrived during the night, he had stationed himself on the beach while waiting for dawn and the promised reinforcements. He was counting on this confiscation to earn him enough money to at least start repaying his increasingly impatient creditors. He had spent his last coins paying the informer a pretty sum to obtain the information that had finally put him on Tom Fearmòr's trail. Finding a friend of the clandestine distillers who was desperate enough to betray them hadn't been easy.

It'll be worth it, as long as the information proves accurate, thought Proudfoot. The exciseman, driven by his obsession, had played for high stakes—so high that this time, if he lost, he would be the one going to prison.

* * *

Day was just dawning when Tom and Paul finally heard the sea. Throughout the long night, they'd been harassed by a cold, damp, disagreeable drizzle.

In the faint light, they spotted the MacGregors' rowboat on the beach and pulled up to it with their cart full of barrels. Offshore, a small, blinking point of light confirmed the presence of the ship that was waiting for their cargo. The two men filled the rowboat and, just as they slid it into the sea, Paul scanned the top of the cliff behind them. Shona, standing there, blew him a kiss. Though he was tired and still had an arduous task ahead of him, Paul replied with a wide smile. After his work, he planned to enjoy a romantic tête-à-tête. Tonight when he left, he'd be engaged.

* * *

Proudfoot couldn't make out the features of the two men on the beach, but he saw clearly that they were loading barrels onto a rowboat. He checked his watch: five-fifteen. The reinforcements were supposed to arrive from the west and, if they didn't show up very soon, they'd no longer be able to intercept the smugglers. With every minute, the traffickers were getting a few precious boat-lengths farther away on the sea.

Proudfoot let out a cry of joy when, on the other side of the point, to his right, a second rowboat manned by a squadron of dragoons appeared. The exciseman recognised the young officer in command of the detachment, the same one with whom he'd planned the operation the day before. Jumping around like a child, Proudfoot attracted the soldiers' attention and pointed towards the smugglers' rowboat.

He gauged the distance separating the two boats. The soldiers' craft, with four times more rowers, was hurrying towards the smugglers. "I've got them!" he gloated.

* * *

Tom Fearmòr gave in to his discouragement.

"It's useless, son. The bastards have us!"

Paul and his father had heard the shout and then noticed the soldiers' rowboat. They didn't know who was observing them from the shore.

"Maybe they'll get the whisky, but not us, Dad. Let's row back to land.

If we stay a bit ahead of them, they won't be able to run faster than us."

Paul manoeuvred the rowboat to turn it around, and his father grabbed one of the oars. The younger Fearmòr was right; they could still reach land and flee, either to the village or to the woods. The craft started to make a beeline for the nearest point of land, about five hundred metres away.

* * *

From his position, Proudfoot watched their flight. He rushed along the shoreline towards where the smugglers were heading. He had covered a hundred metres when a clamour warned him that he wasn't the only one following the course of events.

Shona MacGregor was running towards the village as fast as she could, shouting at the top of her voice. "The soldiers are after the Fearmòrs. We have to stop them!"

Several inhabitants were already attending to their morning chores. When they heard Shona, they looked towards the sea and immediately understood the predicament. Some armed themselves with pickaxes or sticks; others ran empty-handed towards the beach where the two Fearmòrs were going to make a desperate landing.

Shona's shouts had attracted twenty people—men, women, and even a few children. Some were screaming insults at the soldiers, who were now less than a cable-length away from the Fearmòrs. Having reached shore, the two men leapt from their boat and dashed behind the crowd. To the Fearmòrs' great surprise, the villagers advanced, pulled the rowboat onto land and formed a line to protect it.

The soldiers landed a few metres farther away, disembarked immediately and stood in a row, guns raised menacingly in front of them. Faced with this welcome as hostile as it was unexpected, they awaited orders.

The officer, a young Englishman from the nobility who had yet to experience his baptism of fire, hesitated. He shot a haughty look at the villagers, hoping that the presence of armed men would intimidate them. The children had been dispatched to the village to call for reinforcements, and the crowd kept on growing. In this fierce, incongruous mass, the officer couldn't make out the two fugitives. Backed by his twelve soldiers and by the strength of the law, he decided to take the first step.

He yelled at the crowd to disperse. The unrelenting horde replied with more insults. Finally the officer drew his sword and ordered his men to take the rowboat. The soldiers advanced slowly, closing ranks, and without sparing man, woman or child, brutally forced their way with blows from their rifle butts. The dragoons circled their prize and waited for new orders.

Recovering from their astonishment, the villagers regrouped. Furious men brandished sticks or cudgels. Two stones fell at the soldiers' feet. Frightened, the officer resolved to leave with the two rowboats, but without the fugitives. He was opening his mouth to give the order when, panting, eyes bloodshot, Proudfoot arrived next to him.

"You … you … didn't get them?"

A stone hit the officer on the arm. "Shoulder arms!" he barked instinctively. Deep down, the officer was praying that the excited crowd would calm down. The clamour decreased as everyone heard the clicking of primed weapons. The officer looked at Proudfoot. "Can you see the two men who were in the rowboat?"

Proudfoot swept the crowd with his uneasy glance, searching in vain for Tom Fearmòr and his son. In fact, he hadn't been able to confirm with absolute certainty that the smugglers actually were the Fearmòrs. If he'd been in his own district, where he knew everyone, he would have moved forward among the villagers to flush them out. Here, he didn't dare venture into this unpredictable, livid mass.

The soldiers' obvious hesitation and unease emboldened the crowd. A rain of projectiles crashed onto the dragoons and two men fell. The officer succumbed to panic.

"Fire!"

He regretted the order even before it was carried out. The thunder of gunfire echoed in his ears. Screams of terror rose from the distraught fleeing crowd. Without even checking whether the bullets had hit anybody, the officer ordered his men to cast off the rowboats. The soldiers didn't make him repeat the order. After a moment of uncertainty, Proudfoot jumped aboard the boat carrying the whisky.

Two cable-lengths away from shore, the exciseman turned towards the dreadful scene. At least three shapes were lying on the ground, and villagers were running to them, letting out horrifying wails. Leaning against a barrel of whisky, Proudfoot hung his head overboard and retched. His mostly empty stomach could only bring up bile and a bitter taste. He felt utterly lost. Such was his reward for twenty years of good and loyal service to the Crown.

Geordie Proudfoot would have liked to turn his back on it all. But that was impossible; the exciseman's profession was all he knew. At any rate, who in the district would give him work, especially once the news of this tragic event spread? For Proudfoot, the dice had been tossed. He wouldn't play this losing game anymore, at least not the same way.

* * *

Paul Fearmòr threw himself on the motionless body that had taken a bullet in the middle of the chest. Another villager, the father of a family, lay a few metres away from Shona. Around him, people busied themselves caring for the injured and taking them to the village. All the villagers were demanding the heads of these soldiers who had massacred civilians. A rider had already left for the district council office at full speed, to demand their arrest.

Tom joined his son. He'd have liked to say something, but in his throat there was only a thirst more acute than any he'd ever felt before. If his whisky had been there in front of him, rather than in the rowboat far away on the sea, he'd have emptied a whole barrel. Why had the girl who had rallied the brave people of Lossiemouth in defence of the whisky paid for her courageous act with her life? Tom would never be able to explain it to Paul, nor ever console him for his loss.

And yet he had to move fast, with or without Paul's help. Faced with this turn of events, neither he nor Paul could deny their part in this horrible drama. The law would doubtless come to search Tom's house, where he still had at least twenty barrels.

"Paul ..."

The son raised sad eyes to his father, who couldn't articulate any more words. "I know, Dad," he said, getting up.

They had to leave. As always, the whisky took precedence over everything, even death. He'd come back to bury Shona, and bring with him a barrel of Gleann Dubh to help the villagers first drown their sorrow, his sorrow, and next to find it in their hearts to forgive him and his father.

During the return to the Dubh valley the Fearmòrs remained in profound silence. Once at home, though thoroughly exhausted, they loaded the twenty barrels of *poteen* into the cart right away.

Paul picked up the reins again, and when Tom moved to climb up beside him, he raised a hand to stop him.

"No, I prefer that you didn't know where I'm going to hide them."

Tom was going to object, but the image of his son leaning over Shona, face contorted with pain, wouldn't leave him. He climbed back down from the cart. Without saying another word, Paul left. Tom had to hold back his desire to secretly follow the young man. He realised that he'd never see those barrels again. He reasoned with himself: that whisky represented Paul's future, not his. It was therefore up to Paul to dispose of it.

For two hours, Paul climbed the course of the *Sruth fuar*, driving the cart on dusty paths where no one had wandered for ages. The spot he had chosen was a natural cave, well hidden, on the other side of the Dubh valley. The last five hundred metres leading to it had to be crossed on foot. Paul lugged one barrel after the other on his back. Once all the barrels save one had been buried in the cavern, he blocked its entrance. With each shovelful of soil, it seemed to Paul that he was burying two separate parts of his life: his past, dedicated to whisky, and the future he'd no longer be able to live with Shona at his side.

His task completed, he erased all traces of his passing. In a year's time even he would have difficulty finding the entrance to this cache. That didn't matter much to him. As he left the burial place, he declared aloud: "Farewell, *uisge beatha*; I swear never to distil *poteen* again."

Paul then set off for Lossiemouth. The last barrel of Gleann Dubh, which he'd share with the villagers, wouldn't erase his pain—but at least it would dull it a little. The Gleann Dubh owed him this last favour before disappearing.

One bereavement was already one too many. Paul wouldn't weep over the whisky's grave. However, he was still young. He didn't know that life and its powerful water could end up deciding otherwise.

20. Scotland, 1823

The prison reeked so strongly of sadness and despair that Tom avoided breathing deeply. He followed the prison guard, who didn't seem the least bit bothered by the unsanitary conditions. The jailer unlocked a door, which opened with an infernal creaking.

Fearmòr hesitated for a second, afraid that by entering this sordid spot he'd end up staying there. Finally, he resigned himself to stepping inside. In the depths of the dark cell, he barely recognised the haggard face of the man turning to face him.

"Tom Fearmòr! What a surprise. I'm so honoured."

Fearmòr ignored the sarcasm in Geordie Proudfoot's voice. He almost offered the man his hand, but reconsidered.

"I wanted to see you," said Tom, disturbed to find himself in front of this formidable adversary reduced to such a pitiful state.

"Is your thirst for revenge so great?" Proudfoot asked ironically. "Oh, I can't say that I blame you. After all, if I'd had my way, you'd be rotting here in my place."

Proudfoot gave himself up to a laugh, which changed into a dry cough. The former exciseman spat.

Tom felt an urgent need to get straight to the point. "I had to tell you that neither I, nor my son holds you responsible for Shona's death."

Proudfoot couldn't believe his ears. He tried to speak. "It was that scatterbrain of a captain ..."

But the keenly painful memory of the investigation surrounding the Lossiemouth shooting kept him from continuing. The government had wanted to cover up the affair as quickly as possible. The Crown had even brought charges against Captain Jenkins, the man who had ordered his troops to open fire on the civilians, going so far as to sentence the officer in the hope that this would appease the outraged people of the Highlands. However, shortly after the ruling, the guilty man's sentence had been discreetly commuted to a voluntary departure from the army. The Fearmòrs' confiscated whisky had been kept by the Crown and sold legally in the Lowlands. The earnings from this sale had been used to pay a modest compensation to the families of the victims. The law had dropped the smuggling charges brought against the Fearmòrs.

"It's the English and their damned taxation system that are to blame."

Faced with Tom's comment, Proudfoot smiled before adding: "The system of the English and the whisky of the Scots."

"Maybe," Fearmòr obliged Proudfoot, "but I swear to you that neither my son nor I have distilled a single drop since then."

Proudfoot started pacing his narrow cell as he listened to his visitor.

"Have you heard the rumour? The tragedy has shocked the politicians. In the hope of convincing the distillers to acquire licenses, Duke Alexander Gordon is going to present a petition to Parliament calling for a decrease in customs duties and taxes."

"But you don't believe it'll work?"

Fearmòr's silence answered for him. Tom hadn't come here to debate, but to seek what reconciliation he could with Proudfoot, out of pity for him.

"If you'd decided to come over to our side earlier, you …"

"… wouldn't be here?" Proudfoot cut in. He shook his head. "Oh, no. I'd have wound up here all the same. I'd just have ended up here faster and spared myself the frustration of working tirelessly like a fool for the sake of a hypocritical, ungrateful government."

After the Lossiemouth incident, Proudfoot had continued to carry out his duties, but this time with the ambition of obtaining a personal gain from them. He'd begun to falsify distillery accounts in order to pocket part of the customs money. The number of arrests made by the civil servant had fallen considerably. What's more, when he caught a distiller in the act, he occasionally agreed to let him go, in exchange for half his merchandise. Nonetheless, Proudfoot had shown himself a less capable crook than a gauger, and the government had soon unmasked and charged him.

"That's all I had to say to you." His mission accomplished, Fearmòr headed for the door.

"Admit that you really came here to see me swing at the end of a rope tomorrow."

Fearmòr lied with a nod—one last gesture to appease the condemned man, by admitting that he was right. He knocked on the door.

"I also have a confession to make," Proudfoot declared. "Of all the peat-reeks that I've confiscated and tasted over twenty years, there's not a single one that can hold a candle to the Gleann Dubh. If I had some right now, I'd offer you a *deoch an dorus.*"

The door opened and, smiling, Tom left the condemned man. In this confession he'd only heard the voice of sincerity.

* * *

Alone again, Proudfoot settled in on the straw mattress that served as his bed, picked up an inkwell and dipped his quill into it.

"… *Captures of the greatest magnitude are attended with very great expenses; for in a country like the Highlands, where the inhabitants are almost wholly connected with the illicit trade, it is difficult to find a person among them who can be prevailed upon to give information against his neighbour, and nothing short of the officer's share of the seizure can induce the informant to divulge his secret. It has principally been in this way that I have involved myself in debt …*"

Geordie Proudfoot wrote for a few more hours—his final hours. He wanted to leave behind these hastily scrawled pages titled "The memories and case of one of His Majesty's excisemen". Although they wouldn't save his life, they'd at least let him keep his pride.

The next day, Tom Fearmòr was one of the few spectators at the execution. After the hanging, Tom went to a tavern, ordered himself a whisky and silently drank in honour of the most famous exciseman in all of Scotland, the man who had confiscated more than twenty-five thousand gallons of whisky.

21. Elizabeth, Lighthouse Point

A roar or tumult—is this noise real, or does it exist only inside Elizabeth's head? At the entrance to the distillery, she searches for its source. The waterfall-like murmur is coming from the lakeshore twenty metres in front of her, on the other side of snow fields covered in ice.

She takes long strides on this ice, which is beginning to melt under the nearly spring-like sun. Her feet assail the sides of a white castle, a cone three metres tall, an imposing link in a chain of ice towers and caves. At the top, facing the bay, she discovers another world.

The ice, in full upheaval, is moving. With an infernal grinding, enormous sheets are shifting a few centimetres per second and piling up one on top of the other to form an iceberg.

For a long moment, Elizabeth is entranced by this movement as it creates a temporary island. With its invisible hand, the bay is throwing off its icy shell, shattering it into shards resembling window glass.

Suddenly, this sound gives way to another, a whistling akin to that of human voices, which makes Elizabeth shudder.

Those are the wails of the shipwrecked people, of…

These laments from the water's depths get louder and sing her a long, monotonous chant, a supplication launched by the drowning victims from the more than two hundred ships swallowed by Georgian Bay.

Elizabeth plugs her ears and turns away from the heaps of pale blue, transparent ice, randomly stacked like gigantic ice cubes.

Then the noise stops just as abruptly as it began. Everything freezes, making way for the sound of the waves crashing against the new wall of ice in a rhythm as regular as breathing.

Lowering her hands, Elizabeth contemplates the calm around her.

They just wanted to get some fresh air, she tells herself, relieved, as she retraces her steps.

Back in the distillery, she equips herself with a hammer and goes to the storehouse. Once again, she's going to check the barrels to make sure they remain watertight, by tapping on the wood and listening to the sound. Stopping in front of the first barrel, she taps lightly.

Bong!

The sound echoes like a drumbeat in the dark room, which is as gloomy as a funeral home. Elizabeth takes a few steps. The hammer in her hand falls on the wood of a second barrel, making its baritone voice sing. Shortly after, she finishes her rounds.

All watertight, she thinks, getting ready to leave the storehouse. On the doorstep, she hesitates. How can she be so sure? This voice that gives her orders, telling her whether a task is well executed or not—where is it coming from? What's driving her to take on the burden of an enterprise whose success seems so uncertain, even for her?

Since she's been living at the distillery, Elizabeth has the impression of progressively losing her hold on reality. In the middle of winter's darkness, she has repeatedly felt herself slipping into another world. The first winter, she had several visitors and a lot of help. Now, during the second, the people of Lighthouse Point have kept their distance, as though the long wait, or Elizabeth's strange behaviour, has made them lose faith in this senseless venture.

Elizabeth sets down her hammer. From a shelf at the entrance to the storeroom, she takes two sticks that she has cut from an oak branch. She goes to a barrel. And, like a Japanese taiko drummer, she starts to beat the wood in a succession of movements, slow at first, then faster and faster.

Yelling and laughing like a possessed woman, she leaps gracefully and starts drumming on another barrel with even more energy and enthusiasm, captivated by this strange music carrying her frenetically away. She knocks on the barrels to her left and right. The storeroom becomes a huge drum singing the tune of wood and water. Elizabeth dances as though she were floating on a wave carrying all these barrels.

Giddy, sweat beading on her forehead, she can no longer clearly make out the barrels bobbing up and down around her. If only she could hang on to one of them. But they're all too rounded, with no handholds to grasp. Every time she reaches a barrel, her hands slip. And there's the cold filling all her limbs …

"Zab!"

All movement stops, and she herself comes to a halt. Panting, her breathing unsteady, she turns around and realises that Ghisèle is watching her, puzzled, not knowing what to say. So she softly repeats her name.

"Elizabeth?" Finally Ghisèle moves forward, takes her by the shoulders and leads her to a chair. "Are you okay?"

"I … I was just having some fun, giving myself a bit of a workout." Elizabeth looks at the sticks in her hands and throws them to the ground. "Oh! I'm just as crazy as everyone thinks I am."

"I brought you your mail," Ghisèle says hurriedly.

The two women calmly go to the apartment, where Ghisèle settles into an armchair while Elizabeth cursorily examines the letters placed on the table.

"More bills! Everyone's afraid of not getting what they're owed."

"Our suppliers aren't the only ones. When will we at least be able to taste the whisky?"

Elizabeth looks harshly at her friend. "Even I haven't tasted it yet."

"When will it be ready? People need a sign, Zab. They've been waiting for almost two years."

Elizabeth lowers her eyes. She's seen signs all right, but she's not at all sure that she understands them. "In a month," she says, "on the twentieth, which is also the day of the equinox."

Ghisèle remains sceptical. "March twentieth?"

Elizabeth has recovered her enthusiasm. "It'll be a real party. We'll taste our three blends and drink in honour of the return of both spring and the whisky."

Ghisèle feels relieved. Since Elizabeth's appearances in the village have become so rare, Ghisèle is sure to be bombarded with questions when she goes back to the Bar au Baril.

"Well, well!" exclaims Elizabeth, opening the last envelope. "MacPhearson's done a good job. The *Maison du whisky* in Paris is ordering a barrel of each of our blends! Even if the people here have lost faith, at least those elsewhere still have it."

"Amen!" adds Ghisèle, laughing.

Elizabeth goes to the window. The moment of truth is coming up fast, and she'll have to face it. And if she fails? In the distance, she sees the ice sheets. Will she go so far as to add her voice to that dismal choir? In a month, she and Lighthouse Point will have their answer.

22. Scotland, 1824

Paul had been searching fruitlessly for three endless hours, all along the banks of the *Sruth fuar*. His mood, like the leaden sky, was getting bleaker and bleaker.

"And yet it *was* here," he repeated to himself for the hundredth time. Three years had passed since his last visit to this place—three years and an entire lifetime. The spot looked sinister, like a cemetery, like the grave of a hated or at least formidable relative, which he had thought he'd never need to see again. Only death had been able to push him to set foot in this cursed place once again.

At the beginning of his search, he'd been surprised by his lack of any recollection of the slightest detail of this landscape. Had his subconscious erased his memory of this place so associated with tragic events? For that matter, snowmelt, which had been particularly abundant for the last three winters, had swelled the burns and somewhat altered their course. Violent winds had flattened or broken several trees. The mild summers had, on the other hand, encouraged the dense flora to flourish abundantly.

Paul Fearmòr was disoriented. He had lost much more than the memory of the location of the cave where the last barrels of Gleann Dubh were hidden. His father had died, without his son being able to grant him his last wish.

On his deathbed, Tom Fearmòr had asked Paul whether he had destroyed or hidden the barrels of Gleann Dubh. The son hadn't had the strength to lie to him.

"In that case, go and bring me just a little of it, so I can drink a last dram of our Gleann Dubh."

Paul had never heard his father plead like this. His mother's tear-filled eyes had urged him to return to that obscure corner of the valley wiped clean from his memory. He had left without a word. It was already late when he'd arrived at the cache's location. To his great surprise, the area's appearance had changed so much that he was completely lost. Once night had fallen, he'd had to return home empty-handed.

Tom Fearmòr had died just before dawn.

The *aire,* or wake, and funeral of a man as loved and respected as Tom Fearmòr were going to draw a large crowd that would come to share the family's mourning. Local custom dictated that whisky be liberally served and consumed in honour of the dead man. Since the Fearmòrs had stopped distilling their *poteen*, their income had shrunk considerably, to the point that the family had difficulty making ends meet. Paul therefore didn't have the money to buy any whisky, which continued to be produced mostly by clandestine distillers. No one had chosen to acquire the new distilling licenses offered by the government.

The Fearmòrs were much too proud to let people bring their own whisky to the dead man's house. Paul had decided that the Gleann Dubh, cherished by his father like his own blood, needed to be present at the *aire*. Serving anything else would have seriously dishonoured the deceased's memory.

So Paul had once again set off for the opposite side of the Dubh valley, to find the hidden barrels, the only thing that could ease his conscience and give him the feeling of properly honouring his father, who had died with only the faint memory of Gleann Dubh on his lips.

He had begun his search by trying to orient himself using the *Sruth fuar*. Though he'd climbed up and down its banks several times, this exploration hadn't yielded the slightest clue. Strangely, he had the feeling of discovering these green hills and this marvellous fast moving, cold stream, so aptly named, for the first time. His efforts combined with the force of nature had ended up concealing the cache all too well and he started to despair of ever finding it.

A cloud of midges buzzed around his head. This plague of insects fed his irritation to the point of driving him crazy. To escape them, he dropped to his knees next to the *Sruth fuar* and stuck his head underwater.

He stayed that way for a long time before abruptly pulling his head out of the stream. His lungs greedily sucked in air. How much time had he spent underwater? He'd almost lost consciousness. At least the midges had momentarily given up.

A drop dripped down his right cheek. Paul suddenly began to cry. He searched for the cause of this sadness. Was it his father? The whisky now forever lost? Shona, also lost forever? Or this damned country, where life was so difficult?

Paul then realised that raindrops had replaced the tears on his face. A thunderstorm struck violently. While trying to find a little shelter under the bushes, the young man slipped on the wet rock and found himself flat on his stomach. He watched the drops dancing on the ground and on the surface of the stream. Pushed by the pounding rain, the *Sruth fuar* burst its banks. On Paul's left, the water started to flow down a rock. Hypnotised by the movement of this new waterfall, he moved closer to it. A shiver of excitement shook his cold, wet body from head to toe.

On the other side of the curtain of water, he noticed a nearly triangular-shaped rock. This triggered his memory, and pushing his hand through the water, his fingers skimmed over the smooth stone. *Yes,* thought Paul with delight, *it really is this one. I had chosen it precisely because of its unusual shape.*

With his other hand he grabbed the stone and pulled. When it gave way, revealing an empty space, he almost couldn't believe it. He tore away earth and more stones with his bare hands. The thunderstorm ended, and Paul went to look for a shovel. In fact, he was quite close to his starting point.

He applied himself to widening the opening, his efforts slightly hampered by the water still falling in front of it. After half an hour, he deemed the hole sufficiently large for him to enter the cave. Completely soaked, he slid into the cavern, where there was just enough room to crawl. Groping, Paul found a first barrel, pushed it out of the cave, and then re-emerged into the open air himself.

Standing the barrel upright on a flat rock, Paul pulled out the cork stopper. From his pocket he took his father's *quaich*—a small, flat, circular container five centimetres around, with a tongue on one side that served as a handle. For centuries, this type of traditional chalice had been used by the Scots to drink their whisky, but Paul hadn't touched this particular one for three years. Before expending his energy to remove all the barrels and transport them, he wanted to make sure the spirits remained drinkable. The whisky of the Highlands had always been distilled for immediate consumption. The longest time a distiller had ever kept a barrel was about two months, an extraordinary measure that had been required to escape the gauger's vigilance. As for the legal distillers, their barrels left the distillery as soon as they were filled and, once they reached the taverns and inns, they were emptied just as quickly. Thus, no one had ever kept whisky this long, and Paul feared this ageing might have impaired the spirits' quality.

He filled the *quaich*. What he saw left him both horrified and disappointed. The liquid had a straw-like colour that Paul had never seen before. It couldn't possibly be whisky anymore, because when it flowed out of the still, whisky was normally clear, completely colourless. The wood of the barrel had probably transferred its colour to the spirits and, in all likelihood, a vile taste as well. The Gleann Dubh had surely become undrinkable.

Discouraged, Paul threw the contents of the *quaich* into the bushes. There was nothing left to do but go home. He'd swallow his pride and borrow the sum he needed to buy some whisky for the funeral. Huddled in on himself, numb with cold and exhaustion, he began to shiver feverishly. Despite his efforts to warm himself by rubbing his arms through his soaked clothes, his teeth started to chatter.

Bursting with rage, he got up and went to kick the barrel. Suddenly, he stopped himself. The amber-coloured liquid in the barrel, even if it had a disgusting taste, might still contain enough alcohol to at least warm him. Giving in to his fear of catching a bad cold, he decided to drink this expired whisky, and filled his *quaich* again. His shaking hand brought the vessel to his lips. His nostrils detected a strong, slightly peaty smell. He swallowed the whisky whole. After the blazing fire came a smooth, soothing caress. Stunned, he recognised the peaty, heathery, vegetable accents of the old Gleann Dubh, permeated by a hint of oak and smoke. In his mouth, the comforting, exquisitely mild finish lasted a long time.

Paul hurried to drink again, this time sipping the whisky in order to take in all its splendid nuances. The Gleann Dubh had come out of this cave changed, mellowed, its natural flavours refined. It was now also cloaked in this colour that Paul now found beautiful.

He poured himself a third dram, and then another. His clothes were still wet, but he was no longer shivering. In fact, he now felt like he was wrapped in a large, warm, cottony blanket. Sitting on the bank of the *Sruth fuar* savouring his Gleann Dubh, Paul cried again—but with joy this time.

* * *

"If your mother's ready, we can get started, Paul."

The minister's voice pulled Paul out of the dreamy cloud where he'd been floating for the last two days. Consulting his mother with a look, he saw her nod in agreement.

"All right then, the cart with the Gleann Dubh will lead the way."

Paul, two of his uncles and a cousin carried the coffin from the house to the hearse. Friends of the dead man busied themselves loading a barrel onto another cart. The funeral procession, dominated by men dressed in black, took shape. Alex Campbell, a great friend of Tom Fearmòr's, climbed onto the cart with the whisky and, his voice shaking with emotion, launched the procession.

"Let's bring Tom Fearmòr to his place of eternal rest and toast his memory before he leaves his house forever."

Approving shouts rose, and the men pulled a glass or a *quaich* from their suit pockets and gathered around the whisky barrel where Alex started serving them. The word *Slàinte* rang out dozens of times and the procession finally set out. The cart with the whisky took the lead, followed by the hearse and all the mourners on foot. Five kilometres separated the Fearmòrs' house from the church and the cemetery.

Paul smiled as he took his place next to his mother. Thanks to the Gleann Dubh, this *aire* would be remembered for a very long time. For two whole days, relatives and friends had honoured the dead man's memory by transforming his funeral, where more whisky had been consumed than at any other such occasion in the annals of Scotland, into a true celebration of the deceased's life and whisky. In Heaven, Tom Fearmòr had to be proud. And there was still one last barrel in the house, to ease the pain after the burial. As a precaution, Paul had only removed half of the buried barrels from the hiding place at the *Sruth fuar*.

Friendliness and brotherhood permeated the procession's atmosphere; no one uttered the name of the dearly departed Tom unless it was with tender words, praise, and teary eyes. After a dram or two of Gleann Dubh, even those who had held a grudge against Tom began to crown the dead man with the greatest of virtues.

The whisky had earned just as many compliments as its departed creator. People would eventually end up figuring out how the Gleann Dubh had been so substantially improved but, for now, Paul would keep that secret.

"My friends, let's stop in front of my farm to drink to the health of the man, with whom I shared many pleasant conversations at this very spot."

Robbie MacManus, the Fearmòrs' nearest neighbour, had just climbed onto the cart at the head of the procession to make this speech. The men rushed towards the barrel and raised their glasses anew. The procession had only travelled three hundred metres, and Paul had no doubt that it would stop in front of each one of the twelve houses along the route to the church.

He was proved right. At each new stop, he listened to the eulogies with a distracted ear—since, deep down, he was pondering an idea inspired by this new Gleann Dubh, or rather by this old whisky resurrected through ageing. For two days now this project, both exciting and frightening, had obsessed him. However, his oath made it impossible. *I'll never distil poteen again.* In his head, Paul heard his own voice tirelessly repeating his promise. And yet the circumstances, and especially the Gleann Dubh, had changed.

After the fourth stop, the men moved closer to the source of their alcohol supply and began to walk between the hearse and the cart carrying the whisky. The procession moved forward at a snail's pace, but this didn't offend anyone except the minister who, after the fifth stop, decided to go wait for the convoy at the church.

The funeral procession had started to seem like a metaphorical parade. Jolly songs were followed by shouts of "Good old Tom". Paul would have liked to succumb to the joy of this atmosphere of celebration, but he remained troubled. Seeing the whisky act so effectively as an antidote to the poisonous grief of death awoke his desire to once again take up his calling. He owed it to himself. However, this would have required breaking his promise and, with the Fearmòrs, keeping one's word was a guiding principle, instilled from childhood and for life.

The barrel had just been emptied, and the mourners let out a sigh of disappointment.

Paul, who still had his *quaich* in his hand, climbed onto the cart and called out, "Let's go bury my father. Another barrel of his Gleann Dubh is waiting at the house, so we'll be able to drink to his memory again."

Enthusiasm resumed with greater intensity. Joyfully, the mourners carried on to the threshold of the church, where the minister was waiting impatiently. Paul swallowed the last drop of his whisky and watched the men stumble or lean against each other.

"What a *poteen*!" he murmured. "And I swore never to make it again." Paul repeated, "I'll never distil *poteen* again." Then, struck by a sudden inspiration, he asked: "But what if, more precisely, I was to distil whisky?" He'd just found the way to get around his promise without breaking it. He climbed down from the cart and went to stand in front of the church. Even if his father doubtless wouldn't approve, at least he'd understand.

"Where's the deceased?"

The minister's question brought Paul back to reality. He answered at the same time as the others at the head of the procession: "In the coffin."

Turning around, Paul realised that the hearse was missing. A man with a round face and bulging eyes came forward, tottering with great effort. Torquil Govan, the dazed driver of the lost cart, couldn't form a complete sentence.

"It's … I, I …"

It eventually became clear that the last time the driver had climbed down from the hearse to drink to the dead man, he had forgotten to return. He had simply started walking with the procession.

"I … I'll go look for it."

Torquil left at an awkward run, followed by the crowd's noisy laughter. While waiting for the dead man to arrive, Alex Campbell declaimed a few lines by the great poet Robbie Burns, offering them as praise for the distiller's immortality, achieved through his whisky.

… John Barleycorn was a hero bold,
Of noble enterprise;
For if you do but taste his blood,
T'will make your courage rise …

He spontaneously followed this up with a short tribute of his own creation:

God grant good luck to all the Fearmòrs,
Likewise eternal bliss,
For they should sit next to the Lord
That make a dram like this.

Moved, Paul dried a tear. *Oh yes!* he thought. *My father's funeral will have its rightful place in the annals of Scotland for more than one reason.*

23. MacPhearson, Lighthouse Point

I shouldn't have come. This thought overwhelms MacPhearson as soon as he enters the main room of the New Glen Dubh distillery. Seeing the group of Lighthouse Point inhabitants gathered around the three large barrels ostensibly placed at the centre of the room, he feels like he's just entered an insane asylum.

He receives a noisy greeting.

"You're going to be the first tourist to taste our whisky."

Captain André shakes his hand. MacPhearson has already noticed the local obsession with calling any strangers who disembark here "tourists". If he wanted to be a tourist, MacPhearson would more likely be visiting a tropical island than Lighthouse Point at the end of March. He ought to have insisted that Elizabeth simply send him one bottle of each of the three whiskies, rather than agreeing to her request to come in person. He remains firmly convinced that Elizabeth is still hiding some bottles of Glen Dubh.

From the moment he had seated himself behind the driver of the snowmobile taking him from Parry Sound to Lighthouse Point, he had realised the seriousness of his error. The snowmobile had crossed enormous puddles of water at full speed. MacPhearson had thought he was going to die, either by drowning or from a heart attack.

A drumbeat splits the air. Flabbergasted, MacPhearson notices Elizabeth Legrand standing next to one of the barrels, beating it furiously with two wooden sticks. For the occasion, Elizabeth is dressed in a loose fitting, bright red French-Canadian voyageurs' shirt and sash, as well as a scarlet Scottish kilt. A black beret sporting a silver fleur-de-lys shaped lapel pin completes her strange outfit.

"Ladies and gentlemen, today, the 20th of March and the first day of spring, we're going to celebrate the birth of the three first whiskies produced by the New Glen Dubh distillery of Lighthouse Point."

Even though he doesn't understand French, MacPhearson applauds with the rest of the crowd of twenty. Captain André translates for him. *Once they realise that Elizabeth's wasted their money, I'll have to act quickly to take advantage of their confusion.* An astute strategist, MacPhearson is already planning his next move.

"In a few years," continues Elizabeth, "these first three blends will make way for a single malt whisky distilled here at Lighthouse Point. In the meantime, we'll have these crossbred whiskies. The Glen Dubh, rescued from Georgian Bay and improved by time and contact with our natural elements, has been blended with our pristine water and with an assortment of whiskies from Scotland chosen for their particular qualities. It is these three blended, barrel-aged whiskies that we are finally going to taste."

"Come on, Elizabeth, pour us a glass, so we can see if the stuff is drinkable or not."

Angéline Bresette's voice betrays the group's impatience. Elizabeth maintains her composure.

"Our deluxe blend—which, of the three, contains the largest proportion of Glen Dubh—is the *Cuan fìor-uisge* or, in our tongue, Freshwater Sea. Next, there is the *Lainnir Taigh-Solais,* or Lighthouse Gleam, if you prefer. And finally, our Silent Spirit, the *Spiorad sàmhach.*"

With Ghisèle's help, she begins to fill glasses. Like people taking Communion, all the faithful walk by to take their goblets of holy water. Some take note of the drink's colour, others inhale its nose.

Once everyone has been served, Elizabeth raises her glass and solemnly proclaims: "To the New Glen Dubh!"

"*Slàinte*!" the others reply.

Glasses go up and whisky goes down. No one says a word as the process is repeated with the second barrel. This time no one waits for Elizabeth's signal before starting on their drinks. MacPhearson is holding back from sharing the many impressions he has gathered, and his uncomprehending daze reaches its limit when he sees people tasting the third whisky still without saying a single word. Impatient, he catches the attention of René Longlade, bartender at the Bar au Baril, to get his opinion just as Elizabeth addresses the crowd.

"So, what do you think?"

For a long moment, people question each other with their eyes, until René clears his throat and drops a bombshell: "It's rotgut!"

This first condemnation opens the floodgates to a noisy torrent of invective, which flows over the three blended whiskies. Visibly shaken, Elizabeth unsuccessfully calls for silence, until a voice thunders in English over the din of the crowd.

"You're all completely crazy! You haven't got a clue what you're talking about!"

Though the derogatory comments were made in French, MacPhearson grasped their meaning. Still savouring the sublime essence of the Glen Dubh masked by other malt whiskies, he loses his temper.

"The *Cuan fior-uisge* is extraordinary. That blend is sure to become a household name. As for the other two, I'm telling you they've got strong character, and …"

MacPhearson stops abruptly, realising that he has just uttered the very thing he was supposed to avoid saying at all costs: the truth. What has pushed him to act against his own interests? He contemplates the empty glass in his hand as though it were a cup of poison. Everyone is staring at him, like a class watching a student who has just finished reading his essay aloud and is now waiting for the verdict.

MacPhearson opens his mouth to take back his words when Captain André gives him a big, friendly pat on the back.

"Bravo, Johnny, now we know that you're really on our side!"

Bursts of laughter fill the room. MacPhearson remains in shock, totally taken aback, until Elizabeth, roaring with laughter, explains: "We already knew the whisky was excellent. We tasted it before you arrived."

MacPhearson begins to understand. "So … You all put on a little show in order to …"

"… test your allegiance to our whisky," finishes Elizabeth. "Your honesty confirmed it." Radiant, she takes MacPhearson's glass and fills it with *Cuan fior-uisge.*

So my monumental blunder has ended up saving me, MacPhearson ponders as he savours the *Cuan fior-uisge* once again. No doubt about it—the Glen Dubh is in the blend, harmonising deliciously with the other single malts and masked by flavours of chocolate, peat and smoke.

"It's a shame that your *Cuan fior-uisge* will just be a vintage edition. It's exquisite. Whisky connoisseurs will snatch it up," he says at last.

"As soon as we get the money from the sale of these blends, we'll move on to the next phase."

MacPhearson thinks about the considerable capital that Elizabeth will have to invest, without any return for at least three years after the distillation of her first whisky. He, too, will have to be patient.

She's really the victim of her own success, he concludes. *But I'll be there to keep an eye on her at the fatal juncture. At least in the meantime, there'll be a profit to turn from this business before it evaporates like "the angels' share".*

MacPhearson then surrenders to a daydream. He sees himself floating above Scotland, like an angel. He is breathing ethereal whisky vapours by the lungful, part of the seven hundred million litres that annually evaporate from the eighteen million barrels of spirits sleeping in storehouses. How many angels does it take to absorb all of that?

His smile changes to a grimace. *According to scientific analyses, certain Scotches contain up to three hundred distinct components*, he thinks, studying his now empty glass. *However, this particular whisky must contain at least one component capable of driving people bonkers. And I'm on my way to becoming one of them.*

24. Scotland, 1824

"So, Mr Fearmòr, what do you say?"

Paul Fearmòr, as he looked at the woman who had just asked him the question, could find neither the right words nor the composure to hide his discouragement. He had just spent an hour minutely examining the equipment of the Glen Ciùin distillery and, even though these used stills were perfectly suited for the distillery he was endeavouring to set up, he didn't have the means to pay for them.

"The equipment could serve my purpose, but we need to discuss the price."

Catriona MacInnis couldn't hold back an impish smile. She perfectly understood the meaning of Paul's words and, even more, what he hoped to conceal from her. With a wave of her hand, she invited the young man to follow her.

Wary of the coming negotiations, Paul fell into step behind her. On the way to the administrative offices they crossed the distilling room with its new stills. Catriona never stopped surprising Paul. Although only five years his senior, she was at the head of one of the rare legal, industrial-sized Highland distilleries. Her husband's death three years before had catapulted her into this role, which she brilliantly assumed; her knowledgeable and sometimes implacable management had kept Glen Ciùin profitable. By upgrading her production equipment, the widow MacInnis was taking an enormous gamble. The only way it would pay off was if the British drinkers abandoned their revolting gin in favour of whisky, and particularly whisky distilled legally instead of clandestinely.

"So, are you going to make me a counter-offer?" Catriona had seductively vigorous features and light blue eyes that sparked with an ardent fire.

"You'd have to lower your price by a third." Paul had adopted a firm tone. The laughter that met his declaration disconcerted him.

"You have guts, Mr Fearmòr, I'll grant you that. I have no reason to accept such a ridiculous offer. You want to start a business that will make you one of my competitors and you're asking me to give you favourable terms!"

Paul had to acknowledge the weakness of his arguments. Catriona was negotiating from a position of strength and they both knew it. Watching his dream disappear, Paul gave in to despair. Challenging Catriona's gaze, he drew the weapon he had sworn to himself never to hone again.

"If I can't become your legal competitor, I'll go back to competing against you clandestinely, and we'll both be stuck in the same situation, constantly undercutting each other."

Catriona wasn't laughing anymore. In that moment, for a second, Paul thought he even saw a flash of empathy on her face. Without saying a word, the widow poured some whisky into two glasses.

"*Slàinte,*" they said in unison.

"We could perhaps find some common ground, Mr Fearmòr, on the condition that you agree to an exchange." The warmth of the whisky gave Catriona's voice a subtle mellowness.

"What kind of exchange?" Paul kept his guard up. This woman hadn't successfully kept her distillery afloat in such troubled waters without proving to be cunning.

"I want ten percent of the profits from your first batch."

Paul felt the Glen Ciùin burn in his throat. His first reaction was one of outrage. He went to voice it, but she cut him off.

"You know, I'm taking just as big a risk as you are."

"And I could lose everything." Paul was barely controlling himself.

"Yes, it's true," Catriona continued, "you'll have quite the fight on your hands. All the local clandestine distillers will be against you."

"I'll urge them to follow my example."

Catriona considered him for a long moment, as though she were evaluating his prizefighting capacity.

"I know them just as well as you do. They're going to make life hard for you. That's why I'm demanding a return on my investment that's proportional to the level of risk."

Paul drank in silence. He'd have needed a dram of Gleann Dubh to inject him with the courage to see this madness through to the end.

"Here, I'll also give you a loan. You may need it." Catriona opened her desk drawer, took out two small hair trigger pistols and put them down in front of Paul. "My advice is that from now on you never part from them."

Paul's eyes widened. If he ever needed to defend himself, would he have the strength to use these pistols?

"They belonged to my husband," the widow explained.

Paul drank the rest of his whisky and put the weapons in his coat pockets. The contract of sale was written and signed. He had just signed away his life, and he knew the next few years would be extremely difficult. But he remained resolved: the future of whisky lay on this path, the road leading it out of the darkness of clandestinity to the shining light of legality, where it would at long last claim its letters of nobility. Four years ago, on the banks of the *Sruth fuar*, he had sworn never again to make *poteen*, peat-reek. And he would never again make it, because what he was going to create would be legal whisky, distinguished spirits, a dignified elixir. Thus his oath would remain unbroken.

* * *

As she watched him leave, Catriona MacInnis was certain that she'd made a good deal. The businesswoman had discovered a completely unexpected quality in this young man. Hearing the son of Tom Fearmòr, the famous clandestine distiller, reveal his intention to acquire stills and a license to set up a legal distillery had completely flabbergasted her. Her first impression of him had been totally wrong. She wasn't dealing with a desperate small entrepreneur who had come knocking at her door hat in hand. No, Paul Fearmòr was a visionary, placing the whisky's future above his own.

What's more, by making this pagan distiller's conversion to the new legal religion possible, she'd assured her own place in heaven in this infernal industry. However, Paul Fearmòr had neglected to give her a crucial piece of information. The new Gleann Dubh would undergo a process unknown in the whisky industry until now: three years of ageing in wooden barrels. She would need to be patient before reaping the dividends of her investment.

The two distillers sensed that the deal they had just closed would prove to be a turning point in the whisky saga. Nevertheless, neither of them suspected that their roles in this story would be very different from the ones they had assigned themselves.

25. Robert, Speyside, Scotland

Robert Fearmòr wishes he could plug his nostrils to protect himself against the spell of the fragrances around him. His last visit to a distillery was five years ago. Having guessed the likely reason behind this summons to his Uncle Harry's office, he'd been wary of it. Now he senses an even greater danger: exposing himself to the very subtle fumes of peat, wood, heated copper, water and whisky, indistinguishable for ordinary mortals. On one hand, the familiar feeling warms his heart, but on the other, it dredges up a troubling reminder of a previous life, cast aside forever.

He suddenly finds himself resenting his Aunt Agnes. Her funeral had compelled him to return to the Speyside and to run into his Uncle Harry, who was not one to ever let a good opportunity pass him by.

Robert climbs the six steps that separate the still-room from the corridor of the Glen Fada distillery offices. He can't stop himself from turning to gaze at the three stills on the other side of the glass panels and to imagine the barley malt scent. Next to the spirit safe, a man dressed in overalls is attentively awaiting the perfect moment to stop the outflow of the second distillation. Robert had the intuitive gift of being able to determine the precise timing of this action, a talent that gave the master stillman the fleeting impression of possessing wizard-like powers.

"Seeing the whisky flow is still just as beautiful as ever, isn't it, Robert?"

The voice makes him jump. Forewarned of his arrival, Harry Fearmòr has come to meet him.

"Aye," Robert concedes, "but the emotion varies from one person to the next."

The fifty-year-old man steers his nephew towards his office. Robert settles into one of the comfortable armchairs separated by a coffee table. Harry goes to a cabinet, takes out a bottle of whisky and fills two glasses. The two men first drink to the late Agnes.

"I have a bit of a business proposition for you ..."

Robert sets down his glass. He's been waiting for this bait since stepping into the office. So he uses his already carefully crafted reply. "You know very well that distilling doesn't interest me anymore."

Robert, disgusted by working like a lackey for the company, a multinational corporation that owns a good ten distilleries besides Glen Fada, had left the latter, slamming the door behind him. An accomplished stillman by age thirty, he had quite simply had enough of reproducing the same whisky for a soulless conglomerate owned by a majority of shareholders who weren't even Scottish.

His uncle smiles like a poker player ready to play a trump card. "Aren't you going to ask me what I just served you?"

Robert's face betrays his surprise. The finish of the whisky still lingering in his mouth has the characteristics of a vintage Speyside single malt of an exceptional calibre. However, Robert, who can identify all of Scotland's single malt whiskies by their nose, doesn't recognise it. His curiosity sharply aroused, he takes another long swallow.

"It's a damn good dram," he finally admits. "Definitely a Speyside, and yet it has a wider range of aromas in the finish, and some marvellously complex woody nuances. Smooth, robust, rounded, very individualised, with a sweetness that isn't just the result of prolonged ageing in a barrel. All the same, I can't name it."

Harry Fearmòr's smile starts to look clown-like. Robert, sensing a trap, tries to regain the upper hand.

"But to come back to your proposition, Uncle Harry, don't waste your breath. When I left for Edinburgh, I ..."

"And if I told you that you're drinking Glen Dubh?"

Stunned, Robert ignores his uncle's satisfied gloating—so typically Fearmòr, of the Fearmòr character that Robert hates—and exclaims: "Our Glen Dubh?" Robert then becomes aware of the taste in his mouth, a strange mixture of tenderness and hatred, of sweetness and bitterness. The taste of his family history. "You mean the one from Canada?"

His uncle nods. Robert's heard of this story of bottles found in a small community on the shores of one of the Great Lakes, but he hadn't really believed it. His uncle retrieves the bottle and a file on his desk.

"How does taking a trip over there at the distillery's expense sound? I know you've always been interested in our ancestor who went there, to the shores of that bay … What's it called again?"

"Georgian Bay," Robert blurts out to help out his uncle.

He starts to leaf through the file, a collection of articles about the New Glen Dubh distillery, and stops at the caption: "The best of Scotland, distilled in the New World." A photo of Elizabeth Legrand, posing in front of the distillery with a bottle in her hand, accompanies the text.

"Then, seeing that I'll be in the general area, you want me to go and have a wee peek at this new distillery?"

Harry Fearmòr takes a big gulp of his whisky. "And report back to us."

"What exactly do you want to know?"

"Whether her whisky stands a chance of succeeding," Harry says seriously, pointing at the photo of Elizabeth Legrand.

Robert is completely intrigued. The idea of going to see Georgian Bay enchants him, because it's a gift he couldn't easily afford to give himself.

"And what if that's the case?" asks Robert, scrutinising the title of another article: "A non-Scottish Scotch better than the drink from the country of origin?"

"You don't have to worry about that, my dear nephew."

The sudden gravity in his Uncle Harry's tone of voice surprises Robert. He's in a hurry to leave. He downs the rest of his drink.

His uncle is smiling again. Though he knows better, Robert holds out his glass to ask for more of the whisky that hasn't stopped pursuing him, even in his flight.

26. Scotland, December 21st, 1824

Paul's slender fingers brushed the smooth, cold, curved surface of the copper still. He wanted to commit every detail of the apparatus to memory. His hand gently caressed the metal and, all of a sudden, Paul was surprised to feel a quiver of joy, blended with a hint of desire.

Since Shona, there had been no one in his life. Now he realised how much he regretted it, how incomplete he felt. His path represented a solitary journey; his separation from his family, combined with his precarious situation and future, made him a very poor match. Even if he'd found a woman willing to share this road strewn with suffering, would he have been willing to lead her there? Like one of his ancestors long ago, he'd become a monk devoted to whisky, married to this mistress so seductive and yet so merciless.

The thoroughly feminine-shaped still, with its narrow neck and curved basin, would be the matrix of his creation, the incubator of his whisky, the mother of his offspring and his future. His hand suddenly stopped on a shallow depression in the surface of the still, just where it widened. Would this dent be beneficial or detrimental to the Scotch? For experienced distillers, the slightest aspect of the still's exterior played an essential part. It was therefore paramount to avoid altering anything; otherwise there was a risk of compromising the whisky's quality. Some distillers even refused to remove the spider-webs that formed around stills.

Paul didn't know whether such beliefs had any basis, but he respected those who held them. He'd see, in a few hours. He finished his inspection of the two stills and, for a long moment, stood facing the devices perched like queens on sandstone hearths. Everything around him, except for the stills, he'd made with his own hands. He admired the distilling room, a large space with whitewashed walls and windows at both ends. On the south side, he could see the *Sruth fuar* tirelessly following its course, in spite of a few thin sheets of ice here and there.

To build this place, Paul had only been able to count on himself. His brothers and other relatives, who, normally, would have lent him a hand, had turned their backs on him. How could a Fearmòr stoop so low as to open a legal distillery and agree to pay the English a customs fee on the whisky of the Highlands? No one from clan Fearmòr would take part in such an enterprise. To be disowned by his own family had shaken Paul.

In vain, he'd tried to hire labourers from the Dubh valley who were badly in need of work. Some of them had even been outraged, spitting out that they would rather die of hunger than dirty their hands with such filthy work. Deprived of manpower, Paul had needed to downsize his plans to a smaller building. It was only through great efforts that he had somehow managed to finish the building before winter.

One morning, right at the beginning of construction, he'd arrived on the site to discover that the first wall, completed after weeks of hard work, had been destroyed. Furious, he'd gone to the Cratur House pub in the village. Displaying the pistols received from Catriona MacInnis, he'd ostentatiously announced that they'd stay hung on his belt and that he wouldn't hesitate to use them. Since that day, Paul hadn't strayed far from his distillery.

He shivered again, but this time with cold. It was time to light the fire under one of the stills. Yesterday, the fermentation of the malted barley had peaked. Paul lit a match. Once the fire was well lit, he fed it with peat he'd dug out of the soil himself. The building consisted of one floor above the ground floor, where he'd put the fermentation vats so the wort could flow down towards the still.

Before even starting this first distillation, Paul knew he was already ruined. His property abutting the *Sruth fuar* was heavily mortgaged. He'd have liked to buy the land around the stream in order to ensure his access to the water, but hardly had the money.

The strong smell of the smoky peat filled his nostrils, and the warmth drove away the dampness. Outside, the sun had reached its zenith. Tomorrow would mark the beginning of winter and the very gradual return of the daylight. Paul too had just been through the darkest period in his life. His hand touched the pistol at his waist. One night, he had been attacked by a small group of men. Paul had fired a warning shot into the air. Luckily, that had been enough to drive away the aggressors. He'd defend his distillery whatever the cost, but he didn't know whether he'd go so far as to kill.

He climbed to the second floor and opened the valve. The wort began to descend to the first of the two stills, the wash still. Now he'd have to be patient and let the force of the accumulated pressure in the still work the transformation of the maltose in the water, that is, the liberation of John Barleycorn's spirit and its reincarnation as whisky. Paul felt the onset of his own metamorphosis. But he didn't know whether he would be better for it or worse.

Shortly after, Paul, his eyes filled with a wild intensity, gazed at the lyne arm that joined the head of the still to the condenser, a coil running through a tray full of cold water. For a few minutes now, he'd been expecting the first drop, the birth of the whisky, which was late in coming. The fire under the still was an intense blaze, and the water wouldn't be able to resist this force pushing it to evaporate for much longer. The alcohol had to rise before it.

Paul was immensely relieved when the first drops finally condensed in the coil. The droplets being born from steam, the low wines, headed for the second still, the spirit still, where they would undergo a second distilling. The distillate would then end up in the spirit safe reaching the stage where Paul had to intervene.

He watched the process attentively, examining the foreshots that preceded the middle cut, watching over the clarification of the alcohol. Using his judgment, he would decide the cut-off point, that is, when to stop gathering the middle cut. By turning the taps on the outside of the safe, Paul would move the redistilled alcohol towards another container, the spirit receiver.

Today, this genesis he'd observed so many times fascinated him as though he were discovering it for the first time. Four years had passed since the last time Gleann Dubh had flowed. And this time, unlike all the others, it was coming into being in a legal establishment, authorised by the government. The exciseman would come to take note of all the barrels of whisky, and to measure the alcohol content of the spirits. Thus, when the whisky was sold, the distiller would pay the customs duties, as determined by the exciseman's report. And, in order to mark this important change, Paul would baptise this new whisky "Glen Dubh", simultaneously affirming both its adherence to the British system, through the use of the English form of the word for 'valley', and its Gaelic roots, by retaining the second half of its name.

Paul swelled with pride as he ended the process. At the same time, however, he felt guilty for experiencing neither the shame nor the revulsion that his culture and his Highlander's instincts should have spurred in him. He had just created a legitimate child. Why, then, should he be less proud of it than of a bastard?

It was the end of the shortest day of the year, and the sky was already getting dark as Paul put out the fire. The still could rest. His first whisky had just been born. Now it needed to age and mature in barrels.

A noise at the door made him jump. Instinctively he pulled the pistol from his belt and aimed it at a back-lit silhouette.

"I see that you're on your guard, Mr Fearmòr, and my nostrils tell me that you now have a treasure to protect."

Paul had to be dreaming. This voice and this barely visible shape seemed to be coming from the world of the *sìthichean* or fairies. When he was sure that it was truly Catriona MacInnis, he put away his weapon.

"Aye. You're right in both cases. I get few visitors, and they don't come to offer me their best wishes."

Catriona held out a basket to him. "I have. Here's a holiday gift."

Paul accepted the basket of food where he found, among other things, pastries—a delicacy he hadn't eaten for a long time.

"Thank you, it's much appreciated. I'm sorry I have nothing to offer you in return."

"I'd gladly accept a small dram. From what I can see, you have plenty of whisky now."

Paul laughed a little. "So your visit isn't purely social."

"Let's say a little pleasure mixed with business. I wanted to see whether the rumour that you were about to distil was true."

"And make sure that your investment is well protected," Paul added.

Catriona nodded lightly. "So, how about that dram?"

This conversation, his first in weeks, filled Paul with glee. "Well, all I can offer you is whisky fresh from the still."

"That suits me fine," Catriona declared without the slightest hesitation.

Paul couldn't hide his surprise. Distillers sometimes ventured to taste the fruit of their work in its purest state, out of bravado or to put a greenhorn back in his place, but offering freshly distilled alcohol not yet cut with water to a lady … He found two glasses, led Catriona to the storage vat for the middle cut, took some whisky from it, filled the glasses and handed one to her.

They looked at each other for a long time, as if one was waiting for a movement from the other. A mysterious signal passed between them, and they clinked glasses.

Neither of them could refrain from making a face. The strength of the 120-degree, or 70% alcohol whisky hit them head-on. Once the first shock had passed, a salutary warmth spread first in their mouths and then throughout their whole bodies.

"To the Gleann Dubh!" said Catriona, taking a second swallow.

"Glen Dubh, now," Paul corrected.

The drinker complimented Paul on his whisky, which would fetch a good price.

"Yes, in three years' time."

Catriona's mouth opened wide. The sparkle of her blue eyes took on another, dangerous colour. Paul asked her to sit down at a table to listen to the reason why she'd have to wait.

"It's because of this," said Paul simply, setting a half-empty bottle of the old Gleann Dubh down on the table, just next to his second pistol.

Catriona examined the amber liquid by lantern-light while her host described how ageing had transformed the whisky. He made Catriona taste it. After, her eyes regained their pleasant sparkle.

Suddenly, a stone shattered the window near them, and they heard a clamour of male voices. Paul ran to the door and opened it abruptly, trying to judge the extent of the threat. In the darkness, he made out four or five men who were hurling insults at him. Seeing only one way to calm them down, Paul took the pistol from his belt and, aiming above the spot where he judged his attackers to be, fired. Following the detonation, the group fell silent.

"I have a bullet for each of you," Paul shouted, reloading his pistol.

He heard grumbling, followed by the sound of footsteps walking away. However, just as Paul turned to go back inside, a terrifying roar echoed in the dark.

"You're a dead man, Paul Fearmòr!"

Paul recognised Sandy Donaldson wielding a knife and rushing at him. He had to decide, to shoot or … Paul threw the revolver to the ground just as Sandy reached him. He blocked the first blow and tried to grab the knife. The fighters danced a strange *pas de deux*, and then tumbled to the ground. Paul fought desperately, but Sandy got the upper hand and stabbed him in the shoulder. The injured man let out a cry of pain which, a second later, was buried by the thunder of a gunshot.

Sandy's body, pierced by a bullet, stopped moving. Two metres away from the combatants, Catriona MacInnis was holding the still smoking pistol that she'd taken from the table. Paul leapt to his feet and snatched the weapon from her. The three men who had given up on the attack came back at a run and, disbelieving, discovered the tragedy.

Paul didn't hesitate. Although incapable of killing to save his distillery, he'd lie to protect the woman who'd done it for him. He'd confess to having shot Sandy Donaldson, and would plead self-defence.

Paul now owed a second debt to Catriona. And no matter how much whisky he ended up selling, this one he would never be able to repay.

27. Georgian Bay, 1828

Captain James Hackett watched the bow of his ship, the *Alice Hackett*, plow the waves. He was worried about the clouds and the height of the breakers; this weather did not bode well. The Scottish sailor had gained his experience on the coast of his country of origin, off the Hebrides, so his seaman's instincts on this freshwater sea were completely amiss. The rather sketchy nautical charts that the admiralty issued to captains of Great Lakes ships were hardly adequate to navigate safely. Innumerable islands and rocks waited just below the water, in the most unpredictable places. Here too, storms could easily surprise the mariner. Their warning signs were not at all like those that appeared on the real seas—those with salt water. Here, if a boat was unlucky enough to get caught in one of these tempests, there was no way out. In the ocean, one could flee by riding with the storm, but in this bay that was not an option. At its widest point it was, at the most, ten leagues wide. Sooner or later the ship would run aground on one of the shores, one of the rocks or one of the coastal islands, before the weather calmed.

Hackett cursed the lot of the captains of the Great Lakes, namely ensuring the transport of troops and merchandise—and this ill-prepared November sail he cursed even more. The *Alice Hackett* had left the day before yesterday from Drummond Island, situated at the junction of Lake Huron and St Mary's River. He had ten soldiers, twenty civilians—men, women, and children—and even livestock on board. The civilians—almost all French-Canadian men, their Native wives and their Métis children—were moving to Penetanguishene, at the south-east end of Georgian Bay, where the British garrison of Drummond Island had just been transferred. Sometimes Captain Hackett overheard his crude passengers jabbering in a French dialect or in Ojibway.

The taut tendons in Hackett's neck were clearly visible. A burn scar covered the whole right half of his face, and it became even more evident when the sailor felt the onset of fear. If this voyage could end soon, he'd be greatly relieved.

* * *

Josephte Legrand, née Lachigan, held her six-month-old baby tight against her chest. Captain Hackett had just looked her up and down arrogantly. If she'd been able to speak his language, she would doubtless have found plenty to say to him.

The Ojibway woman's first journey on one of the white people's ships was making her increasingly uneasy. About an hour ago, the wind had changed, starting to blow out of the south-east, an unmistakable sign. She had talked to her husband François about it, but he, who had already travelled on schooners, trusted the British sailors.

Josephte, who didn't clearly understand the reason behind this move, already regretted it. Between 1812 and 1814, François had fought honourably against the Americans, like several other militia men from Drummond Island. The British had thanked them in a singular way, namely by ceding their island to the Americans! The Crown had, on the other hand, offered the civilians grants of land around Penetanguishene Bay, where the English had built a naval establishment just after the war.

François and the others had decided to take advantage of this compensation. Even though he'd spent almost all of his adult life among Native people and the Métis, François remained a white man, raised in L'Ancienne-Lorette in Lower Canada, with certain manners Josephte could not comprehend.

Her baby started to cry, and Josephte hummed to lull her to sleep. The afternoon was fading, and the weather had gotten darker. Two hours ago the schooner had left behind the shores of Manitoulin Island, thus entering the widest, most open section of Georgian Bay, that it had to cross before being able to hug the coast and dry land.

Josephte occasionally heard men's laughter from the ship's hold. An innkeeper and his thirteen barrels of whisky were also on board. Fraser, the innkeeper, had probably found takers for his whisky, Josephte suspected. It was going to be a long night.

* * *

"To the king's health!"

No one knew whether the soldier was joking or making a serious toast in honour of the English sovereign. Like the others, François raised the glass to his lips. Once again, he felt a raging blaze crackling in his throat. He'd tasted the pleasures of the bottle many times; and yet today, he was experiencing an entirely extraordinary state of wellbeing and clarity of mind. A new life was waiting for them in Penetanguishene, and it would be better without a doubt—this was an absolute certainty, confirmed by the whisky. He'd hesitated for a long time before buying some, but now he had no regrets, even though the whisky cost three times the usual price.

At first, François had, like everybody else, balked at the price. Fraser had then specified that he was selling Scotch, Glen Dubh. "Pour me a glass," had ordered the voice of a soldier with a very pronounced Scottish accent.

The man had seemed to be under the influence of an obsessive trance. The poor soul had to be desperate—ready to accept anything, even this overt highway robbery—to rekindle his connection, however slightly, to his country of origin. Just before taking his first draught, the Scot had toasted everyone with a "*Slàinte*" that nobody had understood.

However, as the men watched the drinker's hard face, disfigured by two scars, sink into an angelic sweetness and serene joy, their scepticism had started to dissipate.

"Oh! My friends, you don't know the great pleasure you're denying yourselves."

For all that, François, who'd accumulated his meagre savings through blood, sweat and tears, remained unconvinced. It had taken the testimony of one of his comrades, Ézéchiel Solomon, to make him give in. Solomon convinced Fraser to accept one of his five pigs in exchange for the whisky. Since taking his first swallow of Glen Dubh, Ézéchiel had become a picture of contentment, smiling idiotically. There was no longer the smallest trace left of the poor, miserable trapper and farmer.

So, like everybody else, Legrand had taken out his money and drunk of this nectar. No, he regretted nothing. The future now lay before him with all the beauty of the horizon line. He was on his third glass—his last, he promised himself. The boat had increasingly begun to toss, and he had to hold on to a beam to avoid toppling to the ground.

* * *

The *Alice Hackett*'s situation was going from bad to worse. The southeast wind forcefully whipped up the rushing waves. When it came to stormy seas, Hackett had seen worse. Nonetheless, in these waters, he didn't know how to protect his ship from catastrophe. His facial convulsions had become uncontrollable.

He'd given the order to lower the topsail and the crossjack, so as to ride out the storm with a minimum amount of sail. The closest shore was now a good distance away to starboard. Open water and imminent danger loomed in front of the ship.

Soon it would be dark. On deck, the members of the crew worried. They would have preferred to be in the place of the passengers in the hold who, knowing nothing of the peril awaiting them, were laughing loudly.

* * *

Laugh. That's all these men, that the whisky had reduced to such a carefree state, could do. Every time the boat pitched to one side or the other, François and his buddies had uncontrollable fits of laughter. Ézéchiel Solomon, who'd fallen to the floor, guffawed as he rolled like a barrel. At least, Josephte noted, Fraser had had enough good sense to stopper his barrel of whisky.

The rising wind had forced Josephte to leave the deck and join the men in the hold. She wanted to pray, but she hesitated, torn as she felt between the Catholic God and her ancestral spirits. When she'd been baptised by a travelling priest, she'd already spent five barren years with François. The couple and fifty others had participated in a collective marriage ceremony, with, in a few cases, their children born out of wedlock in attendance. Barely three months later, Josephte had been surprised to find herself pregnant. Would her prayers be less effective because she was sitting down, her baby pressed against her chest, instead of kneeling and clasping her hands? There was no room to pray in the crowded hold. If she had risked shifting her position, the boat's constant rocking would have thrown her to the floor.

When Dédin Laronde, a child of ten, started vomiting, the laughter stopped. In the fear-charged silence, the only thing anyone could hear was the howling of the wind and the sharp creaking of the wooden hull.

The ship let out a prolonged groan followed by an abrupt shock. The passengers were shaken as if by an earthquake. Some were knocked down, others propelled against the beams of the hull. François Legrand, taking a violent blow to the head, fell unconscious. Numerous objects started to leap about, including two of Fraser's barrels, which wedged Josephte against the hull. Screams of disarray and panic burst out all around. The trapdoor of the hold opened and a terrified voice ordered the passengers to climb up as quickly as possible.

The collective haste to leave the hold created a stampede. Luckily, Fraser, who hadn't touched a drop of his own whisky, noticed François Legrand's motionless body and, with the Scottish soldier's help, moved him. Throughout all this mayhem, however loudly Josephte screamed, no one distinguished her pleas for help from the ambient cries of horror.

Barely a minute later, to her great surprise, the only sound that Josephte heard was the moan of the wind and the waves beating against the hull. Had the crew and passengers abandoned ship and jumped into the water? The boat wasn't moving anymore, nor taking in any water. The *Alice Hackett* had probably run aground on a sandbank, and the shipwreck victims had in all likelihood left the schooner and walked to dry land. She sighed with relief: she wouldn't drown! Had François forgotten them, his wife and their daughter?

Gathering all her strength, Josephte tried to move one of the barrels. Her daughter started crying loudly enough to burst her eardrums. In the total darkness, and grappling with her despair, Josephte started screaming too, and then crying warm tears.

Just then, a series of violent waves arose. She was floored, and the barrels holding her prisoner started rolling again. A cannon, propelled violently down the chute and through the hull, made a terrible crash. The vessel stabilised once again and, feeling her way, Josephte moved forward, up to the ladder leading to the still-open trapdoor.

Once she'd reached open air, the young woman discovered that the galley, surrounded by water, was tilting dangerously. The last set of waves had probably lifted it up, to set it down again a little further away from the shore. In the blackness of the night, Josephte couldn't even make out in which direction dry land lay.

Suddenly, she went pale. On the water's surface, Ézéchiel Solomon's drowned livestock—three horses, four cows, twelve sheep and eight pigs—as well as Fraser's thirteen barrels, were moving away from the boat in a macabre convoy carried by the waves. The ship was quickly taking on water.

She searched for a wooden object to serve as a buoy, but in vain. She let herself fall against the mainmast. Around her, the wind was still blowing furiously. There was only one way out: up. She untied one of the pieces of rigging attached to the mast and fixed it around her waist. A cold, cruel rain started to fall.

With little Angélique securely tied to her body, Josephte began to climb, a few inches at a time. The baby, nestled against her mother's chest, was asleep now. Josephte, completely wet and shivering, finally reached the top of the mast. Feeling that she was about to lose consciousness, she made sure that she was firmly secured to the wood. Just before giving in to exhaustion, she managed to pray again. This time, she turned to the Ojibway spirits, hoping to see them succeed where the Catholic God had failed.

28. Scotland, 1851

The boss was going to celebrate his fiftieth birthday, and the distillery its twenty-seventh. The excitement aroused by this great event had spread beyond the Dubh valley and even throughout the whole Speyside region. What's more, Paul Fearmòr's birthday, September 21st, coincided with the beginning of the distilling season.

The Sunday before the celebrations, scheduled for the following Saturday, Paul Fearmòr undertook a series of visits to personally invite his friends and competitors to his party. The day was splendid and, in his handsome cabriolet, Paul appeared like a king roaming his realm, satisfied and happy to take in his subjects' prosperity.

Passing in front of his own distillery, he looked upon the buildings with affection. The Glen Dubh distillery had undergone numerous expansions since 1824. In a quarter of a century, the various structures had, in step with production, multiplied. Today, Glen Dubh provided work for more than fifty men, including master stillmen, malt men responsible for the malting, coopers, peat gatherers, and brewers. Paul's dream of buying the land on the banks of the *Sruth fuar*, thus ensuring control over his water supply, had come true after ten years.

In spite of the enormous evolution in distillation methods, the whisky still remained the same. The ageing process initiated by Paul Fearmòr, at first by accident and then in a systematic way, had now become the industry norm. Today no one could even conceive of selling whisky before it had spent at least three years in a barrel. The distillers experimented with various types of barrels: American white oak, sherry casks from Portugal, barrels of American bourbon … in their quest to perfect the colour and taste of their Scotch.

The spirit safes were under the locks of British customs service officers, who meticulously noted the details of the spirit's production to determine the amount owed to the Crown on the sale of the whisky.

On seeing the sign "Glen Dubh Distillery, Paul Fearmòr and Sons", Paul was, as always, filled with an overt sense of pride. Today, his usual musing was followed up by another thought: "That, too, is going to change soon."

Leaving the village of Dufftown, Paul had driven the cabriolet along the road teeming with distilleries. His first stop was at the brand new Dailuaine distillery. There was a rumour that, despite his undaunted efforts, the owner, William MacKenzie, risked going bankrupt. MacKenzie welcomed Paul Fearmòr reverently and informed him of his firm intent to be among the guests. Satisfied, Paul went on his way, but not before drinking the traditional, obligatory *deoch an dorus*—the parting whisky dram taken on the doorstep.

Paul's tour then took him to the Glenlivet, Cardhu, Glendronach, Benrinnes and Glenfarclas distilleries. Each time, he received affectionate good wishes, a promise to be present at his party and, of course, a *deoch an dorus*. Over the course of the afternoon, the drams shared with his hosts along the way heightened his euphoria. At the entrance to the Glen Ciùin distillery, Paul had to dry a tear shed for Catriona MacInnis, who was no longer there to greet him as on that now distant day twenty-seven years ago. The manager had died ten years ago and, lacking an heir, the distillery had been bought by the Campbell family.

Paul had never forgotten his double debt to Catriona. Without her stills, granted at a very reasonable price, the Glen Dubh would never have been reborn. Her support had allowed Paul to become a legitimate distiller, forever changing the whisky industry in the Highlands.

It had taken more than ten years to bring them round to his way of thinking, but Paul's determination and prosperity had finally convinced the clandestine distillers to come out of the shadows. One after the other, the new legal distilleries had come into being, and whisky smuggling had gradually become a thing of the past. Free of clandestine competition, legal producers had finally begun their rise to prominence.

Paul recalled the smuggling adventures of his youth. Today, there were no more mules loaded with barrels of whisky travelling the road to Glasgow. The whisky was exported via the railroad line extended all the way to Dufftown.

Paul carefully climbed down from the cabriolet. His thoughts turned towards his youth. *If Sandy Donaldson hadn't tried to kill me that night, things would have been different and maybe even ended in ...* Paul remembered the sparkle in Catriona's eyes. There had only been ties of friendship and business between them. Would she have wanted him as her consort? Paul had never asked himself the question. *I could have given her the heir who would have inherited an empire of two great distilleries.* The reflection left Paul momentarily sad.

After the *deoch an dorus* shared with Archie Campbell, the owner of Glen Ciùin, Paul decided to return home before Elizabeth, his wife, started worrying. On the way back, he declaimed the same lines from Robbie Burns' poem, *John Barleycorn*, recited at his father's funeral.

... 'Twill make a man forget his woe;
'Twill heighten all his joy;
'Twill make the widow's heart to sing,
Tho' the tear were in her eye.

Then let us toast John Barleycorn,
Each man a glass in hand;
And may his great posterity
Ne'er fail in old Scotland!

Yes, the whisky of the Highlands had remained the same, but its distillation and distribution had been irrevocably transformed. The business he was going to leave to his sons, and the way in which he had chosen to do so, were the irrefutable proof of that.

* * *

Robb Fearmòr inhaled for a long time and tried to decipher the smells. "A little peat, some vanilla, a light touch of honey." He wrote down his observations in a notebook with the scribbled inscription: "Whiskies to consider".

He picked up the glass he had just sniffed and swallowed a good draught. His mouth confirmed the tastes detected in the nose. Robb smiled. "Soon I'll be able to identify all of them just by nosing them." He replaced a flask of whisky on a shelf with thirty other identical containers. Some of these held single malt Scotches like Glen Dubh, distilled from barley malt, others held grain whiskies—whiskies distilled from various grains, especially wheat.

Robb sat down behind his desk and lost himself in thought. The older of the two Fearmòr sons, who had just turned twenty-three, was, by his own admission, a dreamer. His father and his brother Harold accused him of wasting his time obsessively sampling other distillers' whiskies. According to them, the only Scotch worth knowing in depth was theirs. Robb, however, saw his vast knowledge of whisky as an asset for the distillery.

Harold Fearmòr burst into the office. He was sporting his typical, manager-completely-swamped-by-work manner. "Have you prepared a speech for tomorrow?" he asked without preamble.

Robb had to hold back his desire to lie just for the sake of annoying his younger brother. "Yes, I'm even going to recite some Robbie Burns."

Harold seemed satisfied. Robb, more gifted in poetic writing than his brother, was supposed to pen the tribute to their father and present it during the banquet in his honour.

"It's time for you to go and see the master distillers. They're ready for the next distillate."

Robb agreed once more. Harold, who behaved like he was the sole owner of the place and the big brother, despite being two years younger, never stopped pestering him. Contrary to Robb, he already had a wife and two children, and was more interested in the commercial aspects of the product than in its crafting. In fact, the distinct talents of the two brothers complemented each other, even though their opposing interests sometimes led to conflicts.

Harold left him alone, and Robb went back to his musing. His father and Harold seemed oblivious to the enormous changes that were looming in the industry. Sooner or later they would have to face them, even though, at the moment, no one could predict the exact form they would take. The population of Scotland, with its 2.6 million souls, supported its national industry by consuming 5.6 million gallons of whisky every year, namely two gallons per person. As a result, distillers were multiplying. The most recent census, in 1844, had counted no less than 169 of them.

Nevertheless, even though Scottish whisky was exported to England and elsewhere in the world, its principal clients, the British, hardly appreciated its full value. A large part of the Scotch they bought was rectified into gin.

Harold and his father persisted in ignoring the terrible threat Scotch was facing. For the last twenty years, the invention of the Coffey still, or patent still, had been revolutionising the distilling of grain-based whisky. Contrary to the copper stills required for distilling single malt whisky, the Coffey stills could distil continuously, without needing to be emptied and cooled down before beginning the next batch. These two-columned stills could produce up to two hundred gallons of spirits per hour and, because of the time saved, spit out greater amounts of grain-based whisky at half the price of single malt. The British, especially the gin rectifiers, were taking full advantage of the bargain this lower-quality alcohol offered them.

Robb sensed that this revolution would yield an opportunity to earn profits, but he was still searching for it.

When he had suggested buying a grain-based whisky distillery, equipped with Coffey stills, his father had balked. "Fearmòrs making grain-based whisky? Never!"

Tomorrow, his father, whose health was declining, would officially cede the management of the distillery to his sons. Robb would then be in a position to impose his ideas. And, if he didn't manage to persuade Harold, he'd force him to bend.

* * *

... Let other poets raise a fracas
'Bout vines, an' wines, an' drunken Bacchus,
An' crabbit names an' stories wrack us,
An' grate our lug:
I sing the juice Scotch bear can mak us,
In glass or jug ...

A few lines later, Robb finished his recitation of the poem *Scotch Drink* to a hail of applause.

"I would now like to ask you to raise your glasses in honour of the founder of the Glen Dubh distillery, the eminent Paul Fearmòr."

The three hundred guests rose to their feet and intoned in a prayer-like fashion: "To Paul Fearmòr."

The man thus honoured rose in his turn. The banquet was taking place in the malting room, where tables had been set up. Paul Fearmòr's work had been celebrated in style, starting with his grand entrance led by a bagpiper in traditional tartan dress and now, the moving speech his son had just made. He cleared his throat to speak.

"Even the Glen Dubh has never been able to make an orator out of me," he began, making a long pause to take another swallow of whisky.

Paul praised the occasion, and thanked his wife and sons. He briefly evoked the way his dream had taken shape and surpassed even his wildest hopes.

"God is a Scotch drinker, no matter what the Presbyterians say."

Paul had to wait for his audience's burst of laughter to subside before continuing.

"Because of my increasingly delicate health I have to let others carry on my work and the tradition of *uisge beatha*. As of Monday morning, you'll see a new sign at the entrance to the distillery. It will say: "Glen Dubh Distillery, founded in 1824 by Paul Fearmòr, proprietors Robb and Harold Fearmòr." I have no regrets. I wish my two sons as much success and luck as I've enjoyed."

The crowd warmly applauded the passage of the reins. The two new owners of the business, dressed in tartan kilts like their father, embraced him in turn. To finish, Paul Fearmòr, like a good Highlander host, warned his guests sternly: “You won’t leave here until the barrels at the end of the room have been emptied!”

Raising his glass, his voice trembling with emotion, he left the last word to the poet Robbie Burns:

Freedom an’ whisky gang thegither,
Take aff your dram.

The *céilidh* continued with a joy amplified by the liberal servings of Glen Dubh. Late in the evening, Paul Fearmòr took his oldest son aside. The two men, their *quaichs* filled to the brim in their hands, went outside to get a little fresh air.

“Robb, I’m going to give you my advice one last time.”

Fearmòr junior protested that his father’s opinions would always be welcome. Paul swept away this objection with the back of his hand.

“I know you’re chomping at the bit to put your own ideas into practice. But you and your brother are like a two-headed animal. You’re talented at making whisky, while he has a gift for distributing and selling it. You’ll have to work together in spite of your disagreements.”

Robb took a long swallow of whisky. Since the end of his speech he’d drunk a great deal. In the dead of night, his father’s voice sounded like an oracle predicting his inevitable destiny.

“Sometimes, neither one of you will be willing to give in. You get that from your father. But you’ll need to come to a decision anyway.”

Robb and his father were standing in front of one of the storehouse windows, protected by iron bars. Inside, in hundreds of barrels, the whisky rested, waiting for the end of its ageing process. For Robb, the wait was over.

“That’s why, in the contract where I’ve given the distillery to both of you, Harold has fifty-one percent of the shares and you have the forty-nine others.”

Robb dropped his *quaich*. His father went on talking, but he couldn’t hear him anymore. He opened his mouth and, unable to utter more than a sort of grunt, he stormed away.

In the cool night, his feet set themselves down heavily one in front of the other. Although he was very drunk, his intimate familiarity with the place allowed him to avoid the various obstacles in his path. He'd turned instinctively towards the *Sruth fuar*, to seek out the comforting murmur of its waters. Slowly, his feet sometimes wading in the water for several minutes, he made his way up the slope of the valley hollowed by the stream since time immemorial. After covering a sizeable distance, he sat down, panting, on a large rock right in the middle of the stream. Shaking with rage, he let out a moan and threw up.

After a long moment, Robb saw his silhouette reflected in the water of the stream by moonlight. He splashed his face. The cold of the water and of the night pierced the veil of his drunkenness. He was still shaking, but from weakness and cold now. Anger gradually gave way to clear-headedness, and he considered his situation with a calm, analytical eye. He wiped his mouth with the back of his sleeve. He couldn't dispel the bitter taste, or the resentment that would, from now on, become part of the whisky he'd create.

His hand punched the water. If it had been possible, he would have imitated the giant in the legend and set about drinking all the water of the *sruth*, until it dried up. This water, the source of this whisky that he loved like a mistress, was also the cause of his despair. His father had trapped him; now, Robb had become the prisoner of this marriage of interest with his brother, where he was condemned to be the dominated partner. And this union was for life.

His father may have succeeded in cornering him, but he resolved that his brother wouldn't have the last word. He drank a few swallows from the *Sruth fuar*. He then felt reconciled with himself, with his lot. In the end, fate was working in his favour. Harold was stubborn, but not crazy. Sooner or later, he would end up facing the facts and recognising that the whisky had to change. It would then be Robb's turn to dictate his conditions—because, without his help, the business wouldn't weather the storm that was about to break over them.

Part III

29. Lighthouse Point, 1918

"And that's how I spent my first night on Fitzwilliam Island, with my mother, tied to the mast of the *Alice Hackett*."

Robert Lefroy, amateur historian, looked at his informant with amazement. "And afterwards?"

Angélique burst out laughing. "The next day, the people from the boat finally saw us. My father was still passed out. According to gossip, it was more because of the whisky than his injury. All the same, his forehead remained scarred until the end of his days."

The historian was still taking notes. This priceless account of the coastal life of Georgian Bay would be added to the others he'd published in a prestigious historical journal.

"So the *Alice Hackett* didn't sink?"

"No, not right away. It sank up to the deck, and then settled on the bottom of the bay."

Angélique swallowed a mouthful of the whisky Lefroy had given her. She'd been telling the story of her life for a good two hours now. Oh, she'd exaggerated a few details, but a ninety-year-old certainly had earned the right to do that.

Catching her breath, she explained to the historian that, as dawn rose, a group of men finally returned to the schooner to rescue them. It was only three days later that another boat finally passed close enough to Fitzwilliam Island, a few kilometres south of Manitoulin Island, to notice the fire lit by the shipwreck victims.

"It seems that the men salvaged all the barrels of whisky."

Robert Lefroy gleamed with satisfaction. His readers ate up his transcriptions of these tales told by elderly Métis and French Canadians, with their half-civilised, half-native appearance.

For her part, Angélique knew that she'd given Lefroy what he wanted: the story of the first recorded shipwreck in Georgian Bay, a maritime disaster caused by drunken men, driven mad by whisky to the point of abandoning an Indian woman and her child to the whims of the unbridled elements. She hadn't talked about the true cause of this shipwreck, namely the incompetence of a captain incapable of reading the warning signs of a storm.

"Why did your family stop at Lighthouse Point when it was on its way to Penetanguishene?"

The historian's question drew new bursts of laughter from Angélique. "The boat that rescued us was going to Penetanguishene too. But it made a stop here first, at Lighthouse Point. My mother took advantage of the situation to get off the ship. She then told my father that if he continued his trip, it'd be on his own."

"So you've been living here since that time."

"Yes."

"So, you were here when the *Agomo* ..."

"That," declared Angélique, cutting Lefroy off, "is a another story."

Her facial expression had suddenly become very serious. She abruptly emptied her glass and walked away, leaving Lefroy quite dazed.

30. Scotland, 1853

"What's that?"

Harold Fearmòr's exasperation was visible in his eyes, fixed on the bottle his brother had put on his desk, as well as in his tone of voice.

"The future," Robb replied, with a smile fit to burst.

He'd wanted to say, "My revenge," but had stopped himself in time. Robb was thoroughly relishing this moment. It was finally clear to him where the whisky industry was heading, and he was perfectly positioned to take advantage of it.

"Which whisky is it?" Harold asked, irritated as always by his brother's hackneyed theatrics.

"It's not a single malt whisky like the Glen Dubh, nor a simple grain-based whisky—it's a blend."

Judging by his brother's intonation, Harold surmised that his words had to be important, even though he didn't understand why. He didn't have to wait long for Robb to enlighten him.

"It's a mix of various grain-based whiskies and single malt whiskies, developed by Andrew Usher. In fact, I'm absolutely sure that it contains a small amount of Glen Dubh."

"So?"

Robb gave free rein to his frustration. Even his idiot of a brother should have understood. He pulled a *quaich* out of a cabinet that contained ten of them, set it down on the desk, and said, "Taste it."

Harold filled the *quaich*, poured a few drops onto his hands, rubbed them together and took a second to sniff the whisky. The liquid had a lovely colour and a pleasant, though not very pronounced nose. Harold brought the whisky to his lips. His brother's impatient look disconcerted him. He felt like a student incapable of giving the correct answer to a harsh schoolmaster. Harold considered himself superior to his brother in all things, except when it came to whisky appreciation. It irritated him to depend on Robb, even if only in this one respect.

"Not bad," he finally said. "But it lacks character and especially the smoothness of a good whisky."

"Is that all?"

A key element was definitely escaping him, but, as usual, instead of admitting his weakness, Harold went on the attack.

"Why are you wasting your time over this pathetic whisky? We have much more serious problems. Look at this article from the *Times*. The supporters of the temperance movement will use it to vilify us yet again."

As he spoke, Harold had moved the bottle of blend, which was covering the newspaper and the distillery's balance sheet for the last few months. Sales were in free-fall, largely thanks to the temperance advocates, who controlled the press and were increasingly using it to hammer their message home. Harold handed the newspaper to Robb.

WHISKY CAUSES MADNESS AT ISLAY
May 27th, 1853

The brig Mary Ann, of Greenock, now lying a wreck at Kilchoman Bay, Islay, is fast breaking up, and portions of the cargo are floating ashore. Up to Saturday there had been about 200 boxes saved—containing, among other things, bottled whisky, and upwards of six puncheons of whisky. The wildest scenes of drunkenness and riot that can be imagined took place. Hundreds of people flocked from all parts of the neighbourhood, especially the Portnahaven fishermen, who turned out to a man. Boxes were seized as soon as they landed, broken up and the contents carried away and drunk. Numerous people could be seen here and there, lying amongst the rocks, unable to move, while others were fighting like savages.

Sergeant Kennedy and Constable Chisholm, of the County Police, were in attendance, and used every means in their power to put a stop to the work of pillage. They succeeded in keeping some order during the day on Thursday, but when night came on the natives showed evident symptoms of their disapproval of the police being there at all, and preventing a fellow from knocking the end out of a puncheon, in order, as he said, to "treat all hands". They were immediately seized upon by the mob, and a hand-to-hand fight ensued, which lasted half an hour, and ended in the defeat of the police, of whom there were only two against 30 to 40 of the natives.

The police beat a retreat to Cuil Farm—about a mile from the scene of action—closely pursued by about 30 of the natives, yelling like savages. Mrs Simpson of Cuil, on seeing the state of matters, took the police into the house and secured the doors, at the same time placing arms at their disposal for their protection. The mob yelled two or three times round the house, but learning that the police had got fire-arms, they left and returned to the beach.

Next morning the scene presented was still more frightful to contemplate. In one place there lay stretched the dead body of a large and powerful man, Donald McPhayden, a fisherman from Portnahaven, who was considered the strongest man in Islay; but the whisky proved to be still stronger. He has left a wife and family. Others apparently in a dying state were being conveyed to the nearest houses, where every means was used to save lives. McPhayden was interred on Friday. At the time the corpse was being taken away, some groups could be seen fighting, others dancing, and others craving for drink, in order, as they said, to bury the man decently. Up to Saturday there was only one death, but it was reported on Monday that two more had died.

Realising his brother's ploy, Robb threw the newspaper to the ground, furious. "The teetotallers will eventually calm down."

"Maybe. But in the meantime, our sales are taking a beating. Look at these figures." Harold held out the balance sheet, but Robb had recovered his assertiveness.

"There's much worse on the way. If we don't adjust to the arrival of these blends, we run the risk of losing everything."

"You're blowing the situation all out of proportion, as usual."

Robb took a deep breath and, as calmly as possible, explained the threat looming over them. Producing blends, made up mainly of grain-based whisky, would be much less expensive than producing malt whisky. What's more, the single malt, the ingredient that gave blends their pleasant taste, was already aged when it was combined with grain-based whisky. Thus, contrary to the single malt distillers, the blenders didn't have to tie up their capital while their whisky stocks matured. Blended Scotch only had to be stored in barrels for a few months before being sold.

"Soon, the blends will steal our whisky market."

The seriousness of Robb's tone had an effect on Harold. Even if he remained sceptical as to the imminence of the catastrophe, he could see well enough that this new product would, at the very least, hurt their sales.

"So, in your view, there's nothing to be done."

Robb smacked his forehead and exclaimed, "You're really an *amadan*, Harold. Blends represent a golden opportunity for us. When you can't beat the enemy, you join them."

Harold found himself confused and in the dark once again.

"Now that Usher has charted the course," Robb continued, "they'll be many who'll follow it. But to create a quality blend, you have to be intimately familiar with a wide range of whiskies, and be able to imagine the best combinations."

"You evidently possess this rare talent." Despite the sarcastic bite in his voice, Harold knew it was true.

"Thanks to my trials and my notes, we have a long head start on the others, and the possibility of making a fortune."

Harold thought for a while and, after a long pause, finally said, "I'm willing to let you develop a blend, on a trial basis."

Harold was surprised by Robb's ridiculously large grin. And when his brother spoke again, Harold concluded that he'd gone stark raving mad.

"I'll create four or five blends. But on one condition: you'll sell me eleven percent of your shares in the distillery, or I'll offer my services elsewhere."

31. Georgian Bay, 1855

She was already twenty-seven years old and time was flying by. All Angélique Legrand knew was life at the Point, the life of a small community built on a rock pounded by the waves.

"Tomorrow I'll go check my trap line." Angélique's father, François, went to the wood stove, where he lifted the tea kettle and poured himself a cup of the piping hot liquid.

The young woman watched him. His stride was still steady, but it had lost its vigour. In a year or two, François would no longer have the strength to go trapping. And she, a spinster, would have to take care of her father without any support, financial or otherwise.

As she often did, she thought of how much she missed her mother, swept away by acute pneumonia three years ago. Since then, Angélique and her father had simply been following the rhythm of the seasons.

Barely ten families, namely thirty people, lived along this series of winding channels opening onto an elongated bay. The boats that made this isolated place a port of call were few and far between. The Corbières, the Laramées, the Bresettes, the Chevaliers, the Longlades, the Desaulniers and the Levasseurs—each family had its cabin, or rather its camp, where it somehow managed to live off the limited fruits of the Canadian Shield and the surrounding waters: furs and fish, wild berries, and meagre harvests. The spot didn't even have an official name. The inhabitants spoke of *Neyaashiwan*, which meant 'the Point' in Ojibway. This impressive cliff was the most notable feature of the place.

Angélique decided to go sell some blueberries to the workers who, for the last month, had been camping at the Point where they were building a lighthouse. It was late August, and the weather was already turning cooler. The blueberries that Angélique and the bears had been disputing for weeks were becoming increasingly rare.

The young woman slid a canoe into the water and knelt in it, on top of the folds of her dress. Shortly after, on the other side of the channel, she found the workers savouring their midday break. The Métis woman waved to them and was surprised to discover that the lighthouse had grown ten metres taller since her previous visit a week ago. The stone structure was taking the shape of a circular tower. Angélique babbled a greeting in English to the five men and gestured to her blueberries.

One of the workers tapped a colleague on the shoulder and, pointing to Angélique, said to him in English: "Hey, Frenchie, maybe you can talk to the squaw. Tell her to come with me for a stroll. I'll give her much more than the price of a basket of blueberries."

The group started to laugh noisily, with the exception of the man who came towards Angélique. He must have joined the team of workers recently, because she didn't recognise him.

"It seems you speak Canadian."

"Yes," Angélique stuttered in French, "you …"

Théophile Roy, who had to be about her age, came from the Québec City area. He had arrived three days ago on board the ship transporting the latest delivery of building materials and provisions. Angélique introduced herself as well. Despite their slightly different accents, they understood each other. The other workers were still making bawdy comments.

"What's she saying, Frenchie? Don't keep her all to yourself."

Théophile asked Angélique the price of her blueberries. He gave her the amount, poured the blueberries into a bucket, and invited his workmates to help themselves.

Softly, he suggested to Angélique to move away, so that they could chat more easily. The Métis woman was thus able to find out more about the lighthouse, and Théophile more about the area where he had just landed.

"It's splendid country," he commented. "And there's no lack of opportunities if you're not afraid of hard work."

Fifteen minutes later, when the foreman had announced the resumption of work, the labourer regretfully left his new friend.

"Will you come back?" asked Théophile.

"That depends," Angélique replied. "Tomorrow my father and I are going to join the others in the fishing village."

Théophile had just enough time to learn that this village was a camp in the Tortoise Islands, a few kilometres from the coast. The locals went there to fish and then smoke their catches. As he went back to work, Théophile saw that his colleagues had made the most of his generosity: there wasn't a single blueberry left. His conversation with the Métis woman had cost him a pretty penny, but he had no regrets.

* * *

Il y a longtemps que je t'aime
Jamais je ne t'oublierai ...

The song echoed in Théophile's ears like a dream. And yet the others beside him heard it as well, without understanding it. Carried on the air, it seemed surreal.

"That must be coming from the fishing village," declared Tom Bragg, a labourer who had been roaming about the coastal region for several years.

It was Saturday evening. Théophile had rarely seen a sky so full of stars. The distant voices, encouraged by a frenetic violin, only augmented the young man's desire to find himself in better company. For two weeks now, even though Théophile spoke and understood English fairly well, he had found it increasingly difficult to put up with his crude colleagues, whose language and culture were different from his.

He emptied his cup to the bottom. The whisky burned his throat, but comforted him. The day before, the whole team of workers had chipped in to buy these spirits from an itinerant peddler at a high price. The alcohol, once divvied up, had been consumed quickly. Now the group's discontent, sparked by the beginning of an intoxication cut off too soon, was growing in a worrying way. The atmosphere could easily lead to a brawl.

Théophile had a sudden inspiration. Going to the quay constructed at the bottom of the point, he slipped into one of the construction team's two rowboats. In the blackness, he couldn't pick out words anymore, just the unbridled violin music dancing on the water. The rower guided the boat towards this call.

Suddenly, the music and voices stopped. Théophile set down the oars and turned around to look beyond the bow—there was nothing. On the stern side, there was only the same dense darkness.

He then realised his recklessness. He had ventured into the night without a compass, and with no point of reference other than this music. Was his boat pointing towards open water or towards dry land? Unable to retrace his steps with certainty, he didn't dare move forward anymore. However, if he was pointed towards open water, he should have been able to see the construction site's campfire.

Even though he didn't know how to swim, he wasn't really afraid. The waves would eventually carry him back to shore. He just had to wait for dawn. Even so, the wind could rise and capsize him, or carry him so far down the shore that he would be utterly lost.

The young man started to sing as loudly as he could: *C'est l'aviron qui nous mène, qui nous mène ...*

His song cut through the air. At the third couplet, voices coming from the starboard side finally struck up the refrain with him.

"Go on singing, please," Théophile begged. "Without your voices I'm lost."

First there was silence, then bursts of laughter. The song began again, and Théophile started rowing with great energy.

Two songs later, he finally landed at the fishing village. Men, women and children surrounded him. Angélique Legrand wasn't the first to run towards him, but she welcomed him with a smile. The survivor, not the least bit shy, joined the party and danced like a man who had narrowly escaped a brush with the Devil.

* * *

The steamship *Agomo* struggled against the waves preventing it from reaching the quay at the Point. From their vantage point on land, all the inhabitants of the area, along with the ten labourers, watched the boat as it struggled, gaining one metre at a time. It was October, the beginning of the season when the winds on the Great Lakes were at their most fierce.

The ship had left Collingwood, a small port on the south shore of Georgian Bay, that very morning bearing a precious cargo, sent by train from Toronto. The sea monster spat a few more clouds of black smoke and finally drew up along the small dock held in place by cables run through iron rings planted in the rock.

"Unload that as quickly as possible," the captain bellowed from the third storey of the raised deck.

Three men grabbed the mooring lines, fighting to keep their balance on the quay, which was getting just as manhandled by the water as the ship. The large door of the hold opened, revealing a wooden crate measuring three metres by two metres. The sailors set up three planks as a gangway, but the turbulent water made unloading very difficult. They slid the case up to the planks, and the men on the dock tried to catch hold of it.

In the hold, a nervous looking gentleman who could easily have passed for a civil servant was keeping a close eye on the operations.

"Easy does it!" he shouted. "It's a fragile mechanism."

The labourers and sailors, applying both the strength of their arms and their curses, made great efforts to move the crate forwards. The case had almost covered half of its slightly inclined trajectory when one of the gangway planks fell into the water. The ensuing loss of balance caused the case to slide right down to the quay, hitting Tom Bragg on the way and propelling him into the water.

The civil servant, John Beatty, ordered the men to protect the case, while Hinks, the workers' foreman, threw a rope to Bragg. Confusion reigned for a few seconds, with some hurrying to save the man in the water and others to halt the runaway crate.

From the top of the Point, the Métis watched the strange ballet without really knowing how to react. Some men from the group, including

François Legrand, stepped forward to lend a hand. Bragg was thrashing about with the energy of despair. He managed to grab onto the rope and was pulled out of the water.

The men were still battling the giant crate, which was refusing to stay still. The quay, increasingly destabilised, danced even more wildly on the waves.

"My lantern!" shouted Beatty.

The case jerked one last time before finally growing still. The workers, quickly recovering from their astonishment, attached ropes to it. The enormous package was pulled up onto logs set up at the water's edge.

The captain immediately ordered his men to undo the mooring lines. John Beatty hurried to gather his three suitcases. He crossed the planks and found himself on all fours on the dock.

"Good luck, Mr Beatty," snapped the captain.

The boat set off towards the bay. Beatty got up, grabbed his bags again and, stumbling, made it to the end of the quay. He introduced himself to Douglas Hinks, the foreman.

"John Beatty, the lighthouse keeper of Lighthouse Point."

Hinks and the others looked at him like he was an idiot. Dazed, Beatty repeated his introduction.

"Lighthouse keeper of Lighthouse Point?" Hinks mumbled.

"Haven't you been informed? The hydrography service has given the name Lighthouse Point to this lighthouse and the community surrounding it."

Beatty studied the little crowd of observers standing at the top of the cliff. *Those must be the inhabitants*, he thought. *The best of society, as I was warned.*

Beatty's luggage was brought to the lighthouse, next to which now stood a small residence. Moving the lantern turned out to be a difficult task. More ropes were attached to the case and then looped around two trees at the top of the cliff. Crevices in the rock served as natural stairs. One team at the top and another at the bottom set about raising the lamp very gradually, a few centimetres at a time, the first by pulling and the other by pushing.

It was already very late in the day, and the wind was still blowing. In spite of the cold, the men were drenched in their own sweat as they exerted themselves by lifting or pulling. It was completely dark when the crate reached the summit thanks to the efforts of the exhausted workers, their hands skinned from holding the ropes.

The next day, the inhabitants of the new community of Lighthouse Point gathered again to watch the rest of the work. Théophile Roy described the next stages of the installation to them, and informed them of their locale's new official name. The Métis were greatly excited by the lantern's arrival. On the other hand, the new place name left them completely indifferent.

Dawn had just broken when the men, following Beatty's instructions, removed the lantern with a Fresnel lens from its wooden crate. The device, a dioptric lantern made in Paris, was designed to bend light rays by making them pass through sheets of glass and come out on the other side in a parallel pattern. The four sides made of convex lenses looked like insect eyes. The lamp was supposed to make its twenty-five metre ascent up to its pedestal at the top of the tower by way of a pulley installed on a beam at the pinnacle of the structure.

In less than an hour, the men managed to hoist the device and place it in its cradle set on ball bearings allowing the light to revolve. The rest of the work therefore took place inside the tower, far from the eyes of the Lighthouse Point inhabitants, who were disappointed to be deprived of the show.

At the end of the day, fires were lit and the families busied themselves cooking their evening meal. By seven o'clock, it was pitch dark. In the quiet of the night, people heard Beatty and a few men banging, pulling on chains, or cursing.

"Look!"

Young Hippolyte Cadotte, a boy of ten, had just called out while pointing to the lighthouse tower, where a luminous beam was being projected towards the bay. A strange silence fell. Did this new artificial light signal the beginning of a sinister or happy chapter in the history of the community? Several people were asking themselves that question.

Bursting with joy, John Beatty came out of the lighthouse to admire his work. "My friends, this is a great day for Lighthouse Point."

The absence of the slightest reaction didn't discourage Beatty. Suddenly, a ship's horn broke the calm. The vessel was sending out a call in a sequence that undoubtedly contained a message. Beatty crowed.

"It's telling us that it sees the lighthouse! Where's the lad who speaks their language? He should explain it to them."

* * *

Théophile Roy was nowhere to be found. He was by the water, beside Angélique, looking at the stars. Hearing the boat sound its horn, the couple turned towards the cliff. The lighthouse was beaming its assigned pattern of four flashes every ten seconds, visible nineteen kilometres away, a signal enabling sailors to identify the specific light.

"It's truly Lighthouse Point now," Théophile declared.

"And you're going to leave." Angélique's voice was sad and resigned at the same time.

"Yes … but not with the others."

Théophile then shared with her his vision of the future. He believed the lighthouse was going to bring more to the Point than just light and an official name. *However*, thought Angélique, *if Théophile is right, these changes may not all necessarily be for the best.*

32. Elizabeth, Lighthouse Point

"There! Right here." Ghisèle nervously shakes the small hammer in her hand.

"The dent can't be too deep," adds Elizabeth.

I can't believe that she's really going to put a dent in a brand new still, thinks Ghisèle.

"How do you know it's just there? Even if it's the right spot, what makes you so sure that it'll improve the whisky instead of the opposite?"

Elizabeth only has a vague reply. "All the stills of the old Glen Dubh had this dent."

"Were you there in 1920, when the distillery closed?"

"No, but …" Elizabeth would like to confide in Ghisèle. But her friend's reaction would likely be worse than her present scepticism. "Pass me the hammer."

Ghisèle sighs. Elizabeth, in spite of her unfathomable decisions, has succeeded up to now. They've had to wait four years, but the New Glen Dubh distillery is now ready to distil its first indigenous whisky. Even after the success of the three blends, no one had really believed this feat possible.

Since the installation of the two copper stills, Elizabeth has subjected the equipment, made to measure in Scotland, to a meticulous inspection—mostly with her hands.

Very calmly, she repeatedly taps the chosen spot with the small hammer. The copper gives in to the pressure.

"Now the still is ready," she declares with satisfaction.

The distillery is beginning its second stage, one that will determine its future. The business has been able to pay a few people, Ghisèle being one of them, to help Elizabeth look after filling the orders for the blends, the installation of the equipment, and the transportation of the merchandise. Elizabeth expects to create ten jobs during the distilling season, from September to April, and to maintain half that number during the rest of the year.

"So it'll be tomorrow?"

Elizabeth gives the hammer back to Ghisèle, but stays pensive for a long moment before replying affirmatively. The two women return to the office. Ghisèle goes to a large calendar, taking up a whole wall, where important dates, like delivery and shipment days, are highlighted in red. She circles September 21st.

"Look," she declares, "tomorrow is the fall equinox."

This day will mark the beginning of nature's six-month cycle. But the cycle of distillation that is also commencing will take eight years, and Elizabeth is not at all sure of its outcome.

* * *

The sun has just set. Elizabeth senses that she won't sleep tonight. Her boat passes in front of the lighthouse, and she offers the usual wave to her uncle and her grandfather, or at least to their ghosts. This morning, as she'd watched the first drops come out of the condenser, she'd been entranced. The impure alcohol from the first still had then been transferred to the second still, to be transformed into spirits. She feels as light as the waves and the wind of this cool but lovely evening. *What a birth! Four hundred litres of whisky*. The thought gives her a quiver of happiness.

As soon as the bow of her boat enters the channel, she's surprised to notice that her house is lit. Visitors? But who can it be?

She fastens the mooring lines. No other boat at the dock, so the visitor has been dropped off.

"Louise!"

Elizabeth hasn't seen her little sister for five years. Louise, who lives in Vancouver where she manages an Asian import company, hasn't been in touch with her for a very long time.

"Hello Zab! Long time no see."

Her younger sister is looking at her as if this totally unexpected visit were the most natural thing in the world. She kisses Elizabeth on the cheek.

"The homestead hasn't changed much."

"You didn't come here from Vancouver because you're homesick."

Louise smiles. "No, I came to tell you that I won't let you do it."

Elizabeth drops into a chair, her suspicions now confirmed.

"You can't take out a mortgage on this house without my consent."

Elizabeth casts a defiant look. "I need the money for the distillery."

Louise stares at her with contempt. "I saw an article about the New Glen Dubh. What a joke!"

"Without this loan, I won't be able to continue." Elizabeth is almost hysterical, exactly like the memory Louise has of her.

"So let's sell the place to a rich bastard from Toronto, and you can take your half."

Elizabeth's eyes, filled with terror, look into Louise's. Sell the Legrand house, the only anchor point she has in the world? Never.

The silence drags on. It reminds Elizabeth of the long moments during her childhood, when her rage towards her sister was so great that she couldn't speak. Then, as now, it's Louise who breaks the silence.

"You can always try to convince me to do otherwise."

Elizabeth gazes at her without dropping her guard. "How?"

"Pour me a glass of one of your famous blends. They're supposedly very good."

"How long are you staying?" asks Elizabeth, taking a bottle out of a cupboard.

"We'll see. Tomorrow I want to go and check out the distillery."

Elizabeth fills two glasses. The whisky alone won't make her sister change her mind. She'll have to find something else, a solution powerful enough to meet this threat head-on.

33. Lighthouse Point, 1856

"Why didn't the government tell us it was going to pay someone to look after the lighthouse? I'd do it."

François was grumbling as he examined the few furs he'd been able to gather during a rather unfruitful winter. At the beginning of December, John Beatty had left with the last ship of the sailing season. The lighthouse, painted white except for the bright red covering its lantern room and its guardrail, had blended into the winter landscape. Two days ago, Beatty had returned with the first boat of the spring. Every evening now, the lantern cast its ray offshore.

Beatty's return had also revived François's resentment. By befriending and visiting the keeper, he'd realised that he'd have been quite capable of doing this work just as well as the crabby outsider. The job would have been heaven-sent for Angélique and himself. In fact, any local family would have been happy to benefit from the keeper's annual salary of four hundred and fifty dollars.

Angélique tried to give her father a little hope. "Théophile must be almost on his way back from the lumber camp and …"

The unfinished phrase helped François hear what she didn't dare say to him. The young man had left in November to work in the new lumber camps established inland to the east by the Parry Sound Lumber Company. He was supposed to return at the start of the drive, at the same time as the logs would start passing through Lighthouse Point on their way to American sawmills. Having fallen under the area's spell, Théophile wanted to stay here, but not alone. If he united with the Legrands, the family would manage their tough situation better, especially now, with François's approaching old age.

Angélique's declaration irritated her father. Although the prospect of having Théophile as a son-in-law pleased him, the notion of being dependent on him or on anyone else hurt his morale. By becoming keeper of the lighthouse, he'd keep his pride. And yet Beatty seemed solidly ensconced in his position.

To spare his daughter, François concealed his bad mood. "Yes, I'm eager to see Théophile again too."

Angélique certainly had the right to entertain her own plans. And she wouldn't find a better match at Lighthouse Point.

With the reopening of the sailing season, boats would start coming to call again. This would give the Legrands the opportunity to sell a few furs and renew their depleted provisions.

François suddenly became his usually congenial self again. He'd just had an idea. Aboard the ships stopping at Lighthouse Point, he would find a commodity that would help him carry out his plan.

* * *

The people of Lighthouse Point, raised with the fur trade, had never seen nor imagined the spectacle of such a parade. There before their eyes, they watched their liquid arm of Georgian Bay transform itself into a forest. Thousands of tree trunks had just gushed from the mouth of the Bagami River, and were spreading out as far as the eye could see. Bearded lumberjacks, hardened by a season of harsh cold and exhausting labour, were guiding the logs from the river to the channel. Using chains, they fastened together several trunks which then served to encircle the others and form immense log booms.

Théophile, who was part of this team, greeted the Legrands and the other families of the community, recounting how he had toiled all winter working his fingers to the bone. The younger listeners were impressed, while the older ones were scandalised by the description of this occupation that resembled a hard labour sentence. The pay, Théophile asserted, while not enormous, was enough to live on, although frugally, until the next logging season. The lumberjacks still had a few weeks of work floating the logs down to the bay and clearing all the logjams. In a day or two, small tugboats would arrive at Lighthouse Point to start towing away the log booms.

The last boom left Lighthouse Point at the end of May, just at the beginning of blackfly season. To tell the truth, only the children were sorry to see the booms go, because they used them as a playground, jumping from one log to the other, daring each other to see who could travel the farthest or the fastest on this wobbling carpet of wood. Everybody else had begun to find the heap of wood cumbersome, as it got in the way of their fishing and other activities on the water.

Their task completed, the squads of lumberjacks dispersed. A large number of them went south to Parry Sound, a small town they nicknamed "Parry Hoot". For it had hotels offering them the pleasures they craved after their long months of deprivation in the woods.

Théophile had been tempted to follow them. But he'd reasoned with himself. He would be crazy to waste his hard-earned money to pay for a delight that Angélique would, in the course of time, willingly give him. In any case, he had a plan. Before returning to the lumber camps next winter, he'd prepare his future.

The young man consulted François to determine where he should build his own cabin, because he had decided to take up residence at Lighthouse Point, at least in the summer months. Following the old man's advice and his own instincts, Théophile chose a spot near the lighthouse, with easy access to the open water, but sheltered against bad weather. His arms, muscled after a winter of taxing work, went back to handling axe and saw.

Angélique visited him often, bringing him berries she had just gathered, or fresh bread.

"My father's been acting strange for the last few weeks," the Métis woman confided in him during a visit at the beginning of July. "He's spending more and more time at the lighthouse. When he comes back from hunting, he always brings part of his kill to Beatty."

"If he succeeds in softening up the bastard, so much the better," Théophile declared. Like everyone else, he found the lighthouse keeper sour and unlikeable.

"I happen to have a letter I want to leave with Beatty so he can give it to the captain of the next passing ship."

Angélique's curiosity was aroused. "A letter to your family?"

The question made Théophile laugh mockingly. "No. When I left home I slammed the door on the way out. My folks probably don't even ask themselves whether I'm dead or alive anymore."

Angélique's eyes betrayed her confusion. Her whole immediate and extended family lived a short canoe ride away from her cabin. She clearly couldn't imagine how someone could feel so bitter about their kin and so distant from them.

"It's a letter to the government," he said at last. "I'm going to register my lot here."

"What does that mean?"

To validate his title to the plot where he was settling, Théophile explained, he had to formally notify the government that he was occupying it. The idea of a person having to declare themselves the owner of land they conspicuously occupied was completely beyond Angélique.

"Everyone here should do the same to make sure that they don't lose their lot later on."

"You know very well that no one here can write," Angélique objected.

Théophile brandished his letter in his hand. "My handwriting may not be pretty, but I could write for those who want me to."

In a sudden movement, Angélique pulled the letter from Théophile's hand and ran away. Stunned at first, the young man set off on her heels. Angélique, laughing crazily, ran like the wind. Twenty seconds later, she realised that she'd have to let herself be caught. She adjusted her pace to let Théophile catch up with her. They tumbled to the ground.

Filled with emotion, Théophile pinned her to the ground, placed his lips on hers and felt her heart beating against his chest. He kissed her again and contemplated her face, with her dark skin, rounded cheeks, and eyes almost as black as her hair. His hand caressed her fluttering breast. Taking a country daughter as a wife in the country way—it was natural and easy, like almost everything here. Would he regret it? Did he want to become like her? Or did he hope for Angélique to become like him? Was he longing to possess the girl or the land incarnated in Angélique's warm, enticing body?

Théophile got up. After a long moment, the young woman rose as well and handed him the letter. He put it in his pocket and offered her his hand.

"Come on, let's go to the lighthouse," he said simply.

They returned to the frame of Théophile's cabin, a two-room building with a nearly completed roof. By the water, they found Angélique's canoe and Théophile's rowboat. After tying the canoe to the rowboat, Angélique settled in at the stern while Théophile, oars in hand, set a course for the lighthouse.

Théophile had bought the rowboat, a "mackinaw"—a type of vessel designed in the Collingwood area especially for fishing and sailing in the particular conditions of Georgian Bay—at the beginning of summer. Equipped with a wide sail, it could carry a considerable load.

They stopped at the Legrand house, where they left the canoe, and set off again. The afternoon was calm and, shortly after, the couple arrived at the lighthouse. During the summer, workers had come to construct a permanent quay on a foundation of rocks.

Once the mackinaw was moored, they climbed up to the lighthouse where they found John Beatty sitting outdoors, chatting with François. Théophile explained the reason for his visit to Beatty and gave him the letter. The keeper complained that he wasn't a mailman.

François whispered to Théophile in French: "Maybe a little present might help."

Théophile offered Beatty some pipe tobacco, and he finally agreed to do him the favour.

Masking his disgust, François smiled. *The more I get to know the wily old bugger, the more I hate him,* he thought. *One day, he'll find out just how much.*

34. Sabine, Isle of Skye, the Hebrides, Scotland

The sea—Sabine loves its fragrance just as much as the aroma of the best whiskies. Her lungs never tire of feasting on it. And the vast plain of water that unfurls in front of her cottage on the Isle of Skye smells even better than the rest of the ocean.

Sabine pours herself some more coffee. In spite of the September morning wind sweeping the patio in front of the rustic cottage, she's quite comfortable in the sun. The head of a seal pierces the water's surface and Sabine greets him with a wave of the hand.

For the forty-year-old woman raised in the Parisian suburbs, the Hebrides on the west coast of Scotland don't resemble her country in the least, and certainly not the French capital where she lives most of the time. After having spent all her vacations of the last three years on the island, she has the sense that she's always lived there. Even though the people at the local pub still call her "the Frenchwoman" and laugh at her accent, she feels accepted by these hard-edged and somewhat unsophisticated islanders. And she owes the discovery of this otherworldly place—of this almost new life—to spirits in general first, and then to Scotch in particular.

Indeed, fine food and drink are what brought her to this isolated island. A magazine food columnist for years, one day, Sabine had accepted a colleague's invitation to a Scotch tasting at the *Maison du whisky* in Paris. It was the beginning of the 1980s. The Glenfiddich distillery had just launched a flashy marketing campaign aimed at making single malt Scotch trendy. Sabine, a wine and calvados specialist, had been rather sceptical. She had gone to this soirée with the idea of writing a cutting article on the pretentious snobbery of Scotch.

The exact opposite had happened.

Sabine finishes her coffee while reminiscing that evening. If she had fallen under the whisky spell, it was because the most seductive specimens of the species had courted her. Despite her initial reluctance, each new swallow of vintage Scotch had aroused her with the same effect as a sensual kiss.

Upon leaving the *Maison du whisky*, she had felt drawn to a new calling: becoming a single malt taster and expert. Her intuition, or simply her lucky star, had guided her well. At the same time, the rage for single malt whiskies took off. More and more connoisseurs started reading Sabine's columns and books about whisky. She knew how to judiciously evaluate the merits of a Scotch, but her real genius shone through in her talent for transmitting her passion for whisky to others. If the French are now among the greatest consumers of Scotch in the world, Sabine de Grandmont can pride herself on having done her part to help them earn this title.

After discovering whisky, she'd gone on to explore its country of origin, and had visited all the whisky producing regions of Scotland. The distillers of the most prestigious Scotches gladly gave private tours to this petite woman eager to help them in their conquest of the world's drinkers.

During one of her pilgrimages, she had ended up in the Hebrides, at the Talisker distillery on the Isle of Skye. Seduced by its charms, as much those of its whisky as those of its landscape, she had bought this pretty cottage, where she stayed as often as possible.

From a file on the table, Sabine takes a black notebook with yellowed pages, covered with cramped handwriting. This journal, kept by her great-grandfather, has been entrusted to her by a cousin. The author is trying to write a history of the de Grandmont family, a project requiring long, sometimes painstaking research. This journal has just revealed a fascinating episode of the story, that of Armand de Grandmont, a winegrower at Faltrincourt in Provence. Sabine enthusiastically starts reading from where she left off.

July 13th, 1866

I've just come back from the fields. I can't believe it, but it's true. The vineyard is condemned. Last year, when I found those filthy phylloxera aphids, I thought I'd still be able to save part of the vineyard. We sprayed all the fields with copper sulphate.

This spring, I was expecting that the plants would recover. I was wrong.

This plague comes to us from the north. Piché, the baker, says that ships from America must have transported these insects to Europe.

Galls are covering the leaves. I pulled up a hundred vines. The lumps on the roots don't lie. I burned them—and the bugs too, I hope.

August 7th, 1866

The fields are full of nothing but withered plants. The agronomist says that the phylloxera is sucking the life out of them. The only way of fighting it is to uproot the whole vineyard. I feel as emptied as these vines that will no longer bear any fruit.

I spend my days destroying the fruit of many years of my work, and of my ancestors' work as well.

September 20th, 1866

My grandfather wouldn't have been able to imagine that one day his fields would become a desert. Even a war couldn't have destroyed the vineyard so completely.

The most painful part is burning the uprooted vines. It's like setting fire to a part of your own body. I can hear the soil moaning. Could it be the voice of my forebears?

Misery is running rampant in the area. There's not a single vineyard left for forty kilometres around that hasn't been affected. People say we'll have to re-plant new vines imported from the United States. What a disgrace! With what money? I don't have the financial resources to weather this crisis, nor the heart to start over from scratch.

That's how the journal ends. In the waves, another seal, or maybe the same one as earlier, nods to Sabine. She contemplates a photograph of her great-grandfather taken at the end of his life. The facial features reveal a proud but defeated man. Forced to leave his land, he'd become a labourer in Marseille, a job he had hated.

Sabine thinks of the irony that lies in both her career path and the consequences of the phylloxera epidemic throughout Europe. "If he knew that a century and a half later, a woman of his lineage has fallen in love with Scotch and become a whisky authority, he'd probably turn over in his grave. Or maybe he'd see it as a sort of sweet revenge."

The ringing of her cell phone pulls her out of her daydream. For ten minutes she converses with the editor in chief of a prestigious whisky magazine.

"You want me to go there?"

Hanging up, Sabine starts organising her papers in the file.

"The history of the de Grandmont family will have to wait yet again." The telephone and her file in hand, she heads for the interior of the cottage. "I must have a map of Canada here somewhere. I don't even know where this Georgian Bay is."

35. Lighthouse Point, 1857

In the darkness of his cabin, lust was getting the better of his willpower. Théophile was caressing the woman's breasts so ardently that he was nearly hurting her.

"Let's get married, Angélique."

Carried away by her own passion, she answered yes. Meanwhile, Théophile had drawn back his hand. Angélique didn't understand. For her, this declaration was all they needed to consummate their marriage the country way. The formal part, consecrated by the Church, would come in due course.

"We have to wait," Théophile said, his voice barely audible.

He realised Angélique's intentions now. If she'd come to his house so late in the day in bad weather it was to stay the night. He wasn't angry at her for it, because he'd gladly have given in to their shared desire.

"But why?" Angélique complained. "The priest will pass by here in a few months and ..."

"Getting married the country way was all right in your parents' time. For us, it's different."

Angélique bit her tongue. She didn't have to ask him to explain this difference. Doing as her parents had done would mean behaving like Métis. Théophile was willing to live their lifestyle, but not to become like them.

"We could set out the day after tomorrow if you want."

"Set out to where?"

Théophile took her hand. "There's a priest in Penetanguishene. With my mackinaw, we could be there in three or four days."

Although surprised by Théophile's suggestion, Angélique was

delighted all the same. Getting married in the church didn't matter much to her; however, she was thrilled by the idea of taking a trip.

"It will be like a honeymoon," Théophile added.

They left two days later. Théophile's insistence on going before a priest surprised François. He nevertheless approved this trip, since it would give Angélique the opportunity to see Penetanguishene.

Leaving Lighthouse Point behind them on a superb day at the end of October, the engaged couple were already thinking of their return as husband and wife. They knew that with the beginning of their new life together, nothing would ever be the same.

* * *

Today.

The word echoed in François's head like an order, an imperative he couldn't ignore. Angélique and Théophile, who had left a week ago, would return soon. He couldn't wait any longer.

Besides, he wanted to be done with it. Nonetheless, he was afraid that he'd fail at the last minute. He had never killed a man, not even during the war against the Americans. Outside, the uncertain early November dawn had just broken. This was the perfect moment, the one when such a tragedy would seem completely understandable.

From a hiding place at the back of his cabin, François retrieved the weapon he'd bought a few months ago. His hand slid down its smooth, cool surface. He examined the bottle in the light. The liquid's straw colour evoked vague but still painful memories. François hadn't touched a drop of alcohol since his binge during the sinking of the *Alice Hackett*. This debauchery and its unhappy consequences had taught him to fear the mysterious power of whisky, its ascendancy over a man.

But, today, it was precisely this dire power he was seeking to conjure up and enlist as an ally against his enemy. Nonetheless, his memories of the taste and effect of the spirits were distant. Did this whisky still possess a power capable of destroying a man's will? A merchant on board a ship heading for Lake Superior had sold him this bottle. He had most convincingly praised the qualities of his product, a novelty from Scotland.

"This whisky, the Teine Brìghmhor, is a blend," he had sung out, "a judicious combination of different whiskies, designed to create a delightful marriage of flavours—at a much lower price …" François had asked himself: did this "crossbred", impure whisky really have the guts needed to accomplish such a despicable act?

Unexpectedly, the merchant had then given him the answer. "Its name, in Scottish Gaelic, means 'daring fire', and this blend of the best Scotches, which contains a generous portion of the famous Glen Dubh, comforts the drinker …"

This name had revived in François's memory first the voice of a Scottish soldier, then the taste of a bewitching whisky. He had no longer hesitated after that.

But now François's fear had just reared its ugly head again. And what if this whisky didn't have the power of the Glen Dubh? After all, that Scotch was just one of the components of the blend. Would the will of this Teine Brìghmhor overcome that of the drinker? François owed it to himself to confirm it, because in his plan there was no margin for error.

François abruptly pulled the cork from the bottle. He brought the neck closer to his nostrils. This essence—no, rather these many yet blended odours—were meshed into fragrances of soil and water, of flesh and blood. He took a swallow straight from the bottle and felt himself plunge. In his heart of hearts, fiery waves carried away the last obstacles that could have dissuaded him from going ahead with his scheme.

François's shaking hand replaced the cork. The Glen Dubh was truly present in this mixture, harmonising with other, less strong but equally complicit whiskies. He set the bottle down on the table. "One is enough," he said to himself, "two are too many and three …"

Yes, the Teine Brìghmhor carried its name well, and was the ideal ally. François stuffed the bottle and a few provisions into a bag. Outside, the bay was calm, not at all like the blood in his veins. He slid his canoe into the water, now confident that he'd be able to force the hand of fate.

François didn't feel the cold, which ordinarily would have frozen his limbs on this chilly morning. At that very moment, the one he was going to meet was probably shivering. For that reason, he wouldn't refuse a little comfort.

Shortly after, François knocked at the door of the lighthouse keeper's home. Beatty was sitting next to the wood stove, numb with cold. The two men exchanged remarks on the gloomy weather. François gave some smoked fish to his delighted host. For months, he'd been concealing his disdain and hatred, playing at being the friend of this detestable grouch, and lulling the man's mistrust to sleep.

He put the bottle of Teine Brìghmhor on the table. "You … drink with me," he said, pointing first at Beatty and then to the whisky.

John Beatty smiled in an embarrassed way and shook his head: it was still too early.

"Just a glass," François insisted, "a drop to drive off this damned dampness."

François's congeniality finally broke down Beatty's resistance. François poured a finger of whisky into a glass and handed it to the keeper. The two men clinked glasses, and the Teine Brìghmhor quickly took effect. François took his host's empty glass and turned his back to him. He filled Beatty's glass with whisky and his own mostly with water. The pleasant taste in the keeper's mouth triumphed over his reticence.

As he accepted the third glass, Beatty's loosened tongue lamented: a woman would keep him even warmer than whisky.

"… a well-rounded girl with nice curves, like your Angélique."

You old swine! thought François. *You won't have my daughter, nor anyone else's.*

In spite of his inner turmoil, he smiled. The glass rose to the keeper's lips. … *and three are not enough*, celebrated François. For now the gears he had set in motion could no longer be stopped.

36. Penetanguishene, 1857

"You're truly my wife now."

Angélique and Théophile had just moved into a room in the Canada House, the only hotel in the village. The modest suite contained a mirror, in which the bride was gazing at herself. It wasn't dark yet; at the window, the last rays of the setting sun adorned the sky with shades of red and mauve.

That morning, as soon as they had arrived, they'd gone to see the parish priest. He hadn't wanted to marry them that very day; the banns needed to be published first.

"Father, I'm expecting a child," Angélique had then declared, her tone dry and curt. Théophile was taken aback, but the lie had succeeded in convincing Father Charest to agree to their request. The couple had recruited two witnesses from among the clients of the general store and, shortly after, the priest had declared them united by the sacred bonds of marriage.

"My wife," Théophile repeated.

The groom embraced his bride, and Angélique, as he pushed her back onto the bed, was surprised by this abruptness. Théophile tried to undo the many buttons on her dress, without much success. She felt the warmth of his skin and the impulsiveness of his kisses. Was this love or simply a physical need too long repressed?

Her husband's calloused hands caressed her passionately. Despite Théophile's ardour, she managed to undress. Feeling his genitals against hers, she moved in a way that would help nature take its course. However, Théophile had come prematurely.

The two spouses exchanged an embarrassed smile. Then Angélique placed her wet finger on Théophile's mouth.

"Taste it. It's your water, which will live inside me."

Théophile sucked her finger. His eyes expressed both his disappointment about this false start, and his desire to start over. The couple's lovemaking began again, but this time guided by the rhythm of Angélique's fondling, voluptuously prolonging their pleasure through the night.

Just before falling asleep, Angélique thought that maybe her spontaneous declaration to the priest wasn't a lie anymore.

The next day, re-embarking in the mackinaw, the bride had the impression of taking the first step on a journey to a new land. And yet she was returning home.

37. Lighthouse Point, 1857

Beatty was completely drunk. The warmth of the whisky had driven away both his gloomy feelings and the cold. He began to sing a few songs in his hoarse, discordant voice, scolding François for not knowing these British folk tunes.

Legrand was still smiling. Getting up to refill the glasses, he pretended to stumble, making his host laugh. The afternoon was ending and it was beginning to get dark when François poured the last two glasses from the bottle. This time, unlike the others, he had filled his own glass with whisky. For what would follow, he'd need to draw on the strength of the spirits.

Beatty tried to get up, stammering: "I have to li … light the lamp."

"I'll take care of it," said François, sounding and looking reassuring.

Beatty fell back into his chair, relieved. François climbed the one hundred and fourteen steps of the spiral staircase to the top of the tower and lit the lighthouse lamp. He took out a rope and tied it firmly to the lamp's cradle. Next he climbed back down and, pulling on chains, he raised the attached 260-kilogram weight to the top of the tower. Its gradual descent would turn the lamp's mechanism for six hours.

In the kitchen, he found Beatty lying on the floor, fast asleep. François drained the rest of his glass. The moment had come. First, he took the empty bottle and went outside. On this murky night, the lighthouse's beam swept the rock of the point with its bizarre glow, like that of the full moon blacked out by clouds. At the edge of the cliff, with all his strength, François threw the bottle towards the water.

Next, he struggled to pull Beatty's stocky mass to the tower. The drunken body, a dead weight, didn't react during this bumpy trip. Entering the lighthouse at its circular base, he lifted Beatty up to the top of the tenth narrow step. Yanking the rope suspended in the emptiness at the spiral's centre, he checked the slipknot before sliding it around Beatty's neck. He pulled on the rope to make sure it would hold against the weight.

The last step, swinging the keeper's body into the emptiness of the lighthouse well, was both the easiest and the most difficult. François stretched out his arm to pull the chains of the clockwork mechanism to his side, so that his victim wouldn't be able to grab hold of them. Tonight he'd stay at the lighthouse to continue feeding the oil lamps, and to raise the weight again after its descent. However, as of the following night, people would surely notice the absence of any light in the tower. When Beatty's dangling body would be discovered, his death would be deemed a suicide. François could even testify that, during his most recent visits, the keeper had seemed particularly melancholy, sad, and irascible. He would take over operating the lighthouse until the end of the sailing season, and then offer his services to replace the dead man. The authorities would see no reason to investigate.

François, exhausted by his efforts, took a long breath. One final effort and it would be over. Summoning his strength and courage, he gripped Beatty in his arms. The movement seemed to wake him, and François hurried to finish his gruesome task.

The keeper's body fell into the open space. At its widest point, the tower's well was two metres wide. Half a metre above the ground, the hanged man was suspended quite close to his executioner. The pressure of the rope against his neck jerked Beatty out of his drunkenness. He tried to insert his plump fingers under the rope in vain. His bulging, bloodshot eyes gave his face a hideous look. His feet thrashed about like those of a crazy dancer, guided by music inaudible to all except him. A harsh cry vainly tried to escape from his throat.

François had never seen such frightening, painful death throes. Every second seemed endless to him. He felt terribly faint with pity. Now an assassin, he'd be condemned to live the rest of his days with the memory of his crime, and in the very place where he would endlessly be reminded of it.

He stretched out his arm to Beatty, who was still struggling. The dangling man, thinking this was a manoeuvre to finish him off, grabbed it and pulled with all his strength. François was then thrust into emptiness as well, crashing head-first against the stone foundation. The lighthouse keeper of Lighthouse Point swung back towards the centre of the well and, a minute later, gave up his last breath. Just below his feet lay the lifeless body of François Legrand, his neck broken by his sudden violent fall.

Three days later, Angélique and Théophile, coming home from their trip, made the grim discovery. Lacking indications to the contrary, they concluded that Beatty had committed suicide and that François, while attempting to free the hanged man, had fallen accidentally and died. Beatty was buried near the lighthouse, and François laid to rest behind his cabin.

Théophile took care of the lighthouse until the end of the sailing season. He wrote a letter to the authorities explaining the sad events and entrusted it to the last boat to stop at Lighthouse Point. At the same time he sent a second letter, dictated by Angélique, to the Legrand family in L'Ancienne-Lorette, Canada-East, to inform them of the death of François Legrand.

The latter letter received no reply from the Legrands, while the Ministry of Marine and Fisheries quickly answered Théophile to thank him. By way of gratitude, the government offered him the job of lighthouse keeper. So, returning from the lumber camps the following spring, Théophile Roy settled into his new duties and into the lighthouse keeper's residence with Angélique.

The same year, the couple had their first son. The Roy dynasty of the lighthouse, begun under the sign of death, would never escape from it.

38. Elizabeth, Massassauga Bay

"What's it to you?"

For a day now, Elizabeth has been trying to pry the truth out of her sister. If she can at least flush out the enemy, she'll still have a hope of defeating it.

Louise looks at her resentfully, gets up and goes to the end of the deck; from there she contemplates the bay, where the setting sun is painting the water a shade of blue edging on vermilion.

"I don't hate this place as much as you think," she says. "In fact, it's rather the opposite."

"So why didn't you come back before? Why don't you help me save Lighthouse Point instead of trying to stop me?"

Louise turns towards Elizabeth. "That's exactly it; I can't let you squander our family inheritance on a project that's bound to fail."

Elizabeth gets up and glares at Louise in the same manner which, in the past, used to terrify her sister. "But you've tasted the whisky. You've seen the distillery. It'll take some time, but the business will eventually turn a profit."

"And that's why it's going to fail."

Elizabeth is stunned; Louise's crazy streak must be even bigger than hers. She follows Louise's gaze, once again focused on the water. *Like the lighthouse beam*, she thinks. She's still searching for our parents' ghosts too, and for the ghosts of the Agomo.

If Elizabeth confided in her sister, would Louise rally behind the distillery's cause? She starts again, but in a gentler voice. "For once, I know what I'm doing. You've just said so yourself."

Louise shakes her head. "You really don't understand. Think about it.

If, in spite of everything that's conspiring against it, your whisky ends up being a quality product, they won't accept it."

"Who won't?"

Louise's fierce look frightens Elizabeth. Never in the course of their repeated arguments has she seen her sister speak so coldly, as though she had all the time in the world to aim, then shoot Elizabeth between the eyes.

"The distillers in Scotland. And you're the one who's supposed to know all about them."

"They can't do anything against the distillery. Our whisky is absolutely legal, as long as we avoid using the designation 'Scotch.'"

Louise looks at her sister as though she were talking to a child. "You're moving in on their turf. For them, it's a question of big money. If ever your whisky was equal to theirs, it could compromise the very source their wealth comes from."

Elizabeth vents her frustration. "There have been plenty of new distilleries that have opened in the last ten years. The industry hasn't done anything to prevent them from ..."

"Because they're in Scotland!" Louise screams. "Your distillery is attacking their sacred myth: that Scotch can only be distilled in its country of origin. If you succeed, the big distillers won't just look away."

Elizabeth turns away from her sister. *She can't be right. And even if it were true ...* "We Legrands know how to defend ourselves."

Louise stares her down. "You can fight them, but not me."

Even the outside air is abruptly poisoned with this palpable hatred, so familiar to Elizabeth. She turns on her heels and goes into the house. *If only they hadn't left that day. If only Mom had decided to keep Louise with her ...* Crazy with anger, Elizabeth thinks of completing the task that nature and fate didn't see through to the end. *The bay still has room for another Legrand corpse.*

"And with all that, I haven't even told you the good news yet."

Louise's voice makes Elizabeth jump. Her sister's tone is casual once again.

"I've had a significant other in my life for three years now. David and

I want children. I've left him everything in my will, including my share of this house. He agrees with me about the distillery."

Elizabeth clenches her fists, just like when the sisters were little and fought mercilessly with each other.

"I don't want him to meet you," adds Louise.

She's forgetting who she's dealing with, thinks Elizabeth.

"You'll probably never know what love is," Louise continues. "What a shame. It's a thousand times more intoxicating than your whisky."

If Louise was trying to hurt her sister, she's missed her mark. Elizabeth is focused on only one thing: seeing things through to the end. Neither Louise nor anyone else will be able to stop her.

39. Scotland, 1870

Robb Fearmòr nervously counted his money as the carriage travelled along the poorly lit streets of Edinburgh. This detour, difficult to justify given the state of his finances, would cost him dearly. Yet the idea had ended up driving out all other thoughts—including the very reason for this trip.

As soon as he'd gotten off the train, he had seen to having his cases of whisky stored in a safe place, but not before hiding twelve bottles in his two suitcases. Next, he'd hailed a coach driver who had smiled on hearing the address where Robb wanted to go.

It was almost eleven o'clock and, on this Wednesday night, the streets were dark and deserted. Robb felt the destitution of these sad working neighbourhoods. During the last four years, he had ventured more than ten times from his offices in Dufftown to the Scottish capital to promote the whiskies of Fearmòr Blenders Inc. However, since the appearance of the first blended Scotches, the competition hadn't stopped growing—not only in number, but in ferociousness as well. Choice whiskies, like those carefully made by Robb, had to compete with a whole range of cheap rotguts. And those who could afford better-quality spirits preferred French cognac or even gin, turning up their noses at Scotch and especially its blends, which even the makers of single malt whisky scorned disdainfully.

His own brother, Harold, was one of those distillers who were making life difficult for him. When the older brother had confronted the younger with an ultimatum, Harold had declared war on him. He would never cede control of the distillery. Robb had followed through with his threat by joining forces with another distiller to found a whisky blending company.

But Harold and Robb, like Siamese twins, found themselves imprisoned by the straitjacket of the Glen Dubh. Even though Harold remained the manager of the distillery, Robb owned almost half of it, and continued to benefit from it. In order to produce his blends—which were steadily gaining a reputation for their quality—Robb had to obtain barrels of Glen Dubh, one of the main ingredients of those blends.

Through their lawyers, the two enemy brothers had negotiated an arrangement: Robb had ceded his share of the Glen Dubh distillery to his brother, in exchange for the latter's commitment to hand over one quarter of the distillery's annual production to him. In the meantime, the distillery's founder had passed away. Some said that the patriarch had succumbed to the pain of seeing his offspring quarrelling so bitterly.

Even though Robb's trips to Edinburgh or to Glasgow and London always ended up bringing in a few sales, they never resulted in the hoped-for volume of orders. Facing the failing health of his business, Robb seriously feared that this journey would end up being his last. The situation was cruelly ironic, for the first blends developed by Robb, after being aged ten to fifteen years in barrels, were just now peaking in flavour and smoothness. Hounded by his creditors, he wondered how much longer he could hold on.

Just as Robb was finishing his calculation, the carriage stopped. He didn't have enough to pay the driver. Getting down from the carriage, he had a bright idea.

"My dear sir, I'd like to propose a payment in kind."

The coachman, an old hand, knew his business well. If his client was going to the place where he was being dropped off, then the man had to have at least enough money to pay his fare. He explained to his customer that such a proposition was against the rules. However, Robb had already pulled a bottle from his suitcase.

"But I'm offering you a bottle of Teine Brìghmhor, one of the best Scotches in the country."

Sceptical, the coachman nevertheless took the bottle, and tried to examine it in the light of his carriage's lantern.

"Even if I were to accept, how do I know that this bottle really contains a half-decent whisky?"

The coachman's irritated voice held a clear threat. Robb hurried to reply: "Go ahead and take a dram."

The coachman hesitated for a long time. When Robb finally saw him pull the cork, he sighed. Luck was with him, for once. If fate had made him cross paths with one of the many temperance movement supporters instead, his strategy would have failed. Unceremoniously, the coach driver took a long swig, followed by an even longer silence. Darkness hid the man's face, and his reaction. Meanwhile, Robb's sensory memory evoked in his throat the smooth, comforting warmth that was spreading through the coachman's mouth and body.

"Give me a second bottle and we'll call it a deal."

Robb furrowed his eyebrows. He was dealing with a tough customer, no doubt about it. With one bottle, he'd have gotten off lightly enough, but with two, he was losing a little money.

"So, my friend, are you going to pay up?"

The driver's mocking tone showed that the Teine Brìghmhor had already taken effect. Robb took a second bottle from his suitcase. At least he would keep his precious cash, and get some good publicity at the same time—since the driver would no doubt brag about his profitable trade to all his colleagues and friends.

Once the carriage had left, Robb turned towards the house with its bleak façade and inhospitable look. He took the few steps leading to the door, knocked quickly three times and then a fourth, followed by a last, prolonged bang of the door knocker. He sensed a presence sizing him up through the peephole. Finally he heard the bolts slide back and, a second later, he slipped through the open door with his baggage.

"Mr Fearmòr! We haven't seen the likes of you for a very long time."

The sixty-year-old woman, wearing a red evening gown, was still beautiful. Robb's last visit dated back to more than a year ago.

"Yes, Mrs McEwen, you know, business ..."

"And, very happily for us, you're coming by here before attending to it, as I can see."

The madam pointed out the two suitcases with her eyes. Robb laughed nervously, but she reassured him by putting her hand on his arm.

"You're here for Jeannie, as usual?"

Robb nodded.

"She's free just now. Leave your things in the wardrobe."

The client obeyed and followed the madam's red train. Arriving from the opposite direction, a middle-aged gentleman greeted Mrs McEwen before continuing on his way. The two men avoided looking directly at each other. Robb thought he recognised a banker who had once refused him a loan.

The madam and her client arrived in a sitting room with faint, diffuse lighting, where three scantily clad women turned toward them. On seeing Robb, the oldest and least slender of the three got up with a leap and hurried to kiss him.

"Robb, I thought I'd never see you again."

Jeannie took him by the hand to lead him upstairs. Robb had never wanted her so much, not even during his first visit to this brothel five years ago. Luckily, on that occasion he had run into this girl from Dufftown, an acquaintance. That had encouraged him to come again.

"Are you well at least, Robb? You look thinner."

Jeannie talked while caressing the man who, sitting on the bed, was getting undressed. It was as though they had seen each other the previous day. Delighted as he always was by this simplicity, Robb attacked Jeannie's buttons, kissing her impetuously.

"Clearly it's been more than a wee while, for you."

Robb could no longer hold back his ardour or his joy. His knowledge of women was limited to his experiences with Jeannie, but they had all been good. His mouth nibbled her breasts. Jeannie's way of taking him in hand during his visits seduced him just as much as her body. At the age of eighteen, Jeannie had fled an abusive father. Arriving in Edinburgh, she had preferred practising the oldest trade in the world to working herself to death earning a few pence at jobs each more wretched than the last. The distiller and the prostitute had developed more than just a simple carnal relationship.

Robb satisfied his desire and then gave her the latest news from Dufftown. Jeannie, without being nostalgic, was still interested in the people back home.

"I missed you," Robb admitted, letting his fingers play along the curve of the woman's back. "I'd like to spend the night with you."

Jeannie laughed and whistled. "The gentleman has means, so much the better."

Robb's face grew sombre.

"No, I don't—that's just it. I'd have to pay with whisky. Would Mrs McEwen accept five bottles?"

"I'll try to arrange it," said Jeannie.

Leaping from the bed, she put on a dressing gown while Robb explained where the merchandise was. During her absence, Robb stretched out luxuriously in the bed and scanned the walls of the room. *Jeannie deserves better*, he thought. *And she's not getting any younger.* Exhausted from his journey, he was very sleepy.

Finally his hostess returned, and Robb was surprised to see her with a bottle in her hand.

"You can stay, Robb. We'll share a dram."

Noticing that the whisky was his, Robb was suddenly worried. The madam had demanded six bottles and a little money. Jeannie had taken an advance on her salary.

"So you're paying me back with a bottle," she cooed, filling two glasses. "*Slàinte*!"

Robb took a long drink, happy to find refuge for a few hours in such good company. Nonetheless, if his whisky kept disappearing without being replaced by money, this stay would just put him further in debt. He stretched out at full length and was surprised when Jeannie poured a few drops of whisky into his navel and licked them sensually.

"Your whisky tastes even better when you're the *quaich*," she said, laughing.

"Enjoy it while you can, Jeannie. After this trip, I'll probably have to sell off my inventory and change professions."

Jeannie looked at him with horrified eyes. "What? But now's not the time! Soon you'll be flooded with orders."

Faced with this fanciful optimism, Robb smiled and ran his fingers through Jeannie's chestnut hair. Offended at not being taken seriously, Jeannie renewed her protests.

"The banker Carruthers—who was just here—and several others of our bigwig clients won't stop talking about it."

Robb didn't understand. "They're telling you that whisky sales are going to increase?"

Jeannie shook her curls. "Not exactly. But they're complaining. Because of the grapevine sickness in France, it's become impossible to get a cognac or a brandy, even in London."

Robb sat up. He'd heard talk of the phylloxera that had struck the European continent almost a decade ago. However, even though France wasn't producing wine anymore, since people in the United Kingdom barely drank it anyway …

Seeing how long it was taking Robb to catch on exasperated Jeannie.

"Without wine there's no brandy, and no cognac either. When the last stocks are exhausted, what will all these gentlemen do, in your opinion?"

Suddenly enlightened, Robb's eyes widened.

"They won't stop drinking, I can guarantee you that," stated Jeannie.

"They'll fall back on our whisky." Robb's voice boomed with excitement.

"They won't have a choice."

Robb could already see himself presenting this argument to his clients. Starting tomorrow, he'd enquire about the brandy situation. He kissed Jeannie and they made love again.

"You know, I worry about you," whispered Jeannie. "At your age, you should be married."

"If I got married, I couldn't come here anymore," he protested.

This comment made Jeannie laugh so much that she almost suffocated. "You're about the only bachelor who comes here!"

Shortly after, Jeannie's breathing indicated that she'd fallen asleep. Now Robb wasn't sleepy anymore; he was fired up with a new energy. Jeannie had to be right: the wind was finally going to change. The timing was just right to go see Alistair Carruthers and ask him for short-term financing. This time, the banker might be more receptive.

The sun was almost ready to rise when Robb's mind grew calm enough for him to leave behind his daydreams and join Jeannie in the land of sleep.

* * *

Before leaving the next day, Robb negotiated with the madam for a long time, and finally arrived at an agreement. From now on, at Mrs McEwen's, the only whisky offered to the clientele would come from Fearmòr Blenders, which would supply it to her free of charge. In exchange, the madam, a much-loved and respected person in the red-light district, would promote Robb's whisky in the city's other establishments, earning of course a modest commission on all the sales resulting from her efforts.

And so it was that the brothels took the lead in converting the gentlemen drinkers of brandy and French cognac to Scottish whisky.

Three years later, after a lightning swift rise in Scotch sales—and especially in the sale of blends—first in London and then in all of England, Robb Fearmòr married Jeannie Campbell. He never again visited Mrs McEwen's brothel nor any other as a client, only as a whisky supplier.

Jeannie had three children: one son and two daughters. Thanks to her, the master whisky blender came to have offspring and a future. Robb gave his son his own first name and took his education in hand. This boy would end up resembling him in almost all respects. Robb junior would therefore inherit both the best and the worst of the Fearmòrs.

40. Lighthouse Point, 1878

The foghorn activated by Charles and Louis echoed dismally in the thick, late September fog. Although she'd heard this sound hundreds of times, Angélique found it more sinister today, even though she didn't know why.

It was Friday afternoon, and the boys were relentlessly sounding the foghorn, since this was the day the *Agomo* normally made its second stop of the week at Lighthouse Point. The veil of fog, which had lasted for two days, was so thick that, even with an experienced captain like Grégoire Robillard at the helm, a ship could easily fall off course. The sound signal would at least give the captain an indication of his position in relation to dry land. Nonetheless, in conditions like these, the *Agomo* would no doubt be late for its scheduled stops.

From the kitchen window, Angélique watched her sons. Charles—the older of the two at age seventeen—was directing the operation carried out by his brother Louis, his junior by a year. Doubtless, one day, Charles would take his father's place. He carried out all the tasks needed to maintain the lighthouse—even the most disagreeable ones like trimming the wicks or removing ice from the windows around the lantern—without complaint. His attitude was the opposite of those of his two brothers—especially François, the eldest, who was twenty. François had ventured out into the fog today, partly to go buy provisions at the Lighthouse Point general store, but in particular to get away from the lighthouse for a while.

Angélique went back to her preparations for the evening meal. As if replying to the sound signals, Théophile's snoring coming from the bedroom also reached her ears. The lighthouse keeper was taking a nap in anticipation of another long night of sounding the foghorn at regular intervals.

Peeling her potatoes, Angélique thought of her three sons. She was proud of this family she'd started late in life. Her only regret was the absence of a daughter. She fed the wood stove with a fresh log. Normally, at this time of year, she'd still be cooking on the hearth outside the house. Today, she was cooking indoors to drive away the penetrating dampness. She made a pot of strong tea and carried it outside, along with three cups.

Seeing her arrive at the foghorn located in a clearing at the top of the cliff and oriented towards the bay, Louis and Charles took a break. Thanking his mother, Charles poured himself some tea. Out on the bay, clouds were rapidly forming and then dissipating. For a few seconds, between the temporarily drawn shades of the smoky veil, one could make out the calm surface of the water. Charles, not wanting to compromise the safety of the *Agomo*, emptied his cup quickly and resumed his task.

Suddenly, a boat's siren answered their call. The three quick bursts, followed by a long dash, left no doubt as to the source of this signal: it was the *Agomo*.

Charles ordered Louis to continue the work and, together with his mother, climbed down the steps cut into the rock to reach the quay. They heard the ship's noisy engine long before they were able to make out its silhouette. In the muffled calm, the mechanised humming had an air of sadness. Charles and Angélique were startled and shouted when the *Agomo* emerged only a few metres from the dock, like a mastodon charging at full throttle. Luckily the ship, crawling along at its slowest possible speed, had already adjusted its trajectory to avoid hitting the dock, but only barely.

"Hey, lighthouse keepers! Your signal drew me in like a siren's beguiling song."

Angélique and Charles, used to Captain Robillard's teasing, greeted him. Standing on the raised deck, dressed in his black uniform topped with a grey beard, the captain's imposing figure looked ghostly. For a brief moment, Angélique had the impression of seeing a phantom ship, an ancient wreck, like the ones local sailors and fishermen swore they'd encountered on the water.

"We'll spend the night here," declared the captain. "I won't venture any farther in such weather."

The *Agomo* continued on its way at a snail's pace, so that it could carefully navigate the increasingly narrow channel leading to the Lighthouse Point village dock. Mother and son saw the ship's stern swallowed by the grey veil. They climbed back up the steps, relieved that they no longer had to worry about the *Agomo*. The Legrands could now go back to sounding the usual signal pattern once every fifteen minutes.

"Will we be eating soon?" Louis, who was always hungry, and who constantly had to be reminded, especially at the beginning of winter, that their provisions couldn't be easily replenished, looked hopefully at his mother.

"Yes, soon. We'll wait for François; he shouldn't be long now."

To avoid hurting his mother's feelings, Louis hid his great disappointment. If his brother struck up a conversation with the captain or with one of the *Agomo's* passengers, as was his annoying habit, they'd have a long wait ahead of them.

Angélique listened to the acoustic warning as it faded into the grey clouds off the open water. *This is really ghost weather*, she thought as she hoped this gloomy fog would soon end.

* * *

Louis's concern about his brother's return turned out to be warranted. In fact, night had begun to fall when François moored his rowboat at the lighthouse dock. Angélique had just come outside to bring Théophile a lantern.

That's when she saw him, emerging from the fog: her father, François Legrand, walking towards her with long strides. It was him, but very young, in his mid-twenties. Angélique's hands started to shake and, just when she thought she was going to faint, her François, her son, arrived behind the other and called out: "Mom, I'm bringing a visitor from far away."

A moment later, standing in front of her, the visitor took off his cap and held it to his heart. The emotion in Angélique's eyes troubled him. François made the introductions.

"This is our cousin, your cousin, George …"

"Legrand," added Angélique, breathless.

Too excited to notice his mother's state, François reeled off explanations. George Legrand had just arrived from the village of L'Ancienne-Lorette in Québec; he was the son of Gustave Legrand, one of Angélique's father's brothers.

"I'm truly delighted to make your acquaintance," said George at last.

Angélique accepted the offered hand. The voice of this ghost wasn't her father's voice; it was gentler, with a soothing tone. François introduced the visitor to his father and his two brothers. George had just come off the *Agomo*, thus completing a long journey by train, on foot, and finally by boat to find François Legrand's descendants at Lighthouse Point.

"We've never had any news of François's family."

Théophile studied the young man with a suspicious air. He could detect a certain family resemblance in George, but nothing more. The young man took an envelope from his jacket and held it out to Théophile.

"My father and his two brothers got your letter. I was five years old at the time, but I still remember. They decided not to write back. François was dead to them."

Théophile examined the letter where, on paper yellowed by time, he recognised his own handwriting.

"So why come to find us now, after so many years?"

George opened his mouth to reply, but Louis's voice cut him off. "He can tell us while we eat. I'm hungry."

The suggestion relaxed the atmosphere, and the conversation continued around the table. The story of his unknown, even mysterious uncle had always fascinated George. He had often re-read the letter kept at his father's house. Every time, the young man's interest for the distant land where his uncle lived with his Indian wife had continued to grow in his mind. And then, two months ago, an event had spurred him to undertake this quest.

"My father died."

The Roys stopped eating. Théophile offered his condolences.

"Don't be sad. He was a harsh man."

"But what made you decide to leave?" François wanted to know.

George's family consisted of ten more brothers and sisters. So his father had left him neither land nor money. Like most young people from L'Ancienne-Lorette, George had decided to leave in search of a better life, just like his uncle before him.

"... and to try to find out whether my relatives were still in these parts," he concluded.

Silence fell around the table and Théophile, his meal finished, got up.

"I have to get back to the foghorn. In any case, if you're looking for work, George, there's plenty of it in the lumber camps."

The rest of the evening was spent swapping family stories. The Roy family of Lighthouse Point agreed to put up George and help him find work. François, who was preparing to go spend his first winter in the lumber camps, suggested that they get jobs together.

Two weeks later, the two cousins set out for the lumber camps. It was possible that Lighthouse Point might gain a second Legrand bloodline; the return of spring would tell. Angélique, far from suspecting the tragedy that was to come, was already eager for springtime.

41. Scotland, 1897

"This is how my father must have felt." Intense joy and pride swelled his chest, like a deep breath. Robb Fearmòr was afraid he'd explode with happiness. The sight of this gigantic warehouse with its enormous barrels full of blended whiskies represented the embodiment of his work, his legacy not only to his son but to the whole world.

"Come with me, Dad. I'll show you our new offices."

The voice of Robb Fearmòr junior called Fearmòr senior back to reality. He followed young Robb's gesture, as he showed the way. Deep inside, he laughed, because he knew this path well, since he'd followed it assiduously for thirty years. The two men left the warehouse and crossed a corridor ending with a solid oak door bearing the inscription: *Fearmòr Blenders Inc. Robb Fearmòr Junior, President.*

Seeing this sign, Robb senior smiled, happy to see his son reaping the benefits of his father's talent for whisky blending and tireless work. What's more, he congratulated himself on having been wise enough to put the business entirely in the hands of his only son. He actually had just one regret, and it was negligible. "If Harold hadn't been so stubborn, we'd have been able to build a real empire."

Robb let his father into his recently renovated office. As the man walked into the premises he'd left just a year ago, he couldn't refrain from letting out a curse.

First of all, the walls of two neighbouring rooms had been knocked down to triple the area of the president's office. No matter where the father's eye roamed, he saw nothing but ostentation and gaudy luxury: from the red velvet curtains to the paintings hung on the wall, from the chandelier to the enormous desk, from the leather armchairs to the richly ornamented and hand-carved woodwork of the cabinet crammed with whisky bottles. Everything in this office illustrated a pronounced taste for luxury, and the desire to show it off.

Robb observed his father's strong reaction. The young man invited him to sit in an armchair facing the desk, where stood a carafe of whisky.

"What do you think?" he asked, filling two glasses.

The father searched for words. He accepted a glass and drank a long draught of whisky, hoping it would help him find a little calm and the right words. However, he was even more stunned: his son had just served him a pure Glen Dubh. Finally he managed to speak, making a great effort to tone down his disapproval.

"The company may be doing well, but you're exaggerating! People will accuse you of being pretentious."

Robb junior—who had been expecting this reproach from his father, a great believer in Scottish austerity—laughed heartily.

"We're living in a glorious new era for our whisky. Blends have finally received their letters of nobility. There's even one being served in the bar of the House of Commons. As my friends the Pattison brothers say, we should brag about being the barons of an industry that puts millions of pounds into the government's coffers. If we want to be respected like lords, we have to look like them. The more we show off our success, the more the bankers and other investors will trust us."

Robb senior, irritated by the mention of the name Pattison, drank again. "Robert and Walter Pattison have been successful, but they're not an example to follow."

This time, Robb senior had been unable to keep himself from speaking curtly. Just like their many other detractors, he criticised the Pattison brothers for their extravagant lifestyle because it tainted the reputation of all the whisky blenders. The son let this reprimand hang in the air and took a few seconds to sip his whisky and calm down. Not only did he consider the Pattisons to be his friends, he admired their success, owed mostly to their innate flair for advertising. Nonetheless, he knew too well the futility of debating about the Pattisons with his father.

"Why did you serve me Glen Dubh? You can't afford to consume it frivolously."

Robb junior bit his tongue. He almost wanted to scream. If the Glen Dubh had to be used sparingly, it was because of his father. Again, he controlled himself. According to the latest rumours, at the Glen Dubh distillery, his uncle Harold Fearmòr was preparing to entrust the business to Harold junior, the oldest of his children. So Robb could envision the day when he would extend an olive branch to his cousin and make an agreement with him to increase the flow of Glen Dubh to Fearmòr Blenders.

"Right you are, Dad. But your visit deserves a proper toast."

As usual, the taste of the Glen Dubh stirred up contradictory emotions in Robb senior: joy in the mouth and bitterness in the heart. For forty years, his only contact with his brother Harold had been through his lawyers. Whenever he relived his last conversation with his younger brother, he still trembled with rage.

In spite of themselves, the two belligerent brothers had signed an agreement that still remained valid, and, through a strange paradox, kept them in a state of mutual dependence. The increased production of blends, like those made by Robb, as well as their growing popularity, were causing a drop in single malt whisky sales. However, without the Glen Dubh, Robb Fearmòr would have been incapable of continuing to produce his blends. Faced with Harold's unequivocal refusal to sell Robb a drop more than the quantity stipulated in their contract, Fearmòr Blenders had limited growth prospects—since the company lacked raw material.

"*Slàinte*!" said Robb junior at last, emptying his glass.

His father, having regained his good mood, replied to the toast and held out his empty glass.

"You're right. A wee dram of our Glen Dubh from time to time won't keep us from producing our blends."

As his smiling son refilled both glasses, Robb senior added with a wink: "If you ever run out of it, you know where to look."

Robb grasped his father's allusion to his personal stock. In fact, ever since the founding of Fearmòr Blenders, each year when the business received its delivery of Glen Dubh, two barrels of the single malt whisky were always delivered to Robb Fearmòr senior's house, a tradition continued by his son.

"Your mother would like you to come and have dinner with us this Sunday."

Robb gave an embarrassed smile. "Unfortunately, I have a prior engagement ..."

Robb senior gave him a sympathetic look. "No doubt a pretty young lady will be depriving us of your presence. Good for you."

The son finished his whisky and let his father believe that he'd guessed right. Thus, he was able to avoid lying. A good thing too, because he would never have been able to find the courage to admit that he'd be spending this weekend at the Pattison brothers' estate in Peebles.

42. Elizabeth, Parry Sound

Elizabeth's hands clench the steering wheel of Captain André's old Escort station wagon. She hesitates. The last time she drove a car was at least a year ago. Finally she starts the engine. Her mind is made up, so she might as well get it over and done with.

Gradually she gets used to the vehicle's rhythm, so different from cruising in a boat. Shortly after, the car leaves Parry Sound to get on Highway 400, going south. The first sign she sees indicates the distance to Toronto: two hundred and thirty kilometres. She feels a pang in her chest; she could have avoided this trip if Louise hadn't put her up against the ropes.

She doesn't know how MacPhearson will take her proposal, or how far she'll go if he doesn't accept it straight off. No doubt, he'll interpret her offer as a sign of weakness. Will he take advantage of it?

It starts to rain. Water streams across the asphalt. Elizabeth, who thought she was still living the summer of her life, abruptly realises it's autumn. Since Louise's departure a week ago, she's been endlessly tormented by the thought of this inevitable moment.

She's already passed the city of Barrie where the highway gains a third lane. The heavy traffic smothers her. *As long as the old car doesn't die on me, I'll be all right,* hopes Elizabeth, who sensibly keeps the vehicle in the right hand lane. Suddenly this world seems very unreal to her. She has the impression of being motionless as she watches a hallucinatory parade of cars and landscapes whiz by.

When, an hour and a half later, the old Escort enters urban traffic, Elizabeth feels her heart banging against her chest. For a moment she thinks of Sylvain, of George, of Hélène, of all these people from Lighthouse Point forced to live in this city they hate.

Shortly after, she enters the Dearg Room and orders a thirty-five-year-old Bruichladdich—"cask strength"—which she desperately needs. She asks the waitress to let the boss know she's arrived. It's early afternoon and she's the only client, so she takes in the décor, meant to simulate the ambience of a real Scottish pub: red velvet upholstery, mouldings decorated with bottles and cases of Scotch, framed photos of distilleries, ports and castles in Scotland. In one photo, MacPhearson is sharing a dram with Michael Jackson, the famous Scotch writer, and in another, he's drinking in the company of the renowned distiller, Jim McEwan, of the Bowmore distillery on the island of Islay. All this junk, this tasteless pastiche, conspires to recreate an almost surreal world.

Deep down, I'm no better than MacPhearson. I'm trying to create a type of spirits that doesn't exist, using another that no longer exists—the Glen Dubh. I'm just as much a phoney as he is, with his Gaelic sham.

"So what brings you to my humble establishment, apart from whisky? How's the distillery doing?" asks MacPhearson as he sits down at her table.

Elizabeth states that the New Glen Dubh is still doing very well. Not being the type of person to put off the inevitable, she goes straight to the point.

"I ... we need capital for the barrels."

MacPhearson looks at her with sympathy.

He's gauging the extent of my despair, thinks Elizabeth, disgusted both by MacPhearson and by what she has to do.

"Didn't the sale of the blends bring in enough money?"

He must have known the answer before asking the question. Elizabeth shakes her head. MacPhearson turns to the bar stocked with bottles of various shapes and sizes and gets the barmaid's attention. Even in Scotland, Elizabeth has rarely seen such an impressive collection.

"How much do you need?"

Elizabeth presents the sum without hesitating, just as the waitress sets the boss's glass on the table. MacPhearson lets out a whistle. Is he making fun of her or is he genuinely surprised?

"Can you give us a loan?"

MacPhearson brings his glass to his lips. Today his regular whisky, a nineteen-year-old Tomatin, tastes even better than usual.

"Maybe," he replies, after a long silence. "But there's the question of collateral and repayment. Once the whisky is in barrels, it'll be several years before it's converted to money. And then, at what rate should I loan you the money? There's the risk factor that ..."

"I'm offering you forty-nine percent of the distillery."

Both glasses rise and fall. MacPhearson doesn't hesitate to make his counter-offer. Despite the knife at her throat, Elizabeth tries to negotiate.

An hour later, she leaves the Dearg Room after having accepted two more glasses of MacPhearson's vintage whiskies, as well as his final offer. She and the other shareholders will have the capital to continue distilling and ageing their whisky at Lighthouse Point. However, they no longer possess more than forty percent of their Glen Dubh. If it weren't for the fact that Elizabeth is determined to keep the fabulous taste of the Bruichladdich in her mouth, she'd give in to her desire to vomit.

43. Scotland, 1897

All along the route between the Peebles train station, thirty-seven kilometres from Edinburgh, and the Pattisons' country house, Robb Fearmòr admired the beauty of the heathland through the carriage window. This invitation was a unique opportunity to meet the magnates of the industry and network. In fact, at the Pattisons' he hoped to get a glimpse of his own future, of the paradise where success could take him if he played his cards right.

After a bend in the road, the coachman drove the carriage through the gate of a three-storey castle dominating a picturesque valley. Yes, Robb needed to carve out his place in this world—because he saw the future clearly, just as his father had at his age. Large blenders would grow even larger, swallowing up all the little ones in their path. Fearmòr Blenders, whose very existence depended on its limited supply of Glen Dubh, couldn't expect to grow. So, if he wanted to survive, Robb had to enter into an alliance.

A servant in livery came to meet the carriage, took Robb's case and led him into a vast hall decorated with large-format posters advertising Pattisons' whisky. Robb lingered for a moment in front of one of these; it showed two British army generals dressed in their parade uniforms, standing and sipping a glass next to a cannon and an enormous regimental drum, underneath the Union Jack. Below, the caption proclaimed: "*Pattisons' whisky in **general** use*". A little farther along, another advertisement featured a battleship with the Pattison name cleaving the waves and, according to the slogan, "Forging the future".

Robb was struck dumb with admiration: the genius of the Pattison brothers had revolutionised whisky advertising, which, until then, had been greatly handicapped by its static, austere character. He considered the other posters, which clashed with the residence's sumptuousness. A real lord wouldn't have decorated his house like this, he noted. The Pattison brothers' origins—they had been simple grocers before venturing into the whisky trade—remained humble.

The valet left to bring Robb's case up to his room just at the moment when Robert Pattison, dressed in sporting attire, entered the hall. He greeted his young friend with a shout.

"My dear Robb, what a pleasure to have you. Let's go to the terrace and I'll serve you a drink."

Robb accepted his host's embrace and, commenting on the beauty of the place, followed him through several rooms, finally arriving at a terrace that offered an unobstructed view of the sun-bathed valley. The company consisted of the other Pattison brother, Walter, and his wife, as well as James Buchanan and Mrs Buchanan. Seeing the latter couple, Robb quivered slightly. James Buchanan, born in Canada to Scottish parents who had brought him back to their country of origin during his childhood, had only entered into the blending trade in 1884. However, his flamboyant style had already made him rich and famous. During the 1889 World's Fair in Paris, his blend had received a gold medal. The blender, aged almost fifty, had been the first to supply the British Parliament with whisky. His recent acquisition of the old Black Swan distillery in the Holborn district in London had set tongues in the industry wagging. In 1780, during a horrific riot, a crowd had seized this distillery to swill down its whisky. The subsequent outbreak of a terrible fire had killed tens of people. The incident was described in detail in Charles Dickens's novel *Barnaby Rudge*. Today, Buchanan was having the famous historic building rebuilt at great cost.

Robb was delighted to make his acquaintance.

"I was just telling everyone about my famous advertising trick for my Black and White."

Buchanan, a tall, very svelte man with a moustache and ginger hair, impeccably dressed, gestured with a glass in one hand and a cigar in the other. In his loud, hoarse voice, he explained that he had patented the name Black and White because the public, unable to remember the name Buchanan, had gotten into the annoying habit of simply asking for the "whisky in the black and white bottle". Next, to make his blend better known in London's posh circles, he'd recruited a group of young dandies. He sent them to prestigious restaurants and hotels, selected in advance, because Black and White wasn't featured on their wines and spirits menu. Arriving in one of these establishments at a time when it was packed with people, the young men would choose a prominent table and order themselves a real gourmet's feast. Afterwards, they would ask for a round of Black and White whisky. When the waiter informed them that the hotel didn't offer this whisky, the dandies would jump to their feet and indignantly scold the server. They would cancel their meal and leave the place in a row.

"You should have seen them in action," finished Buchanan, laughing so hard he nearly suffocated. "They'd cross the room, shouting: 'What a wretched restaurant! You can't even get a Black and White here!'"

Everyone except for Helen Buchanan, who doubtless wasn't hearing this story for the first time, burst out laughing. Robb stored the trick in his memory; he'd have to think of equally ingenious ones.

When the laughter finally wore off, Robert Pattison declared pompously: "I actually have a better one, a completely new advertising tool. I'll show it to you, but only after dinner."

Even more than the others, Robb fidgeted with impatience, since he was itching to perfect his knowledge.

* * *

In the evening, Robb shared a large table with ten couples. There were one or two distillers, but the other men were owners of whisky blending companies, like Mackie, McNab and Haig … Across the entire room, people were questioning each other about the famous surprise that the Pattisons were reserving as the highlight of the evening.

Finally, around eleven o'clock, Robert Pattison, judging that he had made his guests languish long enough, asked for silence.

"This evening," he bugled, "I have the pleasure of introducing to you the new allies recruited by the Pattison empire to continue its conquest of the Scotch market."

Behind him, servants hurried to put four sheet-covered packets on a table. Each was about fifty centimetres tall and twenty centimetres wide.

"As of this week," Robert continued, "Pattisons' whisky is going to soar to new heights." Going to the table, he tugged theatrically on a sheet to reveal a cage. "Drink Pattisons' whisky!"

The audience was left breathless. A grey parrot continued repeating its exhortation while Robert removed the other sheets, thus revealing three more identical-looking parrots, which immediately launched into the same refrain.

"Drink Pattisons' whisky!"

The birds were chanting the slogan so loudly that Robert Pattison had to raise his voice to make himself understood.

"Starting Monday, three hundred parrots, specially trained for the task, will be distributed for free to alcohol-selling grocers all across Scotland."

The guests applauded the Pattison brothers, who bowed like actors receiving an ovation at the end of a play. Robb's hands turned red as he applauded even more and louder than the others.

The Pattisons are the best, he said to himself. *I have to join forces with them no matter the cost.*

* * *

Pulling his watch from his suit pocket, Robert Pattison checked it, let out a long sigh and knocked on the carriage roof with his cane.

"Stop," he ordered the coachman.

The carriage came to a halt. His brother Walter, who was sitting next to him, hardly seemed surprised, while Robb, seated across from the Pattisons, didn't understand the reason for this sudden stop. Finally, realising that his hosts would offer him no explanation, he asked for one.

"We're too early," replied Robert simply.

Robb looked at his watch. It was nine thirty-five. According to his calculations, they had just enough time to arrive at the Peebles train station to catch the ten o'clock train, the first Monday morning one bound for Edinburgh. Besides, even if they'd been early, it would have been more logical to wait at the station. Despite his incomprehension, he avoided confronting the two brothers.

"You know, Robb, I like you a lot—so much, in fact, that I'm going to give you a bit of advice."

In the calm that reigned over this stretch of country road, Robert was speaking very softly.

"Buy as many shares of Pattison whisky as you can, starting today. This week, with the launch of our new publicity campaign, their value will soar."

Robb thanked him effusively.

"Maybe you could do us a small favour in exchange."

This time it was Walter who spoke, explaining that, in the near future, the Pattisons were seeking to launch a new blend in which they hoped to incorporate a share of Glen Dubh. However, since this single malt whisky was difficult to obtain, they hoped that Robb could supply them with some, or become their associate by placing Fearmòr Blenders under the Pattison banner.

"But everything hinges on your ability to supply us with Glen Dubh."

Robb now understood how he'd earned this invitation to the Pattisons'. Nonetheless, despite his privileged ties with the Glen Dubh distillery, he couldn't promise them anything; at least, not right now. For that matter, he wondered whether this offer didn't actually conceal a threat: accept the Pattisons as employers or suffer the consequences of facing them as rivals. Opting for prudence, he gave a measured reply:

"This is a very interesting proposition. I'd be happy to discuss it at greater length later on."

This reaction pleased the brothers, and Robert shouted to the coachman to get underway again. At five minutes past ten they arrived at the station and Robb, who had afternoon appointments in Edinburgh, showed his frustration at having missed his train. Robert Pattison seemed, on the contrary, not the least bit discouraged by this setback.

"Don't worry about your appointments, my dear Robb; you'll be there on time."

With this, Robert went off to the station office.

"We arrived late on purpose," Walter whispered. "It gives us an excuse to rent a private locomotive."

Robb paled a little. "But that costs a fortune, at least five pounds per mile."

Walter let out a great laugh. "Yes, but this sum is well worth all the publicity that you, and we, will get out of it. When one arrives late and then rents a private train, one gets noticed, old chap."

Robb, unconvinced by this argument, opened his mouth to protest, but Robert was already coming back.

"There, it's arranged. Our private locomotive will arrive any minute now."

So Robb no longer had any choice but to climb aboard the Pattisons' train. Would this extravagant locomotive really bring him to the Promised Land? He drove the question out of his mind. At any rate, now that he was aboard, there was no getting off.

44. Robert, Fergus, Ontario

Robert Fearmòr is having the time of his life. Intrigued by the ad for the Fergus Scottish Festival and Highland Games he'd noticed in a tourist brochure at Pearson International Airport in Toronto, he had rented a car and headed for this little village an hour's drive away from the Ontarian metropolis.

The Scot hasn't been disappointed. For two days, he's been amusing himself by observing this celebration of the kitschiest elements of Scottish folk culture—from bagpipe band competitions to Highland dancing, and then to haggis, with the caber toss and readings of Robbie Burns' poetry on the way; in short, a faithful reproduction of a culture that has little to do with these people. And, the strangest thing of all, the virtual absence of whisky. At the festival bar, set up under a tent in a discreet corner, one can order a dram all right, but the choice is limited to Glenfiddich and Johnnie Walker. In any case, most people here are happy to quench their thirst with beer.

The spectacle of these Canadians bearing Scottish clan names decked out in their kilts and tartans, talking to each other in an English sounding American to Robert's ears rates as one of the most hilarious things he's ever seen.

If the Scottish diaspora really consists of ninety million people across the world, Robert says to himself as he watches two young women, dressed in traditional garb, jump gracefully above two crossed swords, *may God have mercy on us*. Robert has avoided talking to anyone, for fear that his accent would give him away and that he would then be requisitioned to judge a dance competition or interpret the motif and colours of a tartan.

The festival is drawing to a close. Anyhow, the time has come to move on to his real mission. It's just past one o'clock, so Robert estimates that he should be able to reach the shores of Georgian Bay before day's end. His eyes skim over an Ontario road map. *What a huge territory!* he observes, while discovering some very familiar place names: Rothesay, Thornhill, St Andrews, Kincardine, Nairn, Paisley, Aberfoyle, Holyrood, New Glasgow …

Setting out, he forces himself to remember to keep the car on the right hand side. In late afternoon, after crossing a series of hills covered in vegetation and forests, he suddenly catches sight of it: a blue plain with magnificent white waves.

"Georgian Bay!" exclaims Robert. He parks the car on the gravel shoulder and gets out to enjoy the unobstructed view, his first contact with this vast lake. The early-autumn azure colour of the water fascinates him. At the bottom of a hill, about ten kilometres away along the shore, lies a large grain elevator and the town of Collingwood. A little to the east, Robert picks out a very white, sandy shore: Wasaga Beach. To the north, a green cliff overhangs the bay.

Shortly after, the car begins a brisk descent, passing through Duntroon, another tiny village with a Scottish name, before reaching Collingwood and the lake level. In a park by the bay, Robert considers the view of the open water. *He left from this spot, no doubt from the quay over there,* he thinks.

The Scot consults his tourist guidebook. Until the 1970s, this town had a major shipyard. Between the second half of the 19th century and the beginning of the 1900s, ships left from this port every day, transporting merchandise and passengers along the Bruce Peninsula toward the other Great Lakes.

Today, in this place known for its downhill skiing slopes hurtling down the rather tiny Blue Mountains just west of the town, there are few vestiges of its maritime history. On a rocky island, Robert catches sight of a lighthouse. *It's an imperial tower, like the one in Lighthouse Point.* The guidebook gives him more information. In 1855, the Department of Public Works of Canada West had begun the ambitious project of constructing eleven of these lighthouses, named imperial towers since they were financed by the British government. The task had been entrusted to John Brown, a contractor. For some towers, the stone had been quarried and prepared by masons in Scotland, then sent to Canada as ballast aboard ships. Four years later, when the sixth lighthouse was completed, Brown had already exceeded his budget, having spent $223,000, an exorbitant amount at the time. The five other towers had therefore never been built.

A hundred years ago, Robert would have been able to follow in his ancestor's footsteps and sail directly to Lighthouse Point by boat. Today, he has to go all the way around Georgian Bay by land.

Tired, he decides to take a room for the night. He finds the town's most luxurious hotel, the Cranberry Resort. *Since Uncle Harry is paying, I might as well take advantage of it.*

Although used to sleeping soundly no matter where he is, during the night, Robert is haunted by blurred but troubling images, terrible waves of blue-green water whipped by a biting wind, carrying strident, desperate screams. Rising before dawn, Robert pulls himself out of the cosy bed and goes to the water's edge. On the island, the lighthouse is blinking tirelessly and, on the shore, the waves are unfurling calmly.

"It's incredible the number of detours you have to make to reach Lighthouse Point by car," the Scot complains as he reviews his itinerary. "It's even more inaccessible than a Highland bothy in the 18th century." Robert first goes east, so he can access Highway 400 north.

It's late afternoon when he arrives at Parry Sound. At the office of the Chamber of Commerce, a young employee shows him where he can park his car. She also gives him the name and address of a bed and breakfast in Lighthouse Point, and the phone number of the captain of a water-taxi.

Robert goes to the town dock. Suddenly, a familiar image draws his eye. Five white cases, piled one on top of the other, sport a stylised drawing in black, showing a distillery pagoda floating on three waves. Drawing closer, Robert reads below the logo: "New Glen Dubh Distillery: the whisky of Georgian Bay."

He notices the same symbol on the starboard side of a boat with the rounded, slender shape of a commercial fishing vessel, moored at the quay.

A stout woman with jerky movements shouts at Robert. "Are you here for the Dearg Room shipment?"

Nonplussed, Robert shakes his head. The woman is clearly irritated.

"It should've arrived here a long time ago."

"Are you from the distillery?"

The question and the Scottish accent surprise her, and she replies in the affirmative.

"I'm looking for someone to take me to Lighthouse Point. Could I hitch a ride with you?"

A car arrives at full speed and a young man gets out.

"Sorry for the delay, but there was an incredible traffic jam on the highway."

The woman and the young man start to load the cases into the car's trunk. She turns to Rob. "Help us out and I'll take you."

Robert lends a hand. Once they've finished loading, he boards the boat, noticing its name, *The Dubh*, inscribed in big black letters near the bow.

"My name is Robert."

"Ghisèle," says the captain, accepting the offered hand. She starts the engine and points the boat toward the bay. "Are you from Scotland?"

"Yes."

"What brings you to Lighthouse Point?"

"Tourism."

"It's not summer anymore, you know. But I'm like you. For me, September and October are my favourite months here."

The noise from the motor limits their conversation. Robert loses himself in contemplation of the rock, which meshes with the water like a recently formed volcanic landscape. A short while ago, when he'd begun driving north, the abrupt change in the suddenly granitic landscape had struck him. Since the highway lay inland, he hadn't been able to appreciate the unique character of this coastal region. Now, studying it from the water, he falls in love with all these channels, these rocks and these islands.

He's completely disoriented. If he had to find his way again alone, he'd be completely lost. Is he perhaps disappearing into an imaginary world, like the isle of Avalon from Arthurian legend, a place only the initiated may enter, or indeed leave? *Robb must have felt the same way when he arrived here.* Robert is sure he's right.

When he sees Lighthouse Point's imperial tower appear on the horizon, he knows his journey is ending. Ghisèle drops him off on the dock, pointing out the bed and breakfast. Once again, Robert has a thought for the man whose footsteps he's retracing. *When he landed here, Robb Fearmòr was pursuing his quest. I'm just carrying out a simple mission.*

Shouldering his bag, Robert starts to walk towards Angéline Bresette's house.

* * *

The next day, Robert wakes up in fine form. The sound of the waves echoing through his window has had a soothing effect. After doing justice to his hostess's copious breakfast, he inquires about the best way to get to the distillery. He could go there on foot, but Angéline suggests renting a sea kayak.

The Scot begins his journey over the water. Having done some kayaking in the North Sea, Robert handles the craft skilfully, moving it towards the opening of the channel leading to the distillery. Half an hour later, in front of the New Glen Dubh, for a moment he thinks he's hallucinating. The two pagodas, the entrance, and the general shape of the building look like the historic photos of …

"The Glen Dubh distillery," he murmurs.

For a long time, he stays on the water, admiring this building that brings him back a century and thousands of kilometres. Finally, he pulls up to the shore and goes to the entrance, where Ghisèle, sitting at a desk, is talking to another woman. Robert asks Ghisèle if he can visit the distillery.

"Tell him that our tour season ended on the Labour Day long weekend," the other woman whispers in French, just before starting to walk away.

"That won't be necessary, I speak French."

The woman, eyes goggling, turns around.

"Elizabeth Legrand, let me introduce Robert …" says Ghisèle, recovering from her surprise at hearing the Scot speak her language.

"Fearmòr," adds Robert, holding out his hand to Elizabeth. "Couldn't you make an exception for my tour?"

Elizabeth limply shakes Robert's hand without taking her eyes off him. Since early this morning, she's had a premonition. Now she knows why. *Today the New World is finally meeting the Old*, she thinks. *But is this an omen of war or peace?*

45. Scotland, 1898

The future had never seemed so bright. All along the Speyside, and even in Edinburgh or Glasgow, he was welcomed by people addressing him more than respectfully as "Mr Fearmòr". People begged him to take their money and invest it in Fearmòr Blenders, because the rumour of the company's impending merger with the Pattison empire babbled as madly as the water of a stream, feeding the growing excitement among investors.

For his part, Robb Fearmòr had borrowed left and right, even going so far as to mortgage Fearmòr Blenders, in order to add his capital to the wave that buoyed the Pattison ship still further. The Pattisons' advertisement, repeated tirelessly by their famous parrots, or even posted on the most distinguished walls in the United Kingdom, was bearing fruit.

The whisky market, entirely dominated by blends, had become lucrative, and investors large and small were rushing to acquire their piece of it. Predictions remained highly optimistic and potential profits astronomic. The whole world had just discovered Scotland's whisky. Blenders were multiplying at a frightening pace and, responding to the growing demand, distillers had increased their production tenfold. The producers of Scotch whisky—and the sellers of Scotch even more so—saw themselves elevated to the rank of virtual barons.

Nevertheless, for Robb Fearmòr, the youngest of the whisky lords, there were still two doors that remained closed. The first, that of Robb Fearmòr senior's house, he could ignore if he had to. When he'd found out to what ends his son had tried to borrow money from him, Robb senior had unceremoniously thrown the young man out of his home. Nonetheless, this rebuff didn't worry Robb junior unduly; without this money, he would simply earn fewer profits. His current investment would bring him an impressive fortune all the same and, when his father saw that his son had been right, he would at least admit Robb junior to his house again—even though his pride would keep him from acknowledging his mistake.

The second closed door, however, that of the Glen Dubh distillery, remained a thorny problem for Robb junior. During his last conversation with the Pattison brothers, they had issued him an ultimatum: if Robb couldn't guarantee them a steady supply of Glen Dubh, the merger was off. He had tried all the possible channels to get a meeting with his uncle Harold, and had met with an unequivocal refusal. He had even attempted to approach his uncle one Sunday morning as he left church, only to be sent packing with blows from a cane.

But today, as summer was beginning, Robb was full of a new hope. Since the Pattisons had given him the upcoming autumn as a deadline, he was resigned to risking everything. To that end, he now sat at a table in the Café Royal on West Register Street in Edinburgh, waiting for the man who, without knowing it, held Robb's future in his hands. This pub, a very suitable place to discuss whisky, had catered to several generations of drinkers. The epic words of one of them—James Hogg, the shepherd turned poet—were even featured on the wall.

> *If a body could just find oot the exac' proportions and quantity that ought to be drunk every day, and keep to that, I verily trow that he might leeve for ever, without dying at a', and that doctors and kirkyards would go oot o' fashion …*

The famous quote never failed to make Robb laugh. *If ever the public could be persuaded that it was true, our prosperity would be assured* ad vitam aeternam. He pondered for some time on how to achieve this goal, while sipping a Teine Brìghmhor. When he went to bars, he always ordered his own whisky.

Strangely enough, shortly after, he felt his cousin's presence in the pub without seeing him. As his eyes turned towards the entrance, they confirmed his intuition: Harold Fearmòr junior had just entered the Café Royal. The two young men stared at each other and cursed simultaneously. Even though the breach between their fathers had prevented the cousins from ever meeting, they recognised each other right away. They shared so many family traits that they could have been brothers.

Harold shook Robb's hand, slid into an armchair and ordered himself a Glen Dubh. Robb could barely contain his immense relief at finally being face to face with his cousin. Despite the positive reply to his letter, he'd feared that Harold wouldn't keep the appointment.

The two men exchanged a toast. Robb would have liked to begin by talking about their family a little. However, the separation of the two clans for four decades, and his total ignorance about his relatives on his uncle's side, kept him from doing so. He went straight to the point and asked Harold whether he could obtain for him what Harold's father would never sell to Robb.

"You know," said Harold, after taking a long gulp of his whisky, "you blenders have a very bad reputation. Some distillers are even talking about pushing Parliament to adopt a law forbidding you from putting the words 'Scotch whisky' on your bottles."

His cousin wasn't telling him anything new, but this riled Robb all the same. "It's thanks to us that you sell your whisky! We're your best clients."

"I don't deny it," Harold went on, "but almost all these blended whiskies are nothing but cheap rotgut."

"Not ours," Robb protested. "Taste it and see."

The challenge had been launched. Robb urged his glass on his cousin, who, at first, looked at it with contempt. In his family, drinking blends was strictly forbidden, especially those made by Fearmòr Blenders. Accepting this cup of poison was practically sacrilege. On the other hand, Harold had to admit that he condemned blends in general, and Teine Brìghmhor in particular, without having tasted them himself. He was curious about this blended whisky that contained, so to speak, a little of the Fearmòr distillers' blood. Unlike his father, Harold didn't deny reality: sooner or later, they'd have to adapt to the blends, since the growth of the whisky market depended on them. At any rate, if he had to end up giving in to his cousin's demand, it was in his best interest to know what kind of result Fearmòr Blenders obtained by using Glen Dubh.

He took Robb's glass. The whisky had a distinctly darker colour than Glen Dubh. After a second's hesitation, he brought the Teine Brìghmhor to his lips with a quick movement.

Harold opened his mouth as though to spit, which made Robb leap out of his chair. The distiller burst out laughing.

"It's not bad, really, your Teine Brìghmhor—for a blend, at least."

Sitting back down, Robb accepted the compliment, but without gloating—because in order to win the endgame, he needed to avoid bragging about this first victory at all costs.

"So, can you supply us with more Glen Dubh?"

"Maybe."

Harold's suddenly pensive air didn't reassure Robb at all.

"But my father must never find out where this whisky is going."

"I've already considered that problem. I'll create a company to buy the whisky. That way, you'll be able to send it to a warehouse where I'll go and pick it up."

The bill would go to this company that would exist only on paper, added a now confident Robb. Neither the name nor the address of Fearmòr Blenders would appear in the transactions. Harold seemed to like the idea.

"In a few years, the distillery will be completely in my hands. But from now until then, I'm running a huge risk by doing business with you. If my father ever found out about it ..."

Harold let his unfinished sentence hang in the air, as though he were too afraid to utter the horrible paternal punishment he'd receive in such a case.

"I'll make up for it by paying a good price."

Harold raised his eyes to meet Robb's, who, for a second, had the strong impression of looking in a mirror.

"That's not enough. Should the worst-case scenario come to pass, I need an argument strong enough to convince my father that I was right to disobey him."

"What more can I offer?"

For several seconds, Harold seemed to be racking his brains. "You can offer the termination of the agreement between the Glen Dubh distillery and Fearmòr Blenders."

The note of spontaneity in Harold's voice was supposed to make his cousin believe that this condition had just occurred to him. Robb was no fool. Harold had had this objective in mind long before arriving at their appointment; maybe his father was even aware that this meeting had been arranged and had dispatched Harold here with precisely this aim in mind.

The room lurched around Robb, as though he'd just been suddenly thrown into a violent sea. Before going completely under water, he searched for a life buoy and clutched desperately at the glass of Glen Dubh.

Once the glass was empty, Robb set it down and looked straight into his cousin's eyes. He saw nothing but a dark valley, unfathomable and endless.

46. Lighthouse Point, 1898

The bride was young and beautiful. In front of fifty people gathered in the small Saint Venerius church in Lighthouse Point, Délianne Roy was promising lifelong fidelity to her husband Sigefroid Legrand, her fourth cousin. During the ceremony, the barely seventeen-year-old bride was too absorbed by her own emotions to notice the reaction of the oldest person present, namely her seventy-year-old grandmother, Angélique Legrand-Roy.

There was no one left who had known Angélique before the time of her marriage. Her contemporaries would no doubt have spotted the resemblance between Délianne and the young woman her grandmother had been. Délianne's thickening hips, her chubby face, her straight, night-black hair, her piercing brown eyes, were as many indications that, when she'd be older, she would be the spitting image of her grandmother. Thinking of her grand-daughter woke a flood of memories in Angélique. In short, Délianne embodied the daughter she'd hoped for to no avail.

This marriage had very little in common with hers. For that matter, Délianne was preparing to begin a life very different from her grandmother's. Because of their relatively distant degree of kinship, the spouses hadn't needed to ask for special authorisation from the Church—a step often necessary for marriages in Lighthouse Point uniting second and even first cousins.

"Please welcome Mr and Mrs Sigefroid Legrand."

The bride and groom turned to the audience to receive its resounding applause. Outside, rowboats were waiting for the young couple and their guests to transport them to the home of the bride's parents, Louis and Marie Roy. The splendid weather of this late August Saturday topped off the success of the wedding.

Angélique's other son, Charles, escorted her to his boat, together with his wife Velma, their daughter Charlotte, a tall girl of sixteen, and their ten-year-old son, André. Charles began to row, so that he could join the procession taking shape behind the newlyweds' rowboat. During the short journey, Angélique let herself be carried away by nostalgic thoughts. The world around her today seemed unreal to her, unrecognisable compared to the one in which she'd lived most of her life. On both shores of Lighthouse Point's little bay, wooden buildings—the church, the general store, the sawmill, the small school and several houses—had replaced the trees. The first Métis inhabitants of Lighthouse Point had seen the ranks of the village swell with French-Canadian families: the Lalondes, Robitailles, Grisés, Desroches … drawn by the multiplying lumber camps. A railroad spur, hacked through the forest and the rock by the power of axes and dynamite, now went all the way to the sawmill. The land-based route had supplanted the water as the means of transporting the lumber. Nevertheless, maritime traffic still thrived. Every day boats leaving from the small southern ports—from Collingwood, Midland or Penetanguishene—passed by Lighthouse Point and, in some cases, landed at the quay built by the federal government. This village, where you would no longer hear Ojibway spoken, now had a dominant French-Canadian character. The family of Hugh Simpson, the sawmill boss, was the only one who didn't speak French.

The lumber industry had assured Lighthouse Point's prosperity, but Angélique resented it, because it had taken away her eldest son, François—drowned in a log driving accident under tree trunks that had unexpectedly jutted out from a log jam. And, even twenty years later, this wound remained open, still more painful than the scar left by Théophile's natural death ten years afterwards.

Charles had taken over at the lighthouse. The work remained hard, but entailed few risks, and the salary of four hundred and fifty dollars—unchanged for forty years—although modest, was paid regularly. The housing and food supplied to the keeper by the government allowed the Roy family to manage.

By marrying the son of George Legrand, who was the nephew of François Legrand, her grandmother's father, Délianne, the daughter of Angélique's youngest son, Louis, had now become part of the Legrand family. *The young woman*, thought Angélique, *probably doesn't know that her marriage will draw her to a completely different way of life. It's better this way.*

Sitting at the bow of the rowboat, Angélique looked at Charlotte for a long moment. Her other grand-daughter had idiosyncratic manners that most people found strange. Fascinated by water, Charlotte spent long hours lost in contemplation of the waves. Not very talkative, she didn't mingle with people much, and lacked sociability. Some said that this handicap, which they attributed to her childhood spent in a lighthouse, would keep her from finding a husband. But that hardly troubled Charlotte. On the other hand, her little brother André possessed the exuberance of which his sister had been deprived.

Charles's rowboat landed at Louis Roy's house. The light jolt caused by the movement of the boat sliding onto the shore pulled Angélique out of her daydream. Guests were already sitting down noisily at the crude tables set up outdoors. Angélique noted, with great satisfaction, that Pierre Auger, the finest fiddler in Lighthouse Point, was there. Later on, during the jigs, she would show them what she was still capable of. And maybe one of the young men present would ask Charlotte to dance.

* * *

Délianne watched them without knowing how to react; she'd have liked to laugh, but that might have angered Sigefroid. And yet the sight of these men in ties, stiff in their three-piece suits and wide-brimmed hats, and of these women, dressed up in sombre-coloured dresses and haughty hairstyles, strutting on this wild shore where only the trees and fish could admire them, was quite funny. Even at her wedding, the outfits hadn't been so stylish.

All the same, the splendid tablecloths, the folding tables, the bottles of wine and the phonograph music gave this picnic—the Massassauga

Club's last one of the summer—a pleasant mood. This society of twenty people included only three women. For a week now, Délianne had been trying to win over these strange people, without much success. To begin with, this smart set spoke only English, a language she didn't know—some of them with an incomprehensible American accent. She'd have to get used to it, because Sigefroid had accepted the job of caretaker of the club's buildings and grounds. On hearing Délianne's name, the president of the club had judged it unpronounceable and declared: "We'll just have to call you Delia."

So, the young wife had needed to accustom herself to this new name and to these strangers at the same time. Sigefroid had been reassuring: "They'll be gone in a week. Then we'll be all alone until late spring."

Soon the Legrands would be the only inhabitants of Massassauga Bay, located an hour's boat ride north of Lighthouse Point. The new Massassauga Club—made up of professionals mostly from Toronto and, in a few cases, from the United States—had just purchased the Crown lands surrounding this bay from the Ontario government. It was aiming to create a summer holiday retreat for its members. This summer, eight families had spent a few weeks camping on the shores of this long, narrow bay, which stretched for about two kilometres. The club had decided to hire a caretaker who would be responsible for the construction and maintenance of its clubhouse. Next summer, each family would choose a plot of land through a random draw and then, with the caretaker's help, build a cottage on it. Sigefroid and his wife would stay on site and look after these summer residences.

Two days after their wedding, Délianne and Sigefroid had arrived at Massassauga Bay aboard the barge transporting the construction materials. For a week, the men of the club had worked feverishly to raise the wooden structure. Délianne fed the workers plentiful and—from what she could tell, since Sigefroid, too busy eating, didn't always translate the men's comments for her—highly appreciated meals.

Délianne waited impatiently for each night to come. When the club members withdrew to their tents, she and Sigefroid went to sleep beside the water, under a beautiful starry sky. The couple would make love to the whispering sound of the wind and waves, and then snuggle up against each other, naked under the thick blankets, their faces uncovered, their noses taking in the fresh air before they nodded off. Contrary to the members of the club, who lived in constant fear of an encounter with a snake or a bear, these two children of the land felt completely at home in their element.

"Delia, bring us some more of those dumplings, please."

"The *glissantes*," Sigefroid whispered to her, seeing that his wife didn't understand the request made by Ted Anderson, the club president.

She brought over her pot of *glissantes*, cooked on that morning's fire.

"Thank you, dear."

Délianne had already heard about rich people, about their luxurious homes, which held more servants than children. Did these servants feel just as irritated as she did at the moment?

It was then that the boat hired to take the holiday-makers to Lighthouse Point to meet their connection for Penetanguishene moored at the dock in front of the freshly erected frame of the club building. A visitor disembarked, and the president hurried to greet him.

"Mr Bald, we're happy to have you."

The newly arrived individual, dressed in his Sunday best as well, unloaded a few cases and began to open them right away.

"He's a photographer," Sigefroid explained to Délianne.

John Witherspoon Bald, who had come from Penetanguishene to immortalise the club's picnic, busied himself for an hour setting up his camera, a wooden box, on a tripod. Next, he instructed the people at the picnic to smile. The holiday-makers adopted various poses, with the clear intention of showing off their inexpressible pleasure. The photographer forbade them to move for the next ten seconds. Délianne curiously watched the scene.

Once the photo was taken, Bald repacked his equipment, and the holiday-makers hauled their tents and other baggage aboard the boat. Just before leaving, Mr Anderson took Sigefroid aside. Then the mooring lines were unfastened and the boat set out, heading out to the open water.

Délianne asked her husband about the subject of his conversation with the president.

"He told me to do a good job, and not to blow the chance he's giving me. Most of the members of the club were against the idea of hiring a French-Canadian."

Sigefroid saw the anger flash in Délianne's face.

"He also congratulated me for being married to such an extraordinary cook!"

Délianne considered the boat, now just a small dot on the horizon. A wave of calm came over her, a feeling that would comfort her at the end of every summer when the holiday-makers left. Turning to Sigefroid, she held out her arms.

The couple held each other, and then kissed passionately. Yes, Sigefroid would do his work well—not to please his English-speaking employers, but to be able to stay here, with Délianne and, later, their children. Today, this work could wait. They made love on the sun-warmed rock, in the open air of *la mer Douce*, the Freshwater Sea. The young bride and groom finally began their real honeymoon.

Their first autumn on Massassauga Bay was magnificent. The tender memory of these weeks of ecstasy would help them through a great many of their future ordeals.

47. Scotland, December 7th, 1898

"I don't like this. I don't like it at all."

Harold Fearmòr watched his father fidget nervously behind his desk. As he observed him, he felt his own heart begin to beat irregularly. Finally Harold senior sat back down, placing his hands calmly on the desk.

"Even if all our competitors are doubling their production, we don't have to do the same thing."

For two years now, the Glen Dubh distillery had considerably exceeded the level of expansion Harold senior judged wise. Financing this growth had required investing considerable capital. The distiller, who expected to place the fate of the family business entirely in the hands of his son over the course of the next year, didn't want to bequeath him a business in debt, with a shaky future.

"And these new clients who are ordering so many barrels from us, what do we really know about them?"

Harold junior had some difficulty controlling the anxiety stemming from the pang in his chest. If his father learned the real identity of the Associated Blenders company, he'd be capable of anything, including disinheriting his son. Harold junior had achieved the cancellation of the old agreement forcing them to supply Fearmòr Blenders. However, even though his father would have to acknowledge this tour de force later on, he wouldn't forgive him for having taken such an initiative, and would, no doubt, never trust him again.

"Associated Blenders have the solid backing of major partners," Harold said in a voice he hoped came across as confident and sure.

Harold senior grimaced. The information reassured him—although it didn't dispel his apprehension. Suddenly the father's face took on a smiling expression that worried Harold junior even more.

"This new contract comes at an opportune moment all the same," the old man admitted. "It'll give us a solid financial footing during this turbulent period. When does the first delivery to Associated Blenders leave?"

"Today. In fact, I need to go and check that the barrels have left."

Harold junior then took leave of his father, and went first to his office. He closed the door, collapsed into his armchair and wiped his forehead. An unpleasant feeling overwhelmed him, as though he was once again twelve years old and hiding a terribly stupid act. He was twenty-six, and the deal he'd made wasn't a blunder. Quite the opposite—even his father had just admitted that this contract with Associated Blenders would …

Repeated knocking rang out at the door. Jenkins, Harold's personal assistant, burst into the room, a newspaper in his hand. To be defying standing orders to wait for permission before entering the office was already a sign that something was amiss with Jenkins who was, in fact, visibly stunned by some catastrophic news.

"Jenkins," said Harold, getting up, "have you lost your head?"

The assistant thrust the afternoon paper into his boss's hands. "Read it," he mumbled in an appalled voice.

Harold scanned the banner headline, printed in large black letters: PATTISONS' WHISKIES, AN EMPTY BOTTLE! After reading just the first few lines he understood what had happened. The Lloyds and Bridges bank, one of the many institutions that had loaned money to the Pattison brothers, had begun to doubt the company's solvency. It had therefore demanded a repayment. The company had responded by suspending its payments. Suspicions were confirmed: the Pattison empire was nothing more than an empty, bankrupt shell. Its only real asset consisted of unpaid and unsold supplies of whisky. The terrible discovery had just precipitated a wave of panic among the bankers who were demanding their dues in vain. The Pattisons would be brought to trial for lying to their creditors.

Calculating the enormous consequences of this bankruptcy on the whisky industry, Harold let himself drop into his armchair. However, just a second later, he leapt up again.

"The delivery!" he shouted, pushing Jenkins out of his way.

Thoroughly upset and under the surprised looks of his employees, Harold ran down the distillery corridors. If the barrels sold to Associated Blenders had already left the distillery, they'd fall into the hands of Fearmòr Blenders' creditors, or into those of the Pattisons'.

Panting, he burst into the shipping room. Three men were rolling one last barrel of whisky onto a cart. Unable to talk, Harold gestured to the workers to stop. His breathlessness lasted for another thirty seconds, and the foreman ordered one of the men to bring a chair.

When Harold finally managed to utter a few words, he offered a dram to those who had worked to load this order, which he immediately cancelled. Everyone was stunned. Harold loosened his tie and took a long breath. No one could yet guess where this crisis would take them. Even though times were hard, the Glen Dubh distillery would weather the storm unleashed by Pattisons' Whiskies. This would doubtless not be the case for several other distilleries, or for many blending companies like Fearmòr Blenders.

We'll have to settle the score with those blender bastards once and for all! he cussed to himself.

* * *

Robb Fearmòr could hardly contain his joy and energy. He was practically bouncing up and down as he walked the streets through the rush of people in the Leith city centre. He was finally reaping the reward for his boldness. His offices were just a few street corners from the warehouse which, at least on paper, was rented by the Associated Blenders Company. He checked the time: the first delivery of Glen Dubh was now on its way and, in a few minutes, he'd be at the rendezvous point as well. Once the delivery men from the Glen Dubh distillery had left, the barrels would be loaded up and sent off once again—this time to the Pattisons' warehouses.

Driven by a craving for butterscotch candies, Robb stopped at a grocer's along the way.

"Drink Pattisons' whisky." On its perch at the back of the establishment, a parrot with coloured plumage sang its slogan. For Robb, this ingenious advertisement evoked the seat at the masters' table that he was finally going to claim.

Suddenly, a shaggy-looking man rushed into the shop. "The bank's closed!" he cried, without addressing anybody in particular.

The worker, a regular at the shop, whimpered: "No one's allowed to make withdrawals anymore. All my savings are in there!" As he spoke, he'd pulled a newspaper from the pocket of his jacket. He pointed a finger at an article. "I'm going to lose everything because of them and their whisky!"

Dismayed, he threw the newspaper to the ground. The grocer came towards his distraught client and tried to calm both him and the tension in the air. Alarmed people questioned each other.

Robb picked up the newspaper and then noticed the headline: BANKRUPTCY OF THE PATTISON BROTHERS, ACCUSED OF FRAUD.

A new client arrived and, gasping for breath, announced the closure of another major bank. The paper fell from Robb's hands. The noise of protests and unrest came in from the street. The frightening news had provoked a real frenzy: the wreck of the Pattisons was dragging in its wake the bankruptcies of many financial institutions. Very few people didn't have money invested in a distillery or a blenders' company, or simply an account in one of the banks affected by the crisis.

"Drink Pattisons' whisky!"

The parrot, excited by the tumult, repeated its message even more loudly and frequently, fluttering about on its perch.

"Dri-i-ink Pattisons' whiskyyyy!"

Robb turned towards the feverish bird. Everything was reeling around him. *Birds of prey always end up devouring farmyard birds*, he thought. *Walter and Robert Pattison are nothing but small fry who grew too big. They've really done a number on us.* Staggering like a drunken man, Robb drew near to the parrot. When the dust of the crisis settled, he'd have nothing left but a mountain of debts and no possibility of paying them off.

"Drink, drink, drink Pattisons' whisky!"

The bird beat its wings to avoid him, but Robb's hands were already around its neck. The cord restraining the parrot's foot broke with a sharp snap. The psittacine's cry broke as well, just like its bones under Robb's fingers. Hands still clutching the motionless ball of silky feathers, Robb took a step.

Horrified, the grocer and his clients watched him in bewilderment. Robb's physical stature was hardly impressive. Nonetheless, the madness in his eyes froze them with fear. Finally, after several long seconds, Robb let go of the dead parrot. It crashed to the floor on top of the newspaper, spraying the letters of the Pattison name with blood.

Abruptly pulled out of his trance, Robb left the grocer's at a run. He now had only one option: flight.

Part IV

48. Elizabeth, Lighthouse Point

There's something wrong, and he knows it. Elizabeth stares at Robert Fearmòr as they share a Lainnir Taigh-Solais on the deck in front of the distillery. *But he won't tell me what it is.* She smiles to hide her dark thoughts.

And yet she should be delighted. The visit of a descendant of the creator of Glen Dubh is an honour and a chance to gain a precious ally.

"A fine blend."

A wide smile accompanies Robert Fearmòr's verdict.

"How ironic! I had to come to the other end of the world to taste my ancestors' whisky."

"Like the Celtic musicians who came to Cape Breton," says Elizabeth.

Since Robert doesn't appear to know what she's referring to, Elizabeth explains.

"In Cape Breton in Nova Scotia, you'll find some of the 4.5 million Canadians of Scottish descent. In such an isolated place, they've been able to keep the traditional music alive and pure without any outside influences from other cultures, contrary to traditional music in Scotland. When there was a renaissance of traditional Celtic music in Scotland, Scottish musicians came to Cape Breton to relearn the *na h-òrain mhòra* that had been forgotten in your country."

Robert bursts out laughing. *That's a good one*, he thinks, remembering his Scottish festival in Fergus. "At least I'm not trying to re-learn how to make whisky."

So what exactly are you trying to do? The question crosses Elizabeth's mind, but she doesn't ask it.

"I've come to tread the ground my ancestor walked on."

"Luckily for us, Robb Fearmòr ended up here. We're deeply indebted to him."

Despite the angular shapes of his face, Elizabeth notices for the first time that Robert is good-looking. She finds his accent, neither European nor British, seductive. The Scotsman, who studied French at school, has spent time in France. His current job, distributing imported wines, often gives him the chance to converse with French-speaking clients.

"Now that you've toured our facilities, I'd like to know what you think of them."

Throughout the tour, Robert had examined the equipment and every stage of production almost without saying a word. However, Elizabeth remains convinced that he's formed an opinion about everything. At the moment, she really needs to hear it, whether it's favourable or not.

For a few weeks, a feeling of imminent catastrophe has been oppressing her. The voice that has been guiding her since the beginning of this crazy adventure has fallen silent. If anyone can tell her she's on the wrong track, it's a stillman from the Fearmòr clan. His showing up at this critical moment can't be mere coincidence.

"Everything seems perfect to me," Robert replies after a long silence. "Your mash tuns work well. I've rarely seen more beautiful stills. Really, if I had had the chance to work in a distillery like this one, in such a fabulous setting, maybe I'd still be in the business. The fact remains that ..."

Elizabeth pleads with her eyes.

"It'll be necessary to taste the final product, once it's aged, to know for sure."

"All the same, if you drank some now, you'd have a good idea of how it's likely to turn out?"

"Maybe."

"All right. Let's go to the storehouse." Elizabeth is already on her feet, her worried gaze fixed on Robert.

Slowly, he drains his glass and gets up in his turn. "I can't promise you anything."

"Bring your glass."

So they return to the cellar. Moments ago, fear had kept Elizabeth from inviting Robert Fearmòr to taste the new whisky. If the Scot is trying to harm the New Glen Dubh, she doesn't want to give him ammunition. Now she resigns herself to running that risk.

Elizabeth arms herself with a siphon and moves forward in the dimly lit room, between the rows of barrels.

"You're the visitor. You choose, Robert."

Robert looks his hostess in the eyes for a long time before going towards the barrels, tapping them lightly with his fist. This storehouse, and the gesture he's just made, bring back distant memories and sensations. The smell of wood tickles his nostrils as they detect the faint fragrance of whisky, blended with wood and then evaporated—an odour imperceptible to everyone except angels and experienced distillers. Tasting a whisky at the beginning of its ageing is a privileged moment, like hearing the first major recital of a piano prodigy.

"This one," says Robert, stroking the rough surface of a barrel with the palm of his hand.

Elizabeth passes him his glass and the siphon. With the help of a pocketknife, she removes the cork that plugs the hole in the middle of the barrel. A strong smell escapes from the container.

She sees Robert's lips pucker slightly. His senses, like hers, have just detected not only the smell but also the *presence* of whisky, of its essence, still young but very evident, at least to them. His subtle quiver was revealing: by tasting it, maybe even just by nosing it, Robert will know whether this whisky will one day come to deserve the title of "Scotch", even though it will never be able to carry it legally.

She inserts the siphon in the barrel and Robert brings the glasses close to it. With the end of the tube in her mouth, she hesitates, as though she were about to plunge into a troubled sea from a high rock. She takes a deep breath, watching the rapid advance of the lightly amber-coloured liquid. Taking the tube out of her mouth, she quickly puts it into one of the glasses. A few drops sprinkle her hands and Robert's. Once both glasses are full, Elizabeth stoppers the tube with her thumb and then puts it into the hole in the barrel.

Robert rubs the whisky on his hand. He brings the glass to his nose, swirls the liquid and watches the row of small bubbles form on its surface.

He's noting that the ageing is progressing normally, thinks Elizabeth, as she does the same.

Completely concentrated and impassive, Robert lets his nostrils appreciate the nose of the whisky.

"Well?" Elizabeth sounds like a distressed patient demanding a diagnosis from her doctor.

Robert looks at her as though he's just noticed her presence. "*Slàinte*", he says simply, swallowing the whisky.

The young whisky excites all of Elizabeth's senses, strips them right down to the nerves. Three weeks have passed since her last tasting. She feels a slight transformation in the essence of the spirits. The whisky is trying to speak to her, but like an adult attempting to decipher a child's language, she doesn't understand it. A key element is escaping her. But what is it? She searches for the answer in Robert Fearmòr's expression.

"This will be an absolutely unique whisky." Robert hasn't lied, but he is very careful not to reveal the whole truth.

"Yes, but will it be a true Scotch, in the league of the Glen Dubh?"

The Scotsman feels pity first, and then anger. *She shouldn't have waded into these waters, they're over her head.* "I don't know."

Tears run down Elizabeth's cheeks. Seeing so much fragility, so much instability, leaves Robert shaken. He thinks of his uncle: *The old bastard will be happy about this.*

Elizabeth pulls out the siphon and replaces the cork. Her gaze, which has turned icy, passes over Robert. She then takes her glass and, with all her strength, throws it against the stone wall where it shatters into a thousand pieces.

"It's a tradition I started here," she declares, laughing.

Without waiting to see if Robert will imitate her, she exits the storehouse with long strides. Robert turns the glass in his hand and, after a few seconds, sends it smashing against the wall. He falls into step behind his hostess. *Can whisky really do that to someone?*

Abruptly, he wonders if he shouldn't high-tail it out of Lighthouse Point sooner rather than later.

49. Georgian Bay, 1903

Robb Fearmor, head bowed, was being hypnotised by the eddy of the water parted by the bow of the *Agomo*. He felt like he'd reached the edge, like it would have been a relief to just throw himself overboard in order to end this flight—a flight which, for two years, had been dragging him farther and farther, all the while leaving him with the impression of not having moved forward at all. In fact, he thought it more likely that the opposite was happening.

"Mr Fearmòr, you're not seasick I hope?"

Robb suppressed his desire to brush off Mrs Cleaver, an American from Pittsburgh. Even though the company on board the *Agomo*—mostly rich vacationers from Toronto's polite society, or wealthy socialites hailing from American industrial cities—was hardly pleasant for him, it was in his interest to treat his fellow passengers considerately. He might need them, or at least their money, to survive in this country he was venturing into—a place of granitic rock and pristine, odourless water.

"No, madam; it would take a lot more to get the better of a Highlander like me."

Robb had chosen to play the part of the tough, forthright Scot, strong and proud. It came naturally to him, and made a vivid impression on these Canadians and Americans, who were fascinated by the mythical awe his home country evoked.

He smiled at Mrs Cleaver, who seemed reassured.

"According to Captain Dupré, we'll arrive at Lighthouse Point soon. That's where you're getting off, isn't it?"

Fearmòr nodded. This spot marked the next stop along the route his escape had taken. First he had crossed the ocean and gone up the

St Lawrence River until he reached Montreal. After a year spent living on next to nothing, on miserable wages earned here and there doing minor jobs, Robb had decided to relocate to Toronto. Even in this rapidly expanding city, he hadn't found a single job with a respectable salary or the possibility of advancement.

His only real expertise lay in whisky and, here, his knowledge was worthless. Nor could he brag about his track record: the ruin of the family business. Thus, when he'd read an advertisement in *The Globe* newspaper calling for a man to look after the bar in the Lighthouse Point hotel, he'd dusted off his finest words to write a letter and apply for this job.

A man arrived beside Mrs Cleaver and took her arm. "There you are, my dear. I'll bet Mr Fearmòr has just told you another of his dreadful whisky stories."

Robb met Hank Cleaver's gaze. He couldn't stand the sight of the man. Despite his complete success in winning over the female passengers, Robb's relationship with their men remained somewhat strained.

"No, but I'd very much like to hear more of them."

Robb accepted the compliment. On the train from Toronto to Penetanguishene, he had taken on the role of storyteller for his new acquaintances. His words full of imagery had painted the picture of Glen Dubh, of its creator Tom Fearmòr, of the extraordinary adventures of the clandestine distillers' era. To his own surprise, remembering this saga had filled him with a peaceful contentment. Translating this past into his own words had reconciled him, in a way, with the whisky that continued to flow in his veins, even though he'd had to exile himself from it forever.

"So come and see me at the hotel," Robb suggested with a wide smile.

Mr Cleaver asked his wife to accompany him, since the Davidsons were looking for bridge partners. Once again alone on deck, Robb's eyes looked up to meet the hawk's gaze of Captain Gilbert Dupré, who was observing him from the wheelhouse. The mariner was hardly pleased by his presence, since Robb was the only passenger destined for Lighthouse Point. All the others were travelling just a little farther north, to Massassauga Bay, to spend a few weeks in their summer cottage, or in one belonging to a relative or friend. So, because of Robb, the *Agomo* found itself forced to sail up Lighthouse Point's narrow channel, which was difficult to navigate and therefore loathed by the captains of large ships. What's more, just before sailing, engine trouble had made the *Agomo* seriously late, thus contributing to the captain's sour mood—and he was of a testy nature to begin with.

Robb turned around to contemplate the rocky coast and the sparkle of the early summer sun on the water. He would be very happy to disembark from this ship.

* * *

"Surely rowing a few cable-lengths is nothing at all, to a Highlander."

Hank Cleaver and ten other passengers were anticipating Robb's reaction. Cleaver's grin was meant to be provocative. Robb studied the rowboat and the two sailors who were waiting for orders to launch it.

"Come, Mr Fearmòr, either you accept my offer or you simply get off at Massassauga Bay with the others."

Captain Dupré's implacable eyes looked him up and down. *The old swine! He's really pleased with himself*, thought Robb. Indeed, the captain was exulting at having found a way to solve two problems, both at the Scot's expense. As well as dropping off his boastful passenger at Lighthouse Point, Captain Dupré was also supposed to deliver a rowboat there. He had therefore suggested that Robb make the last stage of the journey in the rowboat, and that he deliver the craft to the hotel in the captain's place. However, this offer had all the undertones of an ultimatum; Dupré had, at any rate, decided to go directly to Massassauga Bay.

Robb's gaze went from the circle of passengers to the port side of the ship. Through a cleft in the rocks of the shore, one could make out the beginning of the channel which, according to the captain, led to the village of Lighthouse Point. His blood boiled.

"Bring up my trunk."

At a sign from the captain, a seaman hurriedly disappeared. Shortly after, he and a second sailor returned with Robb's trunk and loaded it onto the rowboat. Once the rowboat had been lowered into the water, Robb climbed down a ladder and settled into the small craft tossed about by the waves. From the deck of the *Agomo*, the passengers were waving.

"Simply go up the channel, Mr Fearmòr," shouted Captain Dupré. "You have a good two hours of daylight left. Many thanks for doing us this favour."

"I hope to see you burn in Hell," Robb muttered to himself, as he maintained his smile and waved back to the passengers. Taking off his jacket, he rolled up his sleeves and grabbed the oars.

The *Agomo* was already a hundred metres away, and Robb could see the passengers moving towards the stern to watch him. The oars bit into the water, and the boat, a light craft of exceptionally high quality, responded with a leap. The rower glanced behind him. The shore was closer, but still remained very far away. To his right, the *Agomo* disappeared behind a point. Suddenly, the anguish of finding himself utterly alone, abandoned to his fate in this rocky, hostile-looking territory broken up by water, began to eat away at him. He could have protested that he didn't know how to swim. But he hadn't wanted to lose face.

What am I doing here, Robb asked himself, *in a country where a captain can treat his passengers with less regard than he gives the cargo?*

The waves, which had rocked the rowboat gently at first, now shook it with increasingly greater force. Robb had crossed half the distance separating him from the opening in the rocks. However, doubt was treacherously insinuating itself into his mind. Would the water really be calmer once the boat entered the channel? Had Captain Dupré told him the truth about the course to follow?

The breeze was brushing the pines, which all leaned strangely to the south as a result of the strain of resisting the north-west wind's repeated assaults. This whispering suddenly seemed sinister to him. Robb's trunk slid on the bottom of the rowboat, and this movement made the rower lose his balance. If, by some accident, he fell into this freshwater sea, would anyone find his body or even a trace of his meagre possessions? Would his parents in Scotland even be informed of his disappearance?

In front of him, to the west, the sun was setting at a worrying pace. He began rowing again, with renewed ardour. Should he shout for help? What for? No one would hear him. His efforts warmed him. His throat, however, burning with thirst, demanded whisky, not water. Giving in to an insane desire, he abandoned the oars and knelt, determined to taste, one last time, this whisky capable of giving him the courage to face death. The wind, pouncing on this opportunity to take the rowboat's fate in hand, brought it closer to shore, but pushing it a hundred metres north of the opening, facing a steep rocky wall violently lashed by the waves. Robb's hands dug desperately in the open trunk, searching between his underclothes for the only balm capable of easing his now inevitable end.

Finally he ferreted out the bottle, which was well wrapped in towels, and, in spite of his precarious balance, managed to yank out the cork and drink a long draught—his last.

The rowboat was now less than ten metres from the rock—which, with the help of the waves, would smash the craft into a thousand pieces. Robb put the cork back into the bottle. With a calm that surprised him, he sat back down on the bench and picked up the oars again.

He felt invigorated by a new energy. No, this sea wouldn't have his hide. The Glen Dubh had helped him understand that his time hadn't come yet. For two years, countless times he had resisted the temptation to open this bottle—the only parting gift from his father. Now he was happy that he'd been wise enough to keep the strength and wisdom of the Glen Dubh in reserve until this critical moment.

Pointing the rowboat towards the passage between the rocks, he regained the upper hand over the sea. A few minutes later, the craft entered a channel between two rocky shores. The swell had become less turbulent, without being completely calm. Robb now considered the landscape from a completely different viewpoint. These shores, so wild until then, now held a savage beauty. Their smooth rock, with velvety contours, attracted him like a breast he wanted to caress. Since he now felt happy to find himself alone in this new country, a loud cry of joy burst from his throat. He listened to the echo of his voice bounce back against the rock and water.

The sun was still setting. Before moving on, he put the bottle away at the bottom of the trunk. Making a *quaich* with his hands, he filled them with the water of the bay and drank a few long swallows. The cool liquid revived his taste buds still impregnated with whisky. An extraordinary flavour spread in his mouth: was it the taste of the water, of the whisky, or of a new sensation spawned from the meeting of the two liquids? Robb felt excitement, the desire to take off his clothes, bathe himself and lie down naked against the rock.

Meanwhile, the rowboat's position had changed. Robb then realised that he was no longer alone. A silhouette standing at the top of the point on the port side was watching over him.

"The lighthouse ..." he murmured.

The Scot began to row frenetically towards this point dominated by the lighthouse. The glass panels at the top of the tower reflected the light of the setting sun. How great was his surprise when, skirting the point shortly after, he discovered a young woman standing on a dock, observing him. The most surprising thing was the look in her eyes: it was as if she'd always been waiting for him.

* * *

It was time. Her brother and father had just begun the one hundred-and-forty-step climb to the top of the tower, where they would pull back the shade-screens and then light the lamps. This season of short nights was the best one for the lighthouse keepers, since their task took up less of their time. Charlotte climbed down to the dock in order to savour twilight by the water's edge.

The young woman felt the vigour of summer unleashed around her and, in her veins, her life blood surged just as it did for the plants and the animals in the forest. At the age of twenty-one, the change of seasons was stirring her. Her head entrusted itself entirely to her feet, accustomed to travelling this particular path ever since the day she began to walk. Her thoughts, free to wander as they pleased, turned towards the future. Even though Charlotte felt the pulse of summer energy and the desire to use it, she didn't know where to channel that energy.

Suddenly, a cry split the air. She stopped abruptly, but her ears, focused towards the water, heard only silence. Who had let out this roar, this growl or cry of distress? This strange howl, perhaps that of an animal, had come from the water. Quickly, she reached the quay.

She was ready for anything except what she saw. A solitary rower detached himself from the setting sun and advanced joyfully towards the dock. Charlotte was completely bewildered by his approach. Judging by his dress and appearance, the man was neither from here nor one of the tourists who came to spend time in the new hotel.

"Good evening, Miss. Am I on the right path for Lighthouse Point?"

This stranger's accent disconcerted her even more. "If you're looking for the village," she finally said, "you need to keep going until you reach the end of the channel."

The rowboat drew up alongside the quay. The man asked Charlotte how much farther the hotel was.

"You won't get there before nightfall. Tie up your rowboat and come with me."

Completely exhausted, the man could only obey.

Charlotte stared at him; her blue-green coloured eyes were almost identical to the colour of the water tinted by twilight. "Are you the one who shouted?"

The man seemed completely disarmed. "Yes."

Charlotte didn't ask him why—she had already guessed the answer. She began to climb the slope leading to the lighthouse.

The Scot introduced himself and explained the reason for his coming to Lighthouse Point. "I'm not arriving in a rowboat by choice."

The rest of the story made Charlotte burst into laughter. "Oh, my father will get a chuckle out of hearing that one," she said, as though to reassure Robb.

Indeed, Charles Roy, a friend of the eccentric captain, had a fit of laughter upon hearing his story. The Roy family invited Robb to stay with them for the night. He could continue his journey the next day. This first evening at the foot of the lighthouse on the point towering over Georgian Bay, under a sky full of stars—Robb Fearmòr would remember it forever. Even though he didn't understand the language of his hosts, right away he intuitively felt at ease among them.

The fugitive would finally find refuge, although he didn't know it yet. The Glen Dubh had helped him to arrive there, and it would also make sure that he'd stay for good.

50. Scotland, July 28th, 1909

The day had finally come. After four years of work, the Royal Commission on Whisky was going to release its report. If its verdict was favourable to the single malt distillers, Harold Fearmòr junior and his colleagues could entertain the hope of a recovery in the whisky industry. Harold had even travelled all the way to London to be present for this highly anticipated climax. Since he'd arrived early, he'd been able to obtain a seat in the packed courtroom. A number of people had to be content with remaining standing. Given the current high stakes, Harold was hardly surprised by the size of the crowd.

A court case, baptised the "What is whisky?" affair by the press, had led to calls for this commission of inquiry. The borough of Islington in London had brought publicans before the court, accusing them of selling grain-whisky-based blends—a product that had neither the nature nor the quality of the drink their clients had ordered, namely Scotch whisky. The powerful Distillers Company Limited, or DCL, the largest blended whisky business in the country, had quickly loosened the strings of its well-endowed purse to rush to the defence of the accused. So, proof in hand, the defenders had tried to demonstrate that the purchasers of their Scotch whisky had bought the product while fully aware of what they were getting. Since the defence had succeeded at sowing doubt, the court had been unable to reach a definitive verdict. At the instigation of the DCL, the British government had therefore established a Royal Commission charged with putting an end to this dispute.

Thus the inquiry, carried out by English politicians—or *Sassenachs,* as the Scots scornfully called them—who knew absolutely nothing about whisky, had taken its laborious course. There had been no less than twenty-two public hearings, seventy-seven witnesses and even visits to various distilleries.

From the outset of this affair, the single malt whisky distillers had demanded the exclusive right to use the designation "Scotch whisky". They insisted that the law should forbid its use on the labels of blended whisky bottles.

Today, the question would finally be decided. In the courtroom, Harold Fearmòr recognised several faces: Buchanan, Hardy … Nearly all of the DCL big wigs were present. And for good reason: they had a lot to lose. Nevertheless, the absence of Robb Fearmòr bothered Harold. After the Pattison brothers' bankruptcy and the industry debacle in 1898, Robb had disappeared to escape the wrath of his creditors. No one knew where he had fled—surely overseas. Even his parents didn't seem to know.

Harold now counted on savouring his revenge. Nonetheless it would be incomplete, since he wouldn't see his cousin's head fall along with those of the other blenders.

The atmosphere was electric; people were speaking so loudly that one could have thought they were in a tavern. However, as soon as the members of the Commission set foot in the room, a church-like silence fell. The president of the Commission, Lord Huntington, first reminded everyone of the mandate and proceedings of the inquiry. After this long preamble, he read the report's conclusions before a gaping audience.

"'… And so, our general conclusion as far as this part of our inquiry is concerned is that 'whiskey' is a spirit obtained from the distillation of a mash of grains saccharified by the diastase of malt; and that 'Scotch whiskey' is whiskey, as defined above, distilled in Scotland; and that 'Irish whiskey' is whiskey, as defined above, distilled in Ireland. The whiskey trade therefore seems, in our opinion, to be carried out in a just, honest fashion.'"

A roar of joy went up from the blenders. Harold Fearmòr muttered a curse. Lord Huntington, without losing his calm, asked for silence before continuing.

"'Moreover, the Commission is equally of the opinion that the storage of all spirits for a certain obligatory period is unnecessary, and that it would constitute an obstacle to the sale of whiskey.' "

Harold found himself in shock before the triumph of the DCL and the blenders. The single malt distillers had just lost the exclusive use of the name 'Scotch whisky'. In a way, the decision consecrated the victory of the Lowland producers over those of the Highlands. What's more, the Commission had rejected the other important demand of the single malt distillers—the imposition of an obligatory barrel-ageing period of three years upon Scotch. Later, when he would consult the printed text of the report, Harold would notice that the commissioners, contrary to the practice for Scottish whisky, had spelled the word "whiskey" with an *e* before the *y* at the end—another eloquent sign of their ignorance in the matter.

Nonetheless, there was one consolation, however small. The Commission's report officialised the geographical delimitation of Scotch, by specifying that it was a whisky distilled only in Scotland. For lack of being able to defeat the blenders, the distillers would have to put up with them from now on. At least, thought Harold, one blender had been rendered incapable of doing any more damage to Scotch in general, and to Glen Dubh in particular—namely, Robb Fearmòr.

Even though Glen Dubh would continue to be blended with other whiskies of inferior breed and status, the Fearmòr name would stay pure. It remained to be seen whether, in such a climate, Scotch whisky—now armed with a legal and rigorously delimited name—would finally succeed in getting back on its feet.

51. Lighthouse Point, 1909

"Hey, Scottish guy! You'd better take up the slack if you don't want the boss to get angry."

Her smile said the opposite of her words. Nevertheless, Robb Fearmòr replied in kind.

"Take care of your bedding, Charlotte, and let me put away my boats in peace."

The young woman then disappeared inside the Lighthouse Point hotel. Robb went back to hauling the rowboat onto the dock. The rest of the hotel's summer staff—three chambermaids and waitresses, a cook and a handyman—had left several weeks ago. There was no one left to help the owner, Mrs Redbridge, close up the hotel for the winter but Charlotte and him. Since his first year at the hotel Robb had, by necessity, become more than a simple barman. Mr Redbridge had enlisted him to look after the rowboats and perform certain construction, repair or maintenance jobs.

He attached a rope to the ring on the bow of the rowboat, went a few steps farther to the boathouse and cranked a handle to reel in the rope and pull the boat onto rails between the quay and the boathouse.

In a few days' time, he would leave to spend his sixth winter in the lumber camps. The hotel, barricaded against the winter storms, would await his return in the spring. Six years already! He could barely believe it. Scotland, his life prior to landing in this land of water—both seemed light-years away from his current existence.

The rowboat reached the end of the rails and Robb untied it. He then slid it over to its bed for the winter. The small craft, the very one in which he had arrived at the hotel for the first time, took its place as though it were anticipating its long sleep with pleasure. Robb caught his breath. He considered this boat special, the best of the five in the hotel's fleet, with its slender hull made of lightweight, superfine wood. Even though no name appeared on its bow, Robb had christened it *Charlotte.* The month after his arrival at the hotel, the real Charlotte had been hired by the Redbridges as a waitress and chambermaid.

Once the hotel was closed, the young woman would return to live with her family at the lighthouse, as she did every winter. She and the Scot had become the pillars of the establishment, the only employees to return year after year, the first ones at their posts in the spring and the last to leave in the fall. Since the death of her husband four years ago, Mrs Redbridge, a woman in her early sixties, depended on them a great deal. Without them, she would doubtless have abandoned the hotel. In fact, she increasingly spoke of selling the place and returning permanently to Penetanguishene, where she spent the winters.

Come September, usually Robb welcomed the departure of the hotel's clients with joy, since, after a few months, they wearied him. The winters in the lumber camps were hard, but they allowed him to save a little money, since his work at the hotel earned him just enough to live on. This year, now in his mid-thirties, he felt that he'd arrived at a crossroads. Physically speaking, soon Robb wouldn't be up to the challenge of the demanding work in the lumber camps. Not only his body, but also his mind, told him that he had to look for his future elsewhere. But where?

Back on the quay, he examined the last two rowboats. A few minutes ago the wind had risen, and the increasingly stronger waves shook the vessels. He had to choose between *Bertha*, the heaviest, and the medium-sized *Irene.* Deciding to begin with the most difficult task, he leaned forward to grab *Bertha*'s gunwale.

"Come on, old girl," he murmured. A wave struck the dock and the backwash hit the rowboat's side so hard that the craft slid out of Robb's hands. Thrown completely off-balance, his momentum carried him away and he toppled into the glacially cold late October water.

Robb, who still hadn't learned how to swim, swallowed a considerable amount of water. Desperately thrashing his arms, he managed to rise to the surface, where he frantically breathed in a gulp of air. The full force of the backwash coming from the dock struck him, pushing him not only back underwater but also further away from shore.

"Aaaagh!" Robb's mouth pierced the water's surface, and let out a cry. But, immediately after, his head returned underwater. His agitated body fought feverishly against the liquid enemy's hold. Robb was moving in the water, but he didn't know in which direction. He felt his last bit of strength leaving him. His head broke the surface for one brief second, barely enough time to breathe in a mouthful of air. It would be his last, and he knew it.

He was vaguely aware of a movement, like the subtle current of a river, carrying him away. This wave had absorbed him; he was now part of it. The gentleness of this barely perceptible throbbing pulse comforted him. Behind his closed eyelids, he noticed a change in the light. Air was reaching his nose once again, but Robb wasn't consciously breathing.

With her right hand, Charlotte pulled on a rope with all her strength. With her other arm, she tried to maintain her grip on Robb's head and keep it above water. For a terrible moment, she was afraid she'd waited too long before leaping to his rescue. And yet, had she intervened before Robb stopped struggling, they would have both been dragged down to their death. So, when she'd run up to the dock, Charlotte had calmly taken the time to tie the rope attached to the winch around her waist. Next, she'd watched Robb's futile fight for twenty long seconds before throwing herself into the water.

Her skirts floated around her, hindering the movement of her legs. She let the rope go for a second, grabbed it a few centimetres farther on and pulled again. By repeating this manoeuvre several times, she drew them closer to the dock. They were alone at the hotel, so Charlotte couldn't hope for any help.

At the end of another interminable minute, she touched the quay. She had to let go of Robb in order to dive underwater, unfasten the rope around her waist and slide it around the man's chest. Gathering her last reserves of strength, Charlotte hauled herself onto the dock and pulled on the rope to bring Robb's head back to the surface; he was now more dead than alive. Her attempts to lift the heavy man onto the dock proved futile. She then thought of the winch. Without letting go of the rope, she went to the boathouse and turned the crank. When Robb was finally out of the water, she started rubbing him down. A few seconds passed and, to Charlotte's great relief, Robb coughed, his lips opening to spit out water and bile. He opened his eyes and saw Charlotte looking at him. For a second, he thought he was still underwater.

Charlotte smiled at him. Drops were still streaming from her long, loose hair. Her face, with its rounded cheeks and slightly almond-shaped eyes, seemed angelically beautiful to Robb. In spite of his confusion and weakness, the survivor was sure of at least one thing: Charlotte had saved his life and, from now on, that life belonged to her.

52. Robert, Lighthouse Point

Robert Fearmòr doesn't know what else to say to his uncle. If Harry Fearmòr were there with him, in this phone booth on the Lighthouse Point dock flooded by the light of the full moon, maybe then he'd understand Robert's motivation and state of mind.

"... having that Frenchwoman in the picture confuses the issue. If she takes up the distillery's cause ..."

Harry Fearmòr is listening, but remains unconvinced of his nephew's need to prolong his stay in Canada. He's obtained the information they wanted. However, Robert is concealing the real reason behind his request. After a long moment, Harry sighs.

"All right, I'll grant you another week. But if you stay after that, it'll be on your own dime."

Both men hang up. Will a week be enough? Robert leaves the phone booth. Bright moonlight slithers on the water, like a long silver snake. *In Scotland*, thinks Robert, *it's seven o'clock and people are starting their day. Here, everything is rest and tranquillity.* He no longer wants to go home.

This place is having a strange effect on him. Its soothingly gentle waters have given him a completely new serenity. The New Glen Dubh distillery, both troubling and marvellous, has stirred up his emotions—like those inspired by the memory of the rapture of a first love, intensely savoured, but then lost. For a week, he's been spending his days out in the sea kayak and visiting the distillery, where Elizabeth Legrand continues to welcome him warmly. He has dispensed a few pieces of advice to her on how to better organise the work at the distillery, or how to check the quality of the whisky's ingredients. The more time he spends at the distillery, the more he feels shaken by its simultaneously new and familiar atmosphere. Two days ago, he was determined to leave.

The arrival of Sabine de Grandmont had changed everything. He'd been sharing a dram with Elizabeth on the distillery's deck at the moment when Captain André's boat had dropped off the Frenchwoman on the New Glen Dubh dock. Elizabeth had been expecting her and knew she was coming to write an article on the distillery.

Sabine had joined them as if she were meeting old friends. Robert had been immediately and inexplicably charmed—not by her appearance, but by her radiant energy.

For her part, Sabine had been delighted to meet Robert Fearmòr—whose name she, of course, knew. Robert had loved the ensuing banter about Scotch whisky, listening to his conversation partners discuss their shared passion with delight. And what a contrast! There was the Frenchwoman, small and slender, and the Franco-Ontarian, tall and thickset. They even spoke their common language with marked differences, which the Scot's ears found highly entertaining. Elizabeth had invited Robert to have dinner with them and, all evening long, Sabine had continued to captivate him.

However, even though the Scotch whisky columnist's lilting voice had seduced him, her suggestions worried him. The story of this distillery run by French Canadians had delighted her to the utmost.

"Lighthouse Point has all the necessary elements for a fantastic feature article. People the world over will be interested," she had declared.

Robert had sensed the danger right away. If Sabine de Grandmont, blinded by her fascination for the place and its inhabitants, decrees that the New Glen Dubh stands a chance of ranking among the world's great Scotches, she'll give it prestige. In snobbish circles, people don't have to love a stylish whisky to drink and praise it—so long as it helps to elevate their status. Robert knows this all too well. And when, in a few years' time, Scotch experts put these new spirits in their place, the industry's credibility—at least that of its whisky columnists who anoint the winners and losers—will take a beating. What's more, Elizabeth will be crushed by this inevitable disappointment. So, he deems it better to prevent her from rising, and thus spare her the painful fall. He must also stop Sabine from committing this professional faux pas.

Back in his room, feverish and unable to sleep, Robert tries to come up with a plan—but without success.

* * *

On the dock in front of the distillery, Sabine is enchanted by the sight of smoky fog dissipating calmly on the water.

"Is it always like this in the mornings?"

Elizabeth looks at her, seemingly happy to see the woman share her own fascination.

"No, only in the autumn, or in very late summer, when the temperature difference between the day and the night increases. The water still retains the summer heat and, after a night-time frost, when dawn comes, the contrast creates this vapour—too thin to be real fog, but thick enough to make you think the water is on fire and producing white smoke."

Sabine admires the leaves and their splendid bursts of red and orange. Everything is streaming with the breath of the cool night, as though a pouring rain has just descended on the forest. Imagining herself in a mythical land, Sabine can feel the dawning of the voice of poetic inspiration that will dictate her article. *What a fabulous realm to create a unique whisky, a crossroads between the Old World and the New, between Scottish ruggedness and the Latin gentleness of the French of North America, steeped in native primitivism and the natural world.*

* * *

Fifteen minutes later, in the boat that is breaking through the last bits of vapour, the two women reach the Lighthouse Point dock.

"Looks like we're in for some great weather," says Robert, jumping aboard.

During the trip, which takes them through a series of channels, some very narrow, the two passengers admire the view. The boat enters a bay where, on a large smooth rock, stands the silhouette of a two-storey building.

"The Lighthouse Point hotel, or at least what's left of it," Elizabeth proclaims.

The craft approaches a submerged wall of rocks, the old foundation of the now disappeared dock. Elizabeth moors the boat and, once on land, plays tour guide.

"The hotel had already closed before I was born. For more than half a century, it welcomed distinguished guests. When I was a teenager, we came here on ..."

The unfinished phrase piques the curiosity of the two others.

"On dates?" interjects Sabine, exchanging a knowing look with Robert.

"... well, we came here to have a good time."

The trio walks around the decrepit building.

"I've seen old photos. The structure and décor were both rustic and charming. The clients thought they had come to the heart of the forest, but without having to sacrifice their little luxuries. In the summers, one or two cows were brought in to provide fresh milk."

In the old foyer of the hotel, dominated by a large stone fireplace, Elizabeth describes how her grandfather, André Roy, helped build the establishment.

"And where was the bar?" asks Robert.

Elizabeth points to an opening at the back of the room. Robert studies the empty room, where cracks in the walls let in light and air. He turns towards the two women.

"If Robb Fearmòr had lived longer, I wonder whether the hotel would have experienced the same fate."

His eyes meet Elizabeth's.

"All the businesses in Lighthouse Point live through the same cycle. They're born and they die. Fishing, forestry, holidaying—they all ended up dying more or less peaceful deaths."

"Your New Glen Dubh runs the risk of suffering the same fate, just like the old one," Robert prophesies.

"No, not here."

Elizabeth's unequivocal tone surprises the two others.

"We still have the real Glen Dubh. Also, this distillery is different: it creates life, through water."

Sabine agrees with Elizabeth, nodding. Disappointed, Robert turns his back to her. *She's completely crazy!* he thinks. *And Sabine is only encouraging her.*

Standing in front of the main staircase, he climbs a step. Suddenly, a hand lays itself over his.

"Don't go up there!"

For a moment, Robert is dumbstruck by the strength holding back his hand. Elizabeth's eyes are almost popping out of their sockets.

"Why not?"

"It's dangerous. The floor could collapse. I can't let you …"

Robert comes back down. A wide smile covers Elizabeth's face, and that face suddenly reminds Robert of a photo. For the first time, he notices Elizabeth's eyes, which are just as impenetrable as the mystery that surrounds them. *She looks like Charlotte, Robb Fearmòr's wife.* This observation overwhelms him. How far can the resemblance go? He hopes he never finds out.

53. Scotland, 1912

Before opening his son's letter, Robb Fearmòr senior had poured himself a large dram—and not just of any old whisky. At the back of his cellar, he'd located his oldest barrel of Glen Dubh. Under a thick layer of dust, numbers indicating the year 1856 were just barely legible. From this barrel, he had siphoned off a carafe full of fifty-six-year-old Glen Dubh, in order to forearm himself against the effect of what he was going to read. Next, to make the barrel easier to find again, he'd tied a tartan scarf around it.

He had then climbed back up to the sitting room to find his favourite armchair. Still without opening the letter, he had savoured a tall glass of his Scotch. Its ethereal smoothness diminished the man's harshness. A tear ran down his cheek. The whisky had, once again, exceeded his wildest expectations.

He finally tackled the ten-page missive, the first sign of life from his son in many years. For several minutes, he forgot even the glass in his hand. When he discovered the existence of his daughter-in-law—a French-Canadian, no less—he paused in his reading and emptied his glass.

Robb refilled it before continuing. Judging by the photograph that accompanied the letter, Charlotte was neither beautiful nor ugly. But her inexpressible gaze had a disturbing quality. *Doubtless I'll never meet her, any more than I'll meet my grandchildren, if she ends up giving me any.* Was this a regret or a simple observation? Robb wasn't sure.

Reaching the last page, he uttered a series of curses and downed his whisky so fast that he all but suffocated.

Robb Fearmòr certainly had to admit that, just like this Scotch, he had aged. He thought with a touch of irony that the years had had opposite effects on the whisky and its creator. Even so, another thought consoled him. Even after his death, his whisky would live on. He re-read his son's fanciful request several times, and brought the glass to his lips once again. *Bloody Robb! Only he could come up with such an insane idea*, thought the father. Yes, he would agree to his unworthy son's request. Not for Robb junior's sake, but for the Fearmòrs who would succeed him. Now, this new Canadian branch of his family tree would ensure the survival of the true Glen Dubh. At least, he hoped so.

54. Collingwood, November 8th, 1913

Charlotte, eager to return home, was looking forward to getting to the Lighthouse Point hotel. And yet this trip, this honeymoon that was four years late, had delighted her beyond her expectations, in part thanks to the exceptionally mild late fall weather. Robb and Charlotte had taken the *Agomo* to Penetanguishene and, next, a train to Toronto, followed by another to Niagara Falls. During their stays in various hotels, the couple had noted that their clients at Lighthouse Point were treated to an exceptionally high level of service. Nonetheless, Charlotte had been happy to be served by others for once.

Since their return to Toronto three days later, Robb had abruptly stopped being the charming husband to become the concerned business man, preoccupied by the biggest deal of his life. Charlotte shared his anxiety. Even though the widow Redbridge had given them the hotel for a good price, the couple had needed to borrow left and right to amass the small fortune required. From one summer to the next, despite succeeding in renting out all their rooms, they still hadn't earned enough to repay their debts. They were losing hope of keeping the hotel. Robb had thus swallowed his pride and written to his father.

Against all odds, Robb Fearmòr senior had agreed to his son's project. For this reason, the couple's trip was, above all else, for business. Nevertheless, Robb had been able to add a little pleasure to it. The night before the arrival of the cargo from Scotland, Robb had begun to feel acutely worried. To minimise the cargo's transit time in Toronto, as soon as the train cars had arrived from Montreal they had been hitched to the locomotive outbound for Collingwood.

Charlotte had accompanied her husband during his tour of inspection.

When the door to the first car was opened, Robb's reaction astonished her. He vigorously jumped aboard the car and began to press the barrels like a man shaking hands with old friends.

"Oh! Charlotte, these casks contain nothing less than the finest whisky in the world. Our tourists will sell us their souls for a chance to taste it."

Charlotte had considered her husband and the barrels for a long, silent moment. All of a sudden this plan seemed absurd to her. The cars contained more than three hundred barrels and two hundred cases of Scotch, the entirety of the whisky received from the Glen Dubh distillery by Robb Fearmòr senior over more than half a century. No whisky purveyor, not even the Glen Dubh distillery itself, could boast of possessing such old, excellent editions of these sought-after spirits. Robb was counting on selling this inheritance, shipped at his father's expense, at a premium price—not only to the wealthy clients of his hotel, but also to the distinguished bars of numerous port cities on the American side of the Great Lakes.

However, first of all they had to transport the merchandise to Lighthouse Point. The casks had taken a second train trip, from Toronto to Collingwood, this time accompanied by the Fearmòrs.

And so, while the whisky was loaded onto the *Agomo*—a process Robb watched over attentively—Charlotte strolled alone on the quays of the port. On this sunny late afternoon, she had to take off her coat. The weather for this November 8th was oddly mild.

Charlotte's eyes wandered towards the water, where the bay remained unusually calm and the imperial tower of the Collingwood lighthouse stood out from the bleak canvas formed by water and sky. *It's not as beautiful as ours*, she thought. On land, she could hear the noise of the work going on in the shipyards. Shipbuilding would continue all winter long. All along the Great Lakes, as the sailing season was coming to a close, ships were hurrying to transport one last cargo before settling in for the winter.

Charlotte sighed as she headed for her hotel, a shabby establishment. With the end of the honeymoon, the Fearmòrs had resigned themselves to tightening the purse strings once again. The *Agomo* was scheduled to weigh anchor the next day at noon. In less than twenty-four hours, she would finally be home. Taking long breaths of this strangely tepid air, she rubbed her stomach. Since her husband was so preoccupied, she judged it better to put off announcing the arrival of this child that the couple had so long been hoping for.

"Everything will be fine once we're home", she said to herself, trying to feel convinced of it.

* * *

Robb watched Charlotte, next to him in the bed, turn over for the umpteenth time. Despite her particularly restless sleep, on the whole she was having a better night than he was. Robb checked his pocket watch: three-twenty am.

What was this feeling that deprived him of sleep—arousal? Anxiety? His eyes traced the line of Charlotte's back, followed the curve of her hips and buttocks, visible through the sheet. He moved his fingers, driven by desire, by the need to calm this overexcited animal inside him. He slid them beneath the sheet and under Charlotte's nightgown, brushing her thigh. He wasn't in the habit of disturbing his wife's sleep, but tonight …

A sharp knocking at the door made him jump. So late at night, it had to be a mistake. The knocks came again, more insistent now. Irritated, Robb got up, determined to give the idiot disturbing them a piece of his mind. Opening the door, he was stunned to find himself face to face with the hotel's proprietor, wearing a dressing gown.

"The captain of the *Agomo* wants me to tell you that he'll be weighing anchor in an hour. If you want to leave today, you need to board right away. He won't wait."

Her message delivered, the stout little woman left, turning on her heel. Robb went to light the lamp by the bed, and Charlotte woke up. In a soft voice, Robb explained the change in schedule to his wife. He had begun dressing when Charlotte took his hand.

"We can't go."

In the faint light, Robb looked hard at Charlotte's drawn, exhausted features. In his mind, the man pictured his wife's body wriggling like a fish throughout this long night, now abruptly cut short. He put on his trousers.

"I slept badly too, my love. Tonight, in our own bed, we …"

"You don't understand," Charlotte interrupted. "I saw …"

She sat up straight. Her almost bloodless face betrayed such an acute, palpable fear that Robb couldn't hold back a light shiver, which he blamed on the cold of the early morning.

Charlotte searched for the words to describe her terrible vision. "There was an awful storm, and water all around us. I felt this icy cold …"

"It was just a nightmare, Charlotte." Robb clasped his wife's hands. He had never seen her so upset. He tried to make his voice gentle and firm in equal measure. "It's over. Get dressed now. In a few hours, we'll be home."

But Charlotte, almost beside herself, pulled her hands away and shook her head feverishly, hiding her face behind her long, unbound hair. "No. We can't go."

Hoping to subdue his growing anger, Robb took the two steps separating the bed from the window. His own worries, the lack of sleep, and now Charlotte's stubborn persistence were conspiring to drive him crazy. Opening the window, he breathed in fresh air.

"Look. The weather outside is calm. There's no storm."

Charlotte got up and, wrapping herself in a blanket, went to confirm that Robb was right. And yet this hardly seemed to reassure her, for the horrifying omen that had haunted her all night was clearly still burning in her mind. "I won't go."

Robb could no longer contain his anger. "Charlotte, our tickets are non-refundable. Our future is on that ship." His voice, not just firm now, had become severe and no longer held any trace of gentleness. "We can't let it leave without us."

The thought of Captain Dupré troubled Robb. He doubted that the ship's cargo would arrive intact at its destination unless he himself was on board the *Agomo* to watch over it. Nor did he trust the people of Lighthouse Point. News of the whisky's arrival would spread quickly there, and if he wasn't on hand to assure his Scotch's safety, he ran a great risk of losing at least part of it.

Charlotte was staring at him, incredulous and frightened, as though she didn't recognise him anymore. Robb considered the possibility of leaving her in Collingwood; she could catch the next ship out, which sailed in a day or two. But this seedy town, full of sailors, was hardly the sort of place to leave a woman alone. Charlotte cut his musings short by desperately playing her very last card.

"Our future isn't in the ship's hold, Robb. It's in my womb."

* * *

From the bridge of the *Agomo*, Captain Dupré could barely make out the figures creeping about in the half-light on the quay. He checked his watch. In ten minutes' time, he would give the order to cast off the mooring lines. The captain was unaware how many of the twenty passengers spending the night at the hotel had received his hastily sent message. Nor did he know how many of them would show up for the earlier-than-scheduled departure. In fact, he really didn't give a damn. The shipping company would be angry to learn that he had, yet again, treated his passengers with so little consideration; well, tough luck for them. On board the *Agomo,* Dupré alone was master and commander.

For now, the captain just wanted to set out and gain the relative safety of the eastern channel of Georgian Bay, before it was too late.

At about one o'clock in the morning, he noted the dizzying drop in barometric pressure, from 30.4 inches to 28.2 inches in barely a few hours. With a storm on the way, the captain didn't want to be stuck in Collingwood with a hold full of whisky. Delay would expose his crew to temptation, or to the risk of attack. No, their best choice was to run. Dupré had therefore decided to move up the departure time. Even if the weather turned bad on the bay, by taking refuge behind the islands and in the east coast channels, the *Agomo* would avoid the worst.

He got in touch with the engine room: everything was in order. Checking his watch one last time, he ordered the withdrawal of the gangplank. Sailors carried out the order and the ship began to move, its heavy body leaving port very slowly, bending against the waves whipped up by a north wind. Captain Dupré opened the porthole, to breathe in a little bay air. The abrupt arrival of a breathless Robb Fearmòr interrupted this calm moment.

"What's going on?"

Dupré was tempted to simply reply that the ship was leaving. Nonetheless, he was now feeling in a sufficiently good mood to show a bit of kindness towards his distraught passenger.

"It looks like the weather's turning bad. Remaining trapped in Collingwood wouldn't serve your interests, nor mine."

Robb gazed at the captain for a long moment, but did not retort.

"Ask the cabin boy to show you to a cabin; you can have it at the company's expense. You probably wouldn't mind getting a bit more sleep."

Robb turned to leave, but suddenly asked point-blank: "Is it serious?"

The captain adopted a reassuring tone of voice. "If it were, do you think I'd risk my crew, my ship and your precious whisky out on the bay?"

Relieved, Robb left the bridge. For a moment the captain, lost in his thoughts, contemplated the half-light of the coming dawn. Then he noted in the ship's log: "*November 9th, 1913. Departure from Collingwood at 4:50 am. Wind blowing from the north-north-west. A few drops of rain.*"

Ten minutes after the departure of the *Agomo*, Collingwood's telegraph station received an urgent message. An exceptionally large storm was rampaging over the entire northern part of the Great Lakes, moving east at lightning speed. Cleveland already found itself completely buried in snow, cut off from the world. Several boats were fighting for their survival on Lakes Superior, Michigan, and Huron. Caused by the unforeseen and extremely rare meeting of three weather fronts—one from the west, one from the Arctic and the last, hot and humid, from the Gulf of Mexico—the cataclysm was just beginning to engulf the northern half of Georgian Bay. Without knowing it, Captain Dupré had just launched the *Agomo* against the fury of a storm that would merit the title of "the storm of the century".

* * *

"Charlotte, I brought you some tea."

Robb held out a cup to his wife, who was fully dressed and lying stretched out on the bed in their cabin. She accepted it without a word. The ship's movement shook the hot liquid in her hand. Dawn had now come, but the sky was still the colour of lead. The gloom reflected the couple's mood, as well as those of fifteen other passengers, all pulled from their beds. Charlotte drank in silence. Robb went to the porthole, through which he saw only open water. Thirty minutes ago he had seen a lighthouse, the imperial tower on Christian Island, which was the last bit of land before the east coast of Georgian Bay.

"The rain's turned to snow."

Charlotte, paralysed by fear, didn't react. Wet, dense snowflakes stuck to the ship's hull and to the porthole, which had turned white.

"Right, I'm going to go down to the hold to make sure everything's in order." At the door, Robb added, "Try to sleep."

Charlotte looked at him and opened her mouth, but no words came. Still, she smiled. Robb recognised this smile—the one that had welcomed him when she had saved him from the water. This time, however, her eyes were sad. Unable to bear that look for a second more, Robb left the cabin.

He went down to the hold without crossing the deck, where the wind and snow were mercilessly battering the ship. In the hold he found three idle seamen, listening to the waves pounding against the hull. As soon as he entered this dark corner, Robb felt queasy. In vain he tried to strike up a bit of a conversation—particularly with one of the sailors, a young Scot from Glasgow. Tense, the trio focused all their attention on listening to the hull's every creak.

"Down here you're not being shaken up as much as above," Robb commented to encourage the three others.

This remark disconcerted the sailors more than it reassured them. Robb took a walk among the whisky barrels, which were firmly tied down with ropes. He had to hang onto these lines to keep his balance.

At the other end of the hold four horses, a team destined for a lumberjacks' camp on Manitoulin Island, watched him suspiciously.

A seaman dashed into the hold and, gasping for breath, announced: "We're drawing too much water. The captain says to remove ballast."

Robb didn't understand the meaning of this order until he saw the men opening the hold's hatch partway. He cried out: "Don't touch my whisky!"

The seaman from Glasgow had already untied one of the ropes and, with the help of one of his comrades, was beginning to roll a barrel towards the door. The third man went to the horses and, despite their state of panic, was able to lead them up to the open hatch. It took the help of the others to force the distraught animals to move through the door. Their terrified neighing was amplified by the lament of the violent wind and waves.

For a few seconds, astonishment floored Robb. Nonetheless, when the first barrel splashed into the raging water, he rushed at the seamen. At the end of a short tussle, the lad from Glasgow, a ruffian accustomed to using his fists, knocked out Robb. The sailors then returned to their task, throwing into it a new energy brought on by despair.

* * *

Having taken stock of his perilous situation, Captain Dupré tried to take refuge from nature's fury by hurriedly making for shore. Heavy snow had reduced visibility to zero, rendering a fatal meeting with an island or reef more than likely. But the master seaman had exhausted all his options. Throughout his forty years of sailing on the Great Lakes, the old sea dog had never seen such a storm. Waves at least ten metres high assailed the ship. He had ordered the jettisoning of ballast in the hope of raising the ship a little higher in the water. The *Agomo's* engines were no longer even supplying enough power to stay on course against the surging water and gusting wind. Like all Great Lakes mariners, Dupré navigated using dead reckoning, with a compass, lighthouses and the time of day as his only tools. He therefore had only a vague idea of his position in the bay. He sounded the ship's distress signal, knowing all the while that even if it reached human ears, no one could rescue the *Agomo*.

As a last resort, he gave the order to drop anchor. The mooring lines didn't catch, and the craft found itself abandoned to the storm's mercy.

* * *

The *Agomo*, a prisoner of open water, was facing the storm's unbridled wrath. Charlotte had noticed the difference in the waves' movement. In vain she tried to comprehend what was happening and why Robb was taking so long to return.

She decided to equip herself with a life jacket. With great effort, she made her way to the *Agomo*'s deck, now completely buried in a layer of snow and ice. She had no time to realise that the disaster was upon them before it happened. The ship crashed into a reef, and a tremendous impact spread throughout its entire hull. A wave even more massive than the earlier ones scooped up the *Agomo* and threw her down horizontally, with such force that the capsized ship's engines punched through the hull, splitting it in two down its full length. The superstructure broke from the rest of the ship and was carried off into the bay. The few people on deck were thrown into the water. Inside the vessel, instantly transformed into a coffin, everyone else drowned.

The glacially cold water prickled Charlotte's skin. Instinctively she thrashed her arms to regain the surface. Her head reached open air and she breathed in greedily. The tumult of the waves and the raging of the wind filled her ears. Moving her limbs, Charlotte tried to orient herself, searching for some object to cling to: a piece of wood, an oar, anything. The shipwreck had happened so quickly that nothing had managed to escape from the water-swallowed hull.

She made out some rounded shapes bobbing on the water between two waves. Gathering all her strength, Charlotte swam towards twenty barrels, which seemed to be amusing themselves by leaping about on the swell. She exhausted herself trying to grab hold of one of the casks.

Cold numbed all her limbs. Her husband's whisky was offering her one last chance at survival. Robb's name floated to her lips, but she didn't have the strength to scream it.

Charlotte thought of the child inside her. Fighting desperately, she followed a barrel, moving like a dancer imitating her partner's flamenco steps without being able to join her body to his.

She was no longer certain whether she could feel her arms and legs, but she remained aware of the water's movement. Suddenly a wave righted the barrel. Drawing on her last reserves of strength that she'd thought already spent, Charlotte hugged it tightly. Her frozen fingers touched fabric, clutched a tartan scarf. Clinging on for dear life, she was able to press herself flat against the wood. A second later, she found herself horizontal. The cask, tossed from wave to wave, was still bobbing around, but Charlotte, sprayed with water, her hands hooked into the tartan, managed to stay on the barrel, astride this strange mount abandoned to its mad course.

Would the waves push the barrel to shore? The water of the Freshwater Sea, which Charlotte loved with all her heart, would determine her fate. Yet, for thirty-seven ships and two hundred and forty-four sailors and passengers who had had the bad luck of crossing paths with the storm of the century, the water had already made its decision.

55. Massassauga Bay, November 11th, 1913

To Sigefroid Legrand's eyes the morning seemed very dark, despite the sparkle of sunlight reflected by the phenomenal accumulation of snow during the last three days. The peace that now reigned between water and sky, after such cruel hostilities, gave rise to reserved rejoicing. Sigefroid, Délianne and their five children saw in this uncommonly violent storm the beginning of an early, exceptionally hard winter. What's more, Sigefroid and his sons anticipated long days of work repairing the damaged cottages.

Now that it had again become possible to poke one's nose outdoors, Sigefroid suggested to his oldest son, Philippe, that he accompany him on a tour of inspection. More than twenty cottages, most of them less than five years old, dotted the shores of Massassauga Bay.

Father and son busied themselves removing the rowboat from behind the house where they'd sheltered it. As soon as the storm had started, they had surmised that it would be severe. Their dock had survived, minus two planks carried away by the wind. As they placed the rowboat in the water, Philippe tapped his father's arm and pointed towards the bay.

Sigefroid followed his son's gaze. But for his eyes, which had been weakening for a year now, the horizon was no more than a foggy line. He pulled a set of binoculars from a jute bag lying on the bottom of the boat and scrutinised the waters beyond the bay again.

"Damn! It can't be!"

Intrigued by his father's reaction, Philippe took the binoculars and examined the horizon in his turn. "Barrels! At least twenty of them."

The Legrands were in the habit of salvaging construction materials or other objects washed up by the bay after storms, but never as much loot as this fleet, calmly rocked by the water, offered them now. The two men launched the rowboat. Philippe rowed with all the vitality of his thirteen years. Beside him, Sigefroid continued to study the water, in order to determine whether the bay was sending them other bits of flotsam as well. They had crossed about half the distance to the barrels when Sigefroid started cursing with a fury his son had never heard before.

He replaced Philippe at the oars and increased their pace. The son wanted to know what had riled his father so badly.

"There's a woman on the first barrel."

Now it was Philippe who uttered a curse. His father was right. The shape lying on the barrel was wearing a dress. Ten minutes later, their hopes disappeared. The shipwrecked woman was dead, her body covered with a layer of snow and welded to the wood by ice. Sigefroid tried to lift the victim off—and then he saw her face.

"Charlotte!" Stricken, he fell back onto the rowboat's bench. His wife's cousin was returning home at the head of a dismal procession bound for Lighthouse Point.

"She's completely frozen to the barrel. We won't be able to remove her here."

Philippe's voice pulled Sigefroid out of his dark thoughts. If, in spite of this cruel fate, Charlotte had managed to come back to her family, she should at least receive a decent burial.

"Let's attach the barrel to the rowboat."

Philippe found some rope and suggested forming a chain of barrels. They went from one cask to the next, connecting ten barrels and also salvaging a few wooden cases that were floating in the water as well.

"Let's head back," ordered Sigefroid. "We'll get the rest later."

During the return trip, which was considerably slower because of the load being pulled by the rowboat, Sigefroid couldn't prevent his mind from teeming with questions. He knew that Charlotte and her husband had gone on a trip and were supposed to return on board the *Agomo*. Therefore, the dead woman and the barrels no doubt came from the wreckage of this ship. Had others escaped from the condemned vessel? And what did these barrels contain?

Sigefroid then noticed writing on the front of the barrel where Charlotte lay: "Glen Dubh Distillery Ltd 1856". A light went on in his mind. He had heard Robb Fearmòr praising this fabulous whisky from his home country. Sigefroid decided that they would have to do everything they could to save the casks.

The rowboat touched land. *We need to look after Charlotte first*, he said to himself. He lit a fire in a hearth near the water and went to inform Délianne of their sad find. "Don't let the children go outside," Sigefroid advised his wife.

With Philippe's help, he got the barrels out of the water and moved Charlotte close to the fire. After an hour, the barrel and its load had warmed up enough for Sigefroid to separate them. He then began to construct a rudimentary coffin, where Charlotte's corpse was placed. Tomorrow, starting at dawn, he and Philippe would head out to bring Charlotte back to her family and get news of the shipwreck. Today, however, he would work relentlessly until nightfall to gather this strange cargo that Georgian Bay, the Freshwater Sea, had just entrusted to them.

* * *

For an hour, André Roy had been scanning the horizon from the top of Lighthouse Point's imperial tower, searching for a sign of life. He didn't know whether the *Agomo* had kept to its schedule and weighed anchor two days ago. If that was the case, it was very late, and they therefore had good reason to fear the worst. This afternoon's calm water contrasted sharply with the rage of the bay's waves over the last two days. The forest and the rocks, presently covered with a thick layer of snow, were also showing a face very different from the one they had worn yesterday.

All throughout the tempest, day and night, André and his father had operated the lighthouse in case a ship, trapped in the storm, could spot it. Nevertheless, even if an unlucky vessel had been in sight of the lighthouse, the snow carried by the wind had fallen heavily and unceasingly, forming an impenetrable wall that no light or sound could have broken through. When, on the afternoon of the second day, a thick layer of ice had covered the tower's windowpanes, they had to concede defeat. Venturing onto the narrow guardrail outside the lantern room to de-ice the panes would have been suicidal.

André was worried for his sister. Even though both men hadn't dared to mention it, just like his father he hadn't stopped thinking about her while desperately fuelling the lantern.

Suddenly, his heart began to pound very hard. His eyes had just picked out a tiny black cloud rising behind a point—a steamship spitting out smoke from its engines. He tumbled down the steps of the tower. In the kitchen, he announced the boat's imminent arrival to his mother. She asked him whether it was the *Agomo*.

"It's still too far away to tell."

André had barely finished his sentence and he was already outside, where Charles was shovelling snow to open a path to the quay. The young man repeated what he had seen to his father and continued on his way in the snow. Charles went on with his task, since there was no hurry. If his son had just spotted the boat, it would take at least thirty minutes to reach the main channel of Lighthouse Point. Nonetheless, he felt suddenly reinvigorated by the hope of seeing his daughter, or at least of getting news of her.

Twenty minutes later, his wife, Velma, came out of the house with her mother-in-law. Angélique still walked nimbly for an eighty-five-year-old woman. Charles helped both women climb down the steps in the rock. At the quay they found young André, who was pacing up and down. The ship, whose silhouette loomed in the bay, had just sounded its siren to signal its approach.

The Roys craned their necks to guess at its identity. Most of the ships that sailed back and forth along the coast, though operated by rival companies, were of similar design and dimensions. It was therefore impossible to distinguish them from each other from far away. The family had to wait for five more minutes.

"It's the *Borealis*!" cried out André.

The Roys didn't give in to discouragement; after all, this ship, also coming from Collingwood, could be transporting Charlotte and Robb just as well as the *Agomo* could.

When the *Borealis* was close enough to the quay to establish communication, it cut its engines to slow down.

Captain Peter MacNabb came out of the wheelhouse and, to the Roy family's great surprise, asked them,"Have you seen the *Agomo*?"

Charles replied with a negative. According to the captain, that ship had left Collingwood on the morning of November 9th. The lighthouse keeper on Christian Island had seen it pass a few hours later. Since then, no one had any news of the unfortunate craft.

Charles Roy's face turned pale. Still, his voice remained firm. "I'll come aboard. There's a tugboat at the sawmill. We'll organise a search."

The *Borealis* came closer to the quay, and Charles jumped aboard.

"Don't worry," he said to Velma and the others. "I'll only be away a day or two. André, look after the lighthouse."

The *Borealis* went on its way, leaving the Roys motionless and silent on the quay. No one dared to express the sad truth aloud: they would never see Charlotte again.

* * *

The next day, Sigefroid and Philippe arrived at Lighthouse Point and were surprised to learn that they were the only ones to have any information about the disappearance of the *Agomo*. For two days, the tugboat from the sawmill had been exploring all the channels north and south of the area, searching for any sign of the ship. Curiously, it had sunk without leaving the smallest trace. During the next few days, it came to light that lumberjacks working just north of Lighthouse Point had briefly heard a ship's siren at the beginning of the afternoon, but afterwards—nothing.

Besides the *Agomo*, Georgian Bay had claimed only one other victim—namely the *JM Jenks*, run aground on some rocks near Midland, with no loss of life. On the other side of the Bruce Peninsula, however, all along Lake Huron, the shores between Tobermory and Port Elgin bore witness to a catastrophe of a grand scale that was only gradually becoming apparent. People had discovered, among other things, the overturned shell of a boat and countless pieces of debris scattered here and there, from north to south, as well as the bodies of seamen—twenty-five of whom had been found near the community of Goderich.

Other boats took part in the search for the wreck of the *Agomo*. At the end of three days, the grim reality set in: as long as the bay decided to keep its secret, nothing more would be known about the shipwreck.

The funeral of Charlotte Fearmòr, née Roy, was therefore doubly solemn, since it commemorated both the death of a local loved one and the loss of a whole ship and its crew. It took place at the Saint Venerius church in Lighthouse Point the day after the corpse was brought home, and attracted all of the area's inhabitants.

Sigefroid Legrand said that he had found Charlotte's body frozen to a piece of wood, which was entirely true. According to his story, the handyman of Massassauga Bay hadn't recovered any other trace of the wreck. Some residents of Lighthouse Point suspected Sigefroid of hiding certain facts, but no one said so openly. The reason for that was very simple: a large number of them were also concealing their part of the truth.

Other barrels and cases of whisky from the hold of the *Agomo*, conveyed by a mysterious force, had ended up in various channels around the area. They had been found and immediately hidden by more than thirty families. According to the law, the insurance company responsible for compensating the owners of the *Agomo* for their loss would demand all goods recovered from the sunken ship. No one saw any reason to give up this gift from the bay to help a foreign company maintain its profit margin. Furthermore, this was a drinkable commodity, probably one without great commercial value. One might have argued that the barrels should have gone to Charlotte's immediate family. However, by returning this legacy begotten through bad luck to the Roy family, there was a risk of losing it. For that matter, such a deed would raise suspicions as to the existence of other hidden treasures. Everybody believed that at least a barrel or two had to have reached the Roys, who always had their gaze fixed on the bay.

By a cruel, absolutely inexplicable twist of fate, the Roy family was more or less the only one in the Lighthouse Point area that hadn't inherited part of the Fearmòr whisky. During their short ramble along the coast, the casks and cases had avoided passing in front of the lighthouse.

The new whisky owners, each individually and without having even the slightest discussion, chose to keep quiet about their finds. Shortly after Charlotte's funeral, a few of them had risked tasting the recovered Scotch, raising a toast "in honour of the poor deceased woman and her husband". They then concluded that they had been very wise to have opted for discretion.

However, they forgot an inescapable fact: whisky and discretion rarely go hand in hand.

56. Elizabeth, Massassauga Bay

"… And so that's how the Glen Dubh ended up at Lighthouse Point."

For more than an hour, Sabine and Robert have been listening to Elizabeth, their eyes wide with wonder, mesmerised by her incredible tale. Robert gets up from the table where they have just finished the plentiful meal served by Elizabeth. He goes to the sliding door that opens onto the deck. Outside, blackness has already swallowed Massassauga Bay, where the only light is coming from Sigefroid Legrand's old house, which now belongs to his great-granddaughter.

"Did anyone ever find anything else from the *Agomo*?"

Elizabeth shakes her head. "Nothing, except for the whisky and the body of Charlotte Roy. It's very rare for a shipwreck to leave so little behind. The most plausible explanation is that the ship sank very quickly. So no one had time to put on a life jacket or to launch a rowboat. If you like, Robert, I'll take you to the Tortoise Islands. That's supposedly where the *Agomo* sank."

"Was your family the only one that kept the whisky for all these years?" The question comes from Sabine this time.

"Sigefroid Legrand was a very frugal man. He was also the only one to have recovered more than a barrel or two."

"And Charlotte's family never found out that the whisky had reached Lighthouse Point?" asks Robert.

Elizabeth, pouring herself more wine, hesitates before answering. "They did eventually. In fact, that's why, for a long time, Glen Dubh was synonymous with bad luck around here. For my ancestors, this whisky possessed an evil power, a rage that only time would soften. But the others didn't realise that quickly enough, and that's why …"

The ringing of the telephone echoes, and Elizabeth goes to answer. Her two guests question each other with their eyes, anticipating the continuation of this inconceivable story. But their hostess disappoints them.

"I have to go to the distillery. There's a small emergency, but nothing very serious."

"Surely you're not going to travel by boat in this darkness?"

Elizabeth tries to reassure Sabine. "There's no danger. I could navigate these waters blindfolded."

"We'll come with you," suggests Robert.

Elizabeth shakes her head. "No, I invited you to spend the night at my place. Stay and make yourselves at home. I might not make it back before tomorrow." She puts on a coat. "There's a bottle of whisky in the cupboard next to the fridge. Help yourselves."

Shortly after, the sound of a motor disturbs the tranquillity of the night.

"So we'll have to wait for the rest," says Sabine. "What a fabulous story!"

Robert, delighted by this unexpected tête-à-tête, pulls a bottle with the label of the old Glen Dubh on it out of the cupboard. "Shall we share a dram?"

"Gladly."

Robert finds two glasses and fills them.

"*Slàinte!*"

The glasses clink together. As soon as his mouth begins to savour the whisky, Robert rediscovers the Scotch he shared with his Uncle Harry: an authentic Scottish whisky, transformed by a prolonged maturation and a long exposure to water and climate, both unique.

The two drinkers look at each other in silence for a long moment.

"A divine whisky," Sabine comments.

"Yes, not like the New Glen Dubh." Robert, by blurting out his spontaneous comment, has just spilled the beans.

"Elizabeth's whisky won't be able to match this one specifically, or good Scotch in general?" Sabine's accusing tone forces Robert to put his cards on the table.

"It'll no doubt improve with time, but …"

"So you have to help her."

The Scot takes another gulp of whisky. "You're the one who needs help, Sabine. Writing an article on the New Glen Dubh would be a serious mistake."

Sabine is taken aback. Robert opens the sliding door and goes outside. The cold grips him, but the whisky's warmth endures, and the contrast between the two creates a feeling of wellbeing in his whole body. The deep, total silence of this night at the water's edge gives rise to a feeling of ecstasy such as he has never known.

A hand touches his arm.

"For Elizabeth and Lighthouse Point, this distillery is their last chance. Besides, if I could write about how a descendant of the Fearmòr clan saved the New Glen Dubh, this story would become even more enthralling."

In the faint light, Robert can just barely pick out the contours of Sabine's face. His thoughts turn to Scotland, to the memory of the division of the clans, to all those among his people who, over the centuries, preferred crossing over to the English side rather than suffering the oppression of their blood rivals. He'll have to say 'no' to her, but not before …

His lips find Sabine's, along with the taste of the whisky, as though he had just sipped more Glen Dubh. The scent and warmth of the spirits unloose his desire. His eyes desperately search for Sabine's to find out whether she will imprison his longing once again. The whisky has overpowered him like a truth serum. Now he'll have to face the consequences, regardless of whether they are good or bad.

57. Scotland, 1920

Harold got out of the car. He considered the house for a long moment, unable to resign himself to taking this fateful step. And yet he knew it was unavoidable, so what was the point of putting it off?

The modest home was certainly much like its proprietor: simple, almost austere. It was by appealing to this typically Scottish pragmatism, this rock upon which the whisky industry had been built, that Harold was going to try to save his distillery, to save this whisky that had been in the Fearmòr blood for centuries.

Walking lithely, he finally climbed the front steps, now resolved on making this gesture—which, without demeaning him, represented his admission of defeat. There was no way around it. A servant answered the door, and Harold asked to be announced to the master of the house. On hearing his name, the woman couldn't keep from raising her eyebrows slightly before showing him to an armchair in the sitting room. Harold settled in and, in his head, began to repeat his arguments for persuading old man Fearmòr.

Long minutes passed, and Harold started striding back and forth across the narrow room.

"Come, Mr Fearmòr will see you now."

As he followed the maid along a gloomily decorated corridor, his eyes noticed a painting—the portrait of Paul Fearmòr, founder of the Glen Dubh Distillery. His ancestor's hard, determined gaze gave him courage: the power of the Fearmòr whisky transcended that of blood. Robb Fearmòr couldn't turn him down.

"Uncle Robb, thank you for seeing me without prior notice."

His hand held out, Harold took a step towards the old man standing behind a desk. The vigour of the hunched man's grip surprised him. If his father had lived to this age, he would have resembled this man.

Robb Fearmòr pointed to a chair. "Will you have a dram?"

Harold accepted. Happily, even in this upside-down world, a few traditions still held. In this whisky he would surely find the suitably convincing words.

"If you've come to see me, it's surely to give me bad news. From that, I can deduce that this year, once again, I won't get any whisky." Robb spoke while his slightly shaking hand poured.

Harold cleared his throat. "Indeed, it's going to take some time to recover from the war."

Robb uttered the ritual *Slàinte* and the two men drank in silence. Instinctively, Harold kept the alcohol in his mouth for a long moment, letting it pervade his taste buds. Surprised, he realised he was drinking a young Glen Dubh, probably even the 1914 vintage, the last one produced by the distillery before the war and the ban on selling barley to distillers. This policy had assured the British of an adequate supply of grain stocks for the duration of the conflict on the Continent. At the same time, it had deprived whisky makers of their base material.

Moreover, in 1915, David Lloyd George, Chancellor of the Exchequer, had wanted to raise customs duties on whisky. Distillers had persuaded him to accept a compromise, namely to have the Immature Spirits Act passed. In that way, it had become illegal to sell whisky that hadn't been aged for at least three years. This victory for the single malt distillers had been their only comfort during this dark period. The end of the war and the removal of the ban on the use of barley for distillation had come too late. Many distillers had already closed their doors, and others had suspended their operations indefinitely.

The old man keeps the best whisky for himself, Harold pondered. Despite the collapse of Fearmòr Blenders, Harold had judged it prudent to continue the tradition of delivering two barrels of new whisky to his uncle every year.

"How's your son?"

The question disconcerted Harold, who was surprised by his uncle's interest in the family of his hated brother.

"Very well. It's been more than two years since he came home. You'd be surprised to see how nimbly he can get around ..."

Robb Fearmòr's eyes expressed compassion for the twenty-year-old boy who had lost a leg at the battle of Passchendaele. "Damned war!" he spat.

Harold expressed his agreement. For distillers, the First World War had come just at the moment when the whisky industry, propelled by the spectacular growth of the American market, was finally getting back on its feet.

"But at least now production will pick up again."

The moment had arrived, and Harold was grateful to his uncle who, accidentally or on purpose, had just offered him a way of bringing up the subject he had come to discuss.

"That's exactly what we want, Uncle Robb. And yet, what with the United States having just voted in favour of Prohibition ..."

The distillers who had held whisky blenders in contempt were reaping what they had sown. Now, they all depended on this American market that imported only blended Scotches. Robb Fearmòr took a long drink. He had deduced that the very survival of Glen Dubh must be at stake for Harold to have swallowed his pride to come and see him.

"And," Harold continued, "we no longer have the stocks to supply the domestic market while we wait for production to pick up and for the new whisky to age."

Robb nodded, appearing to anticipate what Harold was about to ask.

"If you agreed to sell your barrels of Glen Dubh to us, we could generate enough new capital to at least restart production and weather the next three years."

A sharp pain went through Robb's chest. He succeeded in hiding his unease and, though it cost him much effort, he managed to adopt a hard, pitiless tone. "And in exchange?" He refilled his glass and, with a gesture, invited his nephew to fill his own.

"You'll receive a complete repayment of the whisky's total value over a period of ten years, and twenty percent of the company's stocks."

"What else?" Robb was pushing his nephew to the limit to see just how much he was prepared to pay to save the Glen Dubh.

"The creation of a new division of the company, devoted to producing blends, which would be entrusted to your son, if he wants it."

The old man's eyes widened. Harold was proposing nothing less than the reconciliation of the Fearmòr clan. Robb got up and Harold, sensing his uncle's emotion, followed suit.

And if I spared him? thought the old man. *If I refused, he could blame me, me and my stubbornness for his failure.*

A tear ran down his uncle's cheek. Harold interpreted it as a sign of joy and got up to accept Robb's embrace.

"It's too late."

The hoarseness of his uncle's voice made Harold pull back with fear. His uncle's tears were of grief.

"My Robb … disappeared … with our Glen Dubh."

Harold could make no sense of the old man's monotonous lament until he showed him the photograph of a woman and a telegram dated November 28th, 1913. Harold then realised, with horror, that he *was* too late: the water of the New World had already triumphed over the water of the Old.

On leaving his uncle's house, Harold went to the distillery, to *his* distillery. For long hours, he wandered through the dreary, empty premises: the last time employees had set foot in them had been more than three years ago. In the distilling room, his hand caressed the copper of one of the stills, rested on a dent for a moment. Tomorrow, he would have to go and see the bankers.

The death knell had sounded for the Fearmòr clan. It would continue to exist, but its life, its whisky, the Glen Dubh, would no longer flow, and the place of its birth would from now on remain forever the Dark Valley.

58. Elizabeth, Massassauga Bay

During her absence, a major transformation has occurred. Elizabeth can feel it. Did she hope for this change? Subconsciously, perhaps she did. Nonetheless the tone between the three stays the same as the day before.

"Did you have a good night?"

"Superb," Robert says at last. "But you shouldn't have shown us the bottle of Glen Dubh. After two glasses, temptation tormented us for the rest of the night."

You resisted that temptation, thinks Elizabeth, *but not the other one.* Her suspicions confirmed, she decides to have a little fun.

"This whisky spurs us into giving in to our worst passions. I had just started telling you about that yesterday evening."

Her glance makes Robert visibly uneasy. Elizabeth rubs it in a little more.

"The night was cool. I hope you two weren't cold."

Sabine, who is avoiding Elizabeth's eyes, fidgets nervously. "Robert and I talked to each other frankly. You were right." She moves closer to Robert and takes his hand. "He doesn't want to tell you what's missing in the whisky."

The stunned Scot's eyes go from one woman to the other.

"We need you, Robert." Elizabeth's voice has become gentle, almost pleading.

Robert finally finds his own. "No, I can't."

Sabine lets go of his hand. The two women have lost the game. Even so, if Sabine manages to forgive Robert his loyalty to his country's whisky, she can hold on to him, while Elizabeth …

"And if I offer you the very best Glen Dubh in return for your help?" Elizabeth's tone has become hard-edged again. She takes a deep breath. "There's a barrel that's never been opened ..."

Incredulous, Robert and Sabine learn that the oldest cask of Glen Dubh pulled from Georgian Bay carried the date 1856. The contents of this cask have been left intact and have therefore continued to age in the barrel. No one has ever tasted it.

"If you help me, it's yours."

Elizabeth's proposition, the opportunity to drink the oldest whisky in the world, leaves Robert momentarily speechless.

"I'd have to taste it first."

Elizabeth smiles. The game isn't over yet. "Of course. We can do that right away."

The sentence is tossed out like a challenge immediately accepted. Elizabeth guides her two guests towards the cellar. When she lights the naked bulb, the pale light is reflected on the dark wood of the barrel. With the reverence of a priest entering a crypt, Robert caresses the rough surface of the barrel and slides his hand over the black lettering: "Glen Dubh Distillery Ltd. 1856". He recognises the pattern of the tartan tied around the cask: it's the Fearmòr clan's, his clan's.

He must be hallucinating. Does this barrel truly contain the memory of his ancestors, the water of their life? Time and the elements will surely have transformed them. This whisky can no longer be the true Glen Dubh. Nevertheless, it must still contain its basic essence. By tasting it, Robert will be able to commune with his forebears, discover the soul and spirit of the vanished Glen Dubh.

The Scot's ceremonious attitude doesn't escape the two women. Elizabeth hands him a pocket knife and the tools to siphon the whisky.

"We'll let you do the honours."

Robert complies, concentrating very hard in order to control the trembling in his hands. Once he has finished extracting the cork and inserting the siphon into the barrel, Elizabeth presents him with a carafe. He looks at both women for a long time before breathing deeply into the siphon and setting off the flow of whisky. The liquid reaches the carafe rapidly, tasting open air for the first time in almost a century and a half.

Shortly after, Elizabeth plugs the siphon with her finger. A gurgle of air announces the end of the operation. The perfume of the liberated whisky floats in the dark, narrow room. Robert perceives subtle notes of heather, coffee, chocolate, oak, and of a whole range of scents that stimulate emotions and sensations buried in the deepest part of his being. Elizabeth fills three tulip-shaped glasses and then distributes one to Robert and another to Sabine. She then mounts the barrel astride and raises her glass.

"*Slàinte*!"

All three swallow their whisky and, during the next few seconds, give themselves over to an intense rapture, feel themselves dive into exquisitely sweet waters. Robert is overwhelmed by the whisky and the sensual, spiritual joy it ignites in him. A wave from the past has just broken over him, leaving behind the outline of his future, of his destiny.

The silence lingers for long seconds, maybe for minutes. Robert, Sabine and Elizabeth are no longer aware of the passage of time.

"So, do we have a deal?"

Elizabeth's voice calls Robert back to this cold room, which holds life born from death. His eyes waver between Elizabeth, perched on her barrel like a little girl on a wooden horse, and Sabine's satisfied smile—between his present and his future.

"First, let's go back upstairs to settle in comfortably around another dram," Robert suggests, "while you tell us the end of your story."

A few minutes later, in the presence of the old Glen Dubh, Elizabeth finishes her tale from the previous night, enthralling her two guests yet again.

59. Lighthouse Point, 1920

Just as he did every November, André Roy was thinking of his sister, of the 1913 storm that had taken her away from her family. Seven years had passed, and yet the memory of that day still remained, as vivid and painful as ever. Maybe if this terrible shipwreck hadn't set in motion a whole series of changes at Lighthouse Point, André would have come to forget it a little. Since this catastrophe, however, the area and its people had become nearly unrecognisable.

André stared at his mother's hands as they adjusted the knot of his tie. He was wearing this suit for the third time. The first had been at Charlotte's funeral, and the second had been last year, at the burial of his grandmother Angélique. Today his marriage to Jeanne Cascagnette would give André a reason to associate this suit with something other than death from now on.

"That's good."

Velma, who was also dressed in her Sunday best, admired her work and how sharp her son looked. Outside, they found Charles Roy scanning the horizon. The sailing season was ending—which was the main reason why the engaged couple had chosen exactly this moment for their marriage. André and his wife would be able to go south for their honeymoon and return just before the ice set in.

The family climbed down to the dock, where they boarded a wooden launch, equipped with a small cabin and a combustion motor. This new type of vessel had just appeared along the shores of Georgian Bay. The Roys, as lighthouse keepers, were among the first to have one, thanks to the government.

André helped his father start the motor and they set off. When they passed in front of the Lighthouse Point hotel, André raised his voice to make himself heard over the noise of the motor.

"The banquet room looks beautiful. Mrs Saunders arranged everything."

Still, from the look in his parents' eyes, André guessed that mentioning the hotel reminded them of Charlotte and Robb. After the couple's death, André's parents had inherited the hotel. They had been forced to let the bank have it, because of the establishment's outstanding debts. The hotel had later been sold to the Saunders, a couple from Toronto. For three years they had been running it, but with much less elegance than their predecessors.

The wedding took place in the early afternoon, followed by the reception in the hotel banquet room rented by the newlyweds at a discount price.

The launch entered a series of channels where rustic-looking cottages surrounded by trees stood here and there on the rock. For a few years now, summer residences had been multiplying at a frightening pace. As they approached the church, André noticed the boats and the teams of horses, a sign that some of the guests had arrived. Lighthouse Point now had three streets connecting the various points of the expanded village. One of these roads led to the sawmill, which had remained silent for several months. In fact, no one knew whether the owner would re-open the mill in the spring. The men and families who depended on it lived under a cloud of uncertainty and want. A climate of moroseness had thus descended on the village and the surrounding area.

Next, there had been this far-away war that had forced young men to either go away and take up arms, or hide in the woods to avoid being drafted.

Lighthouse Point's tranquillity was also troubled by the quick-tempered behaviour of certain villagers usually known for their gentleness. Théodore Lafrenière had beaten his wife one day, while on a wild binge. The brothers Alphonse and Jean-Baptiste Thanasse had come to blows during a drinking session that had almost killed them. Gédéon Vasseur had been found dead, with his rifle and an empty flask of whisky by his side. Officially, it had been called an accident, but everyone believed it had been a suicide. In short, for several years, men in a drunken state had been engaging in reprehensible acts. And yet Prohibition was in full swing, making these sad events, inspired by drink, even more surprising.

No alcohol would be served at the wedding, but a few guests would probably find a way to get intoxicated. Hardly any community celebrations took place without at least one or two drunk people showing up.

André was very impatient to get these celebrations over with, so that he could be alone with Jeanne in the best room in the hotel and in their new life. The next day, the couple would board their ship, and enjoy their first six days of private intimacy, which would perhaps prove to be their last. On their return, they would move into André's parents' house. The anticipation of his upcoming joy comforted him as he entered the church. *Charlotte would be pleased*, he thought.

* * *

"… So let's wish long life and happiness to the bride and groom."

Clamour filled the banquet room, where fifty guests were offering the couple their good wishes. Since they were unable to raise a glass, people applauded or jingled their cutlery. Shortly afterwards, the meal ended and the tables were put away to make room for dancing. The sound of the fiddle started lifting feet, and no matter whether seated or standing, people tapped to the beat. The Lighthouse Point hotel had never known such a joyful celebration, and André was jubilant as well.

The hall was soon stuffy from all this human activity. The young groom felt the need to get a breath of fresh air. On the porch in front of the hotel, he breathed the cool air deeply, watching the darkness of day's end as it transformed water as well as land into a black sheet. His parents and other guests had already left; soon it would be over and the rest of the night would belong to the newlyweds.

"Hey! André, come over here."

In the dark, he recognised the laughing voice as belonging to his cousin, Philippe Legrand. Fearing the worst, he moved a few metres towards the laughter. Well hidden behind a wall of the hotel, he found three young men: Philippe, his brother Joseph, and Anselme Vasseur. When Philippe spoke again, André's suspicions were confirmed.

"Have a little drink for your wedding."

"You might need it soon," added Anselme, chuckling.

Philippe, flask in hand, offered a glass to André, who felt his anger rise. Nonetheless, he calmed himself quickly. After all, they were celebrating his marriage, and the boys, even though they were a little tipsy, were being discreet and not disturbing anyone.

"Why not?" he reasoned, accepting the glass.

Philippe raised his flask, and the two others raised their glasses.

"To you and Jeanne!" Anselme declared.

Without thinking, Philippe uttered the words all the local whisky drinkers had gotten into the habit of repeating when they raised a toast.

"To Charlotte!"

André was speechless. "What did you say?"

Realising his mistake, Philippe got tangled up in his words as he presented confounded explanations. The glass André had quickly downed fell to the ground. He grabbed his cousin by the neck. An implacable logic in his suddenly muddled mind made the connection between the whisky still present in his mouth and the memory of his sister.

"Where does this whisky come from?"

The question remained without reply, and André turned on Philippe. The two others tried to intervene, but André shoved them violently away. He repeated his question tirelessly, hammering Philippe with punches that fell like rain.

Philippe's face, abandoned to this unleashed fury, was no more than a swollen, bloody mess when he finally revealed to André the secret that all of Lighthouse Point had kept from the Roys of the lighthouse. His hands and clothes stained with blood, his heart torn to shreds, André finally stopped. With heavy steps he went to find his wife, who would spend her wedding night, and several others after, trying to close her husband's wounds.

André and Philippe, even though they would continue to meet and live a few kilometres away from each other for another forty years, never spoke to each other again. Philippe never drank another drop of Glen Dubh and, after his father's death, when he inherited the Fearmòr whisky, he could neither resign himself to handing it over to the Roy family nor to destroying it.

Was the curse of the Glen Dubh over or simply giving them a reprieve? The subsequent generations of Lighthouse Point inhabitants would be the ones to find out.

60. Robert, Lighthouse Point

A tongue of fire, a radiant manifestation of an occult power, springs from the round, polished rock. Despite the ten people present, nothing can be heard but the crackling of the blaze, glowing with a vibrant colour matching the trees a few metres away. Robert, whose every move is being watched by vigilant eyes, feels like a wizard, because he's being asked to perform nothing less than magic.

He gestures to Elizabeth. With the help of two men, she moves the tripod, from which hangs a barrel, until it's standing over the flames. Robert puts on a pair of work gloves. He pokes the fire with a long stick to make the flame rise. Next, still using the stick, he positions the barrel, whose heads and hoops have been removed, directly above the tongues of fire that lick and char its interior.

"Enough!" cries Robert, moving the barrel away from the flames with his stick.

On the other side of the fire, the two men detach the barrel and set it down on the rock, where Elizabeth sprays it with a hose, creating a thick cloud of steam. Sabine takes photographs of the operation.

"Put up the next one."

The men attach another barrel and throw it toward the fire, where it undergoes the charring process. Lacking an appropriate space inside the distillery, Robert has decided to work outdoors, on the rock. Elizabeth didn't hesitate when Robert ordered that the barrels be fired to give the whisky a smoky, distinct finish. So, each of the casks full of whisky have been emptied in order to be "charred".

With his back to the forest and to Scotland, Robert faces the west, faces the open water behind the fire and the brazen autumn sun of

Georgian Bay. The work he's performing reveals one secret, but hides another: he's betraying Elizabeth to save his country's whisky. Who wills the end, wills the means. This ignoble perfidy will allow him to repatriate the barrel of Glen Dubh. This treasure belonging both to his family and his country is spurring him to revive the whisky that has never really stopped flowing in his veins.

If he really knew how to save Elizabeth's whisky, would he do it? He doesn't know the answer. To avoid losing the barrel of Glen Dubh, Robert lied. Some distilleries char the insides of their barrels as a way of enhancing the aromas and the colour of their whisky. In the past, the Fearmòrs used this technique. In the case of the New Glen Dubh, it won't change anything. In six years' time, when the first native whisky of Lighthouse Point is put on sale, Elizabeth won't be able to touch him. And if Sabine is still in his life, will she be able to forgive him? He needs to take this risk.

"You can judge when to stop the firing by looking at the barrel."

Elizabeth takes meticulous note of all of Robert's instructions. Next time, she'll have to carry out this delicate operation without his help. The barrel charring lasts all day. Once the process is over, other distillery employees roll the casks to the filling room, where they will once again be filled with whisky.

Night is just beginning to fall when Robert entrusts the charring of the last barrels to Elizabeth. Exhausted, he goes to the apartment in the distillery and crashes on a couch. A few minutes later, Sabine comes to nestle against him.

"I have to leave tomorrow."

A shudder runs through Robert's body. "When will we see each other again?"

"Soon. You can come to see me at my cottage."

Robert imagines this moment with pleasure. Nonetheless, on his return to Scotland, he'll have a lot on his plate.

"You made the right choice." Sabine kisses him.

She can't possibly imagine what this barrel of Glen Dubh means to me, thinks Robert, *nor to what lengths I'd go to get it.*

Elizabeth abruptly enters the room. "The firing is all done. Let's drink to that." Ecstatic, she takes out some *Cuan fìor-uisge*, the New Glen Dubh deluxe whisky.

"To Charlotte," she says, raising her glass.

"And to Robb Fearmòr," adds Robert.

Sabine talks of her departure, and then Robert discusses his and the arrangements to be made for shipping his barrel. Helped by a second glass, the atmosphere is relaxed.

"You know, you Scots and Canadian Francophones have something in common."

Sabine's comment piques the others' curiosity.

"Besides the fact that we've both been colonised by the damned English and abandoned by France, I don't see your point," Robert declares.

"We, at least, kept our language," Elizabeth teases.

The Scot raises his glass in a gesture of resignation. "*Rinn thu 'n gnothach orm! Alba bochd!*"

"No," Sabine says at last, "it's rather that you both love the French: the Canadians, for reasons of language and culture, and the Scots because we're the world's greatest drinkers of their single malt."

"*Tapadh leibh a Fraing!*" Robert raises his glass again and turns to Elizabeth. "Before I leave, can you take me to see the site of the shipwreck?"

Elizabeth agrees.

"I want to pay my last respects to Robb. You and he have helped me find my mission. By my hand, the Glen Dubh will be reborn."

Dumbstruck, Elizabeth looks at Robert.

"I'm going to found my own distillery. Tasting this old Glen Dubh has given me the urge to get back in the saddle. In a few years, your New Glen Dubh will have some serious competition from the old one."

Sabine kisses Robert, and Elizabeth, hiding her deep disappointment, congratulates him. By seeking to ensure the survival of her whisky, has she, on the contrary, unleashed the evil forces of its destruction?

61. Massassauga Bay, 1961

"Elizabeth, go and find me your sister's bottle."

The four-year-old girl got up from the floor, where she had been sitting watching her mother in the rocking chair, baby in arms. In the kitchen, she found the bottle on the table, and came back to give it to her mother. The baby coughed violently and Rosita leaned over her, mopping up the red-tinted saliva at the corner of the child's mouth.

"Is Louise sick?"

The apprehension in her mother's face worried Elizabeth more than her sister's health did. To tell the truth, though she had enjoyed the arrival of a little sister in the beginning, Elizabeth had quickly become disillusioned; her mother neglected Elizabeth to look after her second daughter.

"Maybe. We're going to take her to see the doctor in Parry Sound."

The little girl clapped her hands, delighted to be taking a trip. As it was early February, the very heart of winter, visits were a rare event for Elizabeth and her family, the only inhabitants of Massassauga Bay. So, the idea of venturing out in her father's scoot, a noisy boat capable of going over snow, ice and water, was cause for excitement, no matter the reason behind it.

Rosita looked hard at Elizabeth, trying to seem very serious and reassuring at the same time.

"Actually, we're going to leave you at your Uncle Edward's at the lighthouse. We don't know how long we'll be in Parry Sound, so you'll wait for us at his house and have a good time with your cousins …"

"It's not fair!"

The little girl's complaint rang out at the same time as the voice of Félicien Legrand, who had just come back indoors.

"We can leave now."

Rosita got up and grabbed Elizabeth's hand. At the door, she passed the baby to Félicien and helped Elizabeth put on her winter clothes.

"She's still spitting up blood," Félicien said in a tone echoing both worry and frustration.

Elizabeth went on grumbling, but Félicien and his wife ignored her. Outside, she followed her parents along a path surrounded by a wall of snow that loomed above her head. The day before, flakes had fallen in abundance—and now the grey sky, heavy with clouds, was getting ready to pour down even more. Félicien, who hoped to get to the hospital before nightfall, was regretting that he didn't have access to a telephone, like the people living on the mainland.

Thirty steps later, the family arrived at the scoot, and Félicien pulled on the handle welded to the deck of the craft, turning it to face the open water. His wife and Elizabeth climbed aboard to settle in on the seats behind the windshield.

He then went to the stern, where an enormous eight-cylinder aluminium motor, recycled from an airplane, sat imposingly. Placing his hands on the wooden propeller, the right at two o'clock and the left at seven o'clock, he shouted to Rosita. "Turn the key."

She made contact, while Félicien took a deep breath and started the propeller with a quick push, drawing his hands back in the same movement. The blades began to turn and the motor came to life with a deafening roar. Félicien was particularly proud of this machine, his third scoot. The flat hull, three metres long, made of wood covered with galvanised sheet metal, made the vehicle particularly fast when sliding on the ice or compacted snow. Its powerful motor had helped him win the scoot races held during the Penetanguishene Winterama for three straight years. Last year, he had broken all the old records by reaching the lightning speed of one hundred and sixty kilometres an hour.

There were now tens of these vehicles all along the east coast of Georgian Bay. For twenty years these singular crafts, all home-made and each one therefore different from the next, had transformed winter life. The isolated inhabitants up the shore could now easily get about during the long months when treacherous ice covered the channels. For Félicien, his scoot guaranteed him a quality of life greatly surpassing what Philippe, his father, had known. He could easily get to the cottages to carry out maintenance work, or go shopping in town when the need arose. And, today, his scoot would maybe help him save his youngest daughter's life.

The thirty-two-year-old man settled in at the vessel's wheel, which was connected to a rudder attached behind the motor. He pushed the gas throttle as far as it would go and, like a plane at take-off, the air-propelled vehicle sprang forward. Elizabeth let out a cry of joy.

The scoot ploughed towards the open water and, rounding the last point of dry land, it entered a section of the bay that was still ice-free due to the constant movement of the waves. The transition from ice to water was abrupt. The vehicle slowed down, but broke itself a path by cleaving the icy waves. Just before arriving at the lighthouse, it slid out of the water back onto the ice. Piloting the brakeless vehicle with an expert hand, Félicien parked it just beside his brother Edward's, at the bottom of the point where the lighthouse stood.

The family got out of the scoot and, with Elizabeth in the lead, climbed up to the lighthouse keeper's residence, where they were welcomed by Edward, his wife Rhéa, their two daughters and two sons. Seeing his brother arrive with his family, Edward thought at first that they were coming for a social call. When he learned the real reason for this trip, he furrowed his eyebrows.

"Little Zab's favourite uncle is going to take care of her," he cried. "What a lucky girl!"

* * *

Elizabeth felt abandoned. When her parents went to the door to leave, she made a terrible scene until her father threatened to spank her in front of everyone.

Her mother kissed her and dried her tears. "It won't be long, Elizabeth. Be good."

After her parents' departure, the little girl promised herself she'd stay resentful for a very long time. She didn't know, then, that it would be for life.

62. Elizabeth, Lighthouse Point

The muffled buzzing worms itself into her ears, working its way into the depths of her memory, where it revives the far-off recollection of another sound. Robert, seated facing Elizabeth in the distillery apartment, hears it too. For him, it's simply an airplane motor.

Elizabeth goes outside. Robert joins her and follows the circular movement of a seaplane preparing for a water landing.

"Are you expecting visitors?"

Elizabeth shakes her head. The rumble of the engine gets louder as the plane loses altitude. The hum of the scoot in her memory becomes more and more acute, just like the image of the vehicle approaching the lighthouse dock with its gruesome load.

The aircraft stabilises on the water like a Canada goose landing with a final flutter of its wings. The seaplane stops at the quay and the door opens. It's not her uncle Edward getting out of the craft, but rather John MacPhearson, with a briefcase in his hand and a tired smile on his lips.

"Hi there! I'm springing a little surprise on you." MacPhearson gives Elizabeth a kiss on the cheek and next turns to the Scot. "Robert Fearmòr, I was very keen to meet you before your departure."

The two men exchange a handshake.

"Is that why you came by plane?"

How did he get wind of Robert's presence? Elizabeth then remembers her suggestion to Sabine to go and see the Dearg Room before taking her flight from Toronto. Did the Frenchwoman reveal something else to MacPhearson as well?

"I can only stay for a few hours."

MacPhearson invites the pilot to join them. Inside the distillery,

Elizabeth settles her guests in comfortably. MacPhearson begins to bombard Robert with questions.

"According to Sabine, you've given us some invaluable advice."

This collective "us" uttered by MacPhearson irritates Elizabeth. *He's not here just to meet Robert*, she thinks. With pleading eyes, she urges Robert to be discreet. Will he get the message?

"And I've finished giving it," the Scot declares after an uncomfortable silence. "I'm going home. Leaving tomorrow, in fact."

"I can take you back to Toronto if you like."

Robert reads the apprehension in Elizabeth's eyes. "Thanks. But I have to pick up my rental car in Parry Sound. Elizabeth's going to take me back there by boat."

If he's disappointed, MacPhearson hides it well.

"I have business to discuss with you, Elizabeth," he continues, picking up his briefcase. "Let's go into your office. Afterwards, maybe we could share a dram."

He gets to his feet. MacPhearson is behaving like he owns the place. His agreement with Elizabeth does, in fact, give him the final word on how the New Glen Dubh is managed. Taken aback, she follows him.

As she closes the door of her office behind them, Elizabeth feels a shiver, the premonition of a tragedy. She can't keep herself from dwelling on that sinister day when, at the age of four, her life was irredeemably turned upside down. If bad luck decides to attack her again, this time it will be facing an adversary old enough and well armed to defend herself.

63. Georgian Bay, 1961

In less than an hour, the weather had gotten warmer, softening the ice and snow considerably. Next the sky had begun to pour down wet flakes.

"We've taken on a lot of ice," Félicien shouted to Rosita.

The scoot's motor was struggling to push the vehicle forward on the sticky snow—which, to make matters worse, was adhering to the large sheets of ice building up on the hull. They were about halfway between Lighthouse Point and Parry Sound, but now only moving at a snail's pace. Exasperated, Félicien cut the motor.

"I'll have to break the lumps of ice."

Grabbing his axe, he climbed out of the scoot and, using the flat side of the tool, began hitting the hull with hard blows. Rosita rocked the baby, who was swaddled in wool blankets. The wet snow, which was falling harder and harder, filled her with a clammy cold. Her husband went on striking the ice, spitting out a curse from time to time.

Even though she liked their way of life up the shore, Massassauga Bay wasn't always a convenient place to raise a family. Before moving here, Rosita had only known farm living with her family in Lafontaine, a few kilometres west of Penetanguishene.

"Turn the key!"

Rosita obeyed and Félicien turned the blades. However, the motor didn't start. Félicien tried again a second and a third time, without success.

"Christ! There must be water on the spark plugs. Break contact."

Félicien let tools and parts fly, giving his frustration free rein. Rosita was relieved when, twenty minutes later, he instructed her to make contact again.

The motor still refused to start. Impatient, Félicien positioned his hands back on the blades and pushed with all his strength. His right foot slid just as he activated the propeller.

The deafening noise of the motor finally rang out and, turning around, Rosita saw the hypnotising whirl of the propeller, but not Félicien. She shouted his name, barely hearing her own voice above the hellish buzzing. A feeling of panic squeezed her chest. Still calling to her husband, she put Louise down on the seat and climbed out of the scoot.

When she discovered his body on the ground, the head almost completely severed from the torso, she no longer had the strength to scream nor to do anything but turn away from the sea of blood soaked up by the snow. Rosita's thoughts tried to organise themselves in her head, but the unrelenting and appalling din of the motor seemed to be laughing at her and at Félicien, its victim. Finally, she ran to the deck of the scoot, hauled herself up onto the side and stretched her hand out towards the key. The motor coughed a few more seconds before falling silent.

Rosita's breath came in quick pants. The hiss of the wind brushing the tops of the pines offered her a familiar, comforting, and gentle music that had replaced the whirring of the motor. After a long moment, the song of the trees reminded her that she was in an isolated place, without any dwellings within a ten kilometre radius. Touching this horrible machine was out of the question. At any rate, she didn't know how to drive the craft.

A cry came from the scoot. With one leap, she boarded the vehicle and took the baby in her arms, suddenly becoming aware of her own tears.

I can't stay here. Rosita mustered all her courage: she had to follow the channel to Parry Sound, towards help. Maybe, with a bit of luck, she would meet another traveller. She took a few steps and got stuck in the snow up to her knees. This long, difficult walk would be impossible with a baby in her arms. *Eskimos live in houses made of snow. Louise will be able to wait for me and stay warm, wrapped up in her blankets.* Rosita set down her baby and began to dig a hole in a snow bank. Once the shelter was made, she kissed Louise's hot face, bundled her up in the blankets and placed her in the hole. The child was sleeping at present, as though she trusted her mother's ability to save them from this dreadful danger.

One last time, Rosita looked at the mutilated body of the man she loved. At least Elizabeth was safe at her uncle's. She took the first steps of a long, desperate walk, her footprints disappearing in the deep snow and the depths of dusk. No, her little daughter was not going to lose her entire family. Her mother wouldn't allow it.

64. Elizabeth, Lighthouse Point

"To the New Glen Dubh!"

Robert's glass clinks against the two others. Elizabeth's eyes are sombre and troubled. She can't drive a disturbing image out of her head—that of the little package, wrapped in a white blanket, recovered by the rescue workers near her father's decapitated body. This package—so tiny, yet so horrible—which was responsible for the death of her parents. This package called Louise. For many years, people up the shore had gone on telling the tragic story of the Legrands and their mother's heroic act. However, no one ever spoke of Elizabeth's childhood spent waiting in vain for the return of her mother, disappeared forever under the ice of Georgian Bay.

"And to the Fearmòr clan," adds Elizabeth before drinking.

"Come to my bar before returning to Scotland," MacPhearson suggests to Robert. "I'll give you the chance to taste some whiskies that will surprise you."

"I've already delayed my departure by several days," Robert replies circumspectly. "But next time, I'll come to see you for sure."

Shortly after, MacPhearson and his pilot leave.

"Tomorrow morning, we'll load your barrel onto the boat, and then we'll go for a cruise around the Tortoise Islands," says Elizabeth.

Robert looks pleased at this last ramble.

All during the return trip to her house, Elizabeth retains her pensive air. When they pass in front of the lighthouse, she makes her usual greeting. "He wants to transform all this into an amusement park!" She's completely disgusted by MacPhearson's plans.

"It's not whisky that can save Lighthouse Point," he had declared to her, "but whisky tourism. We'll build a hotel next to the distillery, organise tours of the lighthouse, boat cruises in the summer, and snowmobile excursions in the winter." He had shown her the sketch of the luxurious house he aims to build for himself on the site of the old hotel.

In this new Lighthouse Point Elizabeth sees no place for herself, not even at the distillery. Once production is running smoothly, MacPhearson will surely want to replace her with a real stillman, like Robert. The way he had hovered around the Scot had been quite telling.

Should she try to convince Robert to become her ally? And if he refuses? Elizabeth is assailed by the question. She has few options left, and even less time.

That evening, she climbs down to the cellar with Robert, to prepare the cask of Glen Dubh for its long journey. Delicately, Robert removes the tartan attached to the barrel and folds it carefully. With a thousand precautions, Robert and Elizabeth place the barrel in another, larger plastic one. Next this sarcophagus is placed in a wooden case.

"Couldn't we take one last wee dram from it, a *deoch an dorus*?"

Robert agrees and sets about obliging Elizabeth. Once the whisky is drawn from the barrel, he seals it and finishes the packing.

"Almost ninety years to the day after its arrival at Lighthouse Point, the Glen Dubh is undertaking its final journey home," proclaims the Scot.

Elizabeth raises her glass. "To the return of the Glen Dubh."

They savour the whisky, letting its calming wave sweep them away. Their eyes meet, and the two drinkers sense a communion of minds and a singular emotion that not even the best stillman or most gifted noser in Scotland could understand.

"Elizabeth, I'd like to …"

Robert hesitates. *The barrel charring will do nothing for her whisky. It's cruel of me to leave her this false hope …*

"I want to …"

Elizabeth's eyes draw him into a depth where he plunges, plunges and loses himself.

"… give you this." Robert pulls a worn photograph out of his wallet.

"Charlotte!"

The whisky hurtles like a torrent in Elizabeth's head. Even without ever having seen a photograph of her great-aunt, she recognises her. This tormented face in which she sees herself has appeared in the whisky several times. Now the vision gives her the courage to see this through to the end—as well as the certainty that she'll succeed.

65. Clan Legrand, Blair Atholl, Scotland

"First of all, I'd like to say a few words to you about Ms Legrand."

The two hundred guests gathered in the great hall of Blair Castle for the presentation of the honorary titles of the Keepers of the Quaich society are all ears. The master of ceremonies, Harry Fearmòr, recounts the founding of the New Glen Dubh Distillery by Elizabeth Legrand, and this whisky's unique journey over the last ten years. The woman just named, sitting next to John MacPhearson, smiles and pretends to listen attentively. The two Canadians are about to be admitted into this prestigious society founded by the great distillers to honour the most illustrious promoters of Scotch the world over. The woman reflects on the parts of the story the presenter doesn't reveal, the events of that November day six years ago, which remain, for her and for everybody else, a mystery. *If Robert Fearmòr were here, I would know …*

"… I therefore have the honour of introducing to you the president and manager of the New Glen Dubh Distillery, Ms Louise Legrand."

The woman gets up and, with confident strides, climbs onto the stage. *Zab would appreciate this ridiculous pomp a lot more than I do.* In her mind, Louise replays the scene of her arrival, the military guard's welcome at the castle door where she had solemnly sworn to the duty officer that she would adhere to the principles of the Keepers of the Quaich. Next, ten bagpipers had trumpeted the guests' entry into the vast hall with its walls decorated with one hundred and fifty sets of stags' antlers.

"I thank you most sincerely for this honour, which I accept in the name of my sister, the true creator and distiller of the New Glen Dubh."

As she reads her speech, Louise asks herself whether her sister would approve of it; she also wonders what kind of fate the New Glen Dubh would have known had Elizabeth lived.

"Elizabeth would be very proud of this tribute. Her memory inspires us, the people of Lighthouse Point, to continue her work."

We'll never know what happened that day, thinks Louise. *It's inconceivable that Zab, who knew Georgian Bay so well, would have allowed herself to be caught in that predictable storm. And it's strange that not the smallest trace of the boat, her body or Robert Fearmòr's was ever found.*

"... To conclude, I extend an invitation to you all. Just as tens of thousands of Scotch admirers do every year, come see us at the New Glen Dubh Distillery."

Applause resounds once again. Louise returns to her place beside MacPhearson.

"Bravo, Louise."

The old bastard loves money even more than whisky! At least thanks to that, we can get along. All the more so, since he's right.

After Elizabeth's death, Louise had been surprised to learn that her sister had taken out a life insurance policy designating Louise as her beneficiary. Since the inquiry into her disappearance had concluded that it was an accidental sinking, this policy had paid out a significant sum to the younger Legrand. With this capital, Louise, the heiress of Elizabeth's share of the distillery, had convinced MacPhearson to accept a settlement of the business's debt, and to sell her a majority stake. The businesswoman had concealed her game well; MacPhearson had never imagined that Louise had smelled the profits to be made from whisky tourism. Fearing the collapse of the distillery, MacPhearson had been very happy to accept her offer.

Thanks to the publicity generated by Sabine de Grandmont, the New Glen Dubh had been awaited with anticipation. When, two years ago, tasters had sampled this first native whisky from Georgian Bay they had unanimously raved about it. The orders had poured in, and there had been speculative bidding on the casks of the still maturing whisky. Contrary to his own expectations, Robert Fearmòr had, through the barrel charring process, endowed the whisky with a distinct, delicious character.

Faced with the new distillery's triumph, the Scottish whisky makers, being the pragmatic business people they are, had found it to be in their best interest to make an ally of the New Glen Dubh rather than an enemy. So long as this Canadian single malt whisky never aspired to the title of 'Scotch whisky', they would manage to live with it—and even take advantage of it, by profiting from the fascination aroused by the extraordinary story of the new and old Glen Dubh.

Louise, on returning to live in her parents' house at Lighthouse Point, had learned something that MacPhearson didn't know: Elizabeth had rigorously trained all the employees of the distillery, notably her right hand, Ghisèle Chevalier. Moreover, since every stage of production had been meticulously documented, by following the recipe the staff could continue to produce the same high quality whiskies, both the blends and the single malts.

The concept of whisky tourism, developed by Louise in collaboration with the people of Lighthouse Point and the Ojibway natives from the surrounding area, was a resounding success. Thousands of visitors, mostly Europeans, flocked to the distillery both in summer and winter. The theme "The waters of life: savour the spirits and a spiritual experience" invited tourists to sip a whisky while gazing out over the waters of Georgian Bay and, the next day, purify their spirits in an Ojibway sweat lodge, by burning some sacred sweetgrass.

"A very beautiful ceremony," says Louise, smiling at Harry Fearmòr.

"Yes. My only regret is that my nephew Robert isn't here with us."

He more likely regrets having sent him to us, thinks Louise.

"By the way," adds Fearmòr, "I think I've found a genealogical tie between our families."

Louise is taken aback. "You can't be serious. The Legrands come from France, from Normandy."

"It's because of the Gaelic."

Interpreting Louise's silence as encouragement, Harry Fearmòr continues.

"Let me tell you a bit of family history."

Louise arms herself with patience and pours herself another whisky, a Blair Athol from the local distillery. Throughout the long ensuing tale, she refills her glass several times.

66. Jedburgh, Scotland, 1153

"So you see, my lord, it's the most practical solution."

Normand Legrand gave his most loyal counsellor, Étienne Montfort, a disdainful look.

"But it would be an affront to the Plantagenet bloodline!"

Montfort carefully kept himself from sighing. Luckily, it was nighttime, so in the castle's dim lighting, Legrand could hardly see the furrowing of his counsellor's forehead, and even less the man's exasperation.

"Your name would remain the same, my lord. It would only take a form the clans will find more acceptable."

Normand Legrand reflected for a while. Would his father, Damien Legrand, consider this concession a betrayal? His grandfather Pierre Legrand, one of the Plantagenet lords at the side of William the Conqueror during his invasion of England, had contributed to the victory at the Battle of Hastings in 1066. His ancestor's share of the spoils of war had consisted of this fief of Jedburgh, an area straddling the border between England and Scotland, and inhabited by warlike, ungovernable clans. Normand Legrand's father had died without being able to impose his authority upon his subjects, leaving the problem entirely to his son, who was the first of this Plantagenet bloodline to be born in the conquered country.

"And the dowry?" demanded the lord.

"It is more political than material, my lord. If you marry the daughter of their leader, the clans will recognise your son as sovereign. You'll also receive a few pack animals and ten barrels of *uisge beatha*."

"Of what?"

The counsellor congratulated himself on his foresight. Having guessed that his lord's curiosity would be piqued, he had made sure he'd be able to satisfy it immediately.

"*Uisge beatha*, a kind of drink, an elixir, made from barley by the local monks. Here, I have procured some for you."

Montfort placed a stoneware jar on the table in front of Normand Legrand and poured a little liquid into a goblet. The lord took the container and sniffed it. The strong smell evoked a strange blend of peat smoke, heather and honey.

"And how does one take this elixir?"

The question left Étienne Montfort a little puzzled. "It is drunk, my lord, like wine."

The lord lifted the goblet to his lips, but stopped abruptly. "Drink for me first." Normand Legrand handed the goblet to his counsellor.

"Drink only a little of it at a time," the monk had suggested to Montfort. He opened his mouth and let the liquid slide down his throat. His expression, which was usually impassive, turned into a smile. He coughed and declared: "It is strong, but it leaves a pleasant taste in the mouth and a blissful feeling in the head."

Normand Legrand took back the glass and drank in his turn. His throat burned and he suddenly felt a delicious ecstasy. "Leave me. Night will bring me counsel."

Montfort obeyed, leaving behind the *uisge beatha*—which would, for Normand Legrand, no doubt bring better counsel than night. Once alone, the lord drank again. This drink certainly didn't have the sweetness of wine. And yet it produced a comparable bliss, but in a faster, more intense way.

His goblet empty, the lord served himself again while pondering the alliance and name change recommended by his counsellor. This marriage of state seemed, on the whole, to be a good bargain—even more so because his intended bride, Janet Bruce, was young and attractive. Normand Legrand was approaching age forty, and it was high time to give the fiefdom a legitimate heir.

Nonetheless, he hesitated to accept the stipulation that accompanied this union. After all, he was the lord, and it was not his subjects' place to dictate their conditions to him.

"Legrand … Fearmòr," he said aloud.

The echo of his own voice made him laugh. He repeated the two names ten times, changing his intonation. *It's simply writing the Legrand surname in its Scottish Gaelic form,* thought the lord, repeating to himself the argument put forward by his counsellor. *If this can make them forget that their lord is a Plantagenet, why not? Besides, fear mòr, which means 'big person' in their language, has a nice ring to it.*

"Normand Fearmòr."

Once again, the name echoed in the air for a few seconds. "Yes, I will name my first son Normand, and he will be a Fearmòr." The lord burst out laughing.

The next morning, Étienne Montfort found the lord of the castle asleep in the chair where he had left him the night before, face on the table, and the stone jar and goblet both empty. He nodded with satisfaction: the dynasty of the Fearmòrs of Scotland would indeed come into existence.

From this day on, the water of life and the water of whisky would flow forever more.

Glossary of Scottish Gaelic, Lallans, French and Ojibway words

The translation of the words and phrases into Scottish Gaelic and Lallans was done by Mòrag Burke, instructor of Scottish Gaelic at the Celtic Studies Department of St Francis Xavier University in Antigonish, Nova Scotia, to whom I am most grateful.

All words in the glossary are in Scottish Gaelic, unless indicated otherwise. The equivalent phonetic pronunciations, provided here in English, are approximate.

Lallans is a dialect of English used in the Lowland region of Scotland. Certain words of this dialect are derived from Irish or Scottish Gaelic words.

agomo: (Ojibway word) It floats

aire: Wake, vigil over a body (pronounced *ä-reh*)

Alba bochd: Poor Scotland! (pronounced *Al-ah-pah bokhk*)

amadan: Idiot! Fool! (pronounced *ama-dahn*)

bagami: (Ojibway word) Arriving, in the process of arriving

bothie: (Also spelled *bothy*) (Lallans word) A facility for clandestine distillation, derived from the Scottish Gaelic word "both" or "bothvan" which means "cottage", "hut" or "tent" (pronounced *bah-thie*)

céilidh: A party (pronounced *kay-lee*)

C'est l'aviron qui nous mène, qui nous mène: Lyrics of a traditional French-Canadian voyageur song, meaning: The paddles carry us, carry us along *cuan fior-uisge*: Freshwater Sea. The French name "La Mer Douce" (or "The Freshwater Sea") was attributed to Georgian Bay by Samuel de Champlain in 1615, since he considered this part of Lake Huron to be a sea of fresh water (pronounced *coo-an fyor ush-geh*)

Dailuaine: Green dale (pronounced *dahl ooh-ahn*)

dearg: red (pronounced *dž-är-ak*)

deoch an dorus: parting glass, parting drink, stirrup-cup; glass which is drunk at the door as one leaves a house which one is visiting (pronounced *džokh an doh-rus*)

Fearmòr: a proper noun (pronounced *fehr-mohr*, rolling the final 'r')

Gleann Dubh (English: *Glen Dubh*): dark valley (pronounced *glee-ah-oon doo*)

Gleann Ciùin (English: *Glen Ciùin)*: calm or tranquil valley (pronounced *glee-ah-oon kee-ooiñ*)

Gleann Fada (English: *Glen Fada*): long valley (pronounced *glee-ah-oon fa-da*)

Il y a longtemps que je t'aime; Jamais je ne t'oublierai: Lyrics of a traditional French folk song, À la claire fontaine, meaning: Long have I loved you / Never will I forget you.

Lainnir Taigh-Solais: lighthouse gleam (pronounced *län-yir taee soh-laeesh*)

na h-òrain mhòra: Traditional Scottish Gaelic songs; literally, "the great songs" (pronounced *na hoh-rah-een vohr-ah*)

Neyaashiwan: (Ojibway word) The Point; point of land

poteen: (Lallans word) Clandestinely distilled whisky (pronounced *puh-cheen*)

quaich: (Lallans word) A small, shallow cup with, usually, two handles, traditionally used in Scotland for the drinking of whisky. Derived from the Scottish Gaelic word "cuach", which means "cup" (pronounced *kweykh*)

Rinn thu 'n gnothach orm!: Touché! (pronounced *rah-een too an gno-tuhkh ohr-um*)

Sassenach: A pejorative term for an English inhabitant of the British Isles. Derived from the Scottish Gaelic word "sasunnach" (pronounced *sass-e-nuhkh*)

shiel: (Lallans word) A large, square shovel made especially for turning over malted barley (pronounced *shee-el*)

sìthichean: fairies (pronounced *shee-ich-an*)

Slàinte: Health! The traditional toast given when drinking whisky (pronounced *slahn-cheh*)

spiorad sàmhach: silent spirit (pronounced *spee-oh-rat sah-vahkh*)

sruth fuar: Swiftly flowing stream (pronounced *sroo foo-ahr*)

Tapadh leibh A Fraing: Thank you, France (pronounced *tah-pah leyv a fräng*)

Teine Brìghmhor: daring fire (pronounced *chen-yeh bree-vohr*)

uisge beatha: whisky. Literally, "water of life" (pronounced *ush-geh bay-hah*)

Wendat: The French gave the name Huron to the Wendats, an indigenous nation, whose territory was located about 150 km north of present-day Toronto

Author's Notes

The quotations from the poem "John Barleycorn: A ballad" (1782) by poet Robbie Burns, which appear on pages 109 and 135, are taken from his poem as reproduced at: http://www.robertburns.org/works/27.shtml.

The poem in tribute to the Fearmòrs, on page 109, is adapted from lines appearing below a painting of William Grant, as quoted on page 31 of *Scotch, The Whisky of Scotland in Fact and Story*, by Sir Robert Bruce Lockhart, Putnam, London, 1967 (a reprint of the original 1951 edition).

The quotation from the poem by Robbie Burns that appears on page 138 is taken from his poem "Scotch Drink" (1785), as reproduced on the website: http://www.robertburns.org/works/84.shtml.

The quotation from the piece by Robbie Burns that appears on page 139 is taken from his poem "The Author's Earnest Cry and Prayer" (1786), reproduced at: http://www.robertburns.org/works/87.shtml.

The article on page 146 is a real newspaper article titled "Disgraceful Wrecking Scenes at Islay", published in the *Greenock Advertiser* and *Argyllshire Herald* on May 27th, 1859, and reproduced on pages 167–168 of *A Wee Dram: drinking scenes from Scottish literature*, by David Daiches, 1990, André Deutsch, London.

The quote attributed to the poet James Hogg on page 214 comes from page 276 of *Noctes Ambrosianae*, vol. 1, published by William Blackmond and Sons, 1887, Edinburgh and London.

The passages on pages 244 and 245 are excerpts from the 1909 report by the Royal Commission on Whiskey, which are quoted on pages 26–27 of *Scotch, Its History and Romance*, by Ross Wilson, David & Charles: Newton Abbot, 1973, and on page 73 of *Scotch, The Whisky of Scotland in Fact and Story*, by Sir Robert Bruce Lockhart, Putnam, London, 1967 (a reprint of the original edition from 1951).

Acknowledgements

My deepest gratitude to Mārta Ziemelis for having initiated the translation of my novel and seen this ambitious project to the end. Without her dedication and persistence this English version would probably have never been.

My most sincere thanks to Mòrag Burke, instructor of Scottish Gaelic at the Celtic Studies Department of St Francis Xavier University in Antigonish, Nova Scotia, for her invaluable assistance regarding the Scottish Gaelic and Lallans words and phrases used in this novel.

The author gratefully acknowledges the support of the Ontario Arts Council during the writing of the original French novel.

CPSIA information can be obtained
at www.ICGtesting.com
Printed in the USA
LVOW12s0356100516
487361LV00001B/142/P

9 781922 200266